BLIND FEAR

Also by Lynn Abercrombie

The Body Box

BLIND FEAR

A COLD CASE THRILLER

LYNN ABERCROMBIE

PINNACLE BOOKS
Kensington Publishing Corp.
www.kensingtonbooks.com

PINNACLE BOOKS are published by

Kensington Publishing Corp.
850 Third Avenue
New York, NY 10022

All Kensington titles, imprints, and distributed lines are available at special quantity discounts for bulk purchases for sales promotions, premiums, fund-raising, educational, or institutional use. Special book excerpts or customized printings can also be created to fit specific needs. For details, write or phone the office of the Kensington special sales manager: Kensington Publishing Corp., 850 Third Avenue, New York, NY 10022, attn: Special Sales Department; phone 1-800-221-2647.

ISBN 0-7860-1728-7

First printing: December 2006

10 9 8 7 6 5 4 3 2 1

Printed in the United States of America

1

Hank Gooch ran the glowing bar of steel through the blazing tube of the propane forge one more time, pulled it out, thrust it into the water. The sword he had just forged hissed angrily as it hit the water. Steam rose into the air.

He could see the blade beneath the boiling water, the steel going from red to black in an instant, bending from the furious forces involved in the quench.

Then he heard a tiny noise from the steel.

Tink.

The sound of about a dozen hours of work going down the drain. He waited ten more seconds, then pulled the sword out of the water. Sure enough, there it was, a thumbnail-sized crack in the cutting edge.

Since he'd retired from the department six months earlier, he'd been trying to teach himself how to make Japanese swords. Without success. He'd bought every book about bladesmithing, every DVD, gone to seminars and hammer-ins, done everything humanly possible to figure out how to make the stupid things. And every sword he forged was worse than the next. If they didn't twist into corkscrews while he was forging them, they broke during the quench. If they didn't break, they warped. If they didn't warp, they chipped out when you tried to cut with them. It was one damn thing after another.

Six months ago he had figured that if he retired early and started making swords, he could pick up enough income to do pretty good on his half pension.

But so far he hadn't made a single blade worth selling. Things had started looking a little dicey on the money front. Turned out making swords was a lot harder than it looked.

Across the room lay the wreckage that accounted for his six months of hard work: warped, twisted, broken, and otherwise useless pieces of steel—half of them impaled in the wall, the other half lying in a pile on the floor. He heaved the bar of steel across the room toward the pile, trying to stick it in the wooden door of his shed. He wasn't bad at throwing knives, so at least he got that satisfaction every once in a while—the ruined blade making a nice dull thunk as it stuck into the wall.

Just as the blade left his hand, though, the door of his shed flew open. The blade sailed out the opening, narrowly missing the head of a young man Gooch didn't recognize.

"Ahhhh!" The young man disappeared, squealing like a girl.

Gooch crossed his arms, waited.

"Sir? Sir?" A timid voice. A hand appeared tentatively from behind the door frame, holding a wallet with a shield on it. "Sir? It's Detective Floss? Cody Floss? Atlanta Police Department Cold Case Unit? Sir? Sir?"

Gooch didn't speak.

The man's head appeared, peeking furtively around the doorframe. More of a kid than a man, really. Thinning blond hair that would all be gone by the time he was thirty, an abject little mustache, a cheap black suit with a tie that wasn't knotted with any proficiency. The kid must have been promoted to detective about ten minutes ago.

"Sir? Lieutenant?"

Far as Gooch was concerned, he wasn't a lieutenant anymore. He despised these old farts that went around calling themselves by their rank after they'd retired. It was like these clowns that retired from the Marine Corps and went around calling themselves Colonel for the next thirty years. Either you were a civilian or you weren't.

"Sir, the chief sent me."

The chief. That idiot. Great.

The kid swallowed. "Sir, I know living down here in the country maybe you haven't been keeping up with the news? I know you and Chief Diggs had some history and stuff? But he's not the chief anymore."

Gooch frowned. Six months living out here in Troup County, rarely reading the papers or watching TV—by God, things started passing you by quick.

"You didn't hear, Lieutenant? Chief Diggs is the mayor of Atlanta now."

Wasn't that a fine thing. All the city of Atlanta needed, some two-faced time-serving glad-hander like Diggs running the show. Well, it wasn't Gooch's problem anymore. He brushed past the young detective, walked out into the weedy yard, picked up the sword he'd just chunked out the door, looked at the crack again. It was even worse than he'd thought at first. Damn near broke in half.

"Shit," Gooch said.

He went back in the shed, tossed it on the scrap pile. The young detective was jingling his car keys nervously in his hands. "Um . . ."

Gooch turned off the needle valve to the propane forge. The plume of yellow flame went away, but the glow of the 2300-degree fire remained inside the insulated shell, heating his face. He turned off the safety petcock, trying to think what he should do next. Commune with his good buddy Jim Beam maybe? Or maybe today he ought to cozy up to Mr. Daniels. Tough choice when you had so many friends.

"Sir? It's about MeChelle. Sergeant Deakes, I mean."

Gooch looked at the kid expressionlessly.

"She's missing, sir."

Missing. That could mean a lot of things. Gooch started ticking off the possibilities. Missing, dead. Missing, kidnapped. Missing, passed out in a gutter. Missing, missing. For the first time in six months he felt like he was thinking about something he understood. The past half year he'd felt like he'd been swimming in molasses the whole time.

So MeChelle Deakes was missing. She had her demons . . . but he didn't think she'd just wander off without telling a soul. Gooch looked around the shed, taking stock of things. Twisted, cracked, ruined pieces of steel everywhere. Who was he kidding? He was never gonna be worth a lick of spit at making swords anyway.

"Shit," Gooch said for the second time.

He went back out the door, snatching the kid's keys from his hands as he went, walked briskly toward the house.

"Sir! Sir? Wait!"

Gooch went inside the house, clumped into the bedroom, opened the drawer to his bedside table, took out a small picture of a girl with blond hair and two missing front teeth. The picture was old and faded and dog-eared, covered with tape. It was a picture he'd carried every day that he'd been a cop, the photo of his daughter taped to the back of his badge. A reminder of why he'd become a cop in the first place.

Then he went back outside. The kid was standing on his porch, waiting, his hands clutched nervously over his genitals. Gooch brushed past him.

"Sir!" the kid called after him as Gooch walked toward the kid's car. "Sir! What are you doing? Where are you—"

Gooch climbed into the kid's car without answering and fired up the engine.

2

Sgt. MeChelle Deakes was blind.

She had awoken with an odd sensation. The first thing she noticed was the smell. Not a bad smell. Just not right. It smelled like new carpet and cement. An odd combination.

Then a sound. A clock.

Tick. Tick. Tick.

Then . . . something about her eyes. Something not right there either. But it was only when she sat up and tried to look around that she realized she couldn't see. Her eyelids seemed to be stuck together. She rubbed them, but they wouldn't come unstuck. An eye infection? There was a thin, hard crust running all along the eyelid. It didn't feel like dried gunk coming out of an infected eye. It felt harder. Like plastic. And her eyes burned a little.

She kept rubbing, waiting for whatever was holding her eyes shut to break loose so she could see. But it didn't.

And she couldn't. For all intents and purposes, she was

completely blind. Her heart started beating fast. A brief stab of panic.

She had to call somebody! Nine one one? Work maybe? Her dad?

She reached over for her phone. But it wasn't there. It was supposed to be on the bedside table. But there was no bedside table. In fact, she wasn't in bed at all. She was lying on a carpeted floor.

MeChelle felt a strange sense of disorientation. She tried to remember what had happened last night. Had she gone on a bender or something? No. She'd gotten back from the department, done a little paperwork, and then gone to bed. This didn't make sense.

Why can't I see?

"Hello?" she called. "Is anybody there?" Her voice sounded a little shaky to her own ears.

No answer.

Just the clock. *Tick. Tick. Tick.*

She clawed at her eyes, harder now, pulling at her eyelids until she felt like her skin might rip off. The pain was terrible. But it did nothing. They were completely stuck together. Finally she gave up. If they were stuck, they were stuck.

She rolled over, stood slowly, feeling her way blindly in front of her. Finally she found a wall. It was an odd texture. Like foam rubber. Not flat, but sort of corrugated—like the bottom of an egg carton.

She wasn't quite freaking out yet . . . but close. Her mind was still fuzzy from sleep. No, not just sleep. She could feel the last vestiges of some kind of drug dulling her emotions, slowing her thoughts. What drug? She didn't remember any drugs last night. In fact, she hadn't touched anything—not even a glass of wine—in over a year.

Which is when it started to dawn on her with terrible clarity: something really bad was happening here.

She felt her way along the wall. No windows, no light switches. No door.

Where's the door? Where's the door? Within seconds she came to another wall. Same as the first wall, same corrugated foam stuff. Like inside a recording studio. That's it—it was sound insulation.

She felt along that wall for a while. Again, no window, no door, no light switch, no outlet plates. She stopped, strained to hear.

Other than the ticking of the clock, there was no sound in the room. Like the air had gone numb. Not just quiet. Not just the relative, peaceful quiet of an empty movie theater or a church on Thursday morning. This was true silence. *Utter* silence. No planes, no traffic, no kids playing in the street, no dogs barking. Nothing. No sound at all.

Except this: *Tick. Tick. Tick. Tick.* A sound that seemed to be everywhere and nowhere, coming from no specific place, just floating in the air around her.

I'm forgetting something. Why am here? I must be forgetting something! There was some kind of mistake, something forgotten, something eluding her memory. By some weird combination of accidents and coincidences she had woken up in a recording studio with her eyes accidentally gummed shut.

"Help! Somebody! I can't see!" MeChelle was struggling to keep her voice under control.

And then the blindingly obvious conclusion hit her, tearing through her like a bolt of lightning.

Accident? Get real! This wasn't an *accident*. This wasn't disorientation or something that she'd forgotten about or some strange coincidence. She hadn't fallen off the wagon last night and woken up in a recording studio.

She had been *put* here.

Her heart began slamming hard in her chest.

Put here? By whom? For what purpose?

There was no possible good answer. Her mind briefly considered various horrible possibilities—rape, torture, dismemberment, violation . . .

She desperately felt along the next wall. There! A doorknob. She turned it frantically. It didn't budge. There was no play in it at all, no jiggling, no play in the screws, no give in the doorjamb. The door and the handle and the wall all might as well have been machined from one giant billet of steel.

And finally the panic started coming on, worming its way out through the druggy torpor. An urge to scream. *Help! Please! No! What do you want? Don't! Don't hurt me!*

But the moment the panic hit her, something else in her mind went still and calm.

No. Screaming wouldn't do. Panic just would not do. If she had been put here, there was a reason. There would be someone out there, just on the other side of that wall. Someone waiting for her to wake. Someone watching her. Someone feeding on her fear. She couldn't let that happen. If she gave in to fear, then they'd have her just where they wanted her.

She took a deep breath.

Get it together, MeChelle, she said to herself. Rule One in all copdom: when you roll up, first thing you do is control the situation. All other options flow from that one act, that one proposition. Control yourself, you control the situation. Control the situation, you go home safe.

"All right," she called. Struggling to use her cop voice, her I'm-in-control voice. "All right, y'all," she called again.

Louder, firmer this time. She held out her hands, widespread. "Here I am. Talk to me."

Tick. Tick. Tick. Nothing but the sound of the clock.

She twisted the handle again. No movement at all. She took a deep breath, tamping down the panic. Then she turned her back on the door.

"I said talk to me."

And with that a voice said, "Congratulations. You've taken the first step."

Like the ticking clock, the voice was all around her. Like it was coming out of stereo speakers that were mounted . . . where? In the ceiling? In the walls? Both?

The voice, she thought. The voice. Have I heard that voice? It was a deep powerful voice. Throaty, carefully modulated, dispassionate and yet somehow slightly ominous. Like the voice of God—God, when he was giving a little of that righteous Old Testament shit to the backsliding Israelites.

"Sergeant Deakes," the voice intoned, "you have thirteen hours. The clock is ticking."

Yes, it was. The sound of the clock was everywhere.

Tick. Tick. Tick.

"Tell me your name," she demanded. "You still have a chance to get out of this without spending the rest of your life in jail."

But the voice of God had said all it was going to say. Now there was only the clock.

Tick. Tick. Tick.

3

The kid, Cody Floss, had to run to catch up with his own car. But he finally made it, his cheap suit covered with dust.

"You look like a mortician's assistant in that suit," Hank Gooch said.

"Sir, this vehicle is city property," the young man said, breathing hard as he pulled on his seat belt. "It's really not permitted for a non-city employee to be driving—"

Gooch hit the accelerator, knocked the kid back in his seat. "Quiet," he said.

Gooch was in a raw state, a walking nerve. No idea why. No clue.

He should have been on easy street. After about twenty-five years of professional life—first as a soldier and then as a cop—he'd retired on half pay to do work that he'd been wanting to do for a long time. Become a humble swordsmith, make blades in the thousand-year tradition of the great Japanese smiths. A fantasy he'd entertained for years and years.

But now that it had come true, now that he was out here in the country, doing what he'd planned for so long, he found that he was in a perpetual bad mood. He'd always considered himself to be the kind of guy who didn't let things get under his skin. But now the world seemed empty, jammed with transparency and falsehood, and everything was pissing him off. Throwing beer cans at the TV news, that kind of thing. Got so bad, a few months back in the middle of watching some politician with a hairpiece lying his ass off on the news, he'd walked over, cradled the TV in his arms, staggered to the window and thrown it out onto the lawn. Where it had continued to lie, spattered with mud and bits of straw.

Good riddance.

And now, for no particular reason, he just wanted to punch this kid in the face. Kid hadn't done a thing to him. Just rubbed him the wrong way somehow.

Then again, lately he'd felt that way about pretty much everyone he'd met.

"All right," Gooch said as they rattled down the dirt road leading from his house to the county highway. There were woods off to the right side of the road, soybean fields to the left, a long irrigator on wheels squatting in the middle of the field like some giant centipede. "Talk to me about MeChelle."

"Well, she was working this case yesterday afternoon. She went off to interview a witness and . . . then she just didn't show up for work today."

Gooch waited for the rest of the story as he banged down the long, rutted gravel track leading from his house to the county road. The fact that MeChelle hadn't shown up for work was obviously not enough for a chief to justify pulling somebody out of retirement.

He swung the car onto Highway 8, headed toward Newnan, where he'd hook up with the interstate that would take them north to Atlanta. He was still waiting for a non-bogus explanation when they hit the interstate.

Gooch pulled off the road, took the keys out of the car, got out of the car. There was a big soybean field in front of him, with a farmer's large white house at the far end of the field.

"Sir, where are you going?" the kid said through the passenger-side window.

"I'm fixing to throw your keys off in them soybeans over there," Gooch said.

"Why?"

"You been wasting my time. I think maybe I'll return the favor."

"But . . . what . . ."

Gooch cocked his arm.

"Wait! Wait!" the kid said, climbing out of the car and grabbing hold of Gooch's hand. "Okay, there's some more to it."

Gooch peeled the kid's fingers from his arm.

"Actually"—the kid swallowed—"actually, uh, the chief didn't, per se, uh, send me."

Here it came. The Story. People like this, before you ever got the truth, you'd get The Story. Gooch sighed. The Story was never the plain-out truth, but it was a version of the truth—the truth plus a big steaming pile of self-serving bullshit. But you had to let them get The Story out before the actual and complete truth ever rolled around.

Cody Floss made an apologetic face. "See, sir, what it is—I just got moved over to the Cold Case Unit. Before that I was in Narcotics. It didn't—look, I wasn't all that great at—well, my daddy is on the Fulton County Commission and I wasn't the world's greatest street cop. But—I don't know—I think maybe my daddy pulled some strings and got me promoted to detective. So after I didn't exactly prosper in Narcotics, they moved me to Theft and, I don't know what it was, but it wasn't such a great fit, personnel-wise or personality-wise, vis-à-vis the boss over there, and so they moved me to Cold Case."

Gooch leaned against the car and stared up into the air.

"Anyway, I get there and Sergeant Deakes, she's like this street cop genius. You know? But a little flaky? And so when she came up missing today I was like, *Oh, crud, what am I gonna do?*"

"You went to Hicks?" Major Denny Hicks, the head of Major Crimes, was MeChelle's supervisor.

"More or less. Yes, sir."

"More or less?"

"Well, I just said she hadn't showed up for work. And Major Hicks was like, 'Well, it wouldn't be the first time she fell off the wagon.' He said they'd look into it if she didn't surface in another day or two."

"So the chief didn't actually send for me?"

"Uh . . ."

"Jesus *Christ*."

Gooch waited a minute for the truth to start settling out of the kid's story. But it didn't. The kid just kept standing there staring out at the soybean field.

"How did you screw up?" Gooch said finally.

"Sir?"

"Son, at first I just thought you were a plain old idiot," Gooch said. "But now I'm beginning to see you're worse than that. If you lie to me one more time, I'm gonna wring your silly neck. Now what's going on here?"

The boy began to cry.

"Is this spose to make me feel sorry for you?" Gooch snapped.

The boy didn't respond.

Gooch reached over, took a lock of hair just behind the kid's ear, and twisted it savagely.

"Ow!" The kid's head jerked up and he pawed ineffectively at Gooch's hand.

"Stop crying, start talking," Gooch said, letting go of the lock of hair.

Cody Floss sniffled for a few seconds, then wiped his face and, in a thin voice, said, "You know why I joined the police force?"

Oh, great, Gooch thought. *Here we go. True confessions.*

"You remember back in '97, that case you did? Jeannie Montfreize, the girl that got strangled? And you solved it?"

Gooch was anxious to get in the car again. But that would break the rhythm of the kid's confession. Gooch crossed his arms and settled in. He'd probably have to listen to a bunch of off-the-point baloney, but eventually the kid would get around to telling him something useful. Across the field a green tractor was driving slowly across the horizon, tiny in the distance.

Cody Floss continued with his story. "Well, anyway, sir, I remember when you caught up with the two guys who'd done it. Melvin Eddy and Purvis Nix? And there was that big shoot-out on live TV? And you killed them both? I saw it on TV. I was in high school and I was kind of trying to figure out what I wanted to do with my life. And I saw you on the TV, taking on those two guys, and suddenly I was like, *Dog, I wanna be that guy!*"

No. Not this.

"I'm embarrassed to say it, but I kept this scrapbook of your cases. I just, like . . . wanted to be *you*."

"They got medications for that, son," Gooch said.

"Sir, I'm just trying to . . ." The kid put his face in his hands.

"I ain't interested in you, son. Can't you get that through your head? Tell me about MeChelle."

"I want to be a good cop! I do! But . . ." There was a long silence. Finally the kid said, "Sir, I think it's my fault, what happened to her. And when I realized that the department wasn't gonna do anything about her going missing, I just . . . I knew I had to have some help."

"That's the first thing you've said so far that's made a lick of sense," Gooch said. "Now tell me how you screwed up."

"MeChelle had this case. What happened was, this blind lady comes into the office. She's got the white cane and everything. And she sits down with MeChelle and she says, 'I know who killed my mom.' MeChelle starts asking her questions. Turns out this lady—"

"Let me interrupt you here. You're a cop, not a philosopher. Cops deal in specifics. Not generalities. When you bring up a person, that person has a name and a physical description. When you bring up a situation, that situation has a time and a date. Now, start over."

The kid fiddled with the knot on his necktie. "Okay. So, yesterday around 3:30 P.M. this individual with a white cane came into the detective bureau office. She identified herself as Lane Priest. White female, five foot eight, one-twenty, blond hair. In terms of a physical description? Even though she was blind—she was kind of, um, extremely hot."

"What, you can't be blind and attractive at the same time?"

"Well, I don't know, sir." The kid suddenly panicking, like there was a right answer to the question.

Gooch took a pack of Red Man out of his back pocket, gnawed off a plug, stuck it in his cheek. This boy irritated him more by the minute. The tobacco calmed him a little, though, gave him something to fiddle with. "Just tell the story."

"Yes, sir! Thank you, sir. So, anyway, this lady, Ms. Priest, she said that her mother had been murdered eighteen years ago. And that she knew who had done the crime. Sergeant Deakes was like, 'How do you know?' And the blind lady was like, 'I heard his voice when my mother was killed. I'd never forget that voice. And then I heard it again yesterday.' Sergeant Deakes says, 'Okay, so who is it?' And Ms. Priest says, 'Well, I don't know. But here it is.' Then she holds up this mp3 player and hits the play button. It was a recording of an advertisement. The lady says, 'Listen. You hear the man in the commercial? That's him. That's the man who killed my mom.'"

Gooch nodded. Now—*maybe*—the kid was finally getting somewhere.

"So anyway, MeChelle—Sergeant Deakes—she takes down the information and the blind lady goes away."

"Who was with her?" Gooch interrupted.

"Who?"

"Lane Priest. Your witness. She's blind. Somebody almost certainly accompanied her to the station. Who?"

The kid blinked. "Uh . . . gosh, I didn't notice anybody."

"And you didn't think that was strange?"

"Honestly? I guess, I just didn't think, sir."

"Go on."

"So the lady leaves. MeChelle sends me over to Records to get the case file. So I get over there, and there's no case. I mean, Ms. Priest had said that her mother's name was Kathleen Bolligrew, said that she was killed, I forget, sometime around 1989? So I search 1989 and this murder just never shows up. So I go through a couple of years in each direction. Nada. Far as the records go, the murder never happened.

"Meanwhile, I go back to the office and MeChelle's not there. She left a note on my desk saying that she had gotten a call about the case from this blind lady."

"Lane Priest. She has a name."

"Lane Priest, right. Her. So anyway the note says that the blind lady found out something else and so MeChelle went out to interview her."

Gooch could see what was coming.

"Sir, it was . . . well, my fiancée and I were supposed to go visit this catering place? We're supposed to get married in November and so we're going around to the places testing the different types of canapés or whatever they're called. See, Crystal—that's my fiancée—Crystal, she's kind of got all these real strong ideas about how everything is supposed to be for the wedding and . . . well, I was running late and I knew she wouldn't be very nice about it if I was late, and so I just kind of . . ." His voice drifted off.

"You knew the case was bogus," Gooch said, "and yet you let Sergeant Deakes go running off on some fool's errand because you were afraid your girlfriend was gonna yell at you."

"Um . . ."

"And so when Sergeant Deakes didn't show up this morning, you figured that, oh, maybe she got called out last night by some thug she'd busted somewhere along the way. And you figured whoever it was, they wanted to get even with her."

"Well . . ."

"And have you actually spoken to Major Hicks yet? At all?"

The kid didn't answer.

Gooch shook his head in disgust. "Son, you must be the dumbest little sumbitch I've ever met in my life."

The kid was sitting slumped on the hood of the car. He had sunk into a soft miserable ball of self-pity.

"Get in," Gooch said, then he jumped in, fired up the car.

"Oh, also, I forgot, sir," the kid said, scrambling to get back into the car before Gooch drove away. "I found this in my mailbox at work today."

He lifted a manila envelope off the front seat and handed it to Gooch. Laser-printed on the front was a message: HAND-DELIVER TO LT. HANK GOOCH ASAP.

"Might have been good if you'd gave me that first," Gooch said, "instead of wasting my time on all your little stories."

Gooch took out the knife that was clipped inside his pocket, flipped it open, slit open the envelope, dumped the contents out in his lap. It was a single piece of paper, folded in half. Gooch pried it open with the blade of his knife, careful not to touch it with his fingers. The message inside was printed with the same font as the one on the outside of the envelope.

It read:

SERGEANT DEAKES HAS THIRTEEN HOURS TO LIVE. DO NOT CONTACT ANYONE ELSE IN LAW ENFORCEMENT OR SERGEANT DEAKES WILL DIE IMMEDIATELY. YOU WILL FIND OUT WHAT TO

DO. FAILURE TO COMPLY WITH THESE INSTRUCTIONS WILL RESULT IN THE IMMEDIATE DEATH OF SERGEANT DEAKES.

Gooch refolded the note, then lifted the paper with his knife. "Bag this and tag it," he said. "We'll be fingerprinting it shortly."

"Is this about Sergeant Deakes, sir?" the young detective said, pointing at the folded piece of paper.

Gooch didn't answer, just put the car in drive and floored it, throwing up a spray of rocks and dust.

"What are we going to do, sir?" the young detective said once he'd finally gotten the note encased in a small plastic evidence bag.

"We?" Gooch spit some tobacco juice out the window. "Son, *I'm* gonna find her."

4

Thirteen hours? Until what?

MeChelle wondered if the voice would repeat itself. But it didn't. There was nothing but the clock noise coming out of the air all around her.

Who was out there? Who had put her here? What did they want?

Whoever it was, that was probably his voice coming out of the speakers. The Voice. Giving them a name. You had to name your enemy, didn't you? So you knew who you were up against.

MeChelle strained her ears, listening for any sound other than the clock. But still there was nothing. No planes, trains, cars, wind noise, nothing.

Tick. Tick. Tick.

It seemed very loud. And yet, she realized, it wasn't. The reason it sounded loud was that there wasn't anything else to compete with it.

"Hello?" No answer. She decided to scream at the top of

her lungs. "Help! Hey! Somebody! Help me!" Not out of panic but just because it was worth a try. Maybe the Voice was out there guarding the door, maybe not. Maybe the walls were thick enough to keep her voice from getting out to someone friendly, maybe not.

But you had to try.

She screamed. A high, keening, horror-movie scream. Not out of fear, but because she knew for a fact there was nothing that got people's attention like a woman screaming bloody murder.

But the sound just seemed to die the moment it came out of her mouth. This room was totally soundproof. Nothing coming in, nothing coming out. Just like a recording studio. She could scream her head off and it wouldn't matter. There might be somebody five feet away on the other side of the wall, and they'd never hear a thing.

She screamed a little more but finally quit. With a sinking feeling, she just knew it wasn't worth it. Whoever had put her here—the Voice—was smart, careful, prepared. They'd thought this out. No one would hear her.

Time to stop wasting her effort. Plus the screaming was making her feel creeped out, shaky, panicked. Panic was what killed you.

Keep calm. What's the agenda here? Number one, look for weapons. Number two, look for a way out. Number three, look for communications devices. Her breath kept threatening to get out of control, the panic worming around and worming around in there. *Keep calm. Breathe deeply. Stay in control.*

MeChelle felt around her. She realized she'd only examined three of the four walls in the room. She felt her way along the next wall. Found a door handle, turned it.

Her heart jumped. This time it turned!

"Hello? Anybody in here?"

No answer.

She felt her way into the next room. As she entered, she heard a soft humming sound. Other than the ticking noise, it was the first sound she'd heard since she'd been in here. There was something distinctive about it. A refrigerator. She felt her way across the room toward the sound. Her hands found a hard, smooth, metal surface. She opened the door. Cool air spilled out. She reached inside, felt around.

On the top shelf, a stack of wax-paper-wrapped objects—squashy and rectangular. Sandwiches, three of them. She smelled them. The sweet smell of ham. The fishy odor of tuna. The slightly rank smell of roast beef.

Not feeling so hungry right now, thanks. She put them back.

In the door there were jars, bottles, cartons, jugs. She opened a jug, smelled the milk inside. It was okay.

She felt around through the collection of jars. This one was octagonal, glass, with a twist cap. Heinz ketchup, she was pretty sure. She pulled the bottle out, closed the door, felt her way around until she found a counter. The ketchup bottle going shhhhhhhhh along the countertop.

Clink.

The bottle hitting something harder. A sink. She smashed the bottle against the bottom of the sink. It shattered, releasing the sharp tang of ketchup. Then she felt around for the faucet, turned it on, carefully washed the neck of the ketchup bottle off, dried it on her shirt. Then she slid the jagged bottle neck into the pocket of her pants.

She smiled. *Good. One down. I'm armed.* Now she needed to find a way out. Or, failing that, something she could communicate with.

How could she communicate? Tapping SOS on the pipes

maybe? Smoke signals? She felt a wave of frustration. There wasn't much doubt that wherever she was, she'd be a long way from other people. Tapping on the pipes probably wouldn't hack it.

Think! Think!

In the other room a phone began to ring.

Then again, MeChelle thought, *there's the obvious. Find the frickin' phone!*

Suddenly her heart was racing. She felt her way across the kitchen, going as fast as she could. A ringing phone! If she could just get to it before whoever was calling hung up. She could talk to someone, she could get help!

The phone rang a second time. A third.

How could the Voice have been so stupid as to leave a phone in the room? Well, it didn't matter.

Through the door. Into the other room.

The phone rang a fourth time.

It still seemed to be a terribly long way away. She started moving across the room as quickly as she dared, sliding her bare feet so as not to slam into anything.

Which didn't work.

She stumbled over something hard, lost her balance, crashed to the floor, banging her head into the wall. She cursed, got to her feet again, moving in an awkward crouch.

The phone rang one more time. Where the hell was it?

She slid forward again, more cautiously this time, waving her hands in front of her. Dammit!

And then, there it was, a smooth plastic thing under her hands. It fell to the floor. She leaned over, picked it up.

"Hello!" she said.

There was a long pause, then a sort of hollow noise, like she was listening to something from the far end of a long tunnel.

"Hello?" she said.

No answer.

"Look. Please, I need help. I don't know where I am but I can't see. I need you to call the police. Hello!"

But there was no answer.

Anger surged through her. She picked up the phone and threw it at as hard as she could at the wall.

5

Gooch had kept his cell phone after he retired. No real need for it. Couldn't even get service out in the boonies where he was at. But he'd kept it anyway, dutifully paying the bill every month.

Why? Maybe because he secretly hoped that one day he'd drive to town and the phone would vibrate and he'd look at the read-out and it would say MESSAGE WAITING.

And maybe it would be MeChelle, calling him up, needing him for something important—maybe an old case he knew a little something about, a family's pain to be eased, a kid to be saved, a killer to be brought down, a case coming to trial . . .

But it never happened.

Still, he had the phone. As he and the kid sped toward Atlanta, the blue light on the dash flashing away, he dialed MeChelle's number.

It rang once, twice. Then three, four, five. And then a click and it went to voice mail. "You have reached Sgt. MeChelle Deakes—"

He hit the one key, cutting her off. The phone beeped, signaling him to leave a message. “MeChelle. Gooch here. Call me now.” Then he thumbed the end call button, hit redial.

This time it went straight to voice mail.

Odd. Why'd it get through the first time? Then not the second?

He hit redial again. Voice mail.

Gooch handed the phone to Cody Floss. “Keep calling that number,” Gooch said.

“How many times?”

“You want to do yourself a favor, son?” Gooch said. “Do not speak to me unless I specifically tell you to.”

The kid kept calling, but seemed to be getting nowhere. Each time, he'd dial, wait, shake his head.

Gooch hit I-85, pushed the pedal to the floor. The big car was soon doing about a hundred and twenty. It didn't really like the road at that speed, twitching and shimmying with every bump and dip. But that was too bad.

After five minutes Cody Floss was still dialing, still shaking his head.

“Okay, change of plan,” Gooch said. “Start calling the cell phone companies. Figure out who her cell provider is.”

“It's Cingular, sir. See, personally, I pay all my bills online? And I was trying to show her how easy it is. So she gave me her bill and—”

“Okay, whatever. Call Cingular, tell them to run a cell tower triangulation on her. That won't tell us exactly where she is . . . but it'll narrow it down.”

“Um . . . they won't do it without a warrant.”

Gooch's eyes narrowed. The kid was right. “Who's doing warrants for the D.A.'s office now?”

“Well, I just came over from Narcotics and when we were there, it was usually . . .”

"Forget it. Dial the D.A.'s office then hand me the phone."

The kid picked up the phone, diddled around for a while, finally handed the phone to Gooch. He got through to Nellie Bowers, the gal who used to do warrants for the D.A.'s office.

"Nellie, hey, it's Gooch from Cold Case. Need a warrant."

"Uh . . ." There was a pause. "I thought you retired."

"I'm back."

"Oh, well . . ."

"Love to chat about old times but we got an officer in trouble. I need a warrant faxed over to Cingular."

"Um, Hank, I kinda need more than that."

"Just write it up. Say you got a CI who says there's a kidnapping."

"What kidnapping? Who's missing?"

"Listen hard, Nellie," Gooch said. "You owe me one for that thing. Remember? Don't make me say it out loud."

Nellie said nothing. Gooch had helped her a long time ago. Helped her, big-time.

"Nellie, unless it gets there in less than ten minutes, you and me gonna have a personal problem. I want them tracking a cell number. It's seven-seven-oh-three-nine-one . . ."

He finished the call and hung up.

Then he called the cell phone company. He had the number memorized—a guy named Robb Newton in security, who used to work Narcotics for the APD. "Yeah, Robb, it's Hank Gooch. We got an officer in trouble and I need a trap-and-trace and a cell tower triangulation on a number. D.A.'s office is faxing over the warrant as we speak. Every second you dick around is a second this officer could be dead. We clear?"

"Uh, Hank, you know I need authorization," his contact at the cell company said.

"Yes, I do. And I promise you it's on the way. Warrant'll be there in ten minutes."

"You're not jerking me around?"

"Have I ever done that to you, Robbie?"

Another pause. "Fair enough. Give me the number."

"Out*stand*ing." Gooch gave him the number.

6

Stupid, stupid, stupid! Why'd she throw the phone at the wall? If she had just broken her only potentional lifeline to the outside . . .

MeChelle crawled in the direction of the phone, feeling the floor with her hands.

There it was! She picked it up. There wasn't a dial tone precisely. But there was some kind of electronic hum. Was it still working?

She felt the keypad with her fingers. Three across. Four down. Simple, old-fashioned phone. No flash button, no redial, no Caller ID buttons. Just the numbers. She could visualize it in her mind.

One. Two. Three.
Four. Five. Six.
Seven. Eight. Nine.
Star. Zero. Pound.

She put her fingers in the middle and started dialing. First she dialed her father's number at work. Nothing happened. The same electronic hum.

She pressed the switch hook for a few seconds, listened. No dial tone, just the hum. So she tried his cell. Nothing happened. Switch hook again. Then her dad's home number.

Then she tried 911. Tried that a few times. Nothing.

Then she sat there for a minute, the phone cradled against her ear, her mind blank. Her fingers started dialing. She was halfway through the numbers before she realized the number she had just dialed.

Hank Gooch. Why in hell had she dialed him? He was retired. And besides, he didn't even like her, did he?

But he was the best cop she'd ever known. Nobody even close.

She dialed his number again. And again. And again. And again.

She must have been dialing for five or ten minutes, the same number over and over, when she realized there were tears running down her face.

Come on, Hank! she thought bitterly. *Come on, you bastard.*

7

Gooch and the kid, Cody Floss, reached the homicide bureau a few minutes later. Gooch followed Cody back to MeChelle's office. When Gooch had been with the Cold Case Unit, their office had been in a dark corner in the basement of City Hall East. But since he'd left, they had moved the unit upstairs to the homicide bureau office. Beige cubicles, indirect lighting—it could have been an insurance company.

"Where's she keep her notes?" Gooch asked Floss.

"Over there, I think," the young detective said.

Gooch walked past Cody into MeChelle's office. He noticed a pile of yellow legal pads sitting on a credenza behind MeChelle's desk. She was not the world's most organized person; those were probably her unfiled case notes. Gooch sat down in MeChelle's chair, picked up the top pad, flipped through it until he found her notes from the previous day. They were sketchy.

Date of the alleged crime. The name and address of the

witness. Facts of the crime as reported by the witness. It took him about two seconds to see why Cody Floss hadn't found the case file he was looking for.

He wrote the correct case name on a piece of paper. "Cody. Go down to Records, pick up the file."

"Yes, sir, only . . . see like I told you, I already looked for it yesterday—"

"Look on the piece of paper. The mother's name is Kathleen Morris *hyphen* Bolligrew. You were looking in the Bs. The case is filed under M." Gooch started thumbing though MeChelle's notes.

Cody Floss stared at the piece of paper. "Oh," he said finally. "I thought Morris was her middle name."

Gooch looked up at him. "Are you still here?"

"Sorry! Sorry!" Cody Floss rushed off.

Gooch scanned MeChelle's notes, committing the major details to memory. There wasn't all that much to go on.

There was one thing in her notes that stuck out:

Wit has Barday-Beetle Syndrome. Something not right!

Gooch swung around, logged onto MeChelle's computer—she was still using the same password she'd used six months ago—ran the name of the witness through the computer. Lane Priest. Turned out she lived at 1134 Peachtree Battle, an address over in Buckhead. That would be their next stop. But first he wanted a quick peek at the file. Hopefully that kid Floss wouldn't get lost on the way back from Records.

He looked at his watch. Until he looked at the file, there wasn't much he could do. He logged onto the Internet, Googled "barday-beetle syndrome."

A message came back. "DO YOU MEAN BARDET-BIEDL SYNDROME?" He clicked Yes. Several hits popped up, most of them related to blindness. He clicked on one and started reading.

My goodness, he thought. *Ain't this interesting?*

When he was done reading about Bardet-Biedl Syndrome, Gooch closed his eyes for a moment and took a deep breath. He'd been so wrung-out after the case he and MeChelle had worked last year that he'd felt like it was time to leave law enforcement. But just being back in the cop shop, smelling the air, hearing the buzz of the detectives in the hallways—it made him realize how much he missed the work.

Damnation.

When he opened his eyes, a man was standing in the doorway looking down at him.

It was Hicks, Major Denny Hicks, head of Major Crimes. He was a square-jawed, tense-looking guy, with his hair swept back and a doofus mustache that would put you in mind of some English regimental officer from World War I. Hicks was chewing gum, his mustache twitching. Hicks couldn't stand Gooch.

"Fuck you doing here, Gooch?" Hicks said.

"Denny," Gooch said. "Good to see you, too."

Hicks kept chewing his gum, smashing the shit out of it. "I ast you a question, goddammit, boy."

Gooch shifted the plug of tobacco around in his own cheek, leaned over, spit in the trash. "Came in to use y'all's phone, make me a phone call."

"Hank, you sitting there in Sergeant Deakes's office making unauthorized use of police computers and looking at records you got no right to be looking at." Still gnashing away on the gum. "You goddamn need to goddamn answer my goddamn question. I want to know what you goddamn think you're doing here."

Gooch smiled, spit again. "Betcha do, son," he said.

"Get your ass out of my shop."

"Mm-hmm," Gooch said. Then he put his cowboy boots

up on the desk, picked up the phone. He'd just come to a realization, something hitting him clear and true and certain as anything that he'd ever know in his life. He felt almost giddy with the force of it.

"Gooch, I'ma give you three minutes. You ain't gone, by God, I'ma have you physically removed."

Gooch ignored him.

Major Hicks stomped away.

"Yeah, hi," Gooch said. "This is Hank Gooch. I'd like to talk to the mayor. Tell him he better not make me wait."

The secretary for Mayor Eustace V. Diggs, Jr. made a point of taking as long as humanly possible to take down his name. But then after a minute the mayor—former chief of the Atlanta Police Department—came on. Like Major Hicks, the mayor was no fan of Gooch. Unlike Hicks, however, he didn't show it.

"Well, well!" Mayor Diggs said. "My close and personal friend Hank Gooch! To what do I owe this dubious pleasure?"

"Aw, hell, I just wanted to congratulate you on getting elected mayor."

"Did you now?"

"Yes, sir, I did." Gooch let a moment pass. "Also, just wanted to let you know I was thinking of writing this book about the investigation you and I was involved in last year. The child murder thing? Kind of a tell-all-type deal. Got this whole chapter about all the behind-the-scenes machinations. How the chief of police—that would be you, wouldn't it?—improperly used his authority to interfere with a major homicide investigation, things of that nature. How, if the chief of police had had his way, that nice little blond girl Jenny Dial would have starved to death in a four-foot-square box."

Diggs laughed merrily. "Uh-*huh*! Brass tacks, right? Hmm? Yes? What you want, Gooch? I'm busier'n a one-legged man in a ass-kicking contest. Spit it out, stop wasting my time."

"My job, that's all. I want my job back."

Diggs hooted. "Hooo-hooooooo! My my my, how the worm has turned! Is that the appropriate expression? I must confess, to my infinite regret, I neglected Shakespeare during my college days. Or is that the Bible? I'm always mixing them up. Oh, but I forget, you probably not much of a reader, huh?" The mayor laughed some, doing all kinds of operatic glissandos and warbles. "So. What? You getting low on funds? No! Wait! Of course not. You just miss the work, don't you? Oh, mercy, mercy, mercy, I do cherish a man who loves his God-given vocation. Gives me that warm, gushy feeling."

"The kid MeChelle's working with is useless. Name's Cody Floss. Put me in his slot. Move this fool to Admin where he won't hurt nobody. You still got that position up there, the Gay and Lesbian Community Liaison?"

"Mmm! Yeah, that's tough. See, I might could get you back as a street cop. We are a little low on head count. Be a loss of pension, modest cut in pay, what-not. But the union situation involved and whatnot? Seniority issues? Very complicated. Very nuanced. Coming back in your old position, that's just totally out of the question."

"Look—" Gooch knew the mayor would give him a raft of shit. But the truth was, the APD was way below quota in recruiting and short on experienced detectives.

"Hey, Hank, what if I made *you* into the Gay Lesbian—we've changed the name conforming to the latest trends in homasexshool political correctness—what if we made you into the Gay, Lesbian, Bisexual, and Transgendered Person Community Liaison? As it happens, that position currently—"

"I just want the work, Mr. Mayor." Gooch paused. The mayor had to humiliate him a little. That was the kind of man he was. He couldn't just give you something. He had to make you feel small when he gave it to you. "That other stuff? Money? Seniority? I don't care. I just want the work. That ain't up for negotiation. Take it or leave it."

"I'ma put you on hold, my brother."

The phone went dead.

Maj. Denny Hicks came back and stared at Gooch, acting like he was all shocked and dismayed that Gooch was still there, eyes wide, jaw pounding away on the gum. "Nah, nah, nah," he said. "You *ain't* still here, Gooch."

Gooch pointed at the receiver. "On the phone, Major," he said.

"Oh, so it's 'Major' now? Five minutes ago you were calling me 'son.'"

"Now that you're my superior again . . ."

Hicks attacked his gum, eyes narrowed. "Fuck you mean?"

Mayor Diggs came back on. Gooch held up his hand, palm out, to Major Hicks.

"Gooch?" Mayor Diggs said.

"Yes, sir."

"Cut in pay grade. Lose your seniority. Cut in rank, two levels. You go back to straight detective, no rank." Gooch could practically see the mayor grinning on the other end of the line. "Oh . . . and, Gooch? You'll now report to MeChelle Deakes. Rather than, as was the case in days of yore, the reverse."

Gooch, unaccountably, felt his heart soar. "Fine, Mr.

Mayor," he said. "I owe you," Gooch said. The mayor was king of the favor bank. Nothing he loved more than having people owe him something.

"You goddamn skippy you do, *Detective,*" the mayor said. "I'll have my deputy assistant call HR, they'll have the paperwork ready for you in an hour."

"Gooch!" It was Major Hicks, standing over the desk now, pushing Gooch's boots of the desk. "Out. Now."

Gooch stood up. "You need me, Major, I'll be out in the field," he said. "I'm hooking up with Sergeant Deakes, working a case." He spotted an mp3 player on the desk, grabbed it.

Then Gooch handed the receiver to Hicks. The major took the phone, stared at it like Gooch had just handed him a cold slippery dog turd. Gooch walked out of the office as Hicks demanded, "Who is this?"

Denny Hicks was still backtracking to the mayor as Gooch headed toward the front door.

He looked around, saw Cody Floss coming around the corner with a file folder in his hand. Gooch snapped his fingers at Cody.

"Bring the file with you," he said. "Let's go."

Then he walked out the front door. He halfway wished he could have stuck around. Been worth five bucks to see the expression on Denny Hicks's face when the mayor told him Gooch was back on duty.

8

MeChelle stood there with the phone in her hand. There was no dial tone. Just a dead line. She felt around for the switch-hook button, pressed for a second, let it up. Still no dial tone. She tried again. Nothing. Just a soft, distant hum.

She set the receiver down. Had anybody out there heard her?

Well, either they had or they hadn't. For now, she needed to keep moving, try to find a way out of this place.

She worked the kitchen first. There was nothing in the kitchen other than in the refrigerator. No knives in the drawers, no dishes, no cleaning products, no doors.

She felt along the wall again, going all the way around the apartment. This time more thoroughly, searching up and down the wall, running a grid.

Nothing. It was just like before. Foam insulated walls, no windows, a steel door. No outlets, no heating ducts, nothing.

So there was no doubt. She was imprisoned here. Two rooms. A kitchen and a larger adjoining room. Two heavy steel doors. Thick, heavy carpet that absorbed the sounds of her footsteps. It was new carpet: she could smell the fresh, formaldehyde odor. That was the strongest odor, the carpet. But there was something else, something slightly sour, that she couldn't immediately identify. No furniture except the table with the phone. And another, larger table. On the table was a cardboard box.

What the hell was going on here?

MeChelle had been wracking her brain. Why? If somebody wanted to kill her or torture her or rape her or something . . . wouldn't they have done it already?

And why the blindness? What had they done to her eyes?

It had to be connected with what happened yesterday. The blind witness who'd come into the office the day before. There had to be a connection.

Think! Think! MeChelle sat down in the middle of the floor and tried to go over every detail of the encounter in her mind.

"Hello, my name is Lane Priest."

The young woman had been standing just inside the entrance to the detective bureau. She was holding a white cane and wearing very dark wraparound sunglasses. She held out her hand toward MeChelle, not quite in the right direction. MeChelle had to move a little sideways to comfortably shake hands with the young woman.

She was a white girl, late twenties to early thirties—MeChelle always had a hard time guessing white women's ages—with very pale skin and very blond hair. She almost seemed albino. "What can I do for you?" MeChelle said.

"I want to report a murderer."

"Ah," MeChelle said. "Well, see, I'm actually from the Cold Case Unit. We only handle old murders."

"Not a murder," Lane Priest said. "A murderer. This happened eighteen years ago. But I only found out yesterday who did it."

"Oh!" This was interesting. "Well, then. Come with me."

The woman held out her elbow, a couple of inches from her side. "Could you . . ."

MeChelle took her arm. "Like this?"

"That's good. Don't pull. Just walk and I'll stay with you."

"Okay." MeChelle walked the girl back to her office, settled her into a chair.

"So," MeChelle said, after introducing herself, "tell me what this is in regards to."

The woman folded up her white stick, put it inside her handbag, pulled out a small mp3 player and set it on the desk. "Eighteen years ago, when I was eleven years old, my mother was raped and murdered. Her name was Kathleen Morris Bolligrew. May 13, 1988. A man came into our house and tied her to the bed. Then he raped her three times. Then he stabbed her."

"I see. And where did this happen?"

"In our home. We lived in a house in Midtown."

"And where were you when this happened?"

There was a long pause. "I was underneath my mother's bed."

"So you . . ."

Another pause. "Yeah. I had heard noises outside the house that night. I looked out and thought I saw somebody on the back porch. So I came into Mom's room and told her there was a man outside. She told me I'd had a bad dream and said I could sleep in the bed with her. She was my mom, so I believed her. I had just fallen asleep when I heard the window shatter. And the footsteps coming down the hallway toward us. I hid under the covers. He came into the room and dragged my mom out of bed by the hair. It knocked me out of the bed. In the dark, I guess he never saw me."

"My God," MeChelle said.

"So, back then were you . . ."

"Blind? No. Not then."

"So how do you know who did it? You saw him?"

The pale young woman shook her head. "No. That's the point. I heard him. I heard him and I knew the voice. I've had that voice in my head all these years. The second I heard it, I knew it was him."

MeChelle frowned. An eighteen-year-old case in which the only witness was blind. This had the makings of a real wild-goose chase. But still. It was intriguing. "Where did you hear him, Ms. Priest?"

"Here. Listen."

Her finger paused on the play button of her mp3 player. MeChelle reached out, put the earpieces into her ears. "Ready?" Lane Priest said.

"Go ahead."

"Wild Adventure Park!" a voice said from the earpiece. "It's more than an adventure—it's a whole world of fun!" It was a commercial. Late spring, beginning of the summer, the annoying ads for the Wild Adventure theme park were all over the radio. Typical-sounding announcer, with a throaty, unctuous voice—big pipes, like a guy who smoked two packs a day. She listened to the rest of the commercial, the announcer going on about all the great rides, all the fun things to do.

Yeah, *MeChelle thought.* Like stand in line for each ride for an hour in the blazing sun.

Eventually the commercial was over.

"Okay," MeChelle said when it was done. "What am I listening for?"

"Him," the girl said.

"I'm sorry. Am I missing something?"

"The guy on the commercial. The announcer guy. He's the one who killed my mom."

MeChelle was silent for a while. "The announcer. You're saying—let me be clear here—you're alleging that this man raped and murdered your mother. And you're saying you remember the voice clearly from eighteen years ago."

"Look, I know it sounds crazy, Sergeant Deakes. But my vision was already going down the tubes back then. When you can't see well, your other senses start getting more acute." There was a long pause. "I remember, Sergeant. I remember that voice."

MeChelle started writing some notes, then stopped and looked at the witness. She sat calmly, eyes straight ahead, as though she were looking straight through the wall. She studied the girl for a while. An extremely attractive young woman. MeChelle hadn't known many blind people. But most of the ones she'd known—somehow you could tell they were blind just by looking at them. The way they moved or something. They didn't have the sort of self-consciousness about their appearance that most people did. They had odd expressions on their faces, little things out of place.

The girl seemed to read MeChelle's thoughts. "It's different when you go blind later in life. You don't have all the twitches and weird faces and crumbs on your shirt." The girl smiled, showing off a row of perfect teeth. "I was always vain about my appearance. I guess I still am."

"Okay," MeChelle said. "I won't lie to you. This is going to be an uphill battle. But I'll take the file home with me tonight. You'll hear from me again as soon as I've absorbed it."

The girl stood. "Keep the mp3 player," she said. "Just return it when you're done."

"Is there somebody here with you?" MeChelle said.

"Yes, thanks. They're waiting outside. If you could just show me to the door, I'll take it from there."

After the girl had left, MeChelle had called her doofus assistant, Cody Floss, and asked him to run over to Records and pull the case file.

She was pretty sure he'd never come back with the file. But to tell the truth, her memory was a little hazy. She'd gone home empty-handed. She vaguely remembered doing forty-five minutes on the treadmill. Then she'd cooked some Chicken Voilà! in the microwave. And after that?

A big blank.

Blindness. This all had something to do with blindness.

Thirteen hours. She had thirteen hours to figure it out. Then what?

Tick. Tick. Tick. Tick. Tick.

She thought about her surroundings again. Phone. Table. Box. Refrigerator. New carpet. That was all that was here. Were these incidental items? Or part of a plan?

She walked across the room. Moving around was getting easier now. She wasn't stumbling and bumping into walls quite as badly. Her mind was starting to make a map of the place: two strides to the door, four to the window, six to the other door. . . . She picked up the cardboard box that was sitting on the table, turned it over, dumping out the contents.

She felt the surface of the table. There were six items there.

A small fuzzy thing. A teddy bear? No, it had long floppy ears. It was some kind of doll—a dog or a rabbit. MeChelle felt a perverse urge to hug the little doll. But she didn't. Whoever was responsible for this, they were probably watching through a camera somewhere. She wasn't going to give them the satisfaction. Sometimes drug smugglers used to hide things in figurines and dolls. She squeezed it carefully to see if anything was concealed in it.

Nope. Nothing there but stuffing. When she was done, she set it carefully on the edge of the table.

The next item was round, flat. A plate? Yes. In the middle of the plate were some little ridges—a design of some sort. Or not? Was it writing? She couldn't really tell.

The next item was puzzling. It was a small, rectangular plastic box. When she picked it up she could hear water sloshing around inside. She felt it carefully. There was a small lid on the top. She opened the lid. Something was inside. A complex plastic thing. It took her a moment but eventually she decided it was a little figure of a man, lying down with his knees in the air. Hmm. She set it down.

The third item was a loop of some smooth material. Cardboard? Plastic?

The fourth item was a stack of paper about half an inch thick, stapled at one corner. Eight-and-a-half-by-eleven paper. But since she couldn't see, she couldn't read it.

The fifth seemed to be another toy. A small, plastic figure—a little doll or mannequin or action figure? The little figure had spiky plastic hair that stuck up off the top of its head.

And then the Voice was suddenly blaring out into the

room, "Congratulations, MeChelle. You're making progress. You have eleven . . . hours . . . and . . . three . . . minutes."

It was the same rich professional announcer voice that had greeted her when she opened the door from the stairs. And again the cadence of the numbers at the end made it sound like they were put together by a computer.

"Progress toward *what*?" MeChelle yelled.

There was a long pause, then, "Congratulations. You asked the right question. Here's the deal. You have been given thirteen hours to solve a murder and make an arrest. You will be allowed to work with a detective on the outside. If you and your partner find out who killed Kathleen Bolligrew, gather compelling and unambiguous evidence for an arrest, and then make the actual arrest within the allotted time—the front door will open and you'll walk away, scot-free.

"Meantime, you can use the phone. You can receive three calls an hour, with each call lasting no more than one minute. This line is untraceable, so whoever you work with on the outside, don't make them waste their time trying to trace it.

"You have until 8:00 P.M. tonight, MeChelle."

MeChelle looked up at the ceiling. Her *partner*? God, if she had to rely on that pitiful Cody Floss for help, she was in big trouble. Big, *big* trouble. "What if we don't make it?"

"If you fail, you will die inside this room."

And then the phone began to ring.

9

"MeChelle?" Gooch said.

He was threading his way through traffic. He had been hitting the redial button every minute or two as he listened to Cody Floss reading from the file on the Kathleen Bolligrew investigation.

"Oh, thank God!" she said. "I was sure it was going to be that idiot Cody Floss."

Gooch felt a flash of relief as he heard her voice. It was distant, with an odd delay, like she was talking to him from across the world. But it was definitely her.

"Where you at?" Gooch said.

"Thank God, thank God, thank God," MeChelle said. There was a brief pause. "Listen. Listen carefully. I don't know where I am. My eyes are glued shut. I'm in a soundproof, locked room. They drugged me. We're allowed three calls an hour, one minute per call. Clear?"

"Listen to me, girl," Gooch said. "I want you to understand one thing. I'm gonna get you out."

"We have one minute to talk," MeChelle said urgently. "Okay? Write down the following items. I think they're clues."

Gooch looked over at Cody, sitting in the passenger's seat, and made a scribbling motion with his hand.

Cody pulled out a pen and a small notebook from the breast pocket of his shirt.

"A ceramic plate," MeChelle said.

"Ceramic plate," Gooch said.

"How do you spell ceramic?" Floss whispered.

Gooch ignored him.

"Second thing—" MeChelle said. Then the line went dead.

"Dammit!" Gooch handed the phone to Cody Floss. "Call Robb Newton at Cingular."

Cody dialed, handed it back.

"Robb, it's me. Did you track that last call?"

"Nailed it. It's in Conyers, over in Rockdale County. Right near I-20."

"Okay. I'm calling again. See if you can get any closer."

"I'll do what I can. This particular technology doesn't have GPS. All we can do is triangulate based on an algorithm that—"

"Do what you can." Gooch hung up, dialed MeChelle's number.

"I'm here," MeChelle said. "Listen. The second clue is a little plastic box with a plastic guy lying in it. There's water or some kind of fluid in it. It might be like a toy vampire in a coffin or something? I'm not sure."

"Toy vampire," Gooch said. "Plastic. Water inside."

Floss wrote furiously.

"A stack of paper, stapled on one corner. I don't know if it's a story or a report or . . ."

"A stack of paper," Gooch said to Cody. "Might be a report or something. Stapled."

"A ring or loop of cardboard. Or maybe it's plastic. One-inch-wide strip, maybe ten or fifteen inches long. Also a little doll with stick-up hair"

Gooch repeated the clue to Cody Floss.

"Hank," MeChelle said. "Whoever's holding me prisoner says that we have to find out who killed Kathleen Bolligrew, gather evidence, and make an arrest. And we've got to do it by 8:00 P.M. tonight."

"Who's telling you this? Is there someone with you? Have you met your captor? How many people are there with you? I need to know how—"

But Gooch didn't get any more answers. The phone went dead.

He tried dialing again. But this time it wouldn't go through.

Shit. Maybe he was in a dead spot. Hank redialed the cell phone company. The call went through.

"Robb, it's Gooch. Same location?" he said.

"This is kinda weird. Now the signal's in Douglas County."

"No." Douglas County was twenty, thirty miles west of Conyers.

"Hey, I ran it twice. Douglas County. Near Wild Adventure, that theme park off I-20. Maybe they're calling from a plane."

"Run it again."

"Look . . ."

"Again."

Gooch heard some keys clicking. He was tearing down Peachtree at about eighty. The road was six lanes across, with a thirty-five-mile an hour speed limit. Cars were peeling off in front of him, getting out of his way. "Douglas County, Hank."

"And if they're not calling from a plane?"

"Then you're dealing with somebody serious. Some kind

of relay array, custom transmitters with cell phone IDs programmed in. Each time they'll use a different number. Probably a different location. If that's how they're doing it, it's like a firewall. You'll never get through it."

"I'll be in touch again soon." Gooch hit the END CALL button, then turned to Cody Floss. "Whoever snatched her, they want Kathleen Bolligrew's murderer arrested."

"Wow. Boy. Gosh. Isn't it ironic that—"

Now wasn't the time to hear Cody's reflections on life. "What do we know about this case, son?"

"Well, um . . ."

"No, not *um*. Lay it out plain. Start with the victim, then the crime. Move to the witnesses and the evidence. You got to have it all in your mind."

"Yes, sir." The kid took a deep breath. "The victim was a thirty-three-year-old white female, Kathleen Morris-Bolligrew. Victim was a former dancer. Like ballet dancer. Not exotic or stripper or whatever." The kid blushed. "Time of her death, she was employed as an analyst at First Buckhead Securities. The victim was found stabbed to death in her bedroom at her home on 2424 Tilden Drive in Midtown. The 911 call came in from the daughter, Lane, age eleven."

Gooch was amazed. This fool was actually presenting a completely organized and cogent briefing on the case. "Now the crime scene."

"Victim was lying on her back—"

"Call her by her name."

"Ms. Morris-Bolligrew was lying on her back, naked on the bed. She had been stabbed fifty-one times in the head, neck, arms, and pubic area. Autopsy indicated a serrated knife. Serrated on top, like one of those Rambo knives. There were defensive wounds to the arms. There was extensive vaginal chafing. No semen was found. The back door, which was glass, had been kicked in."

"*Kicked in?*"

"Uh . . . smashed, I guess. From the notes I assumed—"

"Don't."

"Yes, sir."

"Go on."

"Yes, sir. The back door was shattered, consistent with it being kicked in. Several small items of jewelry were taken from a jewelry box on the nightstand. They were pawned later. But the pawnshop owner couldn't give a description and didn't have a videotape of the person who pawned them. The only witness was the girl, Lane Priest. She was under the bed the whole time. Can you imagine that?" The kid sat there for a minute with his mouth open. "Anyway, she couldn't make a facial ID. Being blind, I guess."

"You guess?"

"Well . . . she did have a white cane and everything."

"Was she blind when she was eleven years old? Do we *know* that?"

"Well . . . uh . . . I don't see it in here."

"What do you see?"

"All we got is her saying the man sounded like a movie preview."

"A movie preview? What's that mean?"

"That's what it says in the interview notes. She said the killer sounded like a movie preview."

"Keep going."

"Well, that's mainly it. As far as I can tell. For a murder file, this is kind of light on detail. Not that many witness statements or anything. According to the detective's notes, no hairs or fibers were found that were any use. The detective who handled the case—a detective by the name of Sergeant Elbert King—he concluded that the rape was a crime of opportunity in the course of a burglary and that the murder was committed so that the perp could avoid being caught."

Gooch hadn't known this detective King. The case had happened before he had joined the department. Gooch snorted.

"Sir?"

"It's obvious his conclusions are wrong. Crimes of opportunity don't involve fifty-one stab wounds and a total lack of hairs or fibers. Any objects lying on the bed?"

"Um. I think there was one." The kid flipped through the file. "Yeah, here it is. A comb."

Gooch sighed, shook his head. "Do *you* see it, son?"

"Sir?"

"Come on. What this King character missed. Do you see it?"

"The comb." There was a long pause. Then an expression on Cody Floss's face, making the connection. "The comb. The perp combed the victim's pubic hair? Is that it, sir? Combed out any hairs he might have left?"

"No semen, no hairs, no fibers," Gooch said. "This is an experienced, organized killer. Possibly a serial rapist. He brought a condom—that's why there's no semen—and he combed her hair. Probably cut her fingernails and washed her hands, too. He stole the jewelry to make it look like a robbery."

He considered calling MeChelle to tell her what he'd read in the case file. But they only had one more phone call this hour. No point wasting it. He'd call her back after he'd finished talking to Lane Priest.

* * *

1134 Peachtree Battle pretty much qualified as a mansion. Buckhead was Atlanta's old-money neighborhood. But even by Buckhead standards this was a fancy joint. It was a brick Georgian with a porte-cochere and separate servants' quarters and very long windows that indicated the ceilings inside were unusually high. Looked like probably six, eight thousand square feet situated on about a five-acre lot. In this neighborhood? Gooch couldn't even imagine what the place was worth. Five million? Ten? More?

He pulled his car down the semi-circular drive of crushed stone, parked as close to the front door as he could get, then walked up to the front door and pressed the bell.

An aging black woman answered the door. "Yes?"

"Detectives Gooch and Floss, Atlanta police. Need to talk to Mrs. Priest."

The woman looked at him like she didn't much like the way he smelled. "And this is in reference to . . ."

"A murder."

After a longish pause, she said, "Won't you please come in?"

The woman showed Gooch and Cody Floss into a large, sparely decorated room. Outside, the house was very traditional. But inside, the house looked modern, Spartan, cold.

Gooch sat. After a while a very tall, very thin woman walked briskly into the room. There was no sign of blindness in the way she moved. She wore sunglasses on a dramatic, but not quite beautiful, face. High cheekbones, small chin, long thin nose. At first he guessed she was in her late thirties. But then he realized that she was younger than he'd first thought. Late twenties maybe? There was something self-assured about her that seemed to go beyond her age. She carried a small electronic personal organizer in her hand.

"Detectives?" she said in a loud voice. "I'm Lane Priest."

Cody Floss pulled Gooch's sleeve. "Sir?" he whispered.

"My name's Detective Gooch," Hank said. "This is Detective Floss."

"Sir? Sir?"

"One moment, ma'am," Gooch said. Then, turning to Cody Floss. "What?"

"Sir," Cody Floss whispered. "That's not Lane Priest."

"Actually," Gooch said, "the lady who came to the homicide office yesterday was a fake."

"How'd you know that?"

"I'll tell you later."

Lane Priest cleared her throat impatiently. "May I ask what this is in reference to?" she said sharply.

"Was your mother named Kathleen Morris-Bolligrew?"

There was a sharp intake of breath. Then she said, "I don't suppose we could talk about this at some other time?"

"Nope," Gooch said.

"Why not?"

"Because I said not," Gooch said.

"Taking that tone may work on street criminals," Lane Priest said. "But it won't work on me."

Gooch paused, thinking what he needed to tell her. Right now everybody he talked to could have had some part in MeChelle's abduction. He wasn't going to go around blabbing about it to just anyone. "I'm in the Cold Case Unit of the police department," he said finally. "We got someone who came into the department claiming to be you. Said she had information on your mom's murder."

The woman stared impassively in Gooch's direction. Then she went and sat stiffly on the couch. "What did this woman look like?"

"Pale. Blond. Pretty. Carried a white cane."

Gooch nodded, studying her briefly. He wasn't sure if she

was blind or not. The fact that she carried a PDA in her hand would seem to indicate she could see just fine. And the sunglasses indoors?—this time of year, sometimes people wore sunglasses inside. She didn't move as though she was afraid of banging into anything.

"So are you blind?" Gooch said.

"Yes."

"Wouldn't have guessed."

"We position the furniture very precisely. The staff is under strict instructions not to leave anything on the floor. I can move around here with assurance."

"What about that thing in your hand, that PDA or whatever it is?"

She held it up so they could see the front. There was no screen, just a flat metal panel with a bunch of raised shiny dots on it. "Braille," she said. "I use a stylus. The screen is made of tiny little steel rods that pop in and out."

Bet that cost a couple bucks, Gooch thought. "The lady who came to us," he said, "she claimed she had Bardet-Biedl Syndrome."

"Apparently she doesn't know much about disorders of the eye. Bardet-Biedl sufferers are generally obese and have extra fingers and toes." She paused. "Among other things."

"This witness, she claimed to have been under the bed. Claimed she heard the murderer's voice. Claimed she knew it."

Lane Priest snorted. "I suppose she had a recording of it, too."

"Let me play something for you." He took out thc mp3 player he'd taken from Deake's desk, then took her hand in his and pressed one of thc car buds into her hand. "Tell me if you've ever heard this voice before."

She slipped one of the tiny speakers into her ear. "This is a total waste of time," she said.

Gooch pressed the play button.

She frowned, listening. Then, suddenly, she sat up straight. One hand went over her mouth and she gasped. Then she ripped the ear bud out and threw it on the table.

"Mrs. Priest?"

She started breathing hard, nothing moving but her chest.

"Mrs. Priest? Have you heard that voice before?"

She ran her fingers up and down her face, like she was trying to wash something off her skin.

"Ma'am."

After a moment her breathing slowed. Finally she whispered, "I don't know. I don't know. It could be him."

"You're not sure?"

She shook her head. "I mean . . . he had a big voice like that. Kind of scratchy. Like a smoker. I remember that. But was that *specifically* him? I don't know. It was a long time ago."

"Were you blind then?"

She shook her head no. "I have macular degeneration. An unusually nasty case of it. But back then I could still see a little."

"So did you get a look at the person who killed your mother?"

"No." She shook her head again. "Surely that's in the file."

"I haven't read the whole file yet," he said.

"You'd think you might have gone to the trouble," she said.

"You'd think. But you'd be wrong," Gooch said. "I want to read you a list of things. Tell me if they mean anything to you."

"I'm not sure I understand."

"A plate."

She frowned.

"A stack of papers, bound together with a staple. Might be a report or something?"

She shrugged.

"A little plastic toy with water in it. A man lying in a bathtub, possibly? Or vampire?"

"I don't understand. What does this have to do with my mother's murder?"

"A plastic doll with hair that sticks straight up off its head. A loop of cardboard or plastic?"

She shook her head impatiently.

"A rabbit."

Her brow wrinkled.

"A stuffed toy rabbit," he added.

She looked away for a while then reached under her glasses and swabbed at her eyes with her fingers. They came away wet.

"A toy rabbit." Her voice was dull. "It's mine."

"I don't understand. I thought you didn't see the guy."

"He took it," she said. "He said, 'If you ever tell anybody, I'll tear your little rabbit's head off. Then I'll come back and tear your head off, too.'" Then she frowned, like she was about to add something else.

"And?"

Before she had a chance to answer, the front door opened and a man breezed into the room. He was a good deal older than Lane, but Gooch took him to be her husband.

"Hi, Joe," Lane Priest said. Gooch figured she knew him by sound. The way he walked maybe? The way he flung open the door?

"Hi, babe," the man said. He kissed her on the side of the

face, then stuck out his hand at Gooch. "Joe Priest," he said, smiling broadly. He looked like the vice president of Kappa Alpha at some Southern university. He had wide, guileless blue eyes, sandy hair, the tanned and leathery skin of a tennis player. Gooch figured anybody who'd done as well as this guy had was hiding a lot of guile behind those guileless eyes. Joe Priest was at least twenty-five years older than his wife.

Gooch put it together now. He'd heard of this guy before. He was a big real-estate developer.

Gooch shook Joe Priest's hand. "Hank Gooch, Atlanta Police. I'm looking into Kathleen Bolligrew's murder."

Joe Priest's smile faded and a look of concern crossed his face. "Really?"

"We had a lady come into the office yesterday, claim she was your wife."

Priest blinked. "Well, goldarn, that's strange."

"Mmm-hmm."

Gooch waited for a minute, seeing if Priest would jump into the silence, volunteer any information. He didn't. He just sat there blinking at Gooch.

Gooch finally went ahead and described the woman, the fake witness.

Priest rolled his eyes. "Oh!" he said. "Well! Heck, yeah. I know who *that* is. Gal by the name of Stormé Venda. Spelled S-T-O-R-M-E with one of those French accent marks over the E. But she pronounces it Stormy, like the weather."

"How you know this woman?"

"I don't especially. She temped for me for a short period of time. Had to fire her."

"You seem pretty sure it's her. How come you jumped so quick to that conclusion?"

"Oh, she wasn't there to work. She came into my employ specifically to extort money out of me. Claimed sexual harassment, sent threatening letters, and so on. It was an obvious setup."

"How'd that get resolved?"

Joe Priest smiled, blinked. "I hired some people. She went away."

"You make it sound like you had her whacked."

"Not that I wasn't tempted." Joe Priest grinned. "Nah, what I did, I used a private investigator, hid some cameras, put her in some situations where she could make various statements that contradicted the claims she was making. Once that was accomplished, I left the rest to my lawyers." He scrubbed his hands together like he was washing something off of them, then held them up, palms out.

"You give her any money?"

He laughed merrily. "Man in my position can't let the word get out that he can be taken." The smile faded. "I'd have had my teeth ripped out one by one with a pair of pliers before I'd have given that gal a nickel."

"You know where I can find her?"

"I'll find out." Joe Priest pulled out his phone, looked at his watch, then dialed. "I beg your pardon, Detective. I got a tennis date to get to and I make a firm point not to be late to appointments. But I'll have someone call you with that information about Stormé Venda. You don't hear from them soon, you call me back and I'll raise Cain." He winked one guileless blue eye, then left the room.

Gooch turned to Lane Priest. "What about the rabbit? Before your husband came back in, there was something you were about to say about that rabbit."

Lane frowned. "Was there?" Her fingers flicked across the

panel on the front of her electronic organizer. Gooch guessed she was checking the time.

"I think so."

She looked thoughtful. "Yes," she said finally. "I never told anybody about that rabbit. I never told *anybody*."

10

MeChelle was thinking about escape again. Was there actually anybody hear to guard her? It was obvious that The Voice was recorded. All those funny spaces every time The Voice talked about time—ten hours . . . and . . . twenty . . . nine . . . minutes—they were obviously caused by the computer stringing the words together from a list.

Could it be that everything here was automated? What if there were switches that cued messages from a computer? Message one came when she stood up. Message two when she picked up the box of toys or clues or whatever they were. Maybe there were electric eyes like they used in bank vaults. Or maybe there was a camera with some kind of computerized sensing devices that—

No, but even though the Voice seemed prerecorded, the messages that it gave seemed to be controlled by what she said or did. Like somebody was watching her, calling the messages up when she did particular things.

Well, it was nearly impossible to know.

The one thing that *was* certain, though, was that somebody had gone to a hell of a lot of trouble to put her here. The thing that was puzzling was this: If they wanted a crime solved, why not just walk into the detective bureau and report the crime?

Control. They didn't just want a crime solved. They wanted control. They wanted to make MeChelle work for it. They wanted to make her squirm.

"Kiss my black ass," MeChelle said.

Tick. Tick. Tick. Tick.

She looked around, seeing nothing but blackness. What now?

She realized that now that the adrenaline was wearing off, she was getting hungry. She felt her way back into the kitchen, opened the door of the fridge, pulled out one of the wrapped sandwiches. Tuna.

Then she took out the milk jug. Were there any glasses? She searched through the cabinets above the sink. She found one plastic bag, shook it. Potato chips. Other than that, the cabinets were stone empty. She sat on the floor and began to eat.

Suddenly it occurred to her that Gooch might call. She went back into the other room, got the phone, pulled the long cord into the kitchen, sat down again and ate her meal. By the time she was done, the phone still hadn't rung.

"So is it three calls between, say, nine and ten o'clock?" she said loudly. "Or is it three calls in any given one-hour period?"

The Voice didn't answer.

She picked up the phone and went back into the other room. It was amazing how blindness heightened the other four senses. The sensation of the carpet on her feet just seemed so subtle and powerful. It was like she could feel every thread in the carpet. She could distinctly smell the tuna fish that she'd just eaten.

There was something else she was smelling, too. Couldn't quite put her finger on it.

Suddenly the phone rang. Her heart jolted. She grabbed the receiver.

"Hank?"

"Just talked to Lane Priest," Gooch said. "Turns out the gal that came in and talked to you yesterday was a fake. Her real name's Stormé Venda. She tried to shake Lane's husband down last year."

"What else did you learn?"

"The rabbit," Gooch said. "Lane Priest confirms that the guy who killed her mom took a stuffed rabbit the night of the murder. She said she never told a soul about it. Whoever's got you in there?—they know *something*."

"Okay."

"So, look, can you hear anything?" Gooch said. "Train, planes taking off, highway noise? Anything that might help us figure out where you are?"

"It's soundproof," MeChelle said. "The only thing I hear is a clock ticking. Plus, there's a voice that talks to me. I think it's computerized. Comes out of speakers in the ceiling. It's the same voice as was on that recording that Lane—Stormé Whatever-her-name-is—the same as on the recording. I think you ought to track down the announcer who recorded that commercial. He's gotta be involved in this somehow."

"I was planning on going to this Stormé Venda girl," Gooch said.

"Maybe if you talk to the announcer first, you'll have something to work with when you talk to her. Or maybe she's working *for* him. If I were you, I'd track down the announcer first."

Gooch didn't say anything.

"You have ten hours," the Voice in the ceiling said.

"Hank? Hank?" She waited. "Hank?" The phone was dead.

11

Gooch's initial instinct had been to go straight for Stormé Venda. But Joe Priest's people still hadn't called with information on her. And MeChelle might be right. This announcer guy was obviously connected to this kidnapping somehow.

He made a few calls in the car as they drove back to the homicide bureau offices, eventually reaching the director of marketing for Wild Adventure, a woman named Eileen Burnside.

"Trying to find the name of the announcer who did your latest commercial on the radio," Gooch said to her.

"Off the top of my head?" Eileen Burnside said, "I believe the VO guy on that spot was Damon Fergus."

"VO?"

"Sorry, in the business we don't call them announcers. VO stands for voice-over. We call them VO guys. Or talent. Or voice talent or voice guys? Or—"

"Okay, whatever," Gooch said. "What can you tell me about him?"

"Great pipes, huh?" she said. "The guy sounds like the voice of God. Give me a second, I'll dig up his phone number." Gooch heard her tapping on her computer or her organizer or something. Then she gave him the number.

When Gooch walked into the detective bureau, the clerk at the desk said, "Major Hicks wants to see you in his office."

Gooch turned around and went upstairs to HR first, getting his ID badge printed up, getting his official order of appointment with the signature of the new chief. If he was going to get into a pissing contest with Denny Hicks right off the bat, he wanted bureaucratic ammo. Then he went to the armorer, signed out a nice new Glock straight from the box. Gooch looked at his watch. He'd burned up almost half of a precious hour. But he didn't want to have some witness turning him away just because he didn't have a badge or a cop ID. When he got back to the homicide bureau office, he found Hicks talking on the phone. Gooch looked at his watch again. Hicks made a point of yammering on about his golf game last weekend while Gooch stood in front of his desk. Finally Hicks hung up.

"Siddown," Major Hicks said.

Gooch sat. Hicks stared at him for a while, chomping and smacking on his gum.

Finally Hicks spoke. "I don't know what shit you pulled, but the mayor wants you back. We don't have space for you, or no need for you. But we'll make do. You got a temporary desk up front. As of this moment, you got a budget of zero dollars, no computer, no nothing. We'll see if we can free up some resources for you. Eventually. But per this moment in time? If you think you gonna get any assistance from any other member of my personnel in whatever mysterious business the mayor's got you working on?—hey, you can forget it."

"Do you have something important to say?" Gooch said. "Because I got things I need to do."

Hicks shrugged. "Hey, go earn your salary . . . *Detective,*" Hicks gave it a little twist, enjoying the fact that Gooch had been knocked down two levels in rank.

12

Something was tickling at the edge of MeChelle's mind. If it had been any other time, any other place, it would have been nothing.

But here? With her eyes glued shut? No, she could feel it.

Only . . . what was *it*?

She smelled the air. There was something else in the room. Something besides tuna fish and potato chips, something besides the smell of fresh cement and new carpet.

It was a sweet smell. Air freshener?

She just couldn't quite say.

She dumped out the box of clues on the table and went over them again. The stack of paper? Couldn't read it. The rabbit? Well, they knew what the rabbit was now. The little figure in the plastic box? No clue. The loop of cardboard? That didn't take her anywhere either. Neither did the plate.

Across the room she heard a squeak.

She jumped. In any normal house, at any normal time, she'd have never noticed it. Just the house settling, timbers in the wall or floor squeaking. But here, every tiny noise was like a gunshot.

She froze, ears straining.

Tick. Tick. Tick.

Nothing.

She returned to the clues. The fourth item was a circular loop of cardboard or plastic. There didn't seem to be anything distinctive about it. She pulled it gently and the ends popped apart. There were small notches in the ends of the cardboard so that the ends could be hooked together. The strip was an inch or so wide, ten or fifteen inches long.

What am I missing? she thought.

She smelled the items. The rabbit smelled like cigarette smoke. Okay, so *if* the rabbit had been taken from the murderer's home recently, then the murderer was a smoker. But if not, then whoever had put her in the room smoked.

The other items had no particular smell.

As she was keying into the smell, she sniffed the air around her. What was that smell? A smell like—

Again the floor squeaked slightly.

Again MeChelle jumped.

And then she realized what it was. Deodorant. Not her brand, though. *Someone else's.* The tiny hairs rose on her arms.

There was someone else in the room. And they had been there all along!

13

"Watch. Listen. Don't talk," Gooch said as he and Cody Floss slid up to the front of the town house in downtown Decatur. It was one of these overpriced pseudo-lofts—weathered brick on the outside that had probably been salvaged from a torn-down textile mill, brand-new on the inside, the ground floor taken up by a parking garage.

The kid nodded earnestly.

A sign said they couldn't get into the parking garage without a swipe card, so Gooch parked in the fire zone out front. There was an entry foyer with a row of mailboxes on the left, the residents' names indicated with little brass plaques.

FERGUS/SWEET. *301.*

Gooch tried the door. It was open, so he walked on through, up two flights of steps. The kid was huffing and puffing trying to keep up.

"Half my age, you shouldn't get out of breath going up two flights of stairs," he said.

"Yes, sir. I got this treadmill a couple months back but I just can't seem to find the time with all the—"

Gooch put his hands to his lips. "What'd I say?"

"Sorry, sir!"

They walked down the hallway, found 301. A tiny brass sign said DO NOT KNOCK. RING BELL. Gooch pressed the button.

After a minute a voice came out of a small speaker by the door. "Yes?"

"Dectectives Gooch and Floss, APD. Need a couple minutes of your time."

"This is in reference to what?" Even coming through the tiny speaker, the voice was large and powerful. It was the voice of a senator or a general in a movie.

"A homicide investigation."

There was a long pause, then the door clicked open. It was impossible to see the face on the other side of the door because the room was entirely dark. "You have a badge, I presume? Not an ID. A badge."

Gooch had been right to take the extra half hour in HR and get his badge and ID. He handed his badge through the door. Gooch saw a pale hand explore the badge carefully, the fingers crawling across the surface of the metal like a large spider. Finally the man opened the door wide. Medium height, shaved head.

"I have to be careful," the man said, holding out the badge. "People will take advantage of me if I'm not careful." He gestured Gooch and Cody into the pitch-black space.

"Little dark," Gooch said. "We catch you in the middle of a nap?"

"I'm blind," the man said. "Don't have much use for lights."

Blind. Another one. That was an interesting development.

The man reached out, hit a switch. The room brightened—though not appreciably. There was one bare forty-watt bulb hanging from the ceiling, its light barely making it to the edges of a dark room. Along one side of the room was a maze of electronic equipment. The walls were strange-looking, three-dimensional, lumpy. It gave the room a cavelike feeling, as though it had been cut from rock.

"What's that stuff on the walls?" Gooch asked.

"Acoustical insulation," the man said. "Have a seat over there." He pointed at a black couch on the far end of the room.

Once Gooch and Floss sat, Gooch became aware of just how quiet the room was. "Bet someone could scream their head off in here, nobody'd even hear."

"I'm a professional voice talent," the man said in his big commanding voice. "This is my studio. It has to be insulated." His physical presence, however, was distinctly different from his voice. He was in his early forties, neatly dressed in all-black clothes. Though he was muscular, with a strongly featured face, he seemed not to take up much space. Almost as though there were something shrunken about him. His eyes were brown and perfectly normal-looking—except for the fact that they stared fixedly at nothing. It was hard to say what it was, but something about him made Gooch uncomfortable. Not the fact that he was blind. Something else.

The man sat on a rolling office chair, put his hands flat on his thighs and sat, waiting, staring.

"Who's Sweet?" Gooch said.

"Pardon?"

"It says Fergus/Sweet on the buzzer downstairs. Who's Sweet?"

"Austin. Austin Sweet." Pause. "He would be my lover."

Was that what was making Gooch uncomfortable—the

guy putting off some kind of gay vibe? Maybe. "How long you been blind, Mr. Fergus?"

"Are you making conversation, Detective . . . Gooch is it?"

"Never been much good at that, no."

"Do I need a lawyer or something?"

"You ever killed anybody?"

"No."

"Then I wouldn't waste your money."

"Fine. You see, it's just that I'm just curious why you're asking."

"I'm asking 'cause I'm asking."

The blind man sat motionless for a long time. Finally he said, "Since I was nine."

"Bardet-Biedl, macular degeneration, what?" Gooch remembering names from the stuff he'd pulled up on the Internet a couple hours earlier.

"You know your diseases of the eye." A strange crooked smile split the blind man's face for a moment, then disappeared without a trace. "No, I was hit in the head with a baseball."

"By who?"

"Surely that's not relevant."

Gooch sat, watching the man. Ten seconds ticked by. Twenty. Thirty. A minute.

Finally Fergus said, "His name was Kevin Woodruff. He was three years older than I. Not much of a hitter as I recall, though. Sadly I happened to have a moment of inattention at the precise second when he hit his all-time best line drive."

"Where'd you grow up?"

"Here. My parents placed me at the Oakdale School for the Blind after the accident." He paused. "Also I wear a size thirty-two/thirty-four trouser, and my fourth grade English teacher was Mr. Robbins. He spoke with a lisp."

There was a Kleenex box on the table. Gooch pulled out a tissue, wadded it up, threw it at the blind man. It bounced off his head and fell on the floor. Fergus never even blinked before the tissue hit him.

"Sorry," Gooch said. "Slipped."

"When you get through having your fun, I have a session to record." In a loud voice he said, "Time!"

A voice from a speaker above him said, "The time is . . . eleven . . . forty . . . seven . . . A.M."

"Neat," Gooch said. "How much does a gadget like that set you back?"

"I have ten minutes," the blind man said. "I wouldn't waste it discussing audio clock technology if I were you."

"Where were you living in 1988?"

"279 Orme Street. It's in Midtown."

"Mmm-hmm. You remember what you were doing on the night of May 13, 1988?"

"I believe so, yes."

"What?"

"Killing someone, as I recall. Though I must tell you, I've killed so many times that I have a hard time keeping the dates straight."

"Sarcasm don't work on me, Mr. Fergus. May 13, 1988."

"How should I remember? That was like eighteen years ago."

"You know a Kathleen Morris-Bolligrew?"

"I do not."

"Lane Priest?"

"Nor her."

"Anybody by the name of Bolligrew? Or Priest?"

"I believe not."

"You ever been convicted of a crime?"

"I have not."

"Accused?"

There was the most minute hesitation before the blind man said, "Even if I had the impulses of the world's most twisted criminal—which I do not—it's difficult enough for me to get to the store and buy groceries. A life of crime, I'm afraid, would be quite beyond my capabilities."

Out of his pocket Gooch pulled the mp3 player that he had found on MeChelle Deakes's desk, played the Wild Adventure spot.

"That your voice?" he said when it was over.

"It is. I hope advertising has not become a crime, or I'll be back to sucking on the public teat. Other than my voice, I'm afraid I have no marketable skills at all. Perhaps I could learn to do massage therapy or play the blues. Those are excellent careers for the blind, I'm told."

Gooch took some notes. This looked like a total dead end.

"How much you get paid for a spot like that?"

"Several thousand. Plus residuals if it runs more than three months or in additional markets. I voiced a TV spot for margarine once that ran for four years in a wide variety of markets. Including Canada and Guam as I recall. I made over ten thousand dollars in residuals. Not bad for thirty seconds of work."

The guy damn sure loved the sound of his own voice. Then again, Gooch supposed, that was probably an asset in his line of work.

"Why you talk that way?" Gooch asked.

"What way?"

"You got a real formal way of speaking. Don't much of nobody talk that way no more."

"Don't much of nobody talk that way no more, indeed."

"Who's making fun of who?" Gooch said.

"I was simply calling attention to the fact that you were

laying on the country bumpkin routine a bit thick. You're clearly a very bright man. Even a blind man can see that." A creepy, lopsided grin appeared and disappeared. "To answer your question, my voice is my instrument. I can play it any way I choose. Why choose to play it badly?"

"You do funny voices? Hick accents, Mohammed the 7-11 guy, stuff like that?"

"Not professionally."

"How long you been in this line of work?"

"Since I got out of college."

"College?"

"Yes, blind people do go to college, Detective. I graduated from Emory University in 1984. Where did *you* go to college?"

"Afghanistan."

"Touché."

"You ever met a detective by the name of MeChelle Deakes?"

"Doesn't ring a bell. She's not one of my victims, is she? *Alleged,* I mean?"

The guy was starting to piss Gooch off a little. "MeChelle Deakes is a friend of mine. She's missing and probably in a great deal of danger. If I hear you make another joke about her, I'll knock your blind ass out of that chair."

There was a brief silence. Eventually Fergus said, "My apologies. Is there anything else?"

Gooch couldn't really think of anything. "So how's this work?" he said. Just trying to stall for time. "You record here, send the stuff to people at advertising agencies?"

"I've got a broadband line. I synch up to equipment in remote studios all over the world. Could be in New York, L.A., London, wherever. The producer, the engineer, the account rep, the client—they're all sitting in a booth somewhere, talking to me just like I was on the other side of the glass in their studio. They can hear me scratch my nose. And vice versa for that matter. Once we're connected, I might as well be in the same room as. I record directly to their equipment."

"So you're kind of an electronics expert?"

"To maintain my studio here, I have to be. This equipment is state-of-the-art. I don't solder wires together. But I don't need to hire people to plug in a mic cable, I assure you."

Gooch didn't know much about recording. But there were a whole lot of black metal boxes over there, with a whole lot of knobs and a whole lot of blinking lights. Wouldn't have been surprised if the guy had a hundred grand in the rig.

"Well," Fergus said, "unless you'd like to throw another Kleenex at me to see whether I'm faking my condition, I really do need to get to work."

"How'd you know it was a Kleenex?" Gooch said.

"I heard you pull it out of the box." The blind man rolled his chair swiftly backward toward the recording console on the far wall, turned his back to Gooch and Floss, hit some buttons, twisted some knobs, then pulled down a large studio microphone on a complicated shock mount.

"Test, one, two," he said. His voice suddenly took on an energy, a brightness, that it had lacked during his conversation with Gooch. It was hard to put your finger on what he did different—but it was definitely something. The I'm-a-sour-little-homo thing was gone. Sounding all big and masculine suddenly. But it was more than that. It was about presence, projecting himself through his voice. Neat trick, whatever it was. It would be a handy skill for an interrogator, being able to do that.

"You give classes?" Gooch said.

"In what?" The blind man's fingers danced over the knobs

and buttons on the mixing board in front of him, fingertips flitting along, feeling their way like spiders.

"How to do what you just did with your voice?"

"What did I do?"

"You cranked it up a notch somehow."

"Ah." The blind man shrugged, back still turned. "That's just diaphragmatic breathing. And, no, I don't give lessons. Those who can, do. Those who can't, teach."

"Mmm," Gooch said.

"Anyway, you're a natural. You already know how to do it."

Do I? Gooch thought. Then, after a moment's thought, *Yeah, probably so.*

"Feel free to see yourself out," Fergus said. "I need to be ready to start my session at precisely noon."

He hit a button.

"Test, one, two." His voice boomed out of speakers on the ceiling.

Gooch and Floss stood, walked to the door.

"Time!" the blind man said.

"*The time is . . . eleven . . . fifty . . . eight . . . a.m.*"

14

MeChelle's pulse was racing and she had a sour taste in her throat. The bastard had been standing there watching her all this time? How close had she passed to this person—it had to be a man, right? Probably within a couple of feet. It made her skin crawl.

And he had never moved.

Which meant he hadn't come into the kitchen. Which meant he hadn't seen her break the bottle. But he must have heard it. Maybe he would have figured she'd knocked it over by mistake. Or maybe not.

MeChelle slid her hand into the pocket of her pants, closed her fingers around the neck of the broken ketchup bottle.

She continued with the clues, ran her left hand over the five items in the box. Waiting. Making a point of keeping her face oriented away from whoever watching her. Him. It was *him*, surely. She could smell the deodorant strongly now. She recognized the brand. Some boyfriend of hers had worn it—when?—back in college? Old Spice, that's what it was.

She tried to put a face on the silent man. Tall, short? Black, white, Mexican, Korean? Thick glasses, good-looking, fat, muscular?

No clue.

She breathed slowly, letting her pulse slow, getting ready. Feeling the soft fur of the rabbit. Pretending she was all absorbed in it.

She had an advantage right now. The silent guy on the other side of the room didn't know that she knew he was there.

Waiting. Waiting for another telltale squeak as he shifted his weight. Then she was gonna be *on* his ass.

It took maybe ten minutes—*man*, he was patient—but it finally happened. The tiniest, most minute little squeak. Ten feet away? Twelve? No, closer. Maybe eight feet. Not quite close enough. It was amazing how accurately she could gauge sound, now that she had no sight to rely on.

She repositioned herself, back to the table, messing with the clues.

Right over . . .

There!

She leapt toward the sound, yanking the jagged bottle neck out of her pants. Left hand out, right hand drawing back at belly level. The idea was that she would feel where he was with her left hand. Then as soon as she made contact, she'd start working him over with the bottle.

She made it one stride, two—flinging herself at him with every ounce of strength, every fiber of nerve and will.

And then it hit her.

A wall of pain.

Thunder exploding from inside her body. Lighting bursting directly into her heart. A 747 crash-landing on top of her head. A piano falling from the umpteenth floor. Cartoon pain, eyes flying out of the sockets, hair shooting out from the head. God's judgment for her sins coming down in pure physical form.

She fell to the floor.

Pain so huge and explosive that all thought ceased.

Or nearly all. Only one tiny distant part of her brain not consumed by pain—and in it this minuscule and fleeting thought:

Okay. That didn't go so hot.

15

"Well?" Gooch said when they reached the car.

"Sir?" Detective Floss said.

Gooch spread his hands but didn't say anything.

"You mean, did he do it, sir? A blind homosexual? I guess he doesn't seem much like a rapist home invader."

Gooch didn't disagree.

"Not a very likable guy, sir, huh?"

Gooch got in the car, turned the key.

"I mean, you want to root for the blind guy, don't you?"

"Oh?" Gooch said.

Floss blinked. "Well . . . I don't know. It just seems like . . ." The kid's voice petered out.

"You think I was rude. Throwing a snot rag at a blind man."

"It occurred to me, yeah."

"Everybody's the same, son," Gooch said. "You want to be a good cop, don't root for nobody. It blinds you. No pun intended. The ones you root for, half the time they're the worst ones of all."

"Gosh!" the kid said. "Never thought of it that way."

Plus—Gooch didn't say it, but the guy gave him the creeps. Not that he'd have admitted it to the kid. Was it because the guy was blind, staring off into the emptiness like that? Or because he was a homo? Nah. There was something about that guy that wasn't right. Couldn't quite get a handle on what it was, though.

As they were sitting there, a mustached, blond man wearing a red cap, bright yellow jacket, and very tight blue jeans, appeared from the elevator in the parking garage, jumped into a red Jag, and peeled out of the lot. The license plate said SWEET E.

"Wonder why Fergus's boyfriend's tearing off in such a big hurry?"

Cody Floss looked at Gooch like, *Huh?*

Jesus Christ, Gooch thought. *Did the kid notice anything?*

16

MeChelle never actually lost consciousness. It was more that consciousness kind of receded while the giant pile of pain fell on her.

And then—like that—it was gone. And when the pain let up, she was on the ground.

She clutched at her chest. Two thin wires protruded from her shirt. It took her a minute to understand it. The guy in the room had tazed her. She ripped the wires out of her shirt.

"Asshole," she whispered. "What do you want?"

But there was no answer. Just a whistling as he pulled the wires back, retracted them into the taser.

"What do you *want*?"

But there was not a single sound in response. He wasn't moving. Wasn't breathing hard. Wasn't even shifting his weight. It was like he was made from a block of ice.

MeChelle felt around her. Eventually her hands closed around the glass of the broken ketchup bottle neck.

Think! There had to be something she could do.

The problem was, she felt weak, wrung-out. Fortunately, *he* wasn't doing anything to threaten her. It seemed like as long as she didn't bother him, *he* wouldn't bother her.

Which meant . . . what? That he was just there to watch her.

And then she had a thought. This was going to really hurt. But she'd give it a try. What the guy probably didn't know about tasers was that they used a lot of juice. You could eat the battery pretty quick if you wanted to.

"You got a name?"

No answer. She needed to distract him.

"Douchebag? Asswipe? Mama's boy? Dick-sucker? Shithead? Hmm?" Trying to provoke him.

But it didn't seem to work. There was no response, no sound, not even a shifting of weight.

She stood, took a deep breath, flung herself at the place she remembered him to be. She heard him move this time, a slight exhalation of breath, a rustle of cloth as he stepped out of the way. She swung the bottle at him, felt it graze something soft.

"You like that, bitch?" she said.

And then the wall of pain came down. The last thought that went through her mind was *Hold on to the ketchup bottle!*

This time he kept the taser going for a little longer. Her muscles seized and spasmed and finally she lost consciousness. When she came to, her muscles ached throughout her abdomen. Felt like she'd done about five hundred sit-ups.

It took her a few seconds to get oriented. She felt the ketchup bottle neck in her hand, cradled against her stomach. For a minute she thought about just lying there. But finally she climbed to her feet and began moving around the room as swiftly as she could.

"Come on, bitch," she said, swinging the jagged bottle. "You got nothing."

She banged her hand into the wall, making a spike of pain shoot through her wrist. But she didn't lose the bottle neck. And she kept moving through the pain. Fight! Concentrate! If she could get the guy to hit her a couple more times, the capacitor in the taser would lose charge and she'd be able to get her hands on the guy. And then it would just be one small blind woman with a ketchup bottle versus . . . *him*.

And she'd find out what he was made of.

In front of her: *squeak!*

She lunged.

The wall of pain.

Hold the bottle! Pull it in! Keep it tight to the stomach!

And then she was on the ground again. It hadn't been as bad that time. Bad, but not so bad that she lost consciousness.

She lay for a while, listening. She really didn't want to do this again. Her abs were a sheet of pain. Her mind was coming up with a million reasons to just lie there now. What if it caused heart failure? What if—

Come on! Come on! Don't give him time!

She staggered to her feet. One leg wasn't working quite right now.

This time she heard an intake of breath in front of her. Okay, at least she was making him breathe hard. She tried to lunge toward the sound, but she ended up veering off to one side, smashing her head into the steel door.

"You think it's funny?" she said. "Huh? We'll see who's laughing when I cut your throat."

She lunged again. The strength was coming back to her legs. But still she was operating mostly on will now. She knew she couldn't take a lot more of this.

The wall of pain.

It was harder getting up this time. Again, though, the charge had gotten weaker. He really laid it on this time. Must have been twenty seconds she lay there twitching. But she could actually feel the buzz in her chest weakening.

The taser leads whistled in the air, retracting.

She tried to stand, fell to her knees.

"You couldn't take me if you tried," she said. Her voice sounded funny—hollow and slurred, like she'd just drunk a bottle of wine. "You're weak. You're nothing."

She pushed herself up, finally got to her feet. The ketchup bottle fell from her grasp. She heard him move then. Coming toward her. Diving for the ketchup bottle maybe? Trying to get rid of her weapon?

She kicked as hard as she could, but caught nothing but air. He'd sprung backward just in time. She leaned down to get the bottle.

The wall of pain.

Only . . . this time it was more like a wall of buzzing—an uncomfortable, twitchy, jerky sensation in her chest.

She fell down, rolled into a ball, pulling the taser leads free, the ketchup bottle neck cradled against her chest. She continued to twitch and jerk as though the taser were still working. But in fact she was holding the taser leads together so that they were short-circuiting, draining more juice out of the capacitor. She could hear them arcing and snapping in her palm.

Finally he stopped pressing the trigger and the arcing noise stopped.

He jerked the wires free from her hand. She listened for

the whistle of wire as they returned to the taser, mapping it out in her mind, figuring out where he was, how close.

She lay for a while, gathering her strength.

"No more," she mumbled. "Please."

Hoping maybe he'd say something, gloat a little, anything.

But there was only silence. She staggered to her feet, not having to lay it on that thick. She really *did* feel like she'd been hit by a truck. Her breath was coming hard and ragged, and her pulse was hammering in her ears.

"Please." She stumbled in the direction of the last sound she'd heard. Her hand brushed cloth.

She grabbed the cloth, yanked. He fell toward her. She jammed the ketchup bottle into him, felt the yielding of human flesh.

"Huh? Yeah?" she said, twisting the bottle, hearing glass cracking in his flesh.

He grunted. The only sound she'd heard from him. There was an impact in her chest, a crackle of electricity.

The ketchup bottle flew out of her hand and she went down.

In the distance. A sound. Ringing. A phone ringing.

She crawled toward it, expecting him to attack her. But instead she just heard the squeaking of the floor as he moved away from her.

The phone rang again. She felt for it. Smooth plastic against her hand. Reaching . . . oh no! It fell clattering to floor.

She fumbled wildly on the floor.

Hello! she yelled. At least she thought that's what she did. But actually her mouth wasn't working. *Hello! Hello!*

Her hand found the receiver. She picked it, held it to her ear.

"MeChelle? You there? MeChelle!" It was Hank Gooch. She tried to answer. But it was like her jaw was wired shut.

Then she heard another voice. For a moment, she thought it was coming from the phone. But no, it was the rich announcer voice. The clock talking from the ceiling. "You have precisely . . . nine . . . hours."

Nothing. Four hours down, and they were nowhere. She slumped against the wall, the telephone cradled against her ear. She felt tears welling up, bathing her useless eyes.

Tick. Tick. Tick. Tick. Tick. Tick. Tick.

17

"Let's listen to the tapes of my conversation with MeChelle again," Gooch said. "Maybe there's something I missed."

Cody rewound the tape they'd been using to record Gooch's calls to MeChelle, hit the play button. They listened to the conversations all the way through. "Wait," Gooch said at the very end. "What's that?"

It was something at the very end of the last conversation. Well, conversation wasn't the right word. It was just some muffled moaning. Right before they got cut off.

Cody played it again. It was a distant fragment of a second voice, not MeChelle moaning, but something else. *"You have precisely . . . nine . . . hours."* An audio clock. An audio clock with a rich, powerful voice.

Cody blinked. "That's him! It's the blind guy!"

"Play it again."

Cody replayed it. Gooch felt a jolt of anger. He'd *known* there was something wrong with that blind sumbitch! Gooch did a tire-shredding one-eighty in the middle of Ponce de Leon Avenue, headed back toward Decatur.

He hit the redial button, calling MeChelle's number.

This time there was no answer.

Gooch switched back to the cell phone rep, who'd been on hold. "Location?"

A clicking of keys. "Yeah," the cell phone rep said. "Definitely some kind of funky transmitter array. That time the signal polled at a location in Snellville."

Gooch broke the connection.

Within two minutes they were tearing through downtown Decatur, skidding to a stop in front of the loft apartment building where Damon Fergus lived. Gooch sprang out of the car, gun drawn.

Cody ran after him. "Sir? Sir? What are we doing?"

Gooch didn't answer as he pounded up the stairs toward the blind man's apartment.

"The reason I ask"—Cody was gasping by the time they hit the third floor—"We're totally out of our jurisdiction."

Gooch stopped in front of apartment 301.

Gooch hammered on the door, pressed the bell, hammered some more.

"Police! Open the door!"

"Sir? Shouldn't we give a courtesy call to Decatur PD?"

"Open the door, Fergus!"

No answer. The door didn't move.

"Um . . . sir . . ."

"Draw your weapon," Gooch snapped. "Kick the door."

Cody Floss fumbled for his duty weapon and swallowed nervously. "Sir, we don't have a warrant, much less—"

The kid was useless.

Gooch kicked the door.

Inside was blackness. He shone his flashlight around the room. The room was empty.

Gooch charged into the apartment, kicked the door in the back of the apartment, found himself in a bedroom. "Fergus!" he yelled.

Gooch checked the closet. Nobody there. Lots of black clothes.

He could hear Cody banging around in the other bedroom. Gooch came out and walked into the second bedroom. Only it wasn't really a bedroom. It was an office. Computer, books, pictures hanging on the wall. This must be the boyfriend's room. Blind people didn't read books or hang pictures.

Cody Floss looked out from the closet. "No one here, sir."

Gooch ducked back out, checked the bathroom. Empty.

And then it hit him. Son of a bitch!

"The boyfriend!" Gooch said.

"Sir?" Cody looked at him, puzzled.

Gooch shook his head angrily. "We gotta start from scratch, son."

18

"So," MeChelle said to the Silent Man, "you got a name?"

Not expecting an answer. But giving it a try anyway.

"I'm MeChelle Deakes." She stuck out her hand. "If you'd introduced yourself instead of just standing there like some creepy sex murderer, I might not have stuck that bottle into your ribs."

She paused, listening to him breathing. She could hear him now.

"That was your ribs, right?" she said. "I thought I felt it grinding against bone. You'll want to have that looked at. It's gonna get infected pretty soon, I guarantee."

She crossed her feet, tried to looked relaxed and calm. "Whew! That was quite a little battle royal we had, bro. You don't mind me calling you that do you? Bro? I don't mean bro in the soul brother black power sense. I gotta call you something though, huh? I mean, I can't see you, but I have this image in mind of a white guy. Is that racial profiling or stereotyping or something? 'Cause I'm just not seeing a brother here. All my villains are white guys. Funny, huh? I bet eighty, eighty-five percent of the people I've arrested in my career in law enforcement have been black. And yet, when I start imagining the freakiest, goofiest nutbag killer I can think of—hey, gotta be a white guy. Does that make me a racist?"

She took a long slow breath, trying to feel this guy's vibe. What the hell was his deal? If he was some nutcase sex murderer, wouldn't he be doing something besides staring at her? Wouldn't he talk? Wouldn't he torture her? There was something here that she was missing.

"I wish you'd say something," she said. "Not because I care about you. I'm just curious, you know. What is it that put you here? One day you're a dog catcher or a clerk down at the registrar's office, next day you're in a soundproof room with a taser in your hand? What makes a guy do that?" She smiled. "I'd like to say, oh, it was your crappy childhood or something, Daddy chaining you to the bed, Uncle Joe doing the nasty with you in the basement while Mommy's upstairs washing clothes, whatever. But, nah, that's too easy. Most of the little assholes I've arrested over the years, they had pretty crummy childhoods, too. You see 'em slinging crack, doing stick-ups, stealing TVs, whatever? Sure."

She laughed in what she hoped was a supercilious way. "But standing there in the room with the taser and the lady with superglued eyes? Nah. That's a whole different can of worms. Whole different sack of shucks. Tell you what I put it down to. You want to hear my theory?"

He didn't move. But she could hear him breathing.

"Oooo!" she said. "You're mad, aren't you? I can hear it in your breathing. You are one mad little white man. You'd like to taze the shit out of me, wouldn't you? Come on! Fess up, bro! Speak it! Let it out!"

He said nothing.

"All right. All right! We were talking about my theory. What turns an innocent child into a guy like you? I'll tell you what I think it is. We've all read the books—abuse, bed-wetting, animal cruelty, head injuries, all that shit. Sorry, I'm not buying. Nah, what puts a guy like you in a room with a woman like me? One word. Laziness."

She nodded, trying to look all sage and wise, lecturing this dumbass.

"Laziness. Mmm-hmm. You get a little idea in your mind, a little fantasy. And the next thing you know, you're indulging it. You think those fantasies make you special. Don't you? Well, nah, sorry, we all got 'em. I had a fantasy once . . ." She tried to think of something outrageous. "I had a fantasy once, um, about cutting this man's head off. You know, boyfriend-girlfriend situation, he's cheating on me, and one day it just popped into my head. Boom. Cut his head off! Problem solved. I thought about it for about three weeks. Where I'd do it, *how* I'd do it. Alibis, evidence. Man, I thought it all through. And then one day I was like, *Yo! Stop being a self-indulgent, lazy-ass hater. You got a problem with this dude, leave him.* So I did.

"But you?" She shook her head. "Nah. Too lazy. You could end this all if you wanted. But you won't. You're too lazy."

She waited. She could feel it in the air, this fool just straining at the bit, wanting to talk. And yet . . .

Tick. Tick. Tick.

The clock noise hung in the air and the Silent Man was still not talking.

She smiled, pointed her finger. "Oop! Hup! I had you, didn't I? You were *this* close." She laughed. "You wanted to say something, didn't you? What was it? *No? No, that's not me?* Was that it? *No, I'm not the lazy type of ax-murdering sex fiend? I'm the rigorous and disciplined type.* Or . . . no! It just struck me! This ain't about sex murdering at all. Is that it? We got something else going on here, don't we? Something just a little bit creepier, huh? Little bit stranger?"

She tried to reach out with her mind and feel this guy. If she could know him, understand him . . . that was the first step to getting out of this place.

"You're not the man, are you?" she said. "You're not the decision maker, the top dog, the big cheese." And then she had it. Everything was coming clear. "I see. I see now. He's got something on you, too, doesn't he? You and me, we're both just prisoners here. Remember that song? 'Hotel California'? Come on, bro! Every white boy in America knows that song!" She sang the part about being prisoners of our own device and all that stuff. "You know what that means, right? We did it to ourselves. *You* did something, didn't you? You made a mistake, and now you're here. You think it's too late to get out." She let the smile on her face fade, imagined herself staring deep into his eyes, getting all serious on his ass. She shook her head. "Uh-uh. Nope. I'm here to tell you it's never too late."

She could feel him out there, his rage and—what was that?—yes—his *fear*! What was he afraid of?

"It's never too late," she said again. "I know this. I mean, I flat *know* this! I been to some dark places, bro. Strung-out, paranoid, stealing things, breaking the law I'm sworn to uphold. Pregnant? Charged with crimes? Shamed? Brought low?" She laughed ruefully. "You got no idea. But look at me! Look! Come on, you just see a little skinny black woman lying on the floor with her eyes superglued shut. But that's the wrong picture, bro. What you oughta be seeing is triumph. Triumph, baby! I've *been* to the dark place, baby!

I've been! And I fought my way back. Day by day, inch by inch, cutting my way through the jungle, baby. And I'm not done yet."

She pointed her finger at him. "You think you know how this is gonna go down? You think you know where it's all leading? Woe is me? You think the ending to this story has already been written? No! *Hell* no, you weak bitch!" Jabbing her finger at him. "You don't know shit, boy! You don't know shit! You don't know MeChelle Armitage Deakes. This thing is going where *I* say it's going! It's happening how *I* say it's happening!"

She clamped her teeth shut, aiming her eyes at the blackness where she imagined this man to be.

"Come on," she said softly. "Come on, baby. We can *do* this."

The room was silent for a long, long, long time, silent except for the ticking of the clock.

She had him. Didn't she? She could have sworn she had him.

But then the moment slipped away. And he didn't speak.

"All right," she said lightly. "All right. We got time." She walked as swiftly across the room as she could, heading toward the door into the kitchen, pausing to grab the cardboard box and dump its contents across the floor. Making a point about how much she didn't care. Clues? A way out of here? Nah, MeChelle Deakes had another plan in mind.

She felt the kitchen door, pushed it open, walked in, set the empty cardboard box on the stove. She ran her hand over the top of the stove. There were big lumpy pieces of metal over each burner. Gas. Perfect.

Then she kicked one of the cabinet doors, smashing it loose, stomped blindly at it, turning it into kindling. She tossed it on top of the cardboard box. She listened. Nothing but the clock. In the other room, Silent Man was still not moving.

She smashed three more cabinet doors, piled them on the stove. Then she turned the knob, felt a gentle heat against her face. Then she smelled smoke as the cardboard began to burn.

She walked to the door, put her foot against the bottom of the door so he wouldn't be able to move it. A rubber-soled shoe could hold a hell of a lot of pressure on a door.

The box was fully aflame now. She could feel the heat, uncomfortably hot.

Let's see what you got! she thought.

"Burn, baby, burn!" she yelled, grinning, pumping her fist in the air.

Then she pointed her finger at the ceiling. The Voice, the top guy—she knew he was watching her, watching her through a little camera mounted right up there. Right where she was pointing. He had to be.

The fire was getting hotter now.

"Come on, asshole," she shouted. "Show us what you got!"

19

"I'm gonna drop you off at the office," Gooch said. "I want you to dig up every damn scrap of information you can find about this guy Fergus. Same with his boyfriend, Austin Sweet. Pull their credit bureaus, criminal records, I mean everything you can find."

"Yes, sir."

Gooch reached for the phone. He figured he'd give MeChelle a quick run-down on what they knew. But as he picked it up, the phone rang. He didn't recognize the number, but he figured it must be Joe Priest's people, calling with information about Stormé Venda.

But it wasn't.

"I heard you was looking into Kathleen Bolligrew," a female voice said. Hick-sounding accent, like somebody from up in the hills of North Georgia.

"Who am I speaking to?" Gooch said.

"I'd rather not say on the phone." She pronounced *I'd*

rather like it was *Ah druther*. Didn't sound like somebody in Kathleen Bolligrew's circle of friends. A cleaning lady? What?

Gooch hesitated. He hated this kind of witness. You pushed them for their name, they were liable to skate on you. But if you didn't, you might not ever find out who they are. "Do you have information related to Kathleen Bolligrew's death?"

"Uh-huh," she said.

"I need your name."

"Not on the phone. They's a bar called Fuzzy's over on North Druid Hills Road. Meet you in the parking lot behind it. Fifteen minutes."

Gooch hung up. Fuzzy's—he knew the place. A fairly good music bar over on La Vista, just the other side of the highway.

Gooch didn't like this whole thing. Didn't smell right. But he had no choice. And until he heard from Joe Priest's people with information about this Stormé Venda, there wasn't much he could do.

Fifteen minutes later, on the nose, he pulled into the parking lot at Fuzzy's. This time of the day the place was pretty well deserted. He scanned the area. The building that Fuzzy's was in was L-shaped, with the parking lot in the crook of the L.

On the other side of the lot there was a Dumpster, then the land fell away steeply into a massive drainage ditch that ran for several miles through the area.

Gooch drove slowly through the lot. Three cars were parked there—an aging Chevy Caprice, its trunk held shut with a bungee cord; a brand-new blue Ford F-150 pickup; and a silver Miata. No people, though. Gooch thought about writing down the license plate numbers, but then decided there wasn't time. Maybe afterward.

Gooch felt his palms sweating a little. Wasn't just the heat. Something definitely wasn't right here. Couldn't put his finger on it, though.

He drove around Fuzzy's a second time, parked out front by the street, then climbed out, walked slowly into the parking lot. Still nobody there. At the edge of the lot a steel traffic barrier ran along the deep drainage trench to keep drunks from driving into the forty-foot-deep gulch by accident.

Gooch walked to the edge, looked down. The gulley was a couple hundred feet wide, full of brush and trash. Here it was, the middle of a city, a totally deserted area.

That was when he saw her.

Lying at the bottom of the hill was a woman. Her skirt was half torn off, revealing a pair of white underwear, legs laced with varicose veins. Her face was inclined away from him. There was blood all over. She wasn't moving.

Gooch instinctively reached for his radio, realized he hadn't been issued one yet. It was procedure—you stumbled on a serious assault or a homicide, the first thing you did was radio it in.

"Help . . ." she called feebly. One hand stirred.

He drew his gun, leapt the barrier, charged down the hill. Whatever had happened here, it had happened in the last ten minutes. Which meant the doer could be right here still.

Cars thundered by on North Druid Hills not half a football field away. But she probably could have lain there for weeks if he hadn't been looking for her. By the time he reached the bottom of the hill, he was getting nervous. This was a perfect place for an ambush.

"I'm coming, darling!" he called. "It's gonna be okay."

At which point he realized that it was all wrong. She was too far from the parking lot to have just fallen down the hill. But if somebody had been trying to conceal the body, they had put it in the worst conceivable place—perfectly visible from the parking lot.

And the blood. The blood was the wrong color. Just one shade too red.

He felt a burst of anger. It was a goddamn setup.

He started to whirl around, knowing exactly what was about to happen. The bush. Somebody was behind the bush.

But he was about a tenth of a second too late. He heard the whistle of the stick, the crunch of the footstep behind him.

He raised his arm to protect his head.

Then he felt the impact, the blow running through his arm. His Glock flew out of his hand, landed with a thump somewhere off in the brush. He scrambled toward it, but couldn't see it.

"Nah, don't think so." A man's voice.

Gooch squared himself to meet his attacker.

Good-sized guy, athletic-looking, ski mask, long sleeves despite the heat. Probably hiding his tattoos with the sleeves. You could ID a guy easy from a unique tattoo. He wore black combat boots. The toe of the left boot was wrapped with silver duct tape. In one hand he carried a thin stick, looked like a broken-off broom handle. In the other he carried a gun, a big .44-mag wheelgun. The man in the ski mask whirled the stick easily. Looked like he'd been trained in some kind of stick-fighting style—Escrima, Kali, something like that.

"Hike up your skirt, cover up them ugly legs and get out of here," the man said.

The woman who'd been lying on the ground jumped to

her feet, pulled up her skirt. Gooch could see the needle marks behind the knees now and inside her elbows. Probably a prostitute, hired herself out for the hour. The blood was totally fake and lurid looking from here. How'd he let this happen? No excuse.

The prostitute scrambled up the hill, cursing.

"Whoo!" the man in the ski mask said, watching her go. "She's a ugly one."

"I radioed for back-up," Gooch said. "You better head up right behind."

"This ain't gonna take long," the man in the ski mask said. "I been hired to impress a message in your thick skull."

"What message would that be?"

The man stepped forward. "Forget—" He swung the stick. Gooch rolled over quickly and the stick smacked into the ground. "About—" Another swing. This one connected with Gooch's right leg a couple inches above the kneecap. "Kathleen—" The stick connected this time with his ribs. "Bolligrew."

The man stepped forward, swinging away. Gooch dodged one, then let the next hit him in the upper arm. Jesus, it stung! But he was starting to get a bead on the guy's timing, the guy getting overconfident, thinking the gun protected him. He was swinging for the joints—elbows, knees, shoulders. The guy was trying to break him down, ruin Gooch's mobility and his capacity to defend himself. Then he'd close in, beat the crap out of him.

Gooch took one more hit, just above the knee. It hit the nerve bundle that ran down the side of his leg. Pain shot all the way down to his foot. Not so bad it would stop him from moving, though.

"Ow!" Gooch said, dropping to one knee, both hands clutching at his leg. "Please! Don't hurt me!"

The old please-don't-hurt-me routine. It was invariable: you started begging, every thug in the world would take a second to gloat. Then they'd draw back, telegraph the shit out of whatever hurt they were about to lay on you.

The guy in the ski mask stepped forward, drew his arm way back, preparing to smack Gooch in the head.

Gooch couldn't help smiling as he used the opening to leap forward.

With one hand he grabbed the .44, and with the other he encircled the man's waist, driving him backward. They fell down, Gooch driving his shoulder into the man's gut. The man grunted, the air going out of him.

Gooch grabbed the wheelgun, twisted, cranking the man's arm into a painful joint lock, his finger still entangled in the trigger.

"Who do you work for?" Gooch said.

"Blow me!" the man gasped.

Gooch cranked the joint lock tighter. The man's finger twitched and the .44 went off with a deafening bang.

Gooch's ears started ringing.

"Who do you work for?"

The man squeezed again and again, the bullets sailing past Gooch and into the air, until finally the gun was empty.

"I asked you a question."

The man's lips were moving, but Gooch couldn't hear what he said.

"What?" Gooch yelled.

The .44 had gone off so loud that Gooch couldn't make out a thing the man was saying. He cranked the joint lock tighter.

"Louder," Gooch yelled.

"I just told you!" the man screamed. Gooch could barely hear it now—like the man's voice was coming from the end of a tunnel full of bells and wind. Gooch tightened the joint lock a little further, felt something pop in the man's shoulder.

Oops. Went a little too far.

The man was screaming now.

"Hey!" Gooch heard a voice yelling from the top of the hill.

He looked up. It was a guy with a shotgun. He wore a shirt with the Fuzzy's logo on it. Bartender probably. Must have heard the gunshots and the screaming, came out with the gun.

"Get off him!" the bartender screamed.

"I'm a cop," Gooch yelled.

"I don't give a shit who you are. Break it up."

Gooch reached for his badge. In the tussle, it appeared to have fallen off his belt. The man in the ski mask, frantic with pain now, used the release of pressure to roll over and jump to his feet.

"I'm a cop!" Gooch shouted again.

He had the empty gun in his hand. The bartender pointed the shotgun. "Drop it!"

The man in the ski mask began to run. The toe of his left boot, wrapped with silver duct tape, flashed in the sunlight.

"Stop him!" Gooch yelled.

"I told you drop the gun!"

Gooch dropped the gun.

The man with the ski mask disappeared into the brush. Gooch spotted his badge. It lay on the ground near his pistol. He held his hands up slowly, got to his feet, scooped up the badge. He could hear rustling in the bushes, the masked man scrambling up the hill toward the parking lot.

Gooch picked up his badge, held it up to the bartender. "I'm a cop."

"How do I know you didn't buy that off the Internet?"

Gooch pointed at the man in the ski mask. "Just stop that guy, you moron, before he gets away."

But by then it was too late. He could hear a motor cranking up, then there was a howl of tires as the masked man peeled out onto the street.

Gooch picked up his Glock, holstered it, started climbing up the hill. "Nice job letting my perp get away," he said to the bartender.

The bartender looked at him sullenly. "You could at least thank me for saving you."

"Actually, you moron," Gooch said, "you saved the bad guy. I was fine."

The bartender glared.

"And stop pointing that gun at me," Gooch said.

"Cops!" the bartender said, sounding disgusted. "Ungrateful bunch of . . ." Whatever the guy thought about the police, Gooch couldn't make it out. It was lost in the ringing that still filled his ears. The bartender turned and walked back toward Fuzzy's, shaking his head.

Gooch could hear sirens coming. The bartender had probably called 911. Gooch couldn't stick around.

A detective involved in a gunfight in the parking lot of a bar? There wasn't time to sit around explaining himself to a bunch of street cops. Time to go.

As Gooch pulled out of the parking lot, his phone rang.

"Get the message?" a voice said.

"What message?" Gooch said. "Who is this?"

"Stay away from the Bolligrew case," the voice said. "Those lumps on your head will heal, okay? Next time, bullet in the brain."

The phone clicked dead.

Gooch looked at the Caller ID number. It said NUMBER BLOCKED.

He was about to throw the thing back on the seat, but a different number showed up.

"Gooch," he said.

"Detective? It's Elaine Crowder with Schumacher, Dillman. We represent Mr. Priest. I understand you needed some information about an individual by the name of Stormé Venda. . . ."

20

MeChelle could feel the heat of the fire, and the smoke was beginning to thicken.

"How about that, huh?" MeChelle yelled. "What you gonna do now? Let's burn this whole place down!"

The Silent Man from the other room began to batter the door. But with MeChelle's foot wedged against the base of the door, it wasn't budging.

She could hear the clock ticking. The Voice—the man in charge—was he listening? Watching her? She was about to find out.

"Your move, asshole!"

She could feel the impact of Silent Man's body thudding against her shoulder. The door frame was beginning to make cracking sounds every time he hit now. He was obviously a pretty strong guy. Strong or desperate.

The fire on the stove was starting to crackle now. It had created a sort of wind in the room, the hot air stirring her hair.

She kept expecting the Voice to come out of one of the speakers in the ceiling. But it didn't. There was nothing but the steady *tick tick tick*. Unhurried, unconcerned, her time slipping away.

There was another thud against the door. And another. The door frame continued to make cracking noises, but the door still wasn't moving.

Suddenly there was a pause. Silent Man had stopped smashing against the door.

The phone was ringing in the other room. For a minute MeChelle almost opened the door and ran out to get it. Just the sound of Gooch's voice . . . All the times that voice had dogged her and irritated her? Now she could hardly wait to hear it again.

But, no, she couldn't. She'd made her play. Now she had to take it as far as it would go.

The fire was running up the wall now, she was sure of it. The heat was coming down on her head and the smoke was so thick that she was starting to have trouble breathing. She didn't have much longer before she'd need to hunker down on the floor to get breathable air. Shit. And the Voice still wasn't talking.

Now the air was getting worse and worse. She knew she'd have to drop to her belly soon, down where the smoke wasn't so thick.

She'd hoped to get at the Voice. But he didn't feel like playing ball. Surely he wasn't just going to let her choke to death in here. The fire was making all kinds of ugly noises now, popping and crackling.

The phone rang in the other room. With every fiber of her being, she wanted to be talking to Gooch now, to hear the confidence, the competence in his voice.

This is getting nowhere, she thought desperately. The Voice was going to let her die in here. She felt the desperation and fear rising and rising. She'd made her play. And it had come to nothing. The phone kept ringing.

She lay down on the floor, choking and coughing.

The ringing stopped. The fire was getting hotter, the smoke thicker. *I'm going to die in here,* she thought. *This is it.*

And then the door slowly opened.

She felt a cool wind on her face as the Silent Man swept past her. She couldn't move, couldn't stop him, couldn't do anything. She heard the faucet running, the door of the fridge opening. He was getting something out. There was a sound of water hissing, then a smell of burning milk. He was dumping the milk on the fire.

Then he was filling the jug in the sink. More splashing. The heat of the fire began to decrease.

A hissing of steam. He kept filling the milk jug, splashing the water all over. MeChelle lay on the floor gasping. After the tazering experience, she hadn't had much energy left. Now all the smoke and the carbon monoxide had knocked the last strength out of her.

In the other room she could hear the phone ringing again. But she couldn't even muster the energy to crawl toward it.

Then the heat on her skin was gone, nothing left but the acrid smell of smoke and burned milk.

Then she felt something close to her. The Silent Man. How could she tell he was there? She wasn't sure. But she could sense him. She felt his breath on her face.

Then he whispered, "He's watching all the time. If I talk to you, he'll kill me."

After that, he stepped away and his footsteps receded into the other room.

21

The poster outside the banquet room next to the lobby in the Embassy Suites Hotel on Clairmont Road said

USE IT OR LOSE HIM!

Getting and keeping a man by unleashing your
Eternal Feminine . . .
With Stormé Venda, Ph.D.

There was a picture on the poster of an unusually pale and unusually good-looking blonde with a come-hither look on her face, her hair in artful disarray. She wore a business suit, heels, and a lot of cleavage.

Gooch pushed open the door and walked in. Ten or twelve frumpy-looking middle-aged women sat here and there among three rows of chairs. In front was the blonde from the poster. She wore a lavalier microphone on the lapel of her blue business suit and was only slightly less attractive than the photo on the poster made her out to be.

"I understand men!" Stormé Venda was saying. "Men are simple. Men want the cootchie!"

She glanced up, saw Gooch. Her eyes hardened for a moment, then she said, "May I help you, sir? This session is for registered attendees only."

Gooch just shook his head, crossed his arms.

She frowned for a moment, obviously debating whether to ask him to leave, then deciding against it.

Gooch figured he'd watch a little, see what he was up against.

"When I was twelve," Dr. Stormé Venda said, dropping back into what was obviously a practiced spiel, "my second stepdaddy taught me a great lesson. He said to me, 'Honey, I'm gonna show you the key to understanding and controlling men.'" She smiled a cold smile, showing off an expensive-looking set of teeth. "Then he slipped me the old love meat." There were a couple of gasps from the audience.

She held up her hands. "No! No! Girls, hold on. Don't be a hater! I thank him for that lesson to this day. Because he showed me the true nature of the male species." She raised one eyebrow, gave the audience a flirty look.

"See, now when I want a thing, do I go out and get it myself? Do I sweat and strain? God forbid! That's *work*. Nah, girls, I find a man who already has the thing I want. Then I go to him and I'm all, 'Oh, golly gosh, I'm so helpless and pitiful, and you're so *big* and so *strong* and so *handsome,* blah blah *blah,* cleavage cleavage *cleavage*.' And then he gives me what I want. Simple as that. It's his nature." She smiled her cold smile.

Some of the ladies laughed. A couple applauded. One or two shook their heads dubiously.

"Now, I know what you're thinking. 'Oh, but I need *true*

love! I need a man to share my *passion* and under*stand* my feeeelings.'" Her voice dripped sarcasm. "Please! Girls! Pardon me while I vomit."

Dr. Stormé Venda held her hand high in the air, wrist bent. It was impossible to miss the massive diamond on her finger. A fake, no doubt. "True love and gushy feelings don't get you *this*. If you want *this* you got to understand the nature of men. You *must use the cootchie.*"

Gooch applauded languidly. This gal was pretty good, he had to admit.

"I give you about a nine point seven," he said loudly. "Though I got to tell you I thought the love meat thing was a little much. Lot of ladies probably gonna find that type of language a little offensive."

Stormé Venda glared at him. He could tell she made him for a cop. Then she turned on the smile again. "Girls," she said, "this gentleman seems like a rude jerk, but he's actually a very close friend of mine. He's just yanking my chain. I need to have a very, very brief tête-à-tête with him. Why don't we take five? We've got coffee and some just totally *yummy* pastries in the Magnolia Room next door. That's all included in the cost of the seminar, so don't be shy."

She unclipped the mic from her lapel, walked briskly through the group of dowdy women, grabbed Gooch's arm, and propelled him through the door.

"This is a private seminar," she hissed. "Unless you plan to cough up a hundred and thirty-nine bucks—"

"Save it, Callie," Gooch said. Joe Priest's lawyer had given him a lot of useful information on this woman. For instance, Stormé Venda was not her real name. She'd been born Callie Jean Burdon. And the Ph.D. that was listed on the poster next to her name? Closest she'd come to a Ph.D.

was the GED she'd earned during an eighteen-month sentence at AWP for pandering and solicitation. "We got your lying cootchie on video."

"I don't have the slightest clue what you're talking about," she said. Now that he was close up, he could see a lot of fine wrinkles on her face that didn't show up on the poster. Either she was older than she made out to be, or she'd lived way too hard. Probably both.

"Listen up, Callie. As a result of your little charade at the homicide bureau yesterday, a cop is in danger of being killed. If she dies, that makes you an accessory to murder. Murder of a cop is what is known under the law as an 'aggravating circumstance.' Which makes you eligible for the needle."

Her pale skin went a shade paler. "Aw, shit," she said. Her accent had gone all South Georgia on her.

"Talk," he said.

"I need something on paper saying how—"

"You really want the needle? That it?"

"All right, all *right*! God!" She reached into her pocketbook, her fingers shaking, pulled out a pack of Virginia Slims, shook one out, lit it, blew out a long stream of smoke. "I was paid," she said.

"By who?"

She took another long drag. "Hell, man, I don't even know."

"Giving false evidence in a murder investigation is a Class One felony," Gooch said, putting one hand on the cuffs on his belt. In the state of Georgia there was no such thing as a Class One felony. But for some reason a lot of criminals seemed to be scared by the sound of it. "Know what? I think I'm just gonna go ahead and take you in."

"Look look look, hold up. How 'bout we work something out?" She looked around to make sure she wasn't being overheard. "There's an empty room next door. I bet you haven't had anything this good in a long time, huh?" She ran her hands up the sides of her business suit, shook her tail a little bit. There wasn't much show to it. Just trotting out the merchandise for the umpteenth time, weary and indifferent to it now, going through the motions.

Gooch just looked at her.

"Okay, *okay*!" she said. "I don't know who the guy was. This is all I know. Last week, I get this little envelope in the mail. It's got a stack of hundred-dollar bills on top and a CD underneath with a Post-it note that says, 'Play this. Get more Benjamins.' I play it. There's this voice on the CD who explains what he wants. One-shot deal. Go into the homicide bureau wearing sunglasses and carrying a cane. Tell a story about my mom getting raped and killed, hand them this mp3 player, leave."

"Same voice as the guy on the mp3 player?"

"Maybe."

"You got the CD?"

She shrugged. "I guess."

"I need it. Now."

"Now? I'm in the middle of work. That's twenty-one hundred dollars sitting in there. You know how much I spent getting those seats filled?"

"Give me a key to your house, I'll get it myself."

She looked at him suspiciously. Probably thinking about how she had a bag of weed in her nightstand or fake credit cards lying on the kitchen table.

He pulled out the cuffs.

"Okay! Okay! God! You don't have to be such a dick."

"Hey," Gooch said. "It's just my nature."

* * *

On the way over to Stormé Venda's apartment, Gooch tried MeChelle's phone again. Still no answer.

Stormé Venda lived in a high-rise apartment on Peachtree in Buckhead. It was the sort of address that you paid a big premium for prestige. When he got to the apartment, he found a note thumbtacked to the door from the management company. Probably behind on her rent.

He unlocked the door and went in.

No surprise, there was a bong on the floor of the living room. A mixture of nice furniture and cheap reproduction art on the walls. It looked like a place lived in by somebody who hadn't quite figured out who they were—a jumble of different kinds of art, different kinds of furniture. All the colors matched . . . but somehow beyond that it didn't feel like the place had any coherence.

She had given him permission to enter and search the place. That gave him legal carte blanche to do anything he wanted. First he found the CD that Stormé had been sent, put it on the stereo and listened to it. It was definitely Fergus's voice. The CD was twenty minutes long, giving detailed explanations about what Stormé was supposed to tell the police. While it was playing, he dug around in her garbage, found the envelope it had been sent in, bagged it. Maybe they could find prints, DNA, something along those lines.

Then he bagged a 35 mm film canister that he found in the living room. There was no film in it. It had obviously stored her marijunana stash: there were just a few seeds and stray flecks of weed in the bottom—but it was enough to convict her for possession if he needed leverage with her later. Then he went through the rooms as methodically as time would allow, pausing occasionally to dial MeChelle's number. It continued to ring through to her voice mail.

He found no evidence of contact between Fergus and

Stormé in her phone records—though Fergus might have phone numbers that Gooch wasn't aware of. He found a lot of bounced checks and letters from creditors. Unpaid bills were heaped on the floor near her room. Stormé Venda obviously bought a lot of things that she never bothered to pay for. He found a file folder full of correspondence between Stormé and various lawyers for Joe Priest. There were a lot of overheated threats in both directions. Stormé had initially claimed she was being sexually harassed. She seemed to have no evidence to back her claims. Eventually the lawyers had sent Stormé a check for $19,500—which had apparently ended her extortion campaign.

So Joe Priest had lied about not paying her anything. Did that mean anything?

He looked around for an answering machine. Most people were using voice mail these days. But that wasn't necessarily a problem. You could usually pick up people's voice mail without a password, providing you called from their home phone. He picked up the phone and dialed zero zero. It got him through to her local phone provider. From there the menu led him right to her voice mail.

There were three messages.

A male voice, pleasant but somehow also slightly malicious: "Stormé. Me again. Don't think I've forgotten about you." Click.

Second message. Same voice. "Stormeeeeeeeeeeee." The voice was now playful, the man sounding like a kid. "Where aaaaaare you? Don't make me lose my temper. Where's my mooooooooooney?"

Third message. A female voice: "Hello, Miss Venda, this is Vicki in the credit department of Chase Manhattan Bank. Maybe you missed my earlier call regarding your overdue account. It's imperative that—"

Gooch hung up, feeling a growing sense of frustration. This was turning out to be a dead end. Best he could tell, it was like she said: somebody hired her to do this job. She was desperate enough to go along with what was obviously a risky proposition. And that was the end of it.

He called MeChelle's number again.

"Hank?" she said.

"What happened?"

She began to cry.

"MeChelle?"

She didn't speak. He could hear her muffled sobs.

"Look," he said, "I think you need to be aware, whoever killed Kathleen Bolligrew, I think they know we're after them. Somebody sent a guy to beat me up, warn me off the case."

MeChelle didn't answer. She just kept sobbing into the phone.

"I'm gonna get you," he said. "I'm *going* to find you."

She didn't answer. So he just kept repeating himself over and over. Until the phone went dead.

22

"Kenny *Chesney*," Cody Floss said. "I mean, it's not that I mind country music. But Kenny *Chesney*? I *hate* that guy."

"I don't know who Kenny Chesney is," Gooch said, "and I don't much care."

Gooch was walking swiftly back to his car, the kid seeming to have trouble keeping up. Gooch climbed in and started the engine. Gooch had stopped back by the office to find out what Cody Floss had learned. He'd supposedly been running everybody connected to the case through the computer. Fergus, Stormé Venda, everybody.

"Kenny Chesney, he's this singer, always got the sleeves of his shirt cut off?" Cody said. "Showing all his muscles? And I mean, it's not like he's all that cut or anything. He was married to that actress for about ten minutes, you know the one? But then they got divorced and everybody was saying he's probably gay? See, I think—"

Gooch gave the kid a look and he shut up.

"Sorry, sorry, sorry!" Cody said. He was carrying a large

bag from Chik-fil-A. Looked like the other detectives had sent Cody out to get sandwiches for them. Poor kid didn't realize they were taking advantage of him.

"You said you had something for me?"

"Uh, yessir. Can I take these sandwiches back to the guys first?"

"Nope." Gooch started the car.

"But, after I ran the search, Lieutenant Evans sent me out to get Chik-fil-A for everybody and—"

Gooch thumped him on the back of the head. Nothing personal. Sometimes a kid like this needed his attention focused.

"Sorry!" The kid rubbed the back of his head. "So. There's this girl in the Fulton County clerk's office. And she's a big fan of Kenny Chesney?"

"If I hear the words *Kenny Chesney* again, I'm gonna slap you so hard, you gonna wake up in hillbilly heaven."

"Yessir. Um. My point is, this girl, she would only dig up all this information you wanted if I went with her to see this concert with . . . um . . . that singer I was just talking about."

"And?"

"She weighs like five hundred pounds."

Gooch shook his head and sighed. "Enjoy the show," Gooch said. He paused. "I mean, you *did* agree to go?"

"Of course, sir."

"Good. Excellent work. Sometimes you gotta fall on the sword. In the future, however, don't burden me with your personal problems. Now tell me what you learned from her."

"Well, I got her to search the old records. Not just the computer. I'm talking down in the basement where all the old paper files are at. Bottom line, Fergus doesn't have a criminal record. Not even way back. But . . ."

"But *what*?"

"But there was a file on him."

This kid was gonna drive Gooch crazy. "That don't make sense. Either there's a file or there ain't."

"Well, there wasn't a *file* file. There was just, there was a file *folder*. But there wasn't anything in it."

Now Gooch understood. "Which means—what?"

"Well . . . gosh . . ."

Gooch had been thinking about heading back to the blind guy's house. But the empty folder changed everything. This was a good development. And it meant they needed to go someplace else entirely.

He started the car, pulled out of the parking lot, headed toward Decatur. He drove a while, letting the kid try and figure out what the empty folder meant.

But by the time he had reached Decatur, the kid still hadn't come up with an answer.

"What it means," Gooch said, "is he had a juvie record."

The kid frowned. "I don't get it."

"Then think." Gooch turned onto Briarcliff, heading north.

Suddenly the kids eyebrows shot up. "Oh! So were the results expunged?"

Gooch smiled wordlessly.

"But . . . why did they keep the folder?"

"Little trick they used to use in the Clerk's Office. This was back in the days before it was all computerized. Letter of the law said you expunge the records of juveniles in certain circumstances, that you got to destroy the file. They used to throw out the contents of the folder. But they'd leave the empty folder in the file drawer. See, that way if the person ever got investigated again, it would be a signal that the investigator ought to take a closer look at the person's background. Obviously that procedure went out the window once everything got computerized."

"Okay, yeah, yeah, I get it. That way you'd know the person had an expunged record." Cody Floss kept frowning. "But, gosh, wouldn't that be against the spirit of the law or something? Leaving it there intentionally?"

Gooch reached over in the kid's lap, pulled a sandwich out of the bag.

"Uh, sir? That's Sergeant Evans's sandwich."

Gooch took a big bite out of it. "Mmm!" he said.

"Sir, you probably shouldn't—"

"How long you been a detective?"

"Um . . . like six months?"

"They send you out for sandwiches every day?"

The kid nodded. "Pretty much, I guess."

Gooch looked at him.

"What?"

Pitiful.

The first day Gooch had worked in Homicide, this crusty old guy named Ronnie Birdsong had come over and told Gooch to go out and get him a take-out lunch from the Majestik. Fried chicken, mashed potatoes with gravy (but only if the gravy wasn't too runny), collard greens, no hot sauce, extra this, plenty of that, something else in a box on the side—old Birdsong going on like that for quite some while. Two minutes later, everybody in the office was crowding around Gooch's desk giving him orders for food. Gooch had written down all the orders in great detail, nodding and acting all serious. Then, instead of going to the Majestik, he'd gone down to the Varsity, a hot-dog joint near Tech. He'd bought eight Cokes, eight small fries, and eight naked hot dogs—no catsup, no relish, no cheese, no chili, no nothing. Each in a separate bag. Then he brought them back, handed them out to everybody, smiling and being Mr. Agreeable.

There was a whole bunch of noise and cussing from

everybody once they opened their bags, everybody bitching about how they didn't get what they ordered.

Gooch had looked around the room and said, "Next time y'all want a delivery boy, call Domino's." Never got a lick of shit from anybody after that.

"What!" Cody Floss said again.

"Got any fries in there?" Gooch said.

"Um . . . sir, mind my asking where we're going?"

"Fergus had a juvie record? Then we need to talk to the people who knew him when he was a teenager."

"I guess so."

"And that would be where, son?"

"Uh . . ."

Gooch swung his car through a gateway into a wooded area. After a short drive, they came out into a broad expanse of lawn. Rising in the middle was a large brick building that looked like it had been built to be an insane asylum in some horror movie. A large sign in front of it said OAKDALE SCHOOL FOR THE BLIND.

"Oh," Cody Floss said. "Okay. Oakdale School for the Blind."

"Dadgum," Gooch said. "You ought to be a detective or something."

The director of the Oakdale School, a Dr. Sylvia Ammerman, was one of these ladies that made a big show of how concerned she was about people, pressing the point so hard you could tell that she pretty much hated everybody on the planet. Soft voice with just that tiniest bit of condescension, graying hair pulled back into a barrette, big brown eyes with the I-care-deeply expression. Made you about want to punch her in the nose.

"Gooch, APD," he said, shaking her hard veiny hand. The real woman was there in her hands, tough as shoe leather, probably mean as a snake once you got past all the "concern."

"What can I do for you?"

"Were you here in the late seventies?"

She cocked her head slightly, gave him a little Gandhi smile. "I don't mean to be obtuse, Officer Gooch, but I guess I'd really need to know why you're here before I could properly answer that."

Officer Gooch. That was a nice touch. Putting him down right smack off the bat, like she didn't know the difference between an officer and a detective. Gooch looked at Cody Floss. "Can you talk to this lady?"

"Sir?"

"Talk to her." Gooch didn't want to say anything nasty to her. Which was what would happen if he sat there much longer. He stood and walked over to a shelf on the other side of the director's drab office, looked at a couple of framed family pictures. Stiff, unhappy-looking people.

Cody cleared his throat. "Well, Dr. Ammerman, we're investigating the disappearance of an officer by the name of MeChelle Deakes. Now, see, what's come up is a possible connection to a gentleman by the name of Fergus who's a graduate of your fine institution. . . ."

Cody continued to ramble on, telling the lady fifty times as much as she needed to know.

Finally the lady interrupted. "Sure, sure, I'd be happy to help. You had a question?"

At that point Gooch turned around. He could stomach only so much beating around the bush. "Damon Fergus," he said. "He had a juvenile record. The charges were eventually expunged. We need to know what it was all about."

The director stood and said, "Could you walk with me?"

"Yes, ma'am," Cody said.

Gooch followed the pair as the director started walking down the hall. There were kids in the classrooms, white sticks folded up next to their desks. There was something about all those vacant staring eyes that seemed a little eerie. And the lighting didn't help. The whole place was dim, nearly windowless. It felt like they were in a cave.

"Some of our students have sensitivity to light. It hurts their eyes. So we keep lighting to a minimum."

Cody nodded earnestly. "Yes, ma'am, I could see how that would be."

"There was a time when blindness was considered a curse," Dr. Ammerman said. "It wasn't so long ago when we still viewed blindness as a completely crippling disorder. This institution used to view its mission as giving a few modest skills to a group of people who would ultimately be nothing but a permanent drag on society. But things have changed. The blind are now viewed as differently abled—challenged in certain respects, but stronger and more capable than the seeing in others. At times they can see things we can't."

Gooch was tempted to ask if the school fielded a differently abled football team . . . but decided against it. If it made this woman feel better to preach a sermon, might as well let her.

"But prejudice remains," the director continued. "Stevie Wonder jokes, condescension, fear. In the back of the minds of seeing people, there's still a sense that the blind are cursed. If the eyes are windows to the soul, then how are we supposed to know what's going on in the mind of a blind person? Are they sinister freakish beasts hiding inside a human frame?"

"Hmm, gosh," Cody said. "You're kinda talking over my head here."

The director stopped, pointed through a dingy pane of glass into a room. Inside were about a dozen kids, maybe ten years old, listening intently to the teacher. Their faces were rapt as they concentrated.

"Look at them. These are whole, beautiful, complete human beings. Not monsters."

Gooch cleared his throat. "Damon Fergus," he said. "Unless you know something I don't, he's not one of them kids in that classroom."

"Let's say, for the sake of argument, that Damon Fergus made some mistakes when he was a youngster. What good would it do to bring them out twenty-five years later? It would just reinforce another negative stereotype. It would harm these precious children."

Gooch tried to keep from rolling his eyes. "The only stereotype I ever heard about blind people is they ain't much good at seeing."

The director cocked her head and gave him her Gandhi smile again, like he was somebody she really felt sorry for. "I'm sorry," she said. "I just can't give you that information."

"You mean you won't," Gooch said.

As they were talking, a thin old man appeared out of the murky hallway, walked toward them pushing a large plastic trash bin on wheels.

"I said I *can't* give you that information, Officer. If Mr. Fergus was ever charged or convicted of anything when he was a minor—I say *if*—and if that record was expunged, then we would have destroyed those records, too."

The old man with the trash bin altered his trajectory, making a smooth arc to avoid them. It wasn't until the old guy was almost even with them that his empty white eyes became visible in the dim light. The wheels came within six inches of Gooch's left foot, but didn't touch it.

"I've studied a good deal of law, Doctor," Gooch said. "On the job, you might say. And you know what? You got no ethical or legal obligation to conceal evidence of crimes committed. Not as a physician. Not as an educator. If Damon Fergus did something bad, you need to tell us."

One of the director's eyebrows rose slightly. She didn't speak, though.

"How long you been here, Doctor?" Gooch said.

"Thirty years."

"So you know the answer to our question, don't you? You know something about Fergus."

She smiled, blinked, kept looking at Gooch like he was some African kid suffering from malnutrition.

"Something you don't like about me?" Gooch said. "Some kind of stereotype you got about redneck cops? All I'm trying to do is save an innocent woman's life."

"I can't help you."

"What the hell's wrong with you?"

Her voice grew softer and more musical, her smile broader. "Unless you have a warrant, I think it's time for you to leave."

The blind janitor stopped his cart, emptied a trash can into the bin, put a new plastic bag into the can, then pushed the bin on toward the entrance. There wasn't the slightest hesitation or fumbling. You'd have never known the guy was blind unless you'd seen his face.

"Was it a sex crime?" Gooch said.

The director's smile flickered, then broadened. Gooch thought maybe he'd hit the mark. But it was hard to tell. "Thanks for stopping by, gentlemen."

"Let's go, Cody," Gooch said. He turned and walked down

the dim, echoing hallway. When they got outside, Gooch squinted at the light.

The janitor was standing near the door, smoking a cigarette.

"Damon Fergus, huh?" the old man said.

"Pardon me?" Gooch said.

Inside the building, the old guy's eyes had seemed white. But out here Gooch could see that they were actually a very pale blue. "Fergus. He's on the board of directors, you know. Dr. Birkenstocks there, she wouldn't want to piss him off."

"Dr. Birkenstocks?"

"Ammerman. She all the time going on with all that crap about how oppressed blind people are."

Gooch chuckled.

The old man tossed his cigarette butt on the ground, stepped on it, ground it into the concrete. "Did I get it?" he said.

"Get what?"

"The butt. You locate stuff by sound, but every now and then you miss."

"You're right on the money."

"Dr. Birkenstocks gives me shit it if I leave a butt smoldering out here. Secondhand smoke kills children, all that fucking PC crap."

"So you know Fergus?"

"Sure. He's a creep. He musta boned half the girls in the school back when he was a kid. Couple of them claimed he forced himself on them. That's what the charges were. His old man had a bunch of money, hired a good lawyer both times, pled them down to fourteenth-degree sexual misconduct or whatever. But I seen one of them girls. Broke nose, fat lip, the whole nine."

"You said you *saw* her?"

"Figure of speech. I found her crying in the bed the

morning after it happened. But she didn't care about that. She said what was worst was the things he said to her."

"What did he say to her?"

"Wouldn't tell me. Just said he was talking to her the whole time. Today this is just a day school. Back then most of the kids were boarders. About half was wards of the state. Hard to find foster parents when you got messed-up eyes. I couldn't tell you myself, but they say blind folks look creepy to seeing people. That true?"

Gooch grunted noncommittally.

"Went to school here myself. My mama couldn't take having a messed-up kid, just dropped me off on the doorstep one day, drove off into the wild blue yonder."

"You remember the names of the girls Fergus molested?" Gooch said.

"Nah." The janitor pulled out his cigarette pack, squeezed it gently as though to see how many were left. "Trying to cut down," he said.

"Well, I appreciate your help."

"Damnedest thing," the janitor said. "They had a separate wing for the boys and for the girls. Both sides was locked all night. Nobody never could figure out how Fergus got over there and back. Everybody was always whispering about it, trying to figure out how he done it. Give you that, he was a smart little bastard."

The janitor pulled out a cigarette, stuck it behind his ear, then shoved the pack back in the pockets of his jeans and started walking back toward the front door of the school.

"See you when I see you," he said.

Cody Floss—watching the janitor walk away—wore his usual clueless expression.

Gooch pulled out his cell phone. "Something bothering you?" he said to Cody Floss.

"I'm not sure I buy that story," Floss said. "I mean—knowing Fergus is gay? Why would Fergus be molesting girls? Makes me wonder, maybe that janitor's feeding us some BS."

"Or?"

Cody Floss blinked. "Sir?"

"Or maybe there's a simpler explanation." Gooch hit the speed dial for MeChelle's number.

23

Ring. Ring.

MeChelle stumbled across the room, waving her hands in front of her. She bumped into the table, found the phone, grabbed it.

"Hello?"

There was a click, then from deep in the electronic netherworld: "MeChelle. It's me."

"Hank?" As always, she felt a surge of hope as soon as she heard his voice. "I'm sorry about that last call. I kinda lost it for a minute."

"You okay? What happened last time I called?"

"I tried to burn the place down. It didn't work. I was feeling a little . . . disappointed."

"Have you learned anything else?"

"No. There's a guy in the room here with me, though. But he won't talk to me."

"You think this guy is the person who put you in the room?"

"No. I'm almost sure not. I think the guy in the room is here against his will, too."

"Why's that?"

"I'll worry about the guy in the room. You work on finding who killed Kathleen Bolligrew."

"Fair enough."

"What's going on? What have you found out?"

Gooch brought her up to speed.

The phone cut off, but he called her right back. *This was the last call of the hour,* she realized.

"You got any more ideas?" he said. "Anything with the clues?"

"Not really," she said. "Maybe we need to know something else before the other clues will make sense."

"Yeah," Gooch said. Suddenly he sounded tired.

"We're gonna get there," MeChelle said.

"I know. I know." Gooch sighed.

There was a brief silence.

"Question," MeChelle said. "You say someone came after you, tried to warn you off the case?"

"Yeah."

"How does the killer know we're hunting for him?"

She didn't get an answer.

24

Gooch was troubled by the question MeChelle had just asked him. How *did* the killer know Gooch and MeChelle were investigating him? It certainly pointed to Fergus. Other than Lane Priest, Fergus was the only person who they had talked to by the time the guy with the ski mask had jumped Gooch behind Fuzzy's.

"We gotta know more about this Fergus character," Gooch said.

"I pulled his records," Cody Floss said. "Maybe it's in there."

"Hell," Gooch, said. "I wish you'd brought them with you."

"I did," Cody said. "I was gonna look at them while I waited in the drive-through at Chik-fil-A. I got everything on Fergus. Plus his roommate, Austin Sweet."

Gooch stared at him. "And you were planning on tell me this . . . *when?*"

Gooch pulled over at an Exxon station, looked at the small pile of information Cody had brought along with him.

"Nothing about a job here," Gooch said. "Sweet gets regular money, but it's all paid straight out of Fergus's account."

"Fergus is a sugar daddy, huh?" Floss said.

Gooch thought about it. Was that it? Or was there something else going on here?

He held up the pile of paper toward the young detective. "This everything?"

"Yes, sir."

Gooch flipped through the papers. "Where's his DMV? You didn't pull his DMV?"

"It should be there."

"It's not."

Cody Floss bit his lip. "I could swear . . ." He flipped through the information, then leaned over, picked something up off the floor. "Oops," he said, handing over a piece of paper with a large footprint on it. "Kinda dropped it."

Gooch looked at the DMV picture for a second, then frowned. What was it about the picture that seemed so strange? *Wait a minute!*

"Oh, for godsake," Gooch said.

"What?"

Gooch said, "Look at the picture."

Cody Floss looked at it for a minute. Then his eyes widened. "Holy crap!" he said softly.

"No kidding."

Gooch immediately dialed Robb Newton at Cingular and said, "Hey, buddy. Gooch again. I need to know the last phone call made by a fellow by the name of Austin Sweet."

"Is that part of the same warrant you faxed over?"

"It'll be there in a minute. Just like the one this morning."

"Hank, you're killing me."

Gooch waited. Finally Newton sighed, started pecking on the keys of his computer. "Okay," he said finally. "I got it."

Gooch hung up.

"Guess who Austin Sweet just called?" Gooch said.

"I don't know."

"Our little friend Stormé Venda."

When they reached the Embassy Suites Hotel, there were four DeKalb County police cruisers out front, lights flashing. An ambulance had just pulled in front of the door.

"Dammit!" Gooch felt a burst of adrenaline run through him. This was too close to be a coincidence.

He pulled up behind the cruisers, jumped out of the car, and ran inside the front of the hotel, pounding down the hallway toward the room where Stormé Venda's seminar was being held. A large DeKalb County cop stood at the door. Gooch looked past him into the room. A bunch of middle-aged women sat silently in their chairs, staring nervously around them. Stormé Venda was not there.

"Sir, you need to slow down," the cop said to Gooch.

Gooch flashed his badge. "What just happened?" he demanded.

"Sir, you're not with DeKalb County. I'm not at liberty to—"

"Who's running this crime scene, goddammit?"

The officer obviously didn't see the percentage in getting in Gooch's way. "Lieutenant Reese. He's down there." The officer pointed down toward a knot of officers down at the end of the hallway.

Gooch ran toward them.

"What's going on here?" Gooch said.

A tall, thin black man in a suit turned and looked at him without expression. "And you would be . . ."

"Gooch. APD."

"What's your interest?"

"I just interviewed a witness in a homicide I'm working."

"By the name of?"

"Stormé Venda."

"Looks like you got a problem with your witness then." The detective lifted the crime scene tape. "I'm Lt. Constant Reece."

"Constant."

"I know, I know. Brothers and their names."

"Nah," Gooch said. "I kinda like it."

"She's in there." Reece pointed at the ladies' bathroom. "Two shots in the face, large caliber. Big mess on the wall."

"Damn it," Gooch said. It had to be Fergus. If Fergus was killing witnesses, he might be ready to kill MeChelle, too.

"You need to put two names out on the system."

Lieutenant Reece took out a notebook.

"First one to look for, fellow by the name of Damon Fergus," Gooch said. "Second name you need, Austin Sweet."

"Two shooters?" Reece said, raising one eyebrow.

Gooch shook his head. "Not exactly."

25

"So, wait, you think one of these two guys killed Stormé Venda?" Lieutenant Reece said. "But you don't know which one?"

"No," Gooch said.

Lieutenant Reece looked at Gooch with an expression of mild irritation. Gooch scanned the area, thinking how he wanted to explain this to Reece, how much he should explain. A knot of gawkers was standing on the other side of the crime scene tape down in the lobby of the hotel.

"Y'all! Hey!" Lieutenant Reece called down to one of the uniforms. "Are those people witnesses? If they are, put them in the room with the other witnesses. If they're not, get 'em outta here!"

The young policeman at the end of the hallway put on a serious face and started shooing the onlookers away.

Gooch noticed something as they started to move. A flash of something red. Where had he seen that? Then he realized:

a red hat—just like the one that Austin Sweet had worn as he exited Fergus's apartment building earlier that morning.

Gooch started sprinting down the hallway.

"Yo, Detective!" Lieutenant Reece called. "Where you going?"

Gooch ignored him. By the time he reached the lobby, the knot of people was moving out the front door of the building. Where was the red hat?

There! Out in the parking lot.

As Gooch banged through the doors, Austin Sweet turned and looked at the detective, eyes widening. His mouth made a small O under his blond mustache. He turned and ran.

Gooch followed, arms and legs pumping. Sweet dodged through a couple of bedraggled bushes and headed into the parking lot of the McDonald's next door.

Gooch was glad he'd spent the last six months working out so much. He was gaining on Sweet. He could hear cops yelling behind him and his heart soared. Man, it felt good to be back in the saddle again. When was the last time he'd been on a good foot pursuit? Been years now. Nothing like it!

Sweet paused in front of McDonald's, trying to figure out which way to go.

Gooch hit him full tilt, drove him backwards into a statue of Ronald McDonald. The grinning plastic statue fell over and hit the ground with a hollow clunk.

Sweet stared up at Gooch. "Who *are* you?" he said. "What are you *doing*?"

Gooch reached down, tore off Sweet's mustache. It made a sound like ripping paper.

"Ow!" Sweet howled.

"So," Gooch said, holding up his hand in front of the fallen man's wide brown eyes and extending his middle finger at the man's face, "how many fingers, Damon?"

* * *

A few minutes later, Austin Sweet—minus his blond wig and his fake mustache—was sitting handcuffed in the back of a patrol car in the parking lot.

"Lemme talk to him," Gooch said.

Lieutenant Reece smiled. "Now hold up, hold up, hold up. My boys inside got two witnesses say a short, heavyset male white with black hair walked into the ladies' bathroom. Behind Stormé Venda. Say they heard two shots. Say they saw the same short, heavyset male white walk out of the bathroom holding a gun. You still think you got the right man?"

Gooch cleared his throat, felt a twist of anger. Dammit! Somehow he'd gotten this wrong. "That's why I need to talk to him," Gooch said.

"I can't hold this fool just because he ran away from you. Much as I'd like to, I can't even hold him for wearing that Village People-looking mustache you pulled off his face."

"Yeah," Gooch said. "Still I need to talk to him."

"You're out of your jurisdiction, knocking down a citizen without cause," Reece said. "He presses charges? Hey, bro, I got to take you down to the station."

"You think I don't know that?" Gooch said. "Lemme talk to him."

Reece looked around, a blank expression on his face. "I got a crime scene to process."

"How about I take him off your hands," Gooch said. "Release him into my custody. Then if there's a problem, it all falls on me."

Reece jabbed his finger in Gooch's chest. "I want to know what you know about this Stormé Venda person, how come you thought it was *this* dude that killed her."

"You give me Damon Fergus, I'll tell you everything I know."

"Wait a minute, I thought you said his name was Austin Sweet."

"It is."

Reece's eyes narrowed. "Man, I'm confused."

Three minutes later Austin Sweet/Damon Fergus was sitting in the back seat of Gooch's car. Damon Fergus looked a lot different now that he wasn't staring straight ahead. He had put his wig back on. It was slightly cockeyed.

"I am a disabled person!" Fergus said. "You can't do this to me!"

Gooch just drove, ignoring the racket. He had left Cody Floss at the crime scene to see if he could pick up any more information about Stormé Venda and who had killed her.

"I'm going to sue you for false arrest!" Fergus screamed. "I have papers proving I am legally blind!"

Fergus continued to scream and protest for a while. But by the time Gooch reached his destination, he had calmed down a little. They entered the DeKalb County dump, a mammoth stinking facility on the south side of the county. Gooch waved his badge casually at the young woman sitting in the booth at the entrance, then picked a road and drove slowly past one of the large earthmovers that was plowing garbage into huge heaps. Crows pecked at the plastic bags. Pipes protruded from the ground at regular intervals to vent the methane that built up under the dirt cover.

"Must be close to two, three hundred acres out here," Gooch said. "You'd be amazed how far you can get from other human beings. Nobody watching, nobody paying the slightest bit of attention. Nobody figures anybody'd ever come in here and steal garbage."

"Why are you taking me here?" Fergus said.

Gooch drove toward a pile of garbage about fifty feet high and couple hundred feet long. "They leave it to kind of simmer a while," Gooch said, "before they cover it over. You cover it up too quick, the methane builds up and you get explosions. Nothing like five hundred tons of exploding diapers landing on your head."

"What do you *want*?" Fergus's voice had gone high and pleading. Didn't sound at all the way he did on the commercials—all the deep gravelly authority totally gone.

Gooch pulled up in front of the pile, put the car in park.

"My daddy was an interesting character," Gooch said. "Played double A ball when he was a kid, then went to Vietnam. Decorated veteran. Unfortunately everybody said he wasn't himself when he came back. I wouldn't know. Only father I ever knew was a broke-down wife-beating drunk son of a bitch. Only job he ever kept was as a garbage man. That's how come I know all about landfills."

Fergus was hunched down in the back seat, arms tight around his chest.

"He was a big reader, though, when he was sober. Knew a lot of stuff. Hell of a talented guitar player, too. Anyway, problem was, he thought the world had conspired against him, took away all his opportunities. Saddled him with a wife and a couple of brats he didn't want, no how." Gooch shrugged. "Of course, it wasn't the world's fault. He'd done it to himself."

"I suppose there's a point to this?" Fergus said. He'd apparently collected himself enough to get his announcer voice back.

"Yeah, him and his boss got into a dispute one time. I'm sure it was all Daddy's fault. But the next day Daddy showed up at work with a little .25 auto, shot his supervisor in the back of his head, buried him in a trash heap just like this one." He pointed at the massive wall of garbage. Seventy-five feet up the heap, a circle of crows were pecking at the carcass of a small animal. A cat? A possom? It was hard to tell.

"Amazing thing," Gooch went on. "Everybody knew he'd done it. They searched three weeks through all the stinking rotten stuff, never found the body. Best day of my life was when that man went off to prison. Only bad thing, they only gave him five years. You believe that? Killed a man in cold blood, got five years. No body, no witnesses, they had to call it manslaughter."

"If you're trying to scare me . . ."

"I'm not. Get out of the car."

"What?" Fergus blinked.

"Get out of my car."

Fergus looked around, equal parts fear and distaste registering on his face.

"I'm a pretty fair shot," Gooch said, "so I'll make it sporting. Go out, climb up that garbage hill, I won't start shooting till you reach that dead animal up there. I'd give you, oh, thirty percent chance of making it."

Fergus swallowed.

Gooch got out of the car, opened the back door of the car, then took out his pistol, racked the slide.

Fergus stared up at him, looked over at the crows pecking away at the dead animal, then stared back at Gooch with a hateful, cornered expression in his eyes.

"I want assurances," he said finally. "I didn't do anything wrong, so I want assurances."

26

"Okay, okay, okay, okay," Damon Fergus said. "You win."

"Talk," Gooch said.

Damon Fergus took a deep breath. "Here's how it went down. Stormé came to see me one day. She said she was a video game designer. Said they needed a voice for this game she was designing."

"Okay," Gooch said.

"The way she explained it, it was gonna be one of these violent-type games," Fergus said. "Basic idea, somebody is stuck in a room and they've got to get out. She said it was based on a movie called *Slaughter in Room 206*. I said I'd never heard of that movie. She said it was like some cult flick, big with the teenagers. The plot was about—"

Gooch gave him a hard look. Let him know he wasn't here to talk about movies.

Fergus flinched. "Yeah, so anyway, she gives me the script. And I just read the stuff in the script. Period. End of story."

Gooch looked up at the hill of garbage. "You can start running anytime," he said.

"What!"

"Now."

"Wait wait wait!" Damon Fergus held up his hands. "Okay, there's a little more to it."

"You knew something wasn't right about it from the very beginning. Didn't you?"

Fergus looked away for a moment.

"Come on."

"Okay, okay, yeah. I've done a few video game gigs. And they were nothing like this. The script, it was too weird. Too detailed. Normally the script is always a bunch of short sentences."

"How do you read scripts?" Gooch said. "I mean when you're pretending to be blind?"

"I've got a little gadget, an OCR translator."

"OCR?"

"Optical character reader. Basically it's a scanner with a computer in it. Feed the pages through, it translates the words into speech. I run it into a little earphone."

"So what made you so sure she was phony?"

"Look, first off, Stormé Venda didn't strike me as the gamer type. Game designers are the world's biggest geeks. She wasn't even close to being that. I mean, I've spent my life pretending to be something that I'm not. Using it on people. And I knew what I was seeing. She was a total fake."

Gooch nodded.

"Plus, while she was talking to me, she was making faces."

"Faces."

"Yeah! Here I am, a blind guy? So she's talking in this real normal corporate voice. But the whole time, she's sticking out her tongue, pushing up her nose so she looks like a pig. She even uncrossed her legs once, flashed me a little Sharon Stone. I'm serious! No underpants. She's just toying with me. Normal people don't do stuff like that."

Gooch nodded.

"Plus—and this is the kicker—she paid cash. Up front. Video games are made by corporations. Corporate people, they never touch cash, they never pay in advance. It's always, 'Send us an invoice, we'll get you the check when Accounting bloody well pleases.'"

"Okay, so?"

"Well, I have to admit, I was curious who she really was, what she was really up to. So the second she walks out the door, I slip into something a little more Austin Sweet, run down to my car, follow her, see where she goes. Anyway, long story short, once I did the recording, I showed up at her house, told her if she wanted the CD, she needed to give me more money. She said, 'I'll take it up with the guy who's running this thing.'"

Fergus took a long, deep breath.

"That's when I knew I'd stepped in it."

"Stepped in what?"

"Next day there's a knock on my door. I open it up, there's this guy. He's not big. He's not strong. He's not, you know, freaky looking. But somehow he just scares the snot out of me. He walks in and he walks around without speaking. Just touching things. Like he's curious. Picking things up, setting them down. Then he starts breaking stuff. Not like he's mad. Just . . . dropping stuff on the ground. Never once looks at me. Then after he's done about ten thousand bucks' worth of damage to my recording equipment, he walks out. Kinda smiling to himself.

Gooch wondered why a guy would stand there, let something like that happen.

"Two minutes later, the phone rings. It's Stormé. She says, 'You get the message?' I put on my Austin Sweet clothes, drove the CD over, handed it to her, told her, 'Don't ever call me again.'"

"Tell me about the script."

"The way it was explained to me, the way the script works, you got this character in the game, they're locked in this room. They got thirteen hours to solve a crime. But they can't leave the room. All they got is five clues and a telephone on an untraceable line. It's like they're the hostage and the detective all at the same time. Deal is, you got to find out who killed some lady who died eighteen years ago. They don't solve the crime, they lose the game."

"What happens when you lose?"

There was a long pause. Fergus shifted around in his seat. "Come on, Detective," he said finally. "What happens in any video game when you lose?"

Gooch said nothing.

"You lose, you die!"

"I need specifics."

"I don't really remember."

"Start remembering."

Fergus's face hardened. "You gotta protect me from him."

"From who?"

Fergus put his head in his hands. "I don't know," he said. "That's the problem. I don't know. But somebody just wasted Stormé. Probably the same guy that tore up my studio. You don't think they won't waste me, too?"

"Why would they do that?"

"Come on! I don't know what's going on here, but don't you see? Somebody's covering their tracks."

"I need details. You give me details, I'll protect you."

There was a long pause. Fergus stared at the animal being picked over by the crows.

"I'll do you one better," Fergus said finally. "Get me out of here, offer me protection, I'll give you the script."

27

Gooch picked up Cody Floss, then drove Damon Fergus back to his apartment to pick up the script he'd been given by Stormé Venda.

The script was about ten pages. It consisted of short sentences and phrases, separated by large spaces. Gooch stood in Damon Fergus's living room, reading over it while Damon looked on.

The first page included phrases and words like "You have . . ." and "hour" and the numbers one through thirteen, then twenty, thirty, forty, fifty and sixty. The words for the audio clock. The next few pages contained short instructions and warnings.

He flipped to the last page. There was only one line. "You have failed. Say your prayers."

You have failed. Gooch's jaw tightened. He felt a pinprick of fear, then smothered it. Didn't do any good worrying. He looked at his watch. *Damn.* Time was flying.

Gooch scanned the pages looking for clues to where this was all leading. There was nothing specific.

When he got done, Gooch said, "I'm taking this. Don't go anywhere. Don't answer the door. Whoever killed Stormé Venda might come after you next."

Damon looked at him nervously. "Don't you want to know?" he said.

"Know what?" Gooch said.

"Why I did it. Why I pretended to be blind all these years."

Gooch had, in fact, wondered. But only in an idle way. He had never really been interested in the reasons people did evil things. It was enough to know that they did them.

"I really did go blind for about a year," Damon said. His voice trembled slightly. "I got hit in the head with a baseball. But after a year my eyesight slowly came back. By that time, though, I'd gotten used to they way people treated me." He pressed one finger to his right eye, wiped it. His finger came away wet. "My parents, they had a terrible, terrible relationship, and until I went blind nobody paid me the slightest—"

Gooch walked out and slammed the door behind him. God, nothing made him sicker than people whining about their problems. That phony little liar had probably been storing up some self-justifying speech for years, just waiting for a chance to pour it all out, letting his eyes well up and his lip quiver, waiting for everybody to feel sorry for him.

Being stuck in a room with your eyes glued shut—that qualified as a problem. Bad parents—hey, these things happened. Gooch's folks hadn't been a picnic either. And he'd turned out fine, huh?

28

MeChelle picked up the phone as soon as it rang.

"It's me." Gooch's voice.

"Hi," MeChelle said quietly.

"Tracked down Fergus. Venda's dead. Two shots in the head."

MeChelle's heart sank. Somebody out there was killing witnesses. "You think it's whoever put me in here?"

"Maybe," Gooch said. "Maybe it's the person who killed Kathleen Bolligrew. Maybe he found out somehow that we're investigating and he's trying to shut us down before we get to him."

Shit. MeChelle hadn't even thought of that. "You think?"

"I don't know."

"If it's not this Fergus guy, then we're kind of reaching a dead end here, aren't we?"

"You need to start retracing steps. There's something we're missing. If whoever put me here really thinks we can solve this in a day, then the answer's got to be out there."

Another pause. MeChelle was feeling so frustrated that she couldn't be out there on the street. "This sucks," MeChelle said. "I want to be out there doing something."

"There's gotta be a reason you're there," Gooch said. "Think about it. He didn't put you there just to sit around. You've got a part to play. You've just got to figure out what it is."

MeChelle felt a flash of anger. "I don't know what it is!"

"Think," Gooch said. "It's gonna come to you."

She let her hands play over the little clues on the table. A little guy with pointy hair. Wait a minute! That wasn't hair. It was a crown. He was a king.

"King!" she said.

"What?"

"This little doll here, it's a king."

"So?"

"The original detective—his name was Elbert *King*. Right? There must be something significant about him. Something beyond the fact that he's the guy who caught the case. Why don't you talk to him?"

"Yeah," Gooch said. "That's a good idea."

"Whoa!" MeChelle said.

"What?"

"You just complimented my detective chops."

There was a brief pause. "Just trying to keep your spirits up," Gooch said. "Don't let it go to your head or nothing."

Then the line went dead.

29

As it turned out, Elbert King, the detective who had investigated the case, still lived in Atlanta. He had only been in Homicide for about a year before retiring and opening his own private investigation firm.

Gooch dropped Cody Floss off at City Hall East to do some more research, then drove to the office of King's firm. Most P.I.s worked out of their houses or out of small storefront offices. But King's business, the King Corporation, occupied the first four floors of a sizable mid-rise office building in Midtown.

The receptionist was unusually attractive. "Mr. King in?" Gooch asked after identifying himself.

"I'm sorry. Mr. King's taking a late lunch, Detective," she said brightly.

"Where's he eating at?"

She continued to smile. "I'm sorry, I can't give out that information."

It was her job, of course. But that wasn't Gooch's problem. "Would you like to go to jail for contributing to the death of a police officer?"

The girl blinked.

"Then I suggest you tell me where he's at."

She held up one finger. Her manicure looked like it had cost a day's wages. "Just *one* moment, Detective."

Gooch arrived at the restaurant, a swank outfit in Buckhead, a few minutes later. A bunch of self-satisfied-looking guys in suits stood outside waiting for the valet to get their cars. Gooch pulled up at the valet parking stand, flashed his badge, and said, "When I come back out, this car *will* still be here," then went inside before the valet had a chance to speak.

"I'm spose to join Mr. King's party," Gooch said to the girl at the front.

She surveyed his soot-stained T-shirt and smiled coolly. "Yes, sir. He's in a private room in the back." She pointed toward the rear of the restaurant.

"I'll find it."

He walked swiftly back through the restaurant. It was past the lunch rush, so there was hardly anybody still eating. He found a small room in the back that was curtained off from the rest of the dining room. Two slightly overfed-looking men in suits sat at the table talking. He poked his head in and said, "Which one of y'all's Elbert King?"

Two of the men traded glances. "Uh . . ." one of them said. "I believe he went to the little boys' room."

There was something about the way they looked at each other that made him suspicious.

The other man gave Gooch a big phony smile and said, "Have a seat, Chief. You can wait with us while he does his business." He slapped his hand on the chair bottom next to him.

Gooch turned and walked quickly to the bathroom. Nobody was standing at the urinals. He checked the stalls. Empty. Gooch felt a stab of irritation. The sumbitch was giving him the slip.

He ran through the restaurant, found the kid out front pulling up in a big S-series Mercedes, handing the keys to a man of about fifty. Long gray hair, designer jeans, snakeskin boots, sport jacket made of some kind of nubby fabric. A filterless cigarette hung from his lip.

"Slip out the back door on me, King?" Gooch said.

King turned and gave Gooch a broad, crooked smile. What made the smile crooked was a large scar that ran down the side of his face. It looked kind of like a lightning bolt. "Do what, buddy?"

"Gooch. Cold Case Unit. The girl at your office called you, didn't she?"

King chuckled, took a drag on his cigarette, then handed a twenty to the parking valet. He had a lot of very large rings on his fingers. "Dude, why would I do that?"

"That," Gooch said, "is precisely what I'd like to know."

King scowled. "This is about Bolligrew, isn't it?"

That was an unexpected response. "How'd you know that?"

"Knew somebody'd come one of these days." King flicked his butt off into the bushes. "Hop in. We'll talk while I drive."

Gooch eyed his car, which was still sitting by the door. King, apparently sensing his concern about leaving the vehicle, peeled off another twenty, handed it to the parking valet. "Keep an eye on my buddy's car till he gets back."

Gooch figured there was no point in slowing King down if he was prepared to talk, so he climbed in the front seat of the big Mercedes.

King pulled smoothly out into the Buckhead traffic, stubbed out his cigarette, and said, "Yeah. Bolligrew. That was the case that ended my police career."

"Oh?"

"Nah, man, I don't mean like that. I'd just been frustrated for years. Busting bad guys, watch 'em end up back on the street. Listening to these little idiots lie to you all day. Having to say 'Yes, sir' forty times a day to supervisors who didn't know dick about how to do their jobs. And the pay? Hell, I think when I left the force, I was making like thirty-two grand a year. Even back then, that was nothing."

"Yeah," Gooch said.

"How long you been in?"

"About twelve."

"And you're making, what, maybe forty-four? Forty-six?"

"We ain't here to talk about my salary."

"Hey, I'm just always on the lookout for good investigators," King said. "I didn't mean to touch a nerve."

"You didn't," Gooch said. And it was true. Gooch had never given a damn about money. Talking about money just made him irritable. "Tell me about Bolligrew."

King picked up a cigarette, put it in his mouth, but didn't light it. "Cutting down," he said. "Only smoking two packs a day now." He let out a harsh, phlegmy laugh. "Tell you who did it," he said. "The kid did it."

Gooch frowned. What was he talking about? "Her daughter? Lane? She was eleven."

"Nah, nah, nah. You read the file, didn't you? I'm talking about the son."

Gooch was puzzled. "What son?"

King looked over at him, a hint of amused disdain. "You didn't read the file?"

"I read the file."

It was King's turn to look puzzled. "I interviewed the son. Kathleen Bolligrew had a son, age nineteen when the murder happened. Kid by the name of Nathan Morris. Morris was Bolligrew's maiden name. Strictly speaking Morris-Bolligrew was her married name. She hyphenated it when she got married. They divorced after a couple years. But then it was too complicated to explain the hyphen so eventually she just went by Bolligrew. On paper, her name was Morris-Bolligrew. Anyway, this kid Nathan had been born when Kathleen was like fifteen. Needless to say, she wasn't married at the time. She didn't really raise him—mostly her parents did that—and he was resentful of her. Had a few anger issues, if you know what I mean."

"There's no interview report for him in the file."

"Well, hey, I interviewed him three times. Once at his crib, once at his lawyer's office, finally I brought him down to the station. Real cocky little snot."

"I'm telling you. There's nothing in the file."

"Whatever," King said. "All I'm saying, I'm dead sure that boy did it."

"This was a rape-murder. You're saying he raped his own mother?"

"I believe so, yeah. This kid? Classic sociopath. Screw loose from day one. We had psych reports on him going way back. Cruelty to animals, chronic liar, flat affect—all the standard markers of a Grade A monster. Don't get me wrong, though. I don't think he did it just because he was angry, though. The rape was just a cover, make it look like some perv. But Nathan did it. Did it for the money."

"Money?" Gooch was starting to get pissed. There was apparently an awful lot missing from the file in this case. "What money? File said there was a little bit of jewelry missing. Nothing in there about missing money."

"Nah, nah, dude. Here it is. Kathleen Bolligrew's old man was a very successful banker downstate. Owned about half of one of these jerkwater counties north of Savannah. Lotta moolah. There was a trust fund. A big one. Ten, twelve million bucks, something like that. Most of the money went to Kathleen—but some went to Lane and her brother, Nathan. But the money that went to Nathan? It was pay-for-performance money."

"What's that mean?"

"To get his trust fund money, Nathan had to jump through a bunch of hoops. Had to stay in college, had to get certain grades, had to pass a piss test every now and then to show he wasn't a dope fiend. But Nathan wasn't doing it. He wasn't jumping through the hoops. Ergo, no money."

"What's that got to do with the murder?"

"Because if his mom died, the bulk of the money dropped to him and his sister, Lane."

"You're saying if he killed his mom, he got the money."

"He *thought* that was how it would work. So he set it up to look like a rape-murder. I expect he meant to kill Lane, too. But she hid and got away from him."

"What do you mean, he *thought* that was how it worked?"

"After the murder, the trustee of the trust finagled things so that Nathan got cut out of the action. I think he believed Nathan committed the murder, too. So he wanted to make sure Nathan didn't get the money. Like I say, the trust was complicated. The lawyer was able to use all these legalities to tie everything up. My understanding, Nathan filed suit against him. But eventually they settled. Of course, that was after I retired."

"What happened to this kid Nathan?"

King shook his head.

"Why you so sure it was him?"

"Kathleen Bolligrew already had a restraining order against him. They'd had all kind of disputes. For a long time he'd lived with his grandparents. But then in high school he turned incorrigible. His grandparents finally decided they couldn't control him anymore. So Kathleen let him live with her for a while. That didn't last long. She threw him out of the house when he turned seventeen."

"Any physical evidence? Witnesses placing him at the scene?"

King shook his head. "No. And he had an alibi, too. His girlfriend claimed she was with him the whole night."

"None of this is in the file," Gooch said.

King's face seemed oddly opaque. He shrugged. "Look, I worked that case as hard as I could. And I just hit a brick wall with that kid. Meantime, I wasn't getting along with the head of Homicide. Luke Johnson? Is he still on the force?"

"Nah," Gooch said. "Long gone."

"Well, anyway, I was approached with an opportunity to do some investigative work in the private sector, so I got the hell out. Minute I left the force, I wished I'd done it a decade earlier."

Gooch thought about it. There was something missing. King was misleading him about something.

"How come you tried to give me the slip?"

"What?" King had a look of exaggerated surprise on his face. Gooch felt like punching him. Guy like King, always working you.

"You're lying to me about something. Or not telling me. Which is the same thing."

"Lying!" King put a hard look on his face. "Dude, I didn't *have* to talk to you."

"Do me a favor. Don't call me *dude* again."

King's hard face dissolved into a big hokey smile. "Hey, relax. Figure of speech."

"Tell me what you ain't told me yet."

King pulled up in front of his office building, stopped the big Mercedes in front of the glass doors. "This doesn't leave this car," he said.

"I ain't here to negotiate with you or make deals."

King raised one eyebrow. "You want my help or not?"

Gooch thought about MeChelle down in that room, eyes glued shut, and something twisted in his gut. "There's a cop's life on the line here," he said. "I can't tell you the details. This ain't just about solving some moldy old crime."

King grinned coolly. "And I'm spose to give a shit about that?"

Gooch took a deep breath, considered his options. Beating this guy to the floorboards was tempting. But it wouldn't help. Truth was, he didn't have many options. Gooch gritted his teeth. "All right," he said.

"All right what?" King said.

"Whatever you got to say, it ain't leaving this car."

"See how easy that was?" King took the cigarette from behind his ear, lit it, expelled a long thin stream of smoke. "Oh, praise the Lord," he said.

"Talk," Gooch said.

King took another drag. "I'll be honest with you. I always liked money." He didn't speak for a moment. "I only spent about eight months in Homicide. Before that I'd been in Narcotics."

Narcotics. There were a lot of ways you could go wrong in Narcotics.

"You're always busting these little losers and—hey—even just small-time street guys, half the time they got more money in their pocket than you make in a month. I'm not gonna say I gave in to temptation. But, theoretically, you could see how somebody might forget to log in some cash from time to time . . ." King smoked silently. "You remember that investigation back in 1988 where they popped a bunch of guys in the department for being on the take? Some guys in the Red Dog squad, couple of Narcotics guys . . ."

Gooch said nothing, just waited.

"Okay, well . . . let's just say I was very close to several of those guys that got popped. Let's just say Internal Affairs was sniffing around me. So I switched over to Homicide. Trying to get the heat off of me. Anyway, I don't know where he found out—but when I started getting close to Nathan, he said that I needed to look at some other suspects or he might could make it hard on me, tell IA that I was trying to hit him up for money."

"You threw the case," Gooch said.

"Nah, nah, nothing like that!"

"Then what *was* it like?"

"I quit. Quit the job, left the case for somebody else to worry about. Can't blame it on me if the next guy didn't pursue the case all that hard."

"I don't suppose Nathan convinced you to inadvertently take off with a witness statement or two? Maybe shade things in the file so that when you turned it over to the next detective there wouldn't be much to work with?"

King reached across Gooch's lap, opened his door. "Good luck, man," he said.

"I asked you a question!" Gooch said.

"Good luck," King said. "Go tell the girl in reception I said for her to get one of my operatives to take you back to your car at the restaurant."

"I asked you a question. Did you take those files?"

"Nathan's girlfriend's name was Grace Wadell. She alibied him. After all these years, she might be willing to talk."

"That's not what I asked you."

King looked straight ahead, the long scar white against the skin of his face. "We're done here."

30

MeChelle picked up the phone as soon as it rang.

"I think we're on to something with King," Gooch said. "I think he took a lot of stuff out of the file. He didn't admit it outright, but I'm pretty sure he did. Kathleen Bolligrew had an illegitimate son by the name of Nathan Morris. King says he's the guy."

"Why didn't he arrest him back then?"

"King says he had an alibi. I'm trying to track his alibi down. If I can't find her, I'll go straight to Morris."

"So you don't trust King?"

"Nope."

"Why not?"

"He more or less admitted taking money when he worked Narcotics. And he implied that he might have altered the case file so that it didn't incriminate Nathan as much as it otherwise might have."

MeChelle felt helpless again. She wanted to be out there riding in the car with Gooch.

"I know," Gooch said, apparently reading her thoughts. "I know."

There was a long pause. Then the phone went dead.

MeChelle figured that would be it for a while, but the phone rang again after about a minute.

"Hank?"

There was a long pause.

"Hank?" she said again.

"Yeah, it's me."

"What is it?"

"It's almost the end of the hour. We got one more phone call. Thought I'd go ahead and use it up."

"Okay. But . . . I got nothing for you. I can't think of anything else."

Again there was a long pause. MeChelle had a funny feeling, not sure what it was.

"You okay, Hank?" she said.

"I'm fine." Another pause. Then Gooch added, "'Course I ain't been sleeping so great lately."

This was way out of character. "How come?"

Another pause.

"I don't—" He drew a long, audible breath. "I don't know. Been dreaming about my little girl. I keep seeing her in this bamboo thicket. The one where they found her body, you know? I keep moving toward her, but I can't reach her. She keeps calling for me. 'Daddy! Daddy!'"

"You ever have dreams like that before this?"

"Isn't that funny?" Gooch said. "Twelve years since she died, it wasn't till after I quit the force that I start dreaming about her."

"You were focused on other things."

"Was I?"

"Gooch, you're scaring me," MeChelle said.

Gooch was cut off in midlaugh.

Weird. What had put him in this confessional mood? She'd never even vaguely heard him talk like this before. In the six months they'd worked together, he'd never told her a single thing about himself or about his life or his feelings, never had a naked moment between them. Not one.

She'd been joking about him scaring her. But seriously, now that she thought about it, he'd better be keeping his eye on the ball.

31

Gooch found only one listing for a Grace Wadell in the phone book. There was no knowing if it was the right one or not. This long after the fact she could have moved, gotten married, changed her name. . . . He called the number but nobody answered.

Gooch called Cody Floss from the back of the car that took him to the restaurant, asked Cody to run Grace Wadell through the system.

"Nothing there, sir."

"What about Nathan Morris?" Gooch waited, listening to the clicking of keys.

"Yeah, okay, sir," Cody said eventually. "Got a Nathan Morris here. He's on parole right now."

"What was he in for?"

"Fraud. Theft by receiving. A bunch of white-collar-type stuff. Lists his place of employment at something called NHM Research on Peachtree and Lenox, right across from the mall."

"Gimme the address."

* * *

A few minutes later, Gooch walked through a pair of gold-trimmed glass doors into the offices of NHM Research. It was a small suite on the ninth floor of a commercial building in the heart of Buckhead. The reception area was decorated with furniture that, on first glance, looked expensive and antique. But a closer examination made it clear that everything in the room was a cheap reproduction, veneer and chipboard.

The young man sitting at the front desk—despite his necktie and pressed white shirt—looked more like a bouncer than a receptionist. He was large and muscular, his head shaved. His eyes had a certain bellicose, watchful quality that didn't jibe with his clothes or his surroundings.

"Need to talk to Mr. Morris," Gooch said, doing his best to smile.

"What's this in reference to, sir?" the young man said.

"It's in reference to I need to talk to him." Gooch put his badge on the top of the reception desk.

The young man reached for his phone. He wore long sleeves, but as he reached forward, a crude green tattoo crept out from under the white cloth. A prison tat for sure.

"You don't need to call him," Gooch said. "I'll just scoot on back there. Won't take a second of his time."

The large young man looked at him, stone-faced. "Sir, do you have a warrant?"

Gooch's eyebrows went up. "Well! My gracious goodness mercy me, you just stampeded right to the warrant nice and quick."

"Sir, do you have a warrant?" the man said again.

Gooch kept smiling. "You know, son, it's a violation of your parole to be working for a convicted felon. You are aware that Mr. Morris is a convicted felon, I trust? I hate to have to violate you for that."

Still not a hint of expression on the young man's face. "I'm not on probation. Or parole. You can't do jack to me. So unless you got a warrant, get out. Sir."

Gooch met the young man's eye. The young man's glare didn't waver. It was obvious this was a cool character, not easily scared. "NHM Research?" Gooch pointed at the gold lettering on the wall over the young man's head. "What kind of research y'all do here?"

"Investments," the young man said.

"One of them boiler rooms, huh? All the little scammers back there flogging penny stocks to old ladies in Miami?" Gooch edged toward the entrance to the rooms in the back.

"Go ahead, sir," the bald guy said. "Make your move. First thing I'll do is call our lawyer. He's sitting about thirty feet away from here so he won't have much trouble observing as you trespass on private property. You'll be interested to know that we have a security camera that will be used as evidence in any court proceedings that might follow. Second thing I'll do is take a great deal of pleasure in throwing your cop ass out that door."

Gooch sensed the young man wasn't bluffing. Which meant he was going to have to flush Morris out of here.

"Fair enough," Gooch said. "What I need you to do then, is tell your boss that we got him in the crosshairs. Tell him we got a witness. Tell him we know where the stuff is at. Tell him he's pretty well screwed."

The big man looked at him suspiciously. "Stuff? What stuff?"

Gooch didn't know what stuff either. But he figured a guy like Nathan was bound to have something squirreled away somewhere that he wouldn't want the cops to find. It was pretty much a Hail Mary. But that's where he was at right now.

"Also," Gooch said, "tell him I said you're doing fine work up here at the reception desk and he ought to give you a raise."

Gooch turned and walked toward the door.

"Have a nice day, sir," the big man said.

Gooch chuckled a little as he got into the hallway. Wasn't sure what it was about a guy like that, but he had to admit he kind of liked him. Reminded him of some of the characters he'd been around back when he was in the Special Forces.

Now came the tricky part.

Assuming Morris took the bait, there were three parking levels in the building and two exits. Nathan Morris could leave onto either Peachtree or Lenox.

Gooch dialed Cody Floss. "This Morris character. Two things. First, what kind of car's he drive? Second, what's he look like?"

There was a clicking of keys. "He's got three cars, sir. A red 911, a blue Land Cruiser, a white Maybach."

"A what?"

"Maybach."

"What's a Maybach?"

"You haven't heard of those, sir? I think BMW makes them. Or Mercedes?"

"Never heard of it."

"Costs like three hundred and seventy-five-thousand bucks, sir. Looks like a Rolls."

"Okay. What's Morris look like?"

More clicking. "Let's see . . . on the thinnish side? Brown hair, green eyes, six-foot-one, one seventy-five. Very nice-looking guy."

"Thanks. I'll bear that in mind if I decide to turn gay."

"I'm just saying, sir."

"Mmm-hmm." Gooch hung up. A white Maybach. Okay, that should be distinctive enough.

He rode the elevator down to the parking garage, climbed in his car, pulled out onto Lenox. There was no place to park on Peachtree anyway. He'd just have to take the chance.

Sure enough, within less than a minute a very large, unfamiliar-looking car pulled up to the light and out onto Peachtree. *A Maybach,* he thought. *Well, what do you know? Learn something every day.*

Gooch threw the Ford in drive, cut across three lanes of traffic into the left turn lane. He needed to get out onto Peachtree—without alerting Morris that he was following him. This wasn't gonna be pretty. But then, hell, nothing about the day had been pretty. So that's the way it was. The Maybach continued through the light, crossing in front of Gooch and continuing down Peachtree at a high rate of speed. He got a quick glimpse of a man with brown hair, a square jaw, a long nose.

Dammit. If he didn't get a move on, he'd lose this guy.

Gooch didn't want to put on the blue lights and alert Morris, so he waited until the big white car had gone half a block, then blew his horn and made an illegal turn onto Peachtree across three lanes of traffic. Hell, it was only the most heavily traveled street in the city of Atlanta. Nothing to it.

A Hummer thundered by, missing his rear bumper by about six inches. Horns blew, brakes squealed, middle fingers shot out of windows at him. Gooch smiled and waved, then floored it to catch up with the Maybach.

The Maybach was doing about sixty, dodging in and out of traffic, tailgating, doing everything it could to make time in the early afternoon traffic.

Gooch nearly lost Morris three or four times. Morris kept moving straight up Peachtree, heading toward downtown Atlanta. Gooch had to blow a couple of lights to keep up, nearly getting hit each time. His hands were sweating and his heart was racing. But it was good. It was good to get the blood up a little again. He looked out the side window and a flash of sunlight illuminated his face. A sudden reflection in the glass. He was surprised to see his own face grinning fiercely back.

Huh, he thought. *I'll be damn.*

In front of him the big Maybach hung a sudden right next to Piedmont Hospital, headed down Collier Road, a winding two-lane road through a residential area. Gooch screeched through the turn. There was only one car between them now—a Buick driven by a white-haired woman.

Great. There'd be no opportunity to pass on this twisty road, and the Buick would inevitably hold him up while Morris tore up the road.

To Gooch's surprise, though, the old lady was racing through the neighborhood at fifty-five, keeping pace with the massive German car in front of her. She had a cigarette bobbing up and down on one side of her mouth, and was talking on a cell phone. She lifted something to her mouth, with her other hand took a pull on it. Was that a bottle of Southern Comfort? Gooch nearly laughed.

Way to go, Grandma.

The Maybach caught the tag end of the yellow light as it crossed over Northside Drive. Grandma blew the red pretty solidly and Gooch came within a foot or two of being taken out by a cement truck. His pulse was racing now.

The Maybach hung a left at the next light, Howell Mill, with its mixture of seedy strip malls and yuppie bars, while

Grandma tore on up Collier talking, drinking, and smoking away.

Gooch was right behind the Maybach now. The Maybach again began jockeying and tailgating and racing down the road, heading into the grim old industrial area of northwest Atlanta. Gooch decided to hang back a little.

It turned out to be the right decision. Morris turned right within a mile, heading into an area of low-rise warehouses and down-at-the-heels mill buildings. The Maybach drove down the road, turned into parking lot surrounded by a rusting chain-link fence. An old brick building stood at the corner of the lot, a fading sign hanging over it that said ASKEW ORNAMENTAL IRONWORK. Parked in the lot were two Beemers, a Range Rover, and a vintage Camaro with a hood scoop, flames painted on the side.

Gooch wasn't sure how well the ornamental ironwork business paid—but it seemed unlikely that a bunch of hippy blacksmiths were driving these kind of sleds.

He parked at the far end of the block, then ran in a crouch around the back side of the small factory.

He noticed video cameras mounted in a number of locations around the perimeter of the building. It looked like there was a gap in their coverage, however, on one corner of the fence. He climbed it, slicing open a finger as he jumped down to the other side.

It hurt like a son of a gun, but he didn't have time to fuss with it. He ran to the back door of the building, tried the handle. No luck. So he ran around front. There Gooch caught a break. Fortunately, in his hurry to get inside, Morris hadn't pulled the door all the way closed.

Gooch gently pushed it open by an inch or so, peered in. He could see a broad open space, dimly lit, with a concrete floor and some smithing equipment—iron-bending machines, a hydraulic forge press, a power hammer, an anvil, a massive industrial forge.

Okay, what now? Gooch thought. *I got no warrant, no probable cause, no reason to be here that will ever stand up in court. Should I go in?* The fact was, this was different from the office building. He knew there was something going on here that he could use against Morris. He wasn't sure what it was. But he was sure it was there.

The decision was easy. This wasn't about court anyway. This was about finding MeChelle. He drew his Glock, slid through the door into the dark building.

As he did so, he heard a noise—WHOOOMFFFF!—immediately recognizing it as the sound of igniting propane. In front of him the big industrial forge lit up, blue and orange flames licking out the sides. A thin orange light lit the space.

A man in a suit stood in front of the fire. He had a lean, handsome face. Had to be Nathan Morris. Gooch frowned, curious to see what the guy was up to. The man in the suit adjusted the flames on the forge, then walked across the room to a large shipping container. He seemed to be in a big hurry. He opened the door, walked in, then came immediately back out, carrying a large cardboard box, which he threw on the floor.

It burst open, the contents spilling across the floor.

Dolls.

More accurately, they were action figures. Little guys with big muscles and army clothes. GI Joes, hundreds of them. Morris picked up a shovel and started shoveling the dolls into the fire. The forge had gotten very hot by now. Gooch guess it was heading north of 2000 degrees already. Morris seemed in a big hurry to get all the toys into the fire.

The toys were vanishing almost immediately, consumed within seconds by the intense heat.

As Gooch watched in amusement, he heard a noise behind him. It was the characteristic sound of a round being chambered in a Remington 870 shotgun, a weapon that Gooch had known intimately for a very long time.

Gooch felt a moment of self-reproach. He'd gotten too cute, standing around watching the guy.

"Move, I'll kill you," a voice said.

32

Gooch turned. A big guy—bigger even than the one who'd sat at the reception desk at NHM Research—looked at him, a feral smile on his lips. He wore a cowboy hat, cowboy boots, and had one of those giant gaudy rodeo buckles on his belt. His shotgun was pointed straight at Gooch's gut.

"Looks like I got the wrong place," Gooch said. He tried to duck backward out the door, but the big man grabbed his shirt, yanked him forward, slinging him to the floor. As he hit the ground, his gun skittered off across the concrete floor.

"Mr. Morris!" the big man called out. "Check out what I just found."

On the other side of the room, next to the big industrial gas forge, Nathan Morris was looking at Gooch.

"You got a warrant, Detective?" he said.

Gooch said nothing.

"This dude's a *cop*?" the big man said.

"I don't know, Waylon," Morris said. "I'm not at all sure

he's a policeman. Maybe we should hold him at gunpoint and call nine-one-one."

The big man looked puzzled. "Nine-one-one?"

Gooch slowly pulled out his badge. "I *am* a cop," he said.

"You could buy that at the costume shop, man," Morris said. He was still busy shoveling action figures into the fire. Gooch wondered what was in them. Most likely dope. "Nah," Morris continued. "We gotta call 911. But maybe we ought to wait until I get done with this."

Gooch just sat with his hands around his knees as Morris retrieved a second box, threw it on the ground, shoveled more action figures into the fire.

When he was finished, Morris stomped the boxes flat, fed them into the fire, too. Then he clapped his hands together like he was brushing dust off them, then smiled. "Go ahead and call, Waylon."

The big man pulled out a cell phone.

"Oh, I don't think you need to do that, Waylon," Gooch said.

"Armed man? Breaking into my property? No warrant?" Morris said. "You better believe I'm calling nine-one-one." He smiled broadly, then pulled out a pack of cigarettes, smacked them on the ham of his hand, tore open the wrapping. "And when they arrive, you can tell them to search this place to their hearts' content. They won't find a thing."

Gooch said nothing.

"Of course, I still won't let them look around here without a warrant." Nathan Morris knocked a cigarette out of the pack, slipped it between his lips, lit it with a gleaming gold lighter.

Meanwhile Waylon was talking on the phone to 911, telling them he'd just found an intruder who claimed to be a policeman.

Gooch lay back on the concrete, put his hands behind his head. "Yeah, actually, see I'm not here to talk about whatever was in them dolls."

The room was silent except for the low roar of the gas forge.

"Say that again?" Morris said.

"I don't have no idea what was in them dolls," Gooch said. "Don't really care much neither."

The forge continued to roar.

"You're a funny guy," Morris said finally. His voice sounded a little tentative.

"Nah, actually, one of the things most people'll tell you about me, I'm a fairly humorless sumbitch."

Morris looked into the forge. It seemed to be dawning on him that he may have just burned up a lot of very valuable action figures for nothing. As the reality of the situation hit him, he started to get angry, his face flushing.

"Shit!" Morris screamed. He picked up the shovel and slammed it against the forge.

"What is it—" Gooch said. "First you got denial, then rage, then grief, then . . . acceptance? Nah, I'm forgetting something."

Morris cursed and screamed for a while, bashing everything in sight with the shovel.

"When you're done," Gooch said finally. "I need to ask some questions. Questions about the death of your mother."

Morris whirled. His face suddenly froze. The rage seemed to fade. He stared at Gooch. "You're here about *Mom*?"

Gooch stood slowly. Waylon was still concentrating on his phone call to 911. Gooch took the opportunity to kick Waylon in the nuts. The big man, folded up, groaning. Gooch took the phone from his hand and spoke into the receiver. "Sorry, false alarm. Everything's under control here."

Then he closed the cell phone, scooped up the Remington 870, ejected the shells, and tossed the weapon on the ground next to the moaning Waylon.

Morris made a run to pick up Gooch's gun. But Gooch got there first.

"Boy howdy," Gooch said. "You're jumpier'n hell, son."

Morris backed up, hands in the air, as though Gooch had a gun pointed at him. But Gooch just holstered his pistol.

"Just tell me about what you know," Gooch said. "And I'll overlook your situation with G.I. Joe."

Morris looked into the forge. It now appeared to be completely empty, nothing left of the action figures at all. "You have any idea how much money you just cost me? Why would I even dream of talking to you?"

"You the one shoved all your little dolls in the oven. Don't put that on me."

"I don't know jack," Morris said, his face hard and angry. "That's my final word."

"Talked to the detective on the case, King. He thinks you know a lot."

Morris scowled. "King!" His voice was dripping disgust. "Of course King would say that."

Gooch spread his hands in silent question.

"Did you even bother to ask around about that guy?" Morris said.

"Why should I?"

"Well, let's see . . ." Morris gave Gooch a wincing smile. "King got bumped off the force because everybody knew he was on the take. He had a bunch of reprimands for various disciplinary issues—including planting evidence on innocent suspects. Oh, yeah, and he was banging my mom."

Gooch raised one eyebrow.

Morris's chilly smile broadened. "Yeah. Nice, huh?"

"He was dating your *mother*? You got proof?"

"Dating. That's a pretty word for it. No, I don't have proof. But it happens to be true."

"One of them your-word-against-his situations, huh?"

"Kiss my ass!" Morris took a drag on his cigarette. "I made a formal accusation against the guy. Did you find it in the file? I bet not. I bet he managed to make it go away before he took quote-unquote *early retirement*. Huh? Yeah?"

Gooch thought about it. Was it possible? Morris was probably a sociopathic liar. This was the kind of story you'd expect from a snake like him. But that didn't mean it wasn't true.

Morris went over to the big man on the floor and said, "Take a hike, Waylon. Go ice your nuts or something."

Waylon stood, hobbled away, holding his crotch.

"You ask King about the trust fund?" Morris said.

Gooch's eyebrows went up again. "He mentioned it. Said it's precisely what gave you a motive."

Morris's loud laugh didn't contain a shred of humor. "Let me tell you a funny story. Mom had me when she was fifteen. You know who good old Daddy was? Her own father. So my dad and granddad are the same guy. Isn't that a pretty picture? Dad was a very influential guy downstate. Owned a bank and a whole lot of property, served in the state legislature, all that stuff. When he died, he left most of his money to this Christian college down in Tifton. Sick old bastard thought he'd buy his way into heaven after leading this totally depraved life. But he did manage to set aside a small fraction of his fortune to leave as a bequest to Mom. Actually, part of it was for me, part for her, part for my sister, Lane."

"King told me about that. Said you were mad because you weren't getting your slice of the pie."

"Yeah, well, King would say that. Truth is, he was trying to get the whole pie for himself."

"So your theory of the killing is . . ."

"King wanted to marry her, get his greedy little fingers on the dough. My guess, she started seeing through his BS, broke it off with him. He flipped out, went ninja, and killed her. Then, of course, he tried to frame me for it. If he hadn't got caught with his hand in the cookie jar, had to resign from the force . . . ?—Hell, yeah, he'd have pulled it off, too."

"How do you know all this?"

"He was trying to have the administrator of the trust removed, put in a new guy who'd be more . . . flexible."

"How do you know this?"

"Mom told me."

"How'd you find this out? King said she had a restraining order against you."

Morris took a last pull on his cigarette, flicked the butt into the forge. It flared up briefly, then evaporated. "Yeah, well, Mom and I didn't always get along so great. But you know how family is. She was still my mom. Just because she had a restraining order on me doesn't mean we didn't talk."

"And she told you . . ."

"Straight out. 'King wants me to get a new trustee. I think he's after my money.' That's what she said to me. Two weeks later, she was dead."

Gooch scratched his head.

"Think about it, Detective. You've got evidence of rape, but no semen, no hairs, no fibers, nada. That doesn't seem suspicious to you? Who would be in a better position to make that happen than a cop?"

Gooch thought about it. No doubt King was a corrupt schemer. But would he have killed Kathleen Morris just because she wouldn't go along with his plan? "Okay," Gooch said, "let's say it's true. There must be something you can give me."

"I got an alibi. I was with my girlfriend, Grace Wadell."

"So I heard."

"Look, go ask her. I haven't seen Grace in years. She owes me nothing. She's got no reason to lie."

"You better believe I'll ask her."

"Plus, I filed suit against the trustee and my sister."

He said it blandly, like it was nothing. Gooch had a couple sisters. He didn't get along with either of them all that well—but he couldn't imagine filing a lawsuit against his own kin. Seemed kind of pitiful, doing a thing like that. "What's that got to do with anything?"

"All the trust documents came out during discovery in the case. I'm sure they're still down there buried in the courthouse somewhere. I know Mom made some kind of initial filing to change the executor. King was behind that. But then she got suspicious of King and didn't follow through. You can go down to the County Clerk's office and verify this."

Gooch narrowed his eyes, then pulled out his phone. "Cody. Hey, it's me. Need you to run down to the Clerk's Office again, pull the pleadings in a civil case for me."

"I couldn't tell you the case number, but it was filed two weeks after Mom's death."

"You didn't exactly let the body get cold, huh?" Gooch said.

"Hey, it's not personal. It's business. I wasn't gonna to let myself get screwed out of my rightful inheritance on a bunch of little technicalities." He poked the fire with the shovel.

Gooch repeated the information to Cody Floss, then hung up.

"So did you win the case?" Gooch said.

Nathan Morris shrugged vaguely. "I needed the money, so I settled cheap. Biggest mistake of my life."

Gooch studied Morris's face.

"Hey, don't look at me that way!" Morris said. "You think I'd be doing this—" He poked the shovel into the flames, stirred the puddle of molten plastic in the bottom of the forge. The remains of the last dolls flared and disappeared. "You really think I'd be doing *this* if I had nice steady income from all that loot my grandfather left me?"

"'Course you would."

Morris looked like he was about to get angry. Then he laughed loudly. "Okay, you're right. I would."

Gooch turned as though to leave, then stopped. "So what was in them dolls anyway?" Gooch said.

"Dolls! Dolls? Bro, those are *action figures*!" Morris said.

"What was in them action figures?"

Morris stared at him, pointed his finger. "A three-hundred-and-forty-thousand-dollar investment, is what I got in 'em."

Gooch figured that was about all he'd get out of the guy on that subject. Besides, he didn't really care. If the guy had just burned up a third of a million bucks' worth of dope, that was his business. Gooch had always been of the opinion that prosecuting people for buying or selling dope was a waste of time. All it did was create high prices for drugs, which in turn created rich thugs. Some idiot wanted to stick a needle in his arm—why stop him?

Morris turned and stared dolefully into the fire, then shut off the gas. The fired died out, but the lining of the forge continued to glow a hellish red.

"Put King in jail," Morris said, "and it'll be worth every penny this cost me." Morris turned, pointed his finger at Gooch. "Go. Get him."

Gooch studied him for a minute. "What do you know about rabbits?"

Morris frowned. "Huh?"

"Stuffed rabbits."

"These are action figures. Okay? *Action* figures. I don't know squat about stuffed rabbits."

Gooch studied his face for a minute. It seemed clear that the stuffed rabbit reference meant nothing to him. If he was the real killer, wouldn't he have known about the rabbit?

33

The minute Gooch walked out the door, a panel van slid up and the door opened. A man wearing sunglasses and a blue nylon windbreaker jumped out.

The man held up an ID card in a leather wallet. "Special Agent Bremmer, FBI."

Gooch looked at the man impassively, then studied the ID. It looked genuine. Hologram, mag stripe, all the details looking right. "What's this about, bud?"

"Get in, I'll tell you," the FBI man said. He looked hopping mad about something.

Gooch shrugged, climbed into the van. Bremmer slammed the door shut, then the van sped off.

A second FBI man sat in the back of the van, a black guy with very short graying hair and a pair of earphones draped around his neck. There was all kinds of funny surveillance equipment on the walls of the van. Gooch could tell instinctively from the black guy's body language that he was the man in charge. He looked pissed, too.

"You want to tell me what the hell you were doing in there, Detective?" the man said.

Gooch sat, looked at him impassively. "Don't I know you?" he said.

"I'm Assistant Special-Agent-in-Charge Lucas Johnson," the man said. Then his eyes narrowed. "You're Gooch, aren't you? I saw you on the news last year with that child murder case. What's your first name? Hamp? Hemp? Shemp?"

Now Gooch remembered. "Hank," Gooch said. "It's Hank."

ASAC Johnson seemed uninterested. "Yeah, see, Shemp, the reason everybody in here is looking all long in the face? You just messed up a very long and arduous investigation."

"About what?"

"That information's above your pay grade, Shemp."

Gooch held the FBI man's eye. "You call me Shemp one more time, I'm gonna climb right out the van, and whatever it was you wanted from me, you ain't gonna get it."

"All right, all right," ASAC Johnson said. "Ease up. We're on the same side. Look, I used to be APD myself. I worked Homicide back in the day. But here's the thing. You just blundered into our investigation. We need to know how bad you messed us up."

"Investigation of what?"

"I can't divulge that."

"Stop the vehicle," Gooch said. "I'm outta here."

ASAC Johnson and the other FBI man exchanged glances. "Okay, okay. Collectibles. This guy Morris, he sells fraudulent collectibles on eBay."

Gooch shook his head. Collectibles. What did that mean? "Huh?"

"You know, like 1964 G.I. Joe in the original box. Only it's not really G.I. Joe and it's not the original box. It's all fake stuff. Very high-quality fakes. But still fakes."

Gooch thought about it. "Somebody pays money for that?"

"A '64 G.I. Joe in the original box went for eighty-seven grand last year."

What would they think of next? It was a wonder anybody sold drugs, the money you could make with silly scams like this. "Johnson," Gooch said, "you remember a guy by the name of King? Worked Homicide for a year or so?"

Johnson scowled. "We're talking about Nathan Morris right now."

"Nah, we're talking about King. *Then* we're talking about Morris."

Johnson drummed his fingers for a moment, exchanged glances with one of the other agents. "Okay," he said finally. "Yeah, I remember King."

"You remember a case he was working? Kathleen Bolligrew?"

"How could I forget?"

"Meaning what?"

"What's your angle?"

"I'm in the Cold Case Unit. We're reopening the case."

Johnson's eyebrows went up. "No kidding."

"So tell me about King and that case."

"King came over from Narcotics. I was actually his supervisor in Homicide. Remember that ring they broke up—a bunch of guys who were shaking down dealers? Well, it was rumored that King was part of it, and that he got out because he saw the handwriting on the wall. Very slick guy. It wasn't until after I hired him that I found out Internal Affairs was looking at him. Anyway, he got the Bolligrew case, and he worked it a while. And then suddenly one day he walks in and says, 'Hey, boss, I think it's time for me to go into the private sector.' Two weeks later, he hangs up his shingle as a P.I. The whole thing smelled funny."

"How so?"

"I've known a bunch of guys who quit being cops, went into private investigation. Usually they're digging nickels out of the couch cushions for a while till they get a decent client base." Johnson smiled thinly. "Not King. Month after he left, he hired two of my guys right out from under me. Suddenly he's driving a nice new Cadillac, got an office with a secretary. That whole thing didn't compute."

"How you think he did it?"

"Somebody paid him off. Not in straight money, but in investigative work."

"Who?"

"Never found out. When him and those other two guys left, it was right in the middle of the first big crack epidemic. Murders were way up. We were shorthanded, everybody working round the clock. I just got sick of the pressure. FBI knocked on my door, I gave my notice, never looked back."

"Now you're a big hero, clamping down on G.I. Joe."

"Whatever you say, Shemp."

Gooch locked his eyes on the FBI man's face. The FBI man didn't break his gaze. "So you think somebody connected to the Bolligrew thing paid him off?" Gooch said finally.

Johnson shrugged. "Could be. The victim's family had a lot of money. My recollection, there was a brother that King was looking at."

"Yeah. His name would be Nathan Morris."

Johnson's eyes widened. "No!" He covered his eyes with one hand. "You serious?"

Gooch nodded.

Johnson shook his head glumly. "I never even made the connection."

"You know what Morris just told me?"

"What?"

"He said King had a relationship with Kathleen Bolligrew."

Johnson looked skeptical. "I wouldn't believe that guy if he told me the ocean was wet."

"I'm inclined to agree. He claims his girlfriend alibied him. I'm gonna look her up, see if the alibi holds up after all these years."

Johnson shrugged, then gave him an insincere smile. "Well, I'm sure you'll do just fine. Meantime, we need to know what he's doing with all those G.I. Joes."

Gooch smiled back. "He burned 'em. Every last one. Ain't nothing left in that warehouse."

"No!" Johnson punched the wall of the van, making a loud thud. "Now he's gonna move the whole operation somewhere else."

Gooch turned around and tapped the driver of the van on the shoulder. "You can take me back to my car now."

Johnson kept punching the side of the van, leaving big knuckle prints in the metal.

"You gonna hurt your kung fu grip if you keep doing that," Gooch said.

Johnson just glared at him. But as Gooch started climbing out of the van, Johnson called out to him, "King had to push to get that case. He practically got in a fight with me trying to get the case assigned to him. At that time, I thought he was just eager for a good case, being new on the squad. But now? Given what you said? Think about it."

I will, Gooch thought.

34

Gooch wasn't sure what he'd expected Nathan Morris's ex-girlfriend to be. But it was not this.

Grace Wadell was a nun.

He had found her at a convent—the Sisters of St. Albert of Lincoln—in a wooded neighborhood north of Buckhead. The convent had grudgingly allowed him admittance, a frowning, elderly nun in a habit leading him back to the rear of the property where he found a much younger woman chopping down a tree with an ax.

She was very attractive, fit, her shirt wet with sweat and covered with bits of bark and chips of wood. She swung the ax methodically, a pleasure to watch. Unlike the older woman, she didn't look even vaguely like a nun.

"Sister," the elderly nun said. "A policeman here to see you."

The young woman turned and looked at Gooch expressionlessly, then leaned her ax against the tree she was cutting down. "Yes?"

Gooch introduced himself. The elderly nun continued to stand very close to Gooch. "You don't need to stay with us," Gooch said to her. "We're fine."

"No," the nun said. "It's not permitted for a sister to be alone with a man."

The old nun practically stank of disapproval. Her presence was likely to stifle the interview. "Ma'am, I'm here on a police matter," Gooch said to her.

"And I'm here on a God matter," the old nun said. She had very bright, slightly malicious eyes. There was no moving her, he could tell.

"All right," Gooch said. He turned to the younger woman. "Wouldn't have took you for a nun, Ms. Wadell," he said.

"You can call me 'Sister Grace,'" she said. "Why are you here?"

"The name Nathan Morris mean anything to you?"

"No," she said. Her face showed nothing.

"You didn't ever date a man by the name of Nathan Morris?" For all he knew, she was the wrong Grace Wadell.

She picked up the ax, hefted it. Her muscles moved smoothly under her skin. Gooch thought about how long it had been since he'd been with a woman. Long time. Long, long time. For a while it hadn't bothered him. But now, every woman he saw, it seemed like they practically made his skin tingle.

"Sister Albert-Joseph," Grace Wadell said, "would you mind standing over there? I'd like a little privacy."

"Privacy is where the devil lives," the older woman said.

"Yes, Sister, I know. But could you go stand there? Please?"

Sister Albert-Joseph frowned, moved back about ten steps.

"Ten more?"

The old woman scowled, moved back five small steps.

"Jesus Christ," Sister Grace said. She pulled out a pack of

cigarettes, lit one up. "Swearing and smokes—the last of my vices."

"You don't seem much like a nun," Gooch said.

"This place, there's no drinking, no drugs, no men. I don't go to the store. I don't travel. I haven't left this convent in seven years. I may not look like a nun, but believe me, I live like one." She smiled humorlessly. "I couldn't really handle the world."

"Mind my asking what you do here?" Gooch said. "Not sure I've ever met a nun."

"I carve figures of Jesus," she said. "I cut down the trees, I cure the wood, I carve the figures, the whole bit. No power tools, nothing. Just me and my hands and a couple of these." She held up the ax. "I sell them on the Internet. Sistergracewadell.com. They're very popular in Latin America. Some people think they cure diseases." She shrugged in a slightly cynical way. "So what's on your mind, Detective?"

"Nathan Morris. His mother was killed about eighteen years ago. He said you were his girlfriend."

Sister Grace shook her head angrily. "Nathan Morris. God. I don't know if *girlfriend* is the right word. See, the reason I'm here is because—like I said—I'm not much good at living in the world. In here I'm a productive member of society. But out there?" She waved her cigarette at the fence that ran around the property of the convent. "Out there I'm what you'd call a skank. I use men, I sponge off people, I dump any drug you can name into my system. It's memories of assholes like Nathan Morris that keep me in here."

"So were you his girlfriend or not?"

"I was his fucktoy." Sister Grace turned to the old lady. "You getting all this, Sister?"

Sister Albert-Joseph glared back at her.

"The only thing I hate worse than this place is being the person I am out there."

"Let's get back to Nathan Morris. He says you can alibi him for the night of the murder."

Her eyebrows went up. "You think *Nathan* killed his mom?"

"We're looking at that possibility."

"That's not really Nathan's style. He's a liar, a cheater, a welsher, a con-man, a thief, a manipulator. . . . I'm running out of words. But a murderer? Nah, I don't see it."

"Were you with him that night? He says you were."

She stubbed out her cigarette on the tree, slid the butt in her pocket. "Then I probably was."

"That's not a helpful answer."

"Look, I was drunk a lot back then. I wasn't real exact on dates and times." She looked up in the air for a minute, thinking back. "But, yeah, I remember this cop brought me down to the station, took my statement."

"King?"

"Was that his name? Fast-talker-type guy. Put his hand on my ass, accidently on purpose." She looked thoughtful. "I remember now, he kept trying to tell me I was lying about where Nathan was that night. No, you know what, here's the funny thing. Back then I'd lie about anything. But this was one of those rare, sunlit moments where I actually told the truth. And I remember being all pissed off at this guy, this detective. It was like, 'Hey, all the times I've lied, here I am telling the truth and you're giving me grief about it.' I felt like I should have gotten a medal, you know? That was my thinking out there in the world. That's how messed up my mind was."

"Tell me exactly."

"Well, Nathan was supposedly in school. But he wasn't actually *going* to school. See, he had this trust fund. And in order to get his monthly check from the fund, he was required to stay in school. So he was running this scam to make it seem like he was in school. He was a bright guy, wasn't like he wasn't college timber or something. He just didn't feel like it. So anyway, he had this friend at Georgia Tech. They had a little trade going. Nathan would give this guy meth, and the guy would give his transcripts to Nathan, and then they'd alter them and send them to some dude, some lawyer, who administered the trust fund. So on this particular night, I remember we went over to this guy's dorm room and Nathan got the transcript and then we sat around in this guy's dorm room drinking while this kid scanned the transcript into his computer. Then they altered it digitally. When they're done, it looks like Nathan's a 3.7 student in Mechanical Engineering."

"So you were there all night?"

"Yeah, we did a few lines of meth while we were at it. Stayed up all night. We never left the dorm room."

"You're dead sure about that."

"Look, it was eighteen years ago. But at the time, yeah, I remember being totally sure about it."

"How'd Nathan feel about his mother? He ever express negative feelings about her?"

Sister Grace laughed. "He was nineteen. You ever heard of a nineteen-year-old kid who doesn't have bad things to say about his mom?"

"Most kids don't have restraining orders against them."

Sister Grace shrugged. "Nathan claimed that her lawyer put her up to that. The lawyer who administered his trust was convinced that Nathan was going to end up filing suit, trying to get at the trust fund. So he was trying to make Nathan look bad in order to avoid throwing away a bunch of money on litigation. That's how Nathan explained it anyway."

"Do you know what the nature of the incident was that led to the restraining order?"

"She had thrown him out of the house after he dropped out of school. She said, 'Get a job or go to school. But I'm not letting you lie around the house watching TV all day.' Can't blame her for that. She finally had to take away his key to the house. So Nathan got an apartment and moved out. One night he went back to his house to get some of his stuff that he'd left there. She was out of town or something, so he broke in the house to get it. He smashed a window, busted up a real expensive vase or something as he was climbing into the house. Typical teenager behavior. She was pissed, obviously. But I don't think she'd have filed a restraining order if it hadn't been for the lawyer." She smiled sadly. "His mom was a really sweet lady. Part of his problem, she was so gentle and easygoing that she couldn't stand to discipline him."

"What about his father?"

Grace's smile went away. "His father never acknowledged him, as such. I mean, honest to God, I don't even know if the story was true. Nathan always said his grandfather was actually his father, that he'd molested his mother and stuff. But knowing Nathan, that could just be more bullshit."

The elderly nun cleared her throat.

"Yeah, Sister, I know you're listening," Sister Grace said. "I'll say an extra Hail Mary tonight each time I say the word bullshit. That make you happy? Bullshit. There. One more Hail Mary. Bullshit. That's another one."

Sister Albert-Joseph's scowl deepened. But she just looked away as though she hadn't heard anything.

"Nathan's the grandmaster of self-serving bullshit," Sister Grace said. "Nothing's ever his own fault."

"So who do you think did it?"

Sister Grace shook her head. "Nathan always said it was that cop, King, that killed her."

"He claimed King had a relationship with his mother."

"Yeah, he told me that, too. I know for a fact that King knew her. Whether they had a relationship? Couldn't say."

"How do you know?"

"We drove by her house one time and this unmarked cop car was pulling out of the driveway. Nathan said, 'Oh, man, there's that cop again.'"

"How do you know it was King?"

"I got a pretty good view of his face. Enough to see the scar. Looks like a lightning bolt."

"Only when he smiles," Gooch said.

She closed her eyes thoughtfully. "Yeah," she said. "You're right. It kind of disappeared into his face when he wasn't smiling, didn't it? Wonder what he was thinking about that day that made him smile." Her eyes blinked open. "Don't y'all have policies against somebody investigating the murder of somebody they know?"

"Yep," Gooch said.

"Huh. Makes you wonder why he would have taken the case."

Gooch said nothing.

"Man of few words, huh?" Sister Grace said. "You'd make a good nun."

"I'll keep that in mind," Gooch said, "in case my law-enforcement career don't work out."

The young woman picked up her ax, spun it idly and smoothly in her right hand, her body eager to get back to the soothing work of cutting the tree. Gooch could have just sat there watching her cut all day. Not just because she was easy on the eyes. It was more because . . . well . . . it wasn't something he could have explained to her. She'd have taken it the wrong way.

Sister Grace looked at him strangely, as though for the first time. "I'm sorry," she said.

"For what?"

She kept looking at him. "There's something very sad in your eyes. I didn't see it at first."

Gooch had no response for that. He looked at his watch. Dammit. "I gotta go," he said.

"What's making you so sad, Detective?"

"Huh?" Gooch said.

"In your eyes," she said. "I can see the sadness in your eyes."

"I lost my daughter," he said. It slipped out before he could stop it. "She seems to have been on my mind lately." Not sure why he'd say a thing like that. It wasn't like him. He felt stupid. Naked almost. So he turned sharply and walked away.

"I'll say a prayer for you both," she called.

Strange, he thought.

He'd overheard people talking about him now and then over the years. They'd always said how cold his eyes looked. But this gal, she'd seen it different.

Had something in him changed? Or did she just see different from other people?

As he was walking, Gooch heard the methodical thunk-thunk-thunk of the ax begin again. Just as he was about to get back into his car, there was a great ripping sound, the tree starting to fall. Then the earth shook under his feet as the tree hit the ground.

35

"Where does it come from, MeChelle?" Gooch said.

"What?"

"All this sadness?"

"Is this part of your plan to get me out of here?" MeChelle said. "Or are we just shooting the breeze?"

The line was silent for a minute. MeChelle could hear the ticking of the clock—literally *and* figuratively. What was up with Gooch? He seemed almost like a different man from the one she'd worked with six months ago.

"I mean I'm getting a smell about King. It's looking like he might have had a relationship with the victim. But I'm just not seeing where we go next. I'm not seeing what would break it open. I mean, he ain't gonna confess. We know that."

"The key's got to be here in this room. Right?"

"Sure," Gooch said. But for some reason, the way he said it, it didn't sound like he was confident.

Tick. Tick. Tick. Suddenly MeChelle was feeling mad.

"God*dammit*, Hank!" she shouted. "Don't you give up on me now! We got over four hours. We can do a lot in four hours."

"My dad used to beat my ass like you wouldn't believe," Gooch said. "I said I'd never do that to my flesh and blood. And I never did."

MeChelle frowned. "What are you even *talking* about?"

"I don't know."

The line clicked dead.

Shit! MeChelle pawed at her eyes, a frantic tide of fear rising in her. She had to see. Now! She *had* to. Or she was going to go crazy. What if she just tore the skin, tore her eyelids, just ripped them free? She pinched her eyelids in her fingers, yanked on them. A wave of fire shot through her eyes.

No. Come on. Relax. There was glue on her corneas, too, she was pretty sure. If she tore anything, she'd probably permanently blind herself. Maybe as a desperation move later. But not yet.

The phone rang again immediately.

She picked it up. "Hank?"

The line was silent. She could hear him breathing.

"Hank, for godsake, we've got three calls for this hour. Why are you wasting them? This is my *life*!"

Gooch still didn't speak. She was sure it was him, though, absolutely positive.

"Hank, are you wigging out on me here? You need to get your act together!" She was kind of shocking herself. You didn't talk to an Old School cop like Hank Gooch that way. Not unless you wanted your head bitten off.

But still the line was silent.

"Hank? Hank!"

No answer.

"This isn't about your little girl! This isn't about you! This is about me! God damn you, get your shit together!"

Still no answer. She slammed down the phone.

And as soon as she did, she got a sick feeling in her stomach. *Oh, God,* she thought. *What am I doing? I'm alienating the one and only human being in the entire universe who can do anything to help me.*

She started desperately picking up the objects from the table again, feeling them, smelling them, tasting them. It was telling her nothing now. The same sensations, the same circle of useless clues. She felt a sour taste in her mouth, a twist of nausea in her gut.

Finally she swept the objects off the table. She heard them thump off the concrete wall, fall to the carpeted floor. All of them except for the sheaf of papers, which fluttered slowly to the ground, making a noise like a small bird flushed from a tree.

Which is when it hit her.

The papers! That was it!

She put her hand on the phone. "Come on, Hank! Call me again!"

But the phone didn't ring.

"Hank!" she yelled. "The trust document. There's some kind of document that spells out the terms of the trust! The answer's in there somewhere!"

She picked up the phone, started dialing Hank's number. But it was no good. She couldn't call out from this phone.

MeChelle screamed in frustration.

"Just let me make one call! One call! Do you want this case solved or not?"

Tick. Tick. Tick.

"Hey! Hey! Listen to me!"

Tick. Tick.

She aimed her useless eyes in the direction where the Silent Man was standing. "Do something! You can get him to let me call! Come on!"

But as always the Silent Man had nothing to say.

36

Gooch's phone rang. For a second he had this feeling that maybe it was MeChelle calling him back. But of course that was impossible. What was going on here? Why had he called her and then just sat there saying nothing? If he was trying to comfort her, he wasn't doing much of a job.

Well, comforting people, that had never been his strong suit, had it? His little girl was about the only person in his life he'd ever been able to comfort. She'd get all wound up when she was a baby and he would just carry her around, letting her suck on the knuckle of his index finger and she'd just fall right to sleep. He could still feel the sensation of it, the surprisingly powerful and rapid suction as she sucked on his finger.

The phone rang again. It was Cody Floss. Gooch broke himself out of his reverie, flipped open the phone. "Yeah?"

"Sir? Hi, I don't know if I mentioned it but I took this course last year at the FBI academy. It was really fascinating and—"

"Just make your point."

"Um. Right, right, sure. I'm sorry. See, thing is? I think I may have found her."

Gooch blinked. "MeChelle?"

"Yes, sir."

"How?"

"There are methodologies for tracking down router nodes. See whoever is doing this has been routing an Internet signal through a bunch of different routers to a bunch of different cell phone transmitters. What I was able to do was track the cell patterns and locate a central—"

None of this meant anything to Gooch. "I ain't got time for that. Just give me an address."

"502 Lincoln Street. Down in southwest Atlanta."

"You confident this address is good?"

"Yes, sir."

"Meet me there in twenty minutes."

"Shouldn't we, ah, call SWAT or something?"

"SWAT will take an hour to get there. They'll want to make a tac plan and draw pictures on a blackboard and surround the house and a lot of other stuff we ain't got time for. Meantime, if the word gets back to this guy that we told anybody else on the force, he's liable to kill her."

Gooch drove quickly toward the south side of Atlanta, lights flashing but no siren, blowing through red lights, passing in the oncoming lane, then out onto the interstate until he hit University.

As he was driving, he called a number that he hadn't called in a long time.

"Arno," he said.

There was a short pause. "Hank? That you?"

"Need your help, hoss," Hank said.

"What for? You ain't called me in, what, eight, ten years. Now all of a sudden you need my—"

Hank cut Arno off. They'd served together in the Army way back. Arno Liggett kind of owed him a favor. "Saddle up, meet me at the Exxon station, corner of Lincoln and Edgemont down in southwest Atlanta."

"Hold on, hold on, hold on!" Arno sounded mad. "What you into, Hank? This don't sound legal no-how."

"Ain't time to argue," Hank said. "Gonna need dynamic entry tools. Flashbangs, det cord, ribbon explosive, the whole nine."

"Are you out of your mind?"

"Probably."

"Gee, anything else?" Arno was being sarcastic now.

"Yeah. I need you there inside half an hour."

"Oh, well, hell, buddy, you want me to bring a tank, too? Maybe a Blackhawk helicopter?"

"Wouldn't hurt."

Hank hung up the phone without giving Arno any more time to raise a stink.

He kept dialing MeChelle's number, but he couldn't get through. They got three calls in an hour—and he'd wasted them. What had he been thinking? He needed to get his head clear.

The neighborhood was a sad one. It had been a poor working-class neighborhood once. But now it was just poor. There were a lot of people just hanging around doing nothing—women sitting on porches fanning themselves in the heat, old men in stained ball caps playing dominos on card tables, kids who should have been in school but weren't. No white folks for probably two miles in any direction.

A couple of young men on the corner saw the white Ford creeping down the street and immediately started walking briskly in another direction. They were all wearing baggy clothes, red hats turned at odd angles.

Gooch took a quick pass down the road to reconnoiter. 502 Lincoln was a slapped-together white frame house. All the windows were boarded up. There was some kind of legal notice tacked on the front door. It had the look of a crack house or shooting gallery that had been seized by the city. The only evidence of occupation was a pit bull on a chain lying in the weedy front yard.

Gooch felt his heart thrumming. This could be it. This could definitely be it. Cheap house in a neighborhood where no one talked to the cops, nobody got into anybody else's business. If he were going to warehouse a human being for a day, this was as good a place as any.

The only thing was, this was a black neighborhood. Gooch had assumed that whoever was behind this whole thing was white. A white person would stick out. Of course, he could show up in a panel van, look like an electrician or something, hired to fix up an old house. And whoever was behind this thing, they only needed the place for thirteen hours.

It was a small house. He'd busted into a lot of places like this over the years. There'd be four rooms, plus a bathroom, front door, back door. Going into anyplace with only three people was a bad idea. But every second counted. They got more cops involved, they'd need a warrant. Warrants took time. And they didn't have time.

Plus, the more people who knew about MeChelle's situation, then more things that could go wrong.

He made one more circuit of the block, then drove back down to the Exxon station at the corner of Edgemont and waited. Arno arrived minutes later in an unobtrusive Chevy. Gooch had a hunch that there was probably a lot of modification hidden under the hood of the bland-looking car. It didn't surprise Gooch that Arno had beaten Cody Floss to the location. He was the kind of guy who just sat around waiting for phone calls like this. And because he was good at what he did, the calls probably came more frequently than you'd think.

Cody Floss pulled into the lot in his unmarked Ford just as Arno climbed out of the Chevy and stretched. He was wearing a ballistic vest, and a blue windbreaker that read BAIL ENFORCEMENT AGENT on the back. He was six-three, two-fifty or so, with graying hair and very large shoulders. A 1911 pistol was strapped to his leg in a black Kydex holster.

"Plastic explosives?" Arno said. "What are we going into, a bank?"

"House," Gooch said.

"How much am I being paid for this, by the way?" Arno said.

Gooch ignored the question. Cody Floss was climbing out of his car, looking nervous. "Um . . . sir? What's our warrant situation here?"

Gooch motioned toward Arno. "Cody, this big dumb-looking boy knows more about how to get inside houses by force than anybody you'll ever meet. Whatever he tells you to do, you do it, you don't ask questions. Clear?"

"Yes, sir. But . . . about the warrant—"

Again Gooch ignored the question.

"Here's what we're up against, Arno," he said. "Standard

four-room house, doors front and back, pit bull in the yard. House is probably significantly hardened. One hostage inside, possibly two."

"Bad guys?" Arno said.

"Unknown."

Arno looked at him steadily. "Buddy, you need SWAT."

"What we got is you, me, and Cody."

Arno shook his head. "Nope. Ain't doing it."

"Son, we got a friend of mine in there. We don't get her out, she could be dead anytime. We don't got time for warrants or calling SWAT or decent intel."

Arno walked back to his car, unstrapped his holster from his leg, tossed it on the front seat of the car. "Can't do it, buddy."

"You owe me," Gooch said.

"Not this much I don't."

"Then give me your det cord and your ribbon explosive," Gooch said.

Arno shook his head. "You got no warrant, you're freelancing out here. You want me to give you plastic explosives? You out of your mind."

Gooch drew his Glock, pointed it at Arno's head. "You think I'm joking with you, Arno? Cody, go over there get the explosives from him."

Cody swallowed, didn't move.

Arno's face hardened. "You serious, Gooch? You drawing down on *me*?"

"I just told you, a friend of mine's in that house. I ain't losing her."

"*Her?*" Arno said.

Gooch had the front sight resting on Arno's face. Not wavering.

Suddenly Arno laughed. "Hell, I'm down here. Let's just do it."

"My car," Gooch said, holstering his Glock.

They piled in Gooch's car. "The hostage is a female black approximately thirty years of age, light complexion, slim build. She's a decorated cop, by the way. Far as I know, she's not restrained, but her eyes are gonna be closed or glued shut somehow. There's a second person with her. We don't know if he's also a hostage or if he's a bad guy. If he shows any sign of noncompliance, assume he's hostile. Could be other individuals in the house. And they could be armed. Other than that, we don't know nothing."

"Sounds like you know a whole lot of nothing." Arno was busy sorting out things in a black nylon bag. There was a silenced MP5 inside and a ribbon of plastic explosive for taking out the door.

"Priority one is the hostage," Gooch continued. "Getting the bad guys is a distant second. We got no warrant, so the second we secure the building, Arno, you disappear. We're not gonna worry about entering front and back. We don't have enough people. We're going in the front, dynamic entry. Arno, you blow the door. No flashbangs, no gas. I don't want to blow off MeChelle's foot. We just go in fast. I'll be on point, Arno. You follow. Cody, you come in last."

"Anything else I need to know?" Arno said.

Gooch's pulse was roaring in his temples, and he had that half-sick, half-elated feeling that always came before a bust. "We're audiblizing here. I'll call the play as we go."

"What else?"

"The pit bull in the yard. It's on a chain. We'll go around it."

They were pulling up in front of the house just as Gooch spoke. When he saw the dog, he realized he'd misjudged.

"Chain's too long," Arno said. "We can't go around it."

As they climbed out of the car, the dog flung itself at the fence. The dog had a piebald coat, black and tan, and small yellow eyes. It didn't bark, just banged into the fence, the chain jingling behind it.

Arno raised his silenced MP5, shot the dog. It fell with a soft thud.

"Jesus!" Cody Floss said. "He shot the dog!"

Arno gave him a furious look. "Quiet!" he whispered. Then he leapt the fence.

Gooch didn't pause to look at the dog. It was a funny thing—his old man had been the meanest son of a bitch in the world but he was always decent to dogs. Gooch knew Arno had done the right thing. MeChelle's life was worth any ten dogs'. Still . . . it seemed wrong.

But there was no time to mourn the dog.

Gooch followed Arno over the fence. By the time Gooch reached the door, Arno was laying a ribbon of plastic explosive just inside the frame. Now that they were close, he could see that it was good thing they had the explosives. The door was made from steel plate. Probably weighed a hundred pounds. He hoped MeChelle wasn't anywhere near it. But he had no way of warning her. It would be another nine minutes before he could call her. Too late.

Behind them, Cody was struggling to get over the fence, making a racket. Arno looked at Cody, then at Gooch. Gooch said nothing. You worked with what you had. Arno nodded, then jammed a detonator into the plastic explosive.

The two men slid backward along the wall to get out of the blast zone. Cody, oblivious, climbed the stairs directly in front of the door. Gooch motioned furiously for him to get out of the way.

"Sorry!" Cody whispered.

Gooch could have strangled him. Rule one of dynamic entry, you didn't talk. He signaled to Arno to blow the door, then stuck his fingers in his ears.

The door blew apart, and then everything seemed to slow down. Gooch flew past Arno, pushed the smoking remains of the steel door inward. It fell in, hit the ground. But Gooch couldn't hear anything.

He scanned the room. It was empty, the floor covered with detritus. One door to the right, one door straight ahead. He hadn't done this in a long time. But it came back like an old friend. Scan, point, move, circle.

He sensed Arno at his back, motioned for Arno to clear the room to the right. Gooch headed toward the door straight ahead.

The second room was empty. A kitchen, all the fixtures ripped out, gaping holes in the floor. The smell of plastic explosives and urine. No one there. "Clear!" he called.

Gooch backtracked. Arno had not yelled the all-clear. *Why not?*

He rounded the corner into the bedroom on the right, found Arno and Cody facing a second steel door. There was no doorknob, just a fist-sized eye-bolt set into the middle of the door.

"Won't move," Arno said. "Bolted from inside."

"Got more explosive?" Gooch said.

Arno shook his head no.

Gooch approached the wall, tapped gently, locating the studs, then punched the wall with all his strength. It went straight through.

It was followed by a loud crack—a gunshot. A tiny hole appeared in the wall, bits of plaster spraying Gooch in the face. He leapt back as three more gunshots cracked through the air. They sounded distant and muffled.

Then silence.

Arno raised his gun as though to start shooting through the wall.

"No!" Gooch shouted.

Cody Floss, oblivious, began shooting wildly at the wall.

Gooch slapped his hand. Cody's pistol flew across the room.

"She might be *in* there, you moron!" Gooch shouted.

Silence.

And then someone in the other room began to scream.

Arno did a side thrust kick into the wall, smashing a large hole into the ancient plaster and lathe. Then another. Then another. The screaming continued. But no one fired back.

Gooch signaled to Arno to step back, then he circled the now-sizable hole in the wall, sighting over the front sight of his Glock. He saw a young white man slumped on the floor.

"Don't move!" Gooch shouted. He kicked the wall again, clearing more plaster, then shouldered his way into the last room of the house.

The young man on the floor was holding his chest. There was a lot of blood on his shirt. He stared up at Gooch. "You shot me! Dude, why'd you shoot me?"

Gooch scanned the room. Other than the boy it was empty of people. His heart sank. No MeChelle.

Arno barged into the room, looked around. "Where is she?"

Gooch shook his head, gave Cody a hard look. "Not in here."

"You shot me!" the kid on the floor said. Then he began screaming again, high and shrill.

"Shut up, boy," Arno said to him.

"Cody," Gooch shouted. "Look for trapdoors. Maybe there's a basement."

But Cody, still standing in the other room, just stood there blinking. "Oh, my God!" he said. "Oh, my God!"

"Not you, too," Arno said, stepping through the hole in the wall. Then he slapped Cody in the face.

Cody looked around, blinking.

"Trapdoors!" Gooch shouted. "Now!"

Then he turned to the kid on the floor. He looked like he was about twenty, all done up in full ghetto fabulous—gold tooth, baggy clothes, tats, cheap bling hanging around his neck. "What are you doing here, son?"

"I'm gonna die!" the kid shouted.

"No, you're not," Gooch said. He dropped to his haunches, so he was looking eye-to-eye at the boy. "Tell me why you're here, I'll call an ambulance."

The kid started screaming again.

Gooch grabbed his face, squeezed, looked him straight in the eye. The kid stopped screaming. "What are you doing here, son?"

The kid didn't speak, but pointed wordlessly. On the other side of the small room was a computer, lots of wires running out of it, down into the floor.

"What is that?"

"I don't know," the kid gasped. "I was just supposed to guard it, make sure none of these niggers around here busted in and messed it up."

"Cody!" Gooch yelled.

"Sir?" Cody's face appeared at the ragged hole in the wall. His skin was pale and he was sweating.

"What's this for?" Gooch said, pointing at the computer.

The young detective came into the room, quickly scanned the equipment and then groaned. "Oh, no," he said.

"What."

"I should have known." Cody pressed his hands against his face.

"*What?*"

"It's a relay. The thing that looks like a computer? That's an Internet router. Then, see that black box underneath the computer?" He pointed at a black piece of equipment about the size of a pizza box. There were blinking lights on the front. "That's some kind of wireless relay device. It's probably parasitic, broadcasts on cell frequencies. What it does is it converts digital packets to—"

"Explain it without using any computer mumbo jumbo."

"Okay . . . uh . . . basically MeChelle's cell phone signal is being converted to digital form and routed over the Internet. It comes to this box, where the internet signal is converted back to a cell phone signal. Then *that's* routed to these other cell transmitters scattered around town. If whoever did this is smart—and it's obvious they are—then the Internet provider will be off-shore somewhere. Nigeria, Panama—somewhere that we can't get at it. At least not in a hurry."

"So what are you saying?"

"I'm saying this is a dead end."

"Can we take it back with us? Figure anything else out?"

Cody shook his head. "You unplug this, you cut off your only connection to Sergeant Deakes."

Gooch turned back to the boy on the floor. "Who paid you to do this?"

The kid shook his head.

"I asked you a question!"

"I ain't talking, dog," the boy said.

"Fine," Gooch said. "No ambulance. Come on, guys." He slid back through the hole in the wall.

"Wait! Wait!"

Gooch waited until Arno and Cody had exited, then poked his head back through the wall, looked down at the boy.

"Okay, wait," the boy said. "It was Melbert Reavis."

"Who's Melbert Reavis?" Gooch said. He was sure he knew the name. But he just couldn't place it.

"Who's Melbert *Reavis*?" the kid said. Like he couldn't believe it.

"He's a guy that MeChelle busted after you left last year," Cody said to Gooch. "He's a dealer out of Cabbagetown. She arrested him for murder."

Gooch frowned. Suddenly this wasn't looking the way he thought it would. A dealer? Everything so far had indicated that the person behind MeChelle's abduction would have a clear connection to the Bolligrew murder. Why would some dope slinger from Cabbagetown care about solving an eighteen-year-old murder? It made no sense.

Gooch climbed back into the room and the other two detectives followed.

"You get me that ambulance!" the boy howled. "I done *told* you!"

Gooch checked his watch. It was four o'clock, straight up. So he should be able to call MeChelle. This was a whole new development.

He pulled out his cell phone, dialed. He got a message saying MeChelle's phone was out of service. He hadn't gotten that message before. Before, when they had gone past the three-calls-per-hour limit, the phone just rang, but nobody picked up. The whole thing made him nervous. He dialed again.

"Um, sir?" Cody said.

Gooch motioned to him to be quiet, dialed again. He should be able to get through any second now. This Melbert Reavis thing was huge. He needed to talk it through with MeChelle. He waited, got the same out-of-service message.

"Sir?"

Gooch hit redial. Out-of-service message again.

"Sir?"

"What." Gooch turned, glared at the young detective.

Cody pointed at the communications equipment on the floor.

Gooch kept hitting the redial.

Then, as he listened to the message again, he saw what Cody Floss was pointing at: a small, irregular hole in the face of the black pizza-box device.

Gooch dialed again, sudden anger running through him like a burst of frigid water.

A curl of smoke came out of the hole in the device. Then the little twinkling lights on the front went dark.

"Sir? I think I kinda shot it."

37

The Voice spoke from the ceiling. "You have . . . four . . . hours."

Okay, Hank was probably paying attention to the clock. Hopefully he'd call. She stood by the table with the phone on it drumming her fingers.

"Come on, Hank!" she shouted.

The phone didn't ring.

She waited what seemed forever, finally picked up the phone, and dialed. As she expected, it didn't do anything.

She set the phone down, waited some more. What was going on? Why wasn't he calling?

And suddenly she felt a rising sense of panic, panic mixed with anger. What if the Voice wasn't letting his call through?

"Where's my phone call?" she yelled. "It's time! I want my phone call! You want us to catch the guy who killed her, or not? Just let me call out!"

But the Voice said nothing.

Dammit, Hank, why aren't you calling?

She stood with her hand resting on the phone, waiting, waiting.

Tick. Tick. Tick.

Gooch looked at his watch again. Three hours and fifty-something minutes to go. And they were going to be tied up here for quite some time because of this shooting. No, getting tied up just wasn't an option. But leaving the kid here to bleed to death wasn't either.

Gooch called in the shooting to Dispatch, then clapped Arno on the shoulder. "Go."

"Hey, look . . ." Arno said.

"Go. It's five blocks to your car. Hike back to it and get out of here."

Arno didn't take any convincing. Gooch now turned to Cody Floss, who was sitting on the floor looking like he was about to faint.

"Cowboy up, kid," Gooch said. "Things are about to get a little hairy. You need to get yourself together."

Cody Floss looked up at Gooch and blinked. "I messed everything up," he said. "I just—"

"Shut up," Gooch said. "Now ain't the time. You need to concentrate on our story. We got a lead, we knocked on the door, we heard a sound that gave us probable cause to believe a crime was being committed, we entered the home, shots were fired at us. Believing yourself to be in imminent danger of severe bodily harm, you responded with deadly force. That's your story. Period."

"What about your friend?"

Gooch frowned. "Friend? What friend?"

Floss looked confused. Then his eyebrows went up. "Oh! Sorry, sir! I get it." Then his face fell again. "But—"

"Now, look, we've got about two minutes. Tell me everything you know about Melbert Reavis."

Cody Floss looked around vaguely.

In the other room, the kid he'd shot was still moaning.

"Focus!" Gooch said.

Cody Floss rubbed his eyes, then said, "I'm sorry." He cleared his throat. "Like I said, MeChelle busted him last year."

"I recognize the name," Gooch said. "He was gang-affiliated, wasn't he?"

"The CGs," Cody said.

That's right. It came back to him. Melbert Reavis had been a CG, a member of a white gang from a neighborhood called Cabbagetown on the east side of Atlanta.

"There's not much left of old Cabbagetown," Cody Floss said. "As you know, that area around the old Fulton Bag Mill used to be—"

"Skip the history lesson." Gooch already knew the history of the odd little neighborhood where the CGs had hung out. Around the turn of the century, the owners of a big cotton mill had gone up to Appalachia and gathered a large number of hillbillies, brought them back to work at the mill. A small mill village had grown up around the mill. The smell of boiling cabbage that hung over the area gave it its name. Cabbagetown had developed into a close-knit little community, holding on to the Appalachian mores and patterns of speech year after year.

Eventually the white working-class inhabitants of the surrounding areas had all moved away, until eventually Cabbagetown had become an isolated white enclave in the middle of a black ghetto. As the mill jobs that had sustained the community dried up, Cabbagetown fell on the same hard times that afflicted the rest of the inner city—unemployment, poverty, and crime.

The CGs had arisen from that soil just like every other inner-city gang. They just had the unusual quality of being white.

Cabbagetown started getting gentrified ten years ago, and the CGs eventually withered away and disappeared. But in their day, they had been tough, violent, and feared. Surrounded by black gangs, they'd had to be. It was that or get wiped out.

Cody Floss said, "Well, I guess you know that the CGs kind of died out once all the old Cabbagetownies moved out. So Melbert, he eventually moved up-market, went wholesale—Mexican tar, crystal, whatever. Eventually he bought some businesses—a strip club, a rib shack, a used-car dealership—most of them located in those black neighborhoods on Memorial Drive. The word is, eventually he got out of drugs entirely.

"Anyway, the way we came into it, right after you left, Sergeant, this guy came in, said he wanted to clear up a couple of old gang shootings. Guy by the name of Isaac Mudge. Nice name, huh?"

Gooch glared. He hated cops wasting their breath on commentary. Especially when time was short.

"Sorry," Cody said. "Anyway, this Mudge guy, he'd gotten saved, gone into a twelve-step program and was looking to make amends. He sat down with MeChelle, told her about this shooting from ten, twelve years ago. It was supposed to be a hit on a couple of East Side Kings, back when the CGs were heavy into crack and all the gangs were fighting each other. But they'd messed up, shot a little girl and a retired postal worker instead. Apparently at the time everybody knew it had been a CG drive-by and everybody knew that Melbert Reavis was responsible. But nobody saw anything, nobody would testify. Anyway, this guy Isaac Mudge laid the whole thing out. Time of day, the car they'd driven, who'd fired the shots, and what had gone wrong to cause the shots to go wide. Turned out the driver had swerved the car, trying to avoid hitting a squirrel. Threw everybody's aim off. So this guy, Mudge, he'd even led MeChelle to the weapon. Took us to this house in Cabbagetown—couple of nice little gay guys living there for eight years or whatever—not knowing there was this gun stuck in the wall like three feet from their heads. It was wrapped in an oil-soaked rag, plastered right into the wall. You believe that? Still had Melbert's fingerprints on it, ten years later."

Gooch could hear sirens now. Putting out a police-involved shooting call would bring in a million cops. They'd be crawling all over the place. What a disaster.

"Get to the point," Gooch said.

"Yes, sir. Right. Sure!" Cody Floss glanced nervously at the bleeding boy on the floor. "Anyway, when we arrested Melbert he said something to her that stuck with me."

"What'd he say, Cody?"

"He said, 'If I plead it out, I'll probably be out in three. But you'll be dead in one.'"

The terrible thing that had been building in Gooch's mind came clear now: *What if this whole thing was a setup? What if solving some moldy old murder was just a big joke that this Melbert Reavis guy was playing? Suppose that Reavis was behind this. And suppose he had no intention of letting MeChelle out of that room at all? What if he was just toying with her before he killed her?*

If that was the case, it didn't matter who had killed

Kathleen Bolligrew. That had all been a waste of time, a pointless diversion. The only thing that mattered now was finding out where MeChelle was.

Gooch realized they were in a serious hole. And sitting here filling out reports and answering questions from an Internal Affairs investigator for the next four hours was only going to ruin everything. Assuming whoever had snatched MeChelle wasn't lying, she'd be dead in four hours.

He walked into the other room, grabbed the boy that Cody had shot, started dragging him by his collar.

"Um, sir . . ." Cody said.

"Ow!" the kid yelled. "What y'all doing to me?"

Gooch manhandled the kid through the hole in the wall, then dragged him through the house, out the front door and down to the sidewalk. At the street, he let go of the boy's collar.

"Day-um, dog!" the bleeding boy said, lying there on the sidewalk. "What's wrong with you? I been shot!"

Gooch started walking away

"Sir?" Cody Floss was trailing along behind him. "Sir, where are you going?"

"You seem good with computers," Gooch said. "You think you can fix that thing you shot in there?"

"Maybe, sir . . . if I had enough time. But—"

"Then get in there and do it." Gooch kept walking.

"Sir, if I could point out something . . ."

"Get in the house. Start working. Don't let anybody stop you. I don't care if the goddamn chief comes down here. You keep working on fixing that black box. We can't lose contact with MeChelle. Meantime, we leave the kid out here. That way you at least got a chance they won't cordon off the house and bounce you out of there immediately."

"Sir, this is a police-involved shooting! We're under strict instructions to—"

"Change of plans, kid." Gooch started running. Then he called over his shoulder, "You get that damn phone box working!"

38

MeChelle kept waiting and waiting. After a while she started counting ticks. Sixty ticks was a minutes. Three hundred was five. She had counted to over a thousand now. Where the hell was Gooch? Why wasn't he calling?

At first she just felt annoyed, like she was being made to jump through another stupid hoop by the jerk who'd locked her up here. But then she began to get a sinking feeling, a feeling that she'd been abandoned. It crept up her fingers and into her chest, a shaky, sick sensation.

In her last conversation with Gooch, she'd been so mad at him, said nasty things to him. What if he had just given up on her? Or had she just been cut off somehow?

Suddenly she wanted to talk to Gooch more than anything in the world. Hank Gooch! Of all people!

Gooch had gone out on the line for her. And how had she repaid him? She'd yelled at him. She'd questioned his commitment, his instincts. She should have known better. A bitter sense of regret ran through her.

She finally stopped counting, sat down on the floor. *Okay*, she thought, *what now?*

39

Fortunately Melbert Reavis hadn't been able to afford bond. He was still locked up at the Fulton County Jail, waiting for his trial.

Gooch rolled into the parking lot, walked into the administration office and asked to see the assistant warden in charge of security. While he was waited, he made a brief phone call, explaining something he needed. As he was finishing up the call, a uniformed CO came out and led him back to the assistant warden's office. She was a tall officious black woman named Ordellia Means. Big shoulders, small waist, hair that reminded him of soft-serve ice cream.

"I need to see a prisoner named Melbert Reavis," Gooch said. "His EF number is 305-27-411X."

"Sergeant, you need to talk to the desk officer about reserving an interview room," she said, making a big show of studying some papers on her desk. "You appear to be sufficiently experienced to know our procedures at this facility."

"No, ma'am," Gooch said. "I don't want an interview room. I want to talk to him in general population."

She looked up from the papers, blinked once, twice, a third time. "That would not be possible," she said.

"I want to talk to him in general population," he repeated, "ma'am."

She peered at him intently. "Some kind of difficulty in your hearing, Sergeant?"

"No, ma'am."

"Then I fail to understand—"

"I have my reasons."

Her eyes narrowed. "Sergeant, I can't guarantee your safety in population. Ergo, we're done talking."

Gooch didn't move. The phone rang. There was a brief conversation, then the assistant warden hung up the phone. She tapped her fingernails on the desk for a few moments.

"So you got to the governor somehow," she said.

"Can we get this moving?" Gooch said. He had called MeChelle's father while he was waiting. Her dad was the kind of guy who could get his phone calls answered by anybody in the state, a big cheese in the black community. He hadn't told him exactly what was going on with MeChelle—just that her life was on the line, that MeChelle needed his help. Gooch figured there was no point in him knowing all the details, getting all worried.

The assistant warden pursed her lips, gave him a long hard gaze, then took out a piece of paper. "I'll need you to sign this," she said. "We'll put a sharpshooter on the wall for you."

"Ain't gonna come to that." Gooch scrawled his name on the paper.

* * *

The yard was full of prisoners in white clothes with black stripes down the seams. Black prisoners controlled all the basketball goals. Whites had the weight-lifting area. Mexicans were along the fence. Gooch wore his badge on his belt, knowing that it made him a target, knowing that the prisoners knew that he knew it. It was a show of strength, confidence.

Gooch knew that strength was the only thing that would get him anywhere with Melbert Reavis. If they sat down on opposite sides of a table in an interview room and blabbed, Reavis would just sit there laughing and he'd get nowhere.

A CO had pointed out Reavis. He was an enormously fat guy with short, neatly cut hair and big arms, the sleeves of his uniform torn off. A couple of white cons stood around him, laughing at his jokes. Toadies, you could tell. They all had arms covered with tats. They were tough old-school bad guys, it was easy to see.

As Gooch approached them, the conversation stopped.

Everyone in the yard had stopped moving, all eyes on the crazy cop, walking through the middle of the yard without protection. Gooch knew what they were thinking: they were about to get a good show. Looking forward to it, no matter what happened.

The two cons who'd been laughing at Reavis's jokes shifted their weight slightly, getting between him and Reavis, their faces suddenly going blank and hard.

Reavis, on the other hand, smiled at Gooch. "My goodness!" he said. "Lookie here."

Gooch sidestepped the taller of the two toadies—a bald guy with a mustache—did a little aikido thing, sliding his hand under the big man's chin, lifting it back, taking him down, then driving his head into the concrete. The bald man's head hit the concrete with a sound like a dropped block of wood. After that he didn't move.

"Step back," Gooch said softly to the other con.

"Or else what?"

Gooch kicked him in the nuts. The second guy folded up. Gooch hammered his fist into the back of the second man's head. The second man dropped to his knees, making a loud coughing noise. Gooch put a knee in his face and the second man went down for good.

Reavis looked around, gauging the distance to the nearest corrections officer, still smiling. "What? I'm supposed to be scared?"

"I don't care how you feel," Gooch said. "That ain't why I'm here."

Reavis kept smiling. "Okay then."

"I just came here to ask you a question. When I ask my question, I want you to answer by indicating yes or no."

Reavis rolled his eyes genially. "Pssshhh."

"I just walked into this yard in front of a dozen security cameras and a thousand bad-ass cons. You thinking I'm somebody who talks shit, convict?"

Reavis's smile faded. He locked eyes with Gooch. Gooch could see instantly that this boy had a lot of will, a lot of nerve. He was calm, not breathing hard, no anger showing in his face. "And?" Reavis said. "You gonna beat me down while them rednecks on the wall stand up there with my head in the crosshairs? Hmm? Think that's gonna work for you?"

Gooch didn't let his eyes waver. "You must have me confused," Gooch said. "Only reason I beat your friends down was because they got in my way."

"So if I ain't in your way, why you here?"

"I just came to ask you a question."

"Then get it over with."

Gooch kept staring at Reavis. Finally Reavis laughed, broke Gooch's gaze, turned to his buddy, the one Gooch had kicked in the nuts. The guy had regained consciousness and was lying there moaning. "Look at this guy, huh? He'd thrive like a sumbitch in prison, wouldn't he? Be king of the cell block!"

The guy on the ground just moaned, still clutching his crotch.

"So what's your question, boss?" Reavis said finally.

Gooch said, "If a single hair on the head of MeChelle Deakes is disturbed, you will die inside these walls."

"That don't sound like a question to me."

"The question is, do you understand what I just said?"

"I don't even know what you're talking about."

"Let me try again. If MeChelle Deakes is hurt, you will die inside these walls. Please indicate your understanding by saying yes or no."

Reavis said nothing. Gooch tried to read his face. A guy like Reavis was pretty good at hiding his game. But he seemed genuinely unresponsive, like he wasn't sure what Gooch was talking about.

"Yes or no?" Gooch said.

"Look, I said some words to her," Reavis said. "That was six months ago. I was just messing with her head."

"I'm not interested in that. MeChelle Deakes gets hurt, you die. Understand? Right here, in this place. Tell me you understand."

Reavis looked up at the wall, the sharpshooter on the wall pointing down at him with the rifle. He squinted at the light. Finally he looked back at Gooch. "Okay. Whatever."

Gooch turned, started walking away.

He'd made it about ten strides when Reavis's voice called out to him. "Hey! Boss, hold up. Hold up."

Gooch stopped but didn't turn.

"Nah, look, nah, hold up! What is it you ain't telling me?"

Gooch continued to stand there, unmoving.

"Hold *up*, boss!"

Gooch turned, waited till the fat man began waddling hurriedly toward him.

"Look, this ain't about that house, is it?" Reavis said.

Gooch crossed his arms.

"If that thing at the house had something to do with MeChelle Deakes, I didn't know nothing about it!" Reavis's voice was urgent.

"What thing at the house?"

Reavis looked around nervously, lowered his voice. "Look, somebody asked me for a favor."

"What kind of favor?"

"They needed a house-sitter."

"Give me an address."

Reavis voice got even lower. "502 Lincoln. Somewhere down in boogie town. All I was supposed to do was send one of my boys, make sure nobody busted in, messed with the equipment."

"What equipment?"

"I don't know, boss. They just said it was gonna be some equipment in there. Electronic stuff. Got the idea it was part of an Internet scam or something."

Gooch thought about it, wondering how much truth there was in what Reavis was saying. A guy like Reavis would always tell you a little truth so he could sell you a bigger lie.

"Look, boss, what this got to do with MeChelle Deakes? 'Cause I do *not* know nothing about no MeChelle Deakes. I want that on the record."

"Where's the other house?" Gooch said.

"The what?"

"The other house." Gooch meant the one where MeChelle was being held.

Long silence.

"Boss, I don't know nothing about no other house."

"So who was it came to you? And what did they offer?"

Reavis sighed loudly. "Come on now, boss!"

"If MeChelle Deakes dies, you die inside these walls. I ain't telling you again."

"Okay! Okay! It was my lawyer. Neil Diamond."

"Your lawyer's named Neil *Diamond*?"

"Swear to God. Not my criminal lawyer. Neil handles my corporate stuff."

"Corporate stuff?"

"Yeah, boss. Being I'm a convicted felon, I can't own a titty bar outright. Liquor control board won't allow it. I gotta have what they call a beneficial ownership type of situation. Offshore corporations, whatnot. Plus, I got some tax angles to play. I can't be paying no income taxes. So Neil's the guy handles that for me."

Gooch shook his head sadly. Criminals with corporate lawyers. What next?

"I'm *telling* you, boss, I don't know nothing about no second house!" Reavis seemed nervous all of a sudden.

"Fine," Gooch said. "Just remember what I said. It wouldn't mean nothing to me for you to die in here." He made like he was going to walk away.

"Look, look, look. Hold up." The fat man grabbed Gooch by the sleeve.

"Get your hand off my sleeve, convict. You know better than that."

Reavis dusted Gooch's sleeve off, took a deferential step backward. "I'm sorry, boss."

"You were fixing to say something."

Reavis blinked. "I was?"

Gooch nodded. "Yep."

Reavis looked thoughtful for a minute. Then he inclined his head forward slightly. "Neil never told me nothing about that house. Not who owned it, not what the equipment was for, nothing."

"But he told you *something*. Didn't he?"

Reavis smirked.

Gooch narrowed his eyes.

"It's what he *didn't* tell me."

"What didn't he tell you?"

"He didn't tell me who owned it. Neil's one of these gossipy little sumbitches. If he knew, he would have told me. So whatever's going on, it ain't Neil's scam. Somebody paid him to talk to me. Knowing Neil? He would have researched the property, tried to find out who owned it. If *he* couldn't find out, then it's been hid pretty careful."

Gooch wasn't sure he followed Reavis.

Reavis grinned. "Man, you cops don't know nothing about the real world. Don't nobody own nothing outright anymore. Joe Blow wants to buy a house for investment? He sets up a limited partnership. General partner's some lawyer. Might be an offshore corporation listed as a limited partner. The real owner, he don't have his name attached to it no way."

"And?"

"The second house. I don't know what you talking about. But twice now you mentioned a second house. Like it's some big mystery where that house is at. Reading between the lines, sounds to me like somebody snatched MeChelle, stashed her in a house." Reavis paused, studied Gooch's face. "I'm right, ain't I?"

Gooch said nothing.

"Find out who owns 502 Lincoln, you know who owns the house MeChelle Deakes is at. Then you just track down all the houses owned by whoever it is, eliminate all the ones that's got long-term tenants, send SWAT into whichever ones is left. Simple."

Gooch had to admit, it was smart what Reavis was saying.

Reavis's eyes widened. "I'm right, ain't I? Somebody snatched that nigger cooze."

"You say another word like that, you gonna be sorry."

"Sorry, boss." Reavis's eyes went dead.

Gooch looked at his watch. Three and a half hours to go. Damn it. He was seriously running out of time.

He turned and started walking away. This time when he started to go, he heard something behind him, a soft rustle of cloth on cloth. The fat man's thighs rubbing together.

Gooch whirled just in time to see Reavis hurling himself toward Gooch, fist cocked. He swung, caught Gooch in the side of the head. A cheer went up from the yard.

Gooch staggered slightly, but managed to sidestep the convict's oncoming body. Reavis was quick for a fat man. But there was a limit to how fast you could change direction when you weighed three hundred and fifty pounds.

Reavis dove at Gooch again. This time Gooch sidestepped, used the big man's weight against him, threw a nice smooth *koshi nage*. Jesus, the guy weighed a ton! Reavis hit the ground with a massive thud. Gooch followed him to the ground, put the big man's arm in an armbar, rolled him over on his face.

"I had to do it," Reavis whispered. "You know that, don't you? I couldn't let what you did to my boys pass. Not in front of everybody."

"Sure," Gooch said. "No hard feelings."

Gooch couldn't let it pass, either. Not if he wanted to make it back to the gate without getting shanked. He broke Reavis's arm.

Reavis was still screaming by the time Gooch got to the gate. He was not surprised to see the assistant warden for security herself waiting at the gate. She wore a furious expression. And there was a whole troop of COs in riot gear stacked up behind her.

"Governor or no governor, you silly bastard," she said. "You will never enter my facility again."

Gooch kept walking.

"You have *any* idea how much trouble you caused?" she yelled. "What *could* have happened in there? I'm probably gonna have a riot."

Never apologize, never explain. That's what Gooch had learned back in the military. Didn't do no good no how.

Behind him, the cons inside the yard had started hollering and chanting. Gooch wouldn't have wanted to be running security in this joint right now.

But, hey—that wasn't his problem. He just kept walking.

40

"You have . . . three . . . hours."

The Voice came out of the ceiling. An hour had passed and still the phone wasn't working. Had she pissed Gooch off so much that he wasn't calling? What if something else was going on, something she wasn't even aware of, that had stopped Gooch from calling? Equipment problems, a car wreck, Gooch hurt. Or maybe the Voice had changed his mind about something, decided not to let any calls through.

Whatever the case, it was obvious she couldn't sit around waiting on Gooch to be the big hero and come save her. She was going to have to start working her own angle again.

"I tell you what puzzles me," she said, turning her face toward where she believed the Silent Man to be standing. "What puzzles me is why you're here."

Talking to the Silent Man. As usual, Silent Man said nothing.

"I mean, surely you aren't here to guard me. They wanted a guard, they'd have stuck you outside."

Tick tick tick.

"Which makes me wonder. Maybe you're a clue."

Tick tick tick.

"Or maybe you're just here to kill me. I mean, I've said it before, but this whole thing could just be a charade. Maybe you're just sitting here watching me squirm until the time runs out. And then you blow my head off or something."

Tick tick tick.

"Or maybe the reason you haven't talked yet is that I haven't asked the right question. Hmm? Am I getting warm?"

Tick. Tick. Tick.

"Or . . . maybe you're supposed to be my eyes."

She fumbled around on the floor until she found the stack of paper that she had flung there an hour or so earlier. She picked it up, set it on the table, then stepped back to the wall. "Here. Read this to me. Huh? Is there any writing on it?"

Tick. Tick. Tick.

She heard a rustling of paper. Her heart jumped. Silent Man was actually picking up the paper! Could it be . . .

Tick. Tick. Tick. Tick. Tick. Tick. Tick.

And then, miraculously, the sound of human speech.

"'In Re: The trust of Ellis J. Morris the Third,'" Silent Man was whispering.

"Oh my God!" MeChelle said. A wave of excitement spread through her. "You're my eyes! I can't believe I didn't see it! You're my eyes!"

The Silent Man cleared his throat again, began to read. Not loudly, but in a low whisper. "'In Re: The trust of Ellis J. Morris the Third . . .'"

MeChelle felt something expanding in her chest. *Yes! Now she was getting somewhere!*

41

Gooch found the offices of Diamond and Associates LLP on the first floor of a building with a large SPACE FOR RENT sign outside. The place seemed deserted, no tenants other than Neil Diamond. He'd been calling MeChelle, but with no success. And Cody had told him he was getting raked over the coals by IA and hadn't had a chance yet to try fixing the black box that routed the phone calls.

"Goddammit, boy," Gooch had yelled, "you need to find a way!"

"I'm *trying*, sir," Cody had whined.

Gooch walked into Diamond and Associates. The receptionist in the law firm's gaudily decorated reception area had very long yellow fingernails and large fake breasts. "Mr. Diamond in?" Gooch said.

"Do you have an appointment, sir?"

"Tell him my name's Hank Gooch. I'm a friend of Melbert Reavis's."

"How *is* Mr. Reavis?" the receptionist asked. She had a brown front tooth that spoiled an otherwise fairly attractive face. "He's such a funny guy."

"Just get Neil out here," Gooch said.

The brown tooth disappeared. "Yes, sir."

Neil Diamond came right out. He didn't look at all like the singer. He was about thirty-five, cheap suit, thinning hair, ratlike features.

"So . . ." he said. "Friend of Melbert Reavis, huh?" He was smiling, but not friendly.

"Let's go in your office."

The lawyer didn't move. "None of his friends call him 'Melbert,'" Neil Diamond said. "He usually goes by 'Red.'"

"Let's go in your office," Gooch said again.

"What's your name again? Gooch? I never heard that name before."

"I'm gonna give you two choices," Gooch said. He took out his wallet, slapped a dollar bill down on the receptionist's counter. "Choice one, you take this dollar and I become your client."

"A dollar wouldn't buy you eight seconds of my time." He turned to the receptionist. "Honey, call the cops on this redneck asshole. Get him out of here."

"Choice two, you get indicted for aiding in an assault against a peace officer. If she dies, D.A. will up that to malice murder. Special circumstances, murder of a law-enforcement officer, you'll get the needle."

The lawyer laughed loudly.

"502 Lincoln Street," Gooch said.

The lawyer's laugh stopped abruptly and his skin got a

little pale. He cleared his throat, picked up the dollar, stuffed it in his pocket. "Let's go in to my office, Mr. Gooch," he said.

"See?" Gooch said. "How easy it is when you just do what I tell you?"

They walked down a long hallway past a row of empty offices. The whole place had a makeshift quality.

"These offices are kind of big for you," Gooch said.

"Client of mine went into receivership," Neil Diamond said. "I took three years' free rent in lieu of cash payment." They walked into the last office on the hallway. It was large but underfurnished. Diamond sat behind a very large desk, took out the dollar bill, smoothed it on the wood with his fingertips.

"Okay," he said. "What do you want, Detective? I presume you are a cop?"

"502 Lincoln. I want to know who hired you to get Reavis to send somebody over there."

"Detective, I take my oath as an attorney very seriously." Neil Diamond held up the dollar bill. "This is not enough money to persuade me to betray a client's confidence."

"I didn't figure it would be. But what it does, it makes this conversation privileged. So when you *do* betray a client's confidence to me, our little secret can't be used against you with the state bar association because it'll be covered by attorney-client privilege."

"No, actually it would shield you from betrayal by me. But you would still be free to disclose anything you chose to the state bar."

"Huh," Gooch said. "Hadn't thought of it that way. Give me my dollar back."

Neil Diamond pressed against two corners of the dollar

bill with the tips of his index fingers, slid it slowly across the desk.

Gooch didn't pick up the bill.

"You were saying about 502 Lincoln . . ." Gooch said.

Neil Diamond shook his head. "No, I wasn't."

"Let me lay this out plain for you. 502 Lincoln is being used to relay calls from some moron who just kidnapped a cop. We think whoever owns this place may own the house she's been stashed in."

Neil Diamond swallowed. "Oh, shit," he said.

"Now if you'd like me to get the state bar to come through here and take a very close look at your business practices, we can go that route."

"God, God, God, God, God, God, God, shit, God, shit, shit shit." Neil Diamond got up, started pacing around the room, holding the sides of his face gently, like his head might crumble between his fingers if he didn't keep it carefully supported. "I knew it. I knew this was a bad idea."

"Spell it out," Gooch said. "Spell it out while the cop you helped kidnap is still alive."

Diamond sat down, got up, sat down again. "Look," he said finally. "I shredded it."

"Shredded what?"

"The instructions."

"Manila envelope with your name written on the outside? Cash payment, half in advance, something like that? Instructions on a CD?"

Neil Diamond had his head in his hands. "I trashed the CD, too."

"What did it say?"

"You already know. It said go ask Reavis to get somebody to go to this house in the ghetto, sit on it for a few days, make sure nobody steals the electronic stuff in the house."

"That's it?"

"That's it."

"But you looked it up, huh? You found out who owned the house."

Diamond shrugged. "Look, I knew this whole thing wasn't cool. But I needed the money. It was four grand!"

"Who's the owner?"

"It's just a shell partnership, a front. It's called DLP Partners."

"Who's behind the partnership?"

"I got the info on it from the state. The general partner's a lawyer here in Atlanta. The limited partner is an offshore corporation from BVI."

"BVI?"

"British Virgin Islands. No way to find out who's behind it. Not without federal government intervention anyway. And even then, it'd take forever."

"Who's the lawyer?"

"Woman by the name of Renee Makepeace."

"You know her?"

"Nah. She's with some big firm here in Atlanta."

"What's the name of the firm?"

"She won't talk to you. Those guys aren't like me. You'll have no leverage with them. She'll just call her lawyer and sit there with her mouth closed."

"What's the name of the firm?"

"Schumacher, Dillman and Priest." The name rang a bell. That's right—Priest's lawyer, the one who called with information about Stormé Venda, had been with that firm. Only she had just called it Schumacher, Dillman."

"Schmacher, Dillman and *Priest*?"

"Yeah. So what?"

Gooch cocked his head. "As in *Joe* Priest?"

"I don't think he's been directly involved in the firm for a good while. He's just a name on the letterhead now."

"But we're talking about the same guy, right? The big real-estate developer?"

"Sure. He started out as a lawyer."

Gooch sat quietly for a while. "Let me ask you a question," he said finally. "You wanted to find out some other properties owned by the same owner, how would you do it?"

Neil Diamond shrugged. "No good way. The corporation in BVI won't even have the beneficial owners listed. It's all controlled by a solicitor down there. It would take months—if not years—to crack that wall."

Gooch felt a tug of anger. He was getting so close. And now this.

Neil Diamond looked thoughtful. "Unless . . ."

"What?"

"Nah. Nobody'd be that stupid."

"What?"

"You said something about you're looking for a second location, right? Where this cop you're talking about is stashed?"

"Right."

"Well, if she was in another house owned by DLP Partners . . . but nobody would be that stupid."

"Why not?"

"Because all you'd have to do is trot down to the Recorder of Deeds, run a search, it'll pop right up."

Gooch rose, walked to the door, paused. "I always hated that song, 'Sweet Caroline,'" he said.

"Ha fucking ha," Neil Diamond said.

"Heard that one before, huh?"

The lawyer looked up with a bleak expression on his face. "Am I gonna get charged here? 'Cause, man, I'm cooperating to the max. Okay? I am totally cooperating."

Rule One with involved witnesses, you never cut them free. Not ever.

"We'll see," Gooch said. Then he flipped open his phone, made a call to this girl he used to know in the Recorder's Office. "Hey, doll," he said. "It's Hank. Yeah, I'm still alive. Need you to do me a favor."

42

It took a while for Silent Man to finish reading the trust document to MeChelle—reading in a soft whisper. She had to get him to skip over parts of it, it was so long. And since she couldn't skim it herself, she had a hard time knowing what to skip and what not to.

By the time he was done, she was puzzled. There was an awful lot of boilerplate gobbledygook about controlling jurisdictions and severability and all this legal crap that meant nothing to her. But the heart of the document seemed to be the provisions of how Kathleen Bolligrew's father's money got distributed.

What it came down to was that the trust had been established so that most of the money went to Kathleen Bolligrew, with about ten percent divided evenly between her children, Lane and Nathan. Nathan's money came with quite a few strings attached. He had to take regular drug tests. He had to attend an accredited four-year college that was ranked at least "Competitive" by the *U.S. News & World Report* college guide. He had to maintain a 3.0 average. He had to graduate with a bachelor's degree within six years in order to continue receiving benefits from the trust. It went on and on. There were a lot of other strings—most of which would have seemed pretty odious to any nineteen-year-old kid.

There was also an awful lot of stuff about the trustee, too. The way it was phrased, there was obviously a lawyer who would be responsible for the running the trust—they just referred to him as "the Trustee." The trustee was responsible for making sure that Nathan jumped through all the hoops, for keeping the books, for annual audits, for disbursements, and so on.

MeChelle kept waiting for the part that would seem to incriminate Nathan, that would give him a motive. But it never came. The way the trust was structured, if he didn't go to college, didn't jump through all the hoops, he never got anything. And even if he did, he never got at the principal. In fact, Lane was the one who really benefited in the event that her mother died. In the event that Kathleen Bolligrew died, the bulk of the trust went to Lane.

But that was no kind of motive for murder—not by an eleven-year-old girl.

And other than that? The whole thing was all incredibly boring.

Eventually the no-longer silent Silent Man paused. "So that's about it, I guess," he said.

MeChelle was still puzzled. "There's nothing else?"

MeChelle heard the sound of papers shuffling again. "Well," Silent Man said finally, "there's a bunch of Annexes. Annex A, Annex B—all the way out to Annex G."

"What's Annex A?"

"It says 'Properties.' There's a list of . . . looks like real estate."

"Annex B?"

"It says 'Investments.'"

"Annex C?"

"It says 'Trustee.'"

"Oh. Yeah. Who *is* the trustee?"

Silent Man read the name.

For a minute the name didn't compute. "What?" she said.

He read the name again.

"No," she said. "That can't be right."

"I'll read it again if you want."

She frowned for a long time. Then finally she smiled. Now *this* was interesting. *This* was something worth digging into.

Suddenly the phone began to ring.

She grabbed it. "Gooch! Where've you been?"

But there was no answer. The phone was dead.

43

“Well, there’s good news and bad news, sir.”

Hank was standing behind Cody Floss, who was crouched over the black box next to the computer in the back of the house where the shooting had taken place. The cover of the black box lay on the floor next to Cody Floss, revealing a grid of electronic components.

“So you said on the phone.” Floss had called just minutes earlier, said he thought he might be able to make the black box work again. Gooch had driven back to the scene at high speed. Now there were five cop cars and an ambulance parked out front. The kid that Floss had shot was long gone by now, carted off by an ambulance. The floor was slick with his blood, though.

“See, the bullet nicked the lead coming from the power supply here.” Cody Floss pointed at a red wire inside the box. “Well, cut it in half actually. But I think . . . um . . . do you have some chewing gum?”

“You don’t need chewing gum. You need to concentrate.”

Floss flushed. "No, sir, I don't mean that. I want to test it. Chewing-gum wrappers are conductors. I can bridge the gap enough to see if there's any other damage."

Gooch yelled at a uniformed sergeant standing outside the door. "Sergeant. Over here. You got any chewing gum?"

The sergeant walked over and said, "Lieutenant, I'm really not comfortable having you tromp around on my crime scene."

Gooch didn't see any need to let the sergeant know that he'd been knocked down two pay grades, that Gooch didn't outrank the sergeant anymore. "Chewing gum," Gooch said, snapping his fingers.

The sergeant frowned, pulled out a yellow gum pack. "Juicy Fruit all right?"

Gooch grabbed a stick, handed it to Cody Floss. The young detective pressed the end of the silver gum wrapper against the severed ends of the red wire. A green light flickered on the front panel. Then he grinned. "Yeah, baby!"

"Don't move," Gooch said. He whipped out his cell phone, dialed MeChelle's number. There was a click, then a crackling sound. The green light was winking on and off, on and off. The connection went dead.

Gooch tried again. The phone rang once, then went dead.

"Sorry, sir," Floss said. "The connection's no good. I need a real wire."

"Don't go anywhere," Gooch said. He turned, ready to head back into the other room of the house.

But a large figure appeared in the door.

"My gracious!" a voice said. "Looks like a gosh-darn abattoir in here!"

It was Major Eddie DeFreeze, head of IAD. Gooch had worked with DeFreeze years ago and there was no love lost.

Eddie DeFreeze was a massive man, skin the color of

burnt mahogany, who spoke with the sort of accent that black officers did in the Army. To Gooch it had always sounded like some black comedian doing an imitation of a white guy.

"Excuse me, Major." Gooch tried to slip by DeFreeze, avoid eye contact.

But DeFreeze stuck out his arm, put it against Gooch's chest. DeFreeze was six foot seven, close to three hundred pounds, very little of which was fat. "Last I heard, Gooch, you were a fuzz-that-was."

"Got my badge back this morning."

DeFreeze's eyebrows went up. "My gracious!" he said again. "And already we're shooting people."

"I didn't shoot nobody."

"Based on my information, however, you did leave the scene of a police-involved shooting. I need not remind you that's strictly against regulations."

"Excuse me," Gooch said.

DeFreeze's hand didn't move. "I'm gonna need all of you gentlemen to clear the room. Sergeant, I'd like you to separate Lieutenant Gooch and Detective Floss. Also please take both of their duty weapons into evidence."

Gooch had been afraid of this. "Eddie," Gooch said, "we got extenuating circumstances here."

DeFreeze smiled. "Under the circumstances I think we best keep this on a formal plateau. I'd appreciate you referring to me by my rank."

Gooch tried to step closer, but DeFreeze held him at arm's length. The big man outweighed him by about a hundred pounds. No way Gooch would move him.

"I'm telling you—*Major*—we got a police officer in jeopardy. I can't tell you details. Nothing personal, but it's a need-to-know situation. You remove this young man from this room, and a police officer will die."

DeFreeze cocked his head. "Do tell?"

"I know you don't like me. But have I ever bullshitted you? Even once?"

DeFreeze made a comical face, drew air through his teeth like he was getting all thoughtful. "Wow. Boy. I'd have to think about that one."

"Ain't no time to think," Gooch said. He made a move to sidestep the big man, but the pressure on his chest was unrelenting.

"Give up your duty weapon, Lieutenant Gooch."

"I'm telling you—"

"You are in no position to be *telling* me anything," DeFreeze said. "The weapon. Now." He took his hand off Gooch's chest, turned it over, palm up.

Gooch knew they were hitting the point of no return. There was only one way to play it now.

"Listen carefully." Gooch lowered his voice. "Sergeant, Major—both of you. For your own safety. The device that Detective Floss is working on is a bomb."

"Whoa now!" DeFreeze said. "Then you need to call in the bomb squad."

"It don't work like that," Gooch said. "This particular device has an, uh, RF component that the bomb squad guys aren't competent to handle."

"RF?"

"Radio frequency. It can be remotely detonated. Via cell phone."

DeFreeze kept eyeing the black box. "Detective Floss," he said. "Please step away from the device."

"Now listen up," Gooch said. "I'm making a statement to you. A police-involved shooting occurred on this premises today at approximately four P.M. I take full responsibility for it. I left the scene for reasons which I will explain to you in due time. That is my statement in its entirety. Now, Cody, I'm instructing you to keep working on that box."

"Oh, my my *my*," DeFreeze said, "we are making quite the monumental mistake today."

The uniformed sergeant closed the heavy steel door to the room. They were now completely out of eyesight of any other police on the scene.

"Sergeant, please take off your radio." The sergeant wore a radio with a shoulder mic. The mic attached to the radio by a short length of wire. He took it off reluctantly.

"Don't you make another move, Sergeant," Major DeFreeze said.

"Take out that folding knife on your belt," Gooch said. "Cut the wire."

"Lieutenant," the sergeant said. "I got ten men out there. I need to warn them. If this thing goes off—"

"Cut the wire," Gooch said. "Top and bottom. Below the mic, then the right above the radio."

The sergeant did as he was told.

"We need to clear the area," DeFreeze said. "I'm instructing *you*, Lieutenant Gooch, to cease what you're doing. Detective Floss, too."

"Sergeant," Gooch said, ignoring DeFreeze, "hand the wire to Detective Floss. The knife, too."

Reluctantly the sergeant did as he was told.

"No, no, no, huh-uh," DeFreeze said. "Detective Floss, step away from that device. Now."

Cody looked DeFreeze, then at Gooch, blinking Gooch hopelessly.

"Strip the wire, Cody," Gooch said. "Then fix the box with the wire."

Cody Floss swallowed.

DeFreeze drew his weapon, pointed it at Cody. "Do not touch that device, Detective."

This was rapidly going the wrong direction. Gooch knew he had no alternative. He drew his own weapon, pointed it at DeFreeze.

Cody's hands were shaking now.

"Detective Gooch?" Cody said plaintively.

"Fix it!" Gooch said.

DeFreeze had a large cold smile on his face. "No, you didn't, Gooch," he said. "You did *not* just draw down on me."

Gooch could see that everybody in the room was scared silly. The uniformed sergeant's face was gray. Even DeFreeze, who was a pretty tough guy, looked like he was having a bad day. But oddly, Gooch felt calm, a pleasant warm sensation running through his veins. His vision seemed unusually acute, every detail of the wretched little room clear in his vision—the sunlight glistening on the sticky red liquid on the floor, the flaking paint on the walls, the slightly yellow cast of DeFreeze's eyeballs. Even the coppery smell of blood. Gooch drank it all in.

Why am I enjoying this? he thought.

"Cody," Gooch said softly. "Fix it now."

It seemed like it took forever as Cody tore the microphone cord apart, pulled out a red wire, stripped the ends, twisted them around the severed wire inside the black box. But, at long last, the green light on the front of the black box winked on.

And stayed on.

Gooch hit the redial button with his thumb, his Glock still pointed straight at DeFreeze's head.

The phone rang once, rang again. Then a voice. MeChelle.

Gooch's heart leapt.

"Hank?" she said. "Hank! What took you so long!"

"It's me," Gooch said.

"Hank? Hello? Hank?" There was something wrong, the sound dropping out, coming back, dropping out again.

"MeChelle!" Gooch's voice went up a notch. "Listen to me."

"Hank? Is someone there? Hello?"

Gooch looked furiously at Cody Floss.

"Something's wrong," Cody said. "I don't know what happened. Maybe a bullet fragment hit another component but—"

"Hank, list—you've—and the ch—whe—if you can—" MeChelle was saying something, her voice urgent. The drop-outs were getting worse.

"MeChelle! Can you hear me?"

"Listen! If you c—repeat—Joe—something's not ri—you need—the trustee—priest—"

And then the phone went dead.

Gooch cursed.

"No need for that kind of language," DeFreeze said quietly.

Gooch looked at the man like he was an alien. Here it was, the air practically stinking with life and death, and this small-minded fool couldn't think about anything but words coming out of a man's mouth? What kind of crazy value system did people have that would make their minds work in such perverse ways?

"Cody, you fix that box!" Gooch shouted.

"Sir, I don't know if I can."

"You fix it!"

DeFreeze shook his head.

"Listen to me, Major," Gooch said. "Pull back your guys, establish a perimeter, call the bomb squad, whatever you need to do. But you've *got* to let this boy keep working."

DeFreeze's eyes narrowed.

Gooch holstered his pistol, stepped between DeFreeze and Cody. DeFreeze's Glock was pointed straight at Gooch's face. "Look, Eddie," Gooch said. "To hell with rank. To hell with the rules. To hell with procedure. We got to leave the playbook behind on this one. Please."

Eddie DeFreeze stared deep into Gooch's eyes.

"Please," Gooch said again.

"Tell you what I'll do, Gooch." DeFreeze slowly holstered his pistol. "I'll pull back my people, secure the perimeter, let him work."

"Thank you," Gooch said softly.

"But you? You just disregarded direct orders of a superior officer. Then you drew down on me. I can't let that pass. You got to come downtown with me."

"Soon as it's over, you can do anything you want," Gooch said.

Then he stepped past DeFreeze and started to run.

He had just made it out the front door, when something hit him. There hadn't been one moment in the past twelve-odd years where he hadn't known exactly where he was going. *Exactly* where he was going.

But right now? He had no clue.

And for the first time in years, the first time since the morning they had brought his little daughter's ruined body in from the canebreak in the woods where they'd found her, panic began to set in.

44

MeChelle stood in the blackness, holding the phone in her hand.

Whoever was behind this craziness—they had probably convinced themselves that they'd thought of everything. But they were wrong. The Voice was losing control. She could feel it in her bones now. Something was going wrong. And if the Voice got scared, he'd probably kill everybody in sight to protect his own skin.

She set the phone gently in the cradle, took a deep breath, waited.

Tick. Tick. Tick.

"All right," she said, sighing. "Let's read it again. Maybe there's something we missed."

"Annex D," the Silent Man whispered. "I didn't read that yet."

"Okay. Annex D. Audit procedures."

The Silent Man began reading, his voice droning away.

MeChelle tried to focus, but the legal details were mind-numbingly boring.

Suddenly the phone rang again. She grabbed for it, her heart beating fast.

She heard Hank's voice. "MeChelle? Can you hear me?"

Only it didn't sound exactly like that. It sounded like *Me—ell—Nyou—ear m—?* Something had gone kaflooey with their connection.

"Hank!" she shouted. "There's something wrong with the connection!"

But it seemed like he couldn't hear her. He was saying something over and over. Something she couldn't quite make out. He said it at least three or four times before she finally understood. "MeChelle, I can't do it again."

"Do what?" she shouted.

"—lose—"

It was obvious he couldn't hear her at all.

"Can't lose—"

"Hank? I can't hear you. What can't you do again?"

"lose—"

"Hank . . ."

"—someone—"

"Hank . . ."

"—can't lose some—"

"Hank . . ."

"—someone I—"

"Hank, I can't . . ."

"—again—"

"Hank, you need to look at Joe Priest."

"—love—"

And then the connection broke.

What! What did he just say?

It didn't even make sense. But it seemed like what he just

said was, "I can't lose someone I love again." But everything was so scrambled, it was hard to know if that's what he'd said or not.

What in the world was he talking about? *Who* was he talking about?

If she hadn't known better, she might have thought he was talking about her. Which obviously made no sense at all.

Gooch didn't give a shit about her. That much she knew for sure.

45

Gooch set the phone down on the seat.

Jesus Christ, he thought, *I'm losing my mind.*

He was tearing up University Avenue now. Behind him he could hear sirens. He was going to have to ditch somewhere quick. They'd have a vehicle description on him and every cop in the vicinity would be on top of him in no time.

But his mind couldn't seem to focus on the problem at hand. He reached up and wiped his face. Unaccountably his hand came away wet.

I can't lose someone I love again? Where in the world had *that* come from? Pointing his weapon at another cop, that was crazy enough. But for all intents and purposes, he'd just told MeChelle Deakes that . . . well. Not like *that*. And she probably couldn't even hear him.

But still.

He'd said it. Words had come out of his mouth saying things that he had not even thought before, that had not even been shadows inside his mind. Or had they? There'd been a lot of strange stuff in his mind lately. All this stuff about his little girl. It was like he'd turned off the faucet for a long time. And now, suddenly, it was opening up again.

There wasn't time to think about it, though.

The sirens were getting louder.

In the distance he could see the MARTA station. He looked down a side street, saw a huge mint-green flake Hummer—twenty-two-inch wheels, chrome, the whole nine. He hung a hard right, screeched to a halt behind the Hummer. The massive vehicle was now blocking the view from University. If everything worked as planned, the pursuing cars would fly by on University, eventually realizing they'd lost him. But by then he'd be gone.

Two young black men walked out of a nearby store, climbed in to the Hummer. Gooch saw he was about to lose his cover. He climbed out of the Ford, walked over to the window of the Hummer.

"How you doing, fellows?" he said.

The two young men looked at each other. They were both wearing hip-hop gear, bling, saggy clothes. Drug dealers? Maybe. Most drug dealers couldn't afford cars like this, though. On TV they always made out like drug dealers were rich. But the truth was, most of them drove twenty-year-old Chevys. "Something I can help you with, Officer?" one of them asked.

No, not drug dealers. Drug dealers didn't talk like that. Also, there were a couple of nice pinstripe suits hanging in a dry cleaning bag in the back seat. Evangelists? Musicians? Athletes?

Gooch walked slowly around the front of the car, looking at it carefully. The sirens were getting louder, closer.

"Nice car," Gooch said.

"Thank you, sir." The young man's voice was flat, sullen,

but not entirely disrespectful. The kid was just hoping to get out of this without ending up spread-eagled on the ground.

"What do they call this paint color?" Gooch said.

The kids looked at each other again. "Opalescent green," the driver said.

Gooch nodded. "Opalescent."

A cruiser flew by on University, lights flashing.

"Is there something we can help you with?" the young man said again.

"Why that tone, young man?" Gooch said.

The passenger whispered something to his friend. Probably something along the lines of "Man, shut the fuck up!"

"I haven't done anything, sir," the driver said. "And here you are giving me all this stink-eye. I'm not being disrespectful, sir, but I just want to know what your probable cause is."

"Probable cause! Oh, I see, I see," Gooch said. "We lawyers, huh?" He could still hear sirens. No way he could let these boys go yet.

"I'm a law *student,*" the young man said. "To the degree that that's any of your business."

The passenger, audible now: "Shut. *Up*. Raymondo."

Gooch cocked his head. "Sir, I think we're getting off on the wrong foot. I'm a vehicle enthusiast, I ask about your paint job, you start taking a tone. Where's the love?"

The young man glared at him, hands on the wheel in full view. "Can we go? Are you holding us?"

Two more police cars tore by on University. There were a lot of sirens going now. Hard to tell which direction they were coming from. Was he clear yet? Couldn't take the chance.

"*Holding* you?" Gooch came around the side of the

Hummer, stuck out his hand. "Let me introduce myself. My name's Hank Gooch."

The young man shook reluctantly, his fingers loose, his eyes dead, jaw clenched. "Raymondo Albertson."

"You looking forward to becoming a lawyer?" Gooch said.

The young man shrugged.

"What area you planning on going into? Criminal? Corporate? Litigation? What?"

"Real estate, probably."

Real estate. Suddenly something was tickling at the back of Gooch's brain. "That excite you?"

"What are you . . . what are you *talking* about?" Raymondo was having trouble keeping his tone civil.

The passenger, like a ventriloquist, barely moving his lips: "Ray. Mon. *Do!*"

"I'm talking about passion," Gooch said. "You think you gonna get up every day, feel excited, eager, enthusiastic? About *real estate*?"

Raymondo Albertson stared at Gooch. "Sir, my friend and I were in the music store. Okay? We bought a couple CDs." He reached over, picked up a plastic bag, held it up. "We don't have drugs in the car, we're not carrying weapons, we have no warrants out against our persons and we're not double-parked. So unless listening to Snoop Dogg has recently been outlawed—"

"Nah, listen up," Gooch said. "What I'm wondering, y'all ever considered a career in law enforcement?"

The two young men looked at each other wordlessly. Gooch knew the look. It was the official What-Is-The-Crazy-White-Man-Up-To? look, straight from the Black Manual.

Gooch clapped his hands together again. "Passion! Commitment! Service! Duty! Adventure! You think you gonna get that kind of satisfaction working in some beige cubicle on the forty-ninth floor of the some skyscraper downtown? Not in a million years. No adventure on the forty-ninth floor. None. Zero."

"Sir—"

Gooch walked around to the passenger side door, opened it, climbed up on the running board. "Slide over," he said.

"Excuse me?" the passenger said.

"Slide over," Gooch said again.

The passenger lifted his hands, palms up, surrendering. Then he got up, climbed over the transmission hump into the backseat. Gooch said, "Drive."

"Sir," the driver said. "I don't think you fully understand—"

"Shut up," Gooch said. "Drive."

46

"May I ask where we're going?" Raymondo was driving north toward the skyscrapers downtown.

"You may." Gooch was feeling loose now, almost giddy. They'd left the sirens behind five minutes earlier.

"Uh, where are we going?"

"We are going to the offices of Schumacher, Dillman and Priest. You familiar with them?"

There was a long pause. "Okay, yes, as a matter of fact I am. They're in the Bank of America Building on North Avenue."

"Excellent."

Raymondo kept driving.

"Mind my asking y'all something?" Gooch said.

Raymondo shrugged.

"I been a cop on the street for, what, a dozen years now? And the way y'all dress, I can't tell if you're a pimp or a law student. Wouldn't it be better if I could pull y'all over and not have to hassle you?"

"Then pimps would dress like law students and you still wouldn't know," Raymondo said. "We'd still just be a car full of niggers to you."

"Hmm," Gooch said. They had a point. He decided he'd be better off putting his mind on other things.

A couple of minutes later, they pulled up in front of a brown skyscraper with a pointy top made from a tangle of exposed I-beams. For the longest time Gooch had thought they'd forgotten to finish the top of the building. Took a year or two before he realized it was designed that way.

"In there." Gooch pointed at the visitor parking garage.

Raymondo pulled the Hummer in. It took a long time to park, the car too big for all the parking spaces.

"Okay," Raymondo said when he'd finally parked, "we've been very patient, sir."

"Whose suits are those?" Gooch said, pointing at the dry cleaning bag in the back.

"Mine," Raymondo said.

"Y'all look about the same size. This'll work better if you put the suits on."

"What will work better?"

"If I told you, it'd spoil the fun."

Raymondo and the other young man exchanged glances. Gooch had learned during the drive that the second young man's name was Walter Wilcox.

"We better just do it, okay?" Walter Wilcox said softly.

"Listen to Walter," Gooch said. "Walter is a very smart young man, I can tell."

Raymondo climbed over the seat. The two young men changed clothes. When they were done, they looked like young lawyers instead of pimps.

Raymondo climbed out, buttoned his suit coat, shot his

cuffs, straightened his tie. The whole rig looked like it would have cost Gooch a month's salary.

"Now," Raymondo said imperiously, "either you tell us what this is about, or we're done here."

Walter, on the other hand, had a tiny smile on his face. Somewhere along the way the kid had started enjoying himself.

"It's Intern Day in the police department," Gooch said. "Experience the thrill of real law enforcement."

"This is bullshit," Raymondo said.

Gooch took out his badge, held it out to Walter. "Feel that."

Walter held it in his hand, hefted it.

"Clip it on your belt."

Walter clipped the badge on his belt, pulling back his coat so it was exposed to view, then pointed his index finger—pretending it was a gun—at his friend. "On your knees, boy!" Walter shouted.

Raymondo didn't seem to think it was funny.

"Let's go, fellows," Gooch said.

"I don't think so," Raymondo said.

"Come on, bro!" Walter cajoled. "This is gonna be a hoot."

Raymondo scowled.

Gooch started walking. Walter followed. By the time they reached the elevator bank, Raymondo had caught up with them. On the wall next to the elevator bank was a bulletin board, ads for various services you could get inside the building: massage therapy, flower delivery, oil changed while you wait, catering. On a blue sheet of paper was a photocopied flyer advertising sign-ups for Lawyer League softball.

Gooch took the blue flier off the bulletin board, folded it

in carefully in thirds, handed it to Walter. "Put that in your breast pocket," he said.

"What's it for?"

"You'll know when the time comes."

The offices of Schumacher, Dillman and Priest were opulently tasteful. The message was clear: we make huge amounts of money—but discreetly, without a bunch of tacky fuss and bother.

Gooch approached the receptionist. "Where is Renee Makepeace's office?"

"Who may I say is calling?"

"I'm not calling. I asked where her office is."

The receptionist swallowed, then reached for the phone. Probably calling for security or somebody. Gooch put his hand on hers, stopped her, then laid his ID card holder on the desk. "Young lady, this is a police investigation. If you attempt to hinder my investigation, Detective Wilcox will place you under arrest."

Gooch looked at Walter. Walter stood there like a deer in the headlights for a second, then his face changed slightly. His left hand moved, sweeping back the bottom of his jacket, revealing the badge clipped to his belt.

"Um, okay, okay, um, Ms. Makepeace's office is up on forty-nine."

"You call her, you warn her, I'm dead serious, I *will* have you arrested. You understand me?"

"Yes, sir."

Gooch eyeballed her for a minute, then walked to the elevator. They got on, pushed the button for forty-nine.

As soon as the door closed, Raymondo said, "Walter, are you *crazy*? This shit is totally not legal."

Walter was smirking. He swept back his coattail again, revealing the badge. "Huh? How you like that? Huh? Yeah?"

"Aw, *man*!" Raymondo said. "Everybody's going crazy!"

"Straighten your tie, Detective," Gooch said to him.

Raymondo straightened his tie. The doors opened.

"Okay, here's the drill," Gooch said. "We're trying to find some information about some real estate. It's held by a shell corporation. We want to know who really owns it."

"Yeah, typically real-estate transactions are structured that way. See, the tax implications for investors are—"

"That's nice," Gooch said. "Y'all just follow my lead, okay?" He walked out of the elevator.

"Sir!" The forty-ninth-floor receptionist jumped up and followed them as they swept past her. "Sir! Gentlemen! You can't go in there."

"Where's Renee Makepeace?" Gooch said over his shoulder.

The receptionist was a moon-faced girl with frosted hair and very high heels. "Sir—"

"Now!"

"Down there, sir, but—"

Gooch continued rapidly down the hallway until he found a door with the name Renee Makepeace printed on it. A woman of about thirty sat at a computer, typing furiously. She was extremely well dressed, but there were large sweat stains under her arms that somewhat spoiled the effect.

Gooch banged his fist on the door, then walked in. "Excuse me, ma'am," he said loudly, "Detective Gooch, APD. I need five minutes of your time."

Renee Makepeace looked up blankly.

"What's this about?"

"DLP Partners. You're listed as general partner. We need to know right this instant who owns that property. We also need to know any and all additional properties they own in the city of Atlanta."

She blinked. Then her eyes narrowed. "What's this in reference to?"

"It's in reference to if you don't answer my question within"—He looked at his watch—"within two minutes, a decorated police officer is going to be murdered. And it will be your fault."

Her face hardened slightly. "I'm sorry, Officer, but I can't answer your question."

"It's Detective, ma'am."

"Detective, the information you're requesting is privileged."

"Are you trying to get my officer killed?"

"Detective, I don't know anything about that."

"I don't have time to argue with you."

Renee Makepeace picked up the phone. "Security? I need assistance on forty-nine. Now. I also need Roger." She hung up the phone.

"Show her the warrant, Detective Wilcox," Gooch said.

Walter looked nervously at Gooch.

"Show her the warrant."

Walter reached into his breast pocket, started to pull out the piece of folded blue paper. He pulled it out an inch, hesitated.

Renee Makepeace didn't move. "Let's see it," she said.

Gooch was stuck. *What now?*

"Wait." Raymondo put his hand gently on Walter's wrist. "Look, we know how this is gonna go. We bring out the warrant, your guy diddles around in some meeting, finally gets down here, reviews the paperwork, dah da-dah da-dah—meantime my officer gets shot in some squalid little rental property down in funktown. Then the D.A. gets all bent out of shape, starts saying, 'Here we go, big white law firm dragging its feet because the officer involved is African-American, hullabaloo, hullabaloo' because he's running for reelection, and then it's in the papers, it's on CNN, it's worldwide, and then the decedent's relatives are filing suit against Schumacher, Dillman and Priest for contributory negligence. Next thing you know, you're on international TV walking to your car with your face covered up while fat black ladies holding signs and yelling all kind of nasty stuff at you. Meantime? All the partners in this firm are on the hook for something you did, you—a mere fifth-year associate—and now they're all pissing on you, there goes your partnership, everything you've worked for, all down the drain, they're ready to sell you down the river just so Al Sharpton will stop picketing their country club. Hmm? Yeah? Oh, the sadness!"

"Look my hands are tied," Renee Makepeace said. But her face had gone pale.

"Hold on!" Raymondo held up his hands. "We are asking for nothing that is in any respect discoverable, nothing that has any legal standing whatsoever. We're like ghosts. We're here and then we're gone. No trace."

The lawyer rubbed her face nervously.

"Seriously," Raymondo said. "There's a life in the balance. All we need is an address. Nobody needs to know where it came from."

"I can't."

"Detective Gooch," Raymondo said. "Give her your notebook. She writes the addresses down in your notebook. Soon as this is done, that piece of paper goes up in flames. Poof. Never existed."

Gooch took his notebook out, set it on the desk. Then he picked up the phone, hit the redial button, handed it to the lawyer. "Whoever you just called, " he said, "tell them, 'False alarm.'"

Renee Makepeace swallowed, then took the phone. "Hey, it's Renee. False alarm. I don't need security after all. Or Roger either. No, no, it's fine. Yeah. Seriously. Everything's cool."

She hung up the phone, sat down, typed something into the computer, pulled up a file, then wrote five addresses on Gooch's notebook.

"What are these places?" Gooch said.

"Flips," she said.

Gooch frowned.

Raymondo said, "Investment properties in transitional neighborhoods. Somebody's buying them and sprucing them up, flipping them for a profit."

"Exactly," Renee Makepeace said.

"And who owns them?"

"Well . . ." She looked uncomfortable. "Do you really need that information?"

"Could be germane, yes, ma'am," Raymondo said.

"Look—"

"Don't make me get all medieval on you," Walter said.

Gooch shot him a look.

"Hey, I'm just kidding," Walter said. "No joke, though. Might save this officer's life."

The lawyer cleared her throat. "It's owned by this company called FlipMasters."

"Which is who?" Gooch said.

"I'd rather not say."

"Why not?"

She clamped her mouth shut, looked at him stonily.

"Let's go," Gooch said.

"Yeah," Raymondo said, "but it might be handy to—"

"We're gone," Gooch said. "All we need is the addresses."

He walked out of the office. Five addresses. He was almost sure that MeChelle was in one of them.

"Snap!" Walter said as soon as the elevator doors closed.

Raymondo bent over at the waist like he was taking a bow at the opera. "Oh, Mama. Oh, *shit*!"

"That was *mad*!" Walter said.

The two young men started dancing around in the middle of the elevator, grinning like fools.

"You hear that?" Raymondo said. "I was like, 'We are asking for nothing that is in any respect discoverable . . .'"

"Nigga, I about peed my pants."

"That was the maddest shit I ever did in my life."

"Being a cop?" Gooch said. "You get to do that every day of your life." Not strictly true, of course. Most days you stood out in the rain directing traffic or pulling people over for going forty-three in a twenty-five zone. But there was no point spoiling their fun.

The two young men danced for a while, then Walter said, "Is there really some officer kidnapped and everything?"

Gooch nodded. "She's my friend, yeah."

"Damn." Suddenly the two young men straightened up, and stood looking soberly at the floor indicator, the numbers going down and down.

When the doors opened, Raymondo looked at Walter and said, "What you think my Pops would say if I told him I was quitting law school, signing up for the police academy?"

"Say? Nuh, man, it's what he'd *do*. What he'd *do* is pick up the nearest lamp, hit you upside the head."

Raymondo sighed. "Yeah. Yeah, you're probably right."

47

The phone rang again.

"Hank?"

This time Hank's voice was clear, no drop-outs. "It's me."

"I found something out," MeChelle said hurriedly. No telling when the phone might act up again. "The trust document is here. And guess who the trustee of the original will was? Joe Priest. Lane Bolligrew's husband."

"Priest? He was her lawyer? When she was a kid?" Gooch was silent for a moment. "You know, funny you mention that. I just been over to his law firm."

"What did you find out?"

There was a brief hesitation. "Doesn't matter."

"What?" she said

"Nothing."

"You need to look hard at this guy Priest. I mean doesn't that smell fishy? He's the trustee for this estate and then suddenly he marries the little girl who's got all the money?"

"Seems odd to me."

"There are provisions in the trust document for audits. If there was anything hinky in the way Joe Priest handled the money, the auditor ought to be able to tell you. Right? Her name's Leslie Bell. She's with KPMG Peat-Marwick."

"MeChelle, time's running short here. I got to make some hard decisions."

"Like what?"

There was a long pause.

"Hank?" MeChelle said. She found her pulse quickening for some reason. "Hank, what were you saying in the last phone call? You kept breaking up."

Another long pause.

"Did you say something about love?" MeChelle was feeling very weird suddenly, very awkward. "I mean, maybe now's not the time, but—"

"You hang tough," Gooch said finally. "I'm gonna get you out of there."

The line went dead. Was that the end of a minute? Or had Hank just hung up on her? Dammit! She still had things she wanted to talk about. Why had she even mentioned this love thing? Love? Come on! This was Hank Gooch she was talking about. That cracker-ass redneck probably hadn't used the word *love* three times in his life. It was just her imagining things.

"Okay," she said to the Silent Man, "let's start again. I got five things on the table. What can you tell me about them?"

The Silent Man said nothing.

48

"Who's that on the phone?" Raymondo said. He was driving back down University to where Gooch had left his car.

"That's the gal that's been kidnapped. Her name's MeChelle Deakes."

"Wait! She's been kidnapped . . . but you can talk to her?"

"Long story," Gooch said.

The big Hummer pulled up next to Gooch's car. "So," Walter said, "what are we doing next?"

"We?" Gooch said.

"Nah, man!" Raymondo said. "Don't play us like that! We gotta help out some more!"

Gooch didn't have time to play around. He climbed out of the Hummer.

"Wait!" Walter called. "Hold up, you need us!"

"Nope," Gooch said. Then he slid in to his car.

Walter was holding something out the window. One of those electronic doodads that every pretentious jerk in the chief's office wore these days. A BlackBerry or something like that. The kid was cranking at the air with his hand, indicating that Gooch should roll the window down.

"What?" Gooch said, cracking his window a couple inches.

"Those addresses. We could pull up maps for you, show exactly where they are."

"So can this," Gooch said, holding up a paper map that lay on the dash.

"What about this company FlipMasters? Don't you want to know more about it? They might have other properties we could find out about."

"You can do that from here?"

Walter and Raymondo looked at each other and grinned. Raymondo parked the Hummer then the two young men ran over and stood next to Gooch's unmarked police car.

Gooch sighed. He didn't have time to argue. He fired up the car. "Put your seat belts on," he said as the two climbed in with him.

He peeled out of the garage.

"First thing, look up a woman named Leslie Bell with some company called KPG Pete Something-or-other. Get her phone number, any other information you can find."

"KPMG Peat-Marwick," Raymondo said.

Both the young men had their BlackBerries out, tapping away on the keys. "Raymondo," Gooch said, "you find this woman, Leslie Bell. Walter, you find out more about FlipMasters."

"Yes, sir," they both said.

The young men were intent on their tiny computers, not paying any attention as Gooch drove.

After a minute Raymondo dialed a number on his phone.

"Yes, hi," Raymondo said, his voice gone unctuously professional, "this is Raymondo Edwards with Schumacher, Dillman and Priest. I'm attempting to reach a Leslie Bell whom I'm told is affiliated with your firm. However, she seems not to be listed on your Web site. Oh, really? Well, could I speak to the partner who would have assumed her responsibilities? Thank you." Gooch looked at him in the mirror. He winked.

"Here we go, here we go, here we go!" Walter said. "FlipMasters, FlipMasters. Okay, president of the firm is a gentleman by the name of David G. Eddington, Jr., yadda yadda yadda. FlipMasters . . . Okay. Bam! Here we go."

"What."

"FlipMasters. A member of the Joe Priest Industries family of companies. Last year FlipMasters bought over—"

Gooch interrupted. "Whoa, hold on. What did you just say?"

"FlipMasters is a subsidiary of a company owned by a guy named Joe Priest. Big cheese in the Atlanta real-estate scene. You heard of him?"

"Matter of fact, I have," Gooch said. This was a hell of an interesting turn. Suddenly Joe Priest was popping up all over the place.

"Hi," Raymondo said into his phone. "Raymondo Edwards. I'm trying to reach Leslie Bell. I'm told that you assumed her audit responsibilities after she left the firm. Could you assist me in tracking her down? Oh, is that right? No, no, no, certainly nothing connected to KPMG Peat-Marwick. Not at all. No, I'm in trusts actually. She's . . . yes, been named . . . yes, she's been named as a beneficiary in a trust of a distant relative. Quite an affluent man, actually, and we've been unable to reach her, so . . . Mmm-hmm. Mmm-hmm. And might I ask under what circumstances she parted with the firm? From your tone of voice . . . I see. Of course, I understand. I'd appreciate that."

He scribbled something on his hand, then hung up the phone.

"Well?" Gooch said.

"Reading between the lines? I'd say she got fired by KPMG for doing something shady. He didn't put it that way. But I asked for the partner who took over her accounts. Instead they put me in touch with somebody in Legal. Who won't tell me jack. So it's obvious, isn't it? They send you to the legal department, that means they're worrying about liabilities, who this woman screwed over."

It wasn't obvious to Gooch. But he was willing to take the young man's word for it.

"Anyway, he gave me a number, how to reach her."

"Look up the number, find her address."

"You don't want to call, make an appointment, make sure she's there?"

"Never," Gooch said.

"Why is that?"

"Think about it."

There was a moment's silence.

"They might boogie?" Walter said.

Gooch grunted. They might boogie. Yep, that was it.

"I could call, just check if she's there," Raymondo said. "I used to do phone sales. Check this out." He dialed the number, caught Gooch's eye in the mirror, winked again.

"Wink at me one more time, I'm liable to think you're on the down-low, son."

Raymondo stopped grinning. "Yes, hi there, Leslie, how are you today? Good! Terrific. It's Raymondo Edwards at Shillingham Securities. We spoke last month and I was just following up to see if you received that prospectus I sent you last month . . . Hello?" He laughed.

"She's home?"

"1654 March Street."

Walter said, "We got a talent for investigation, huh, Detective?"

Gooch grunted again. The two young men rapped knuckles over the seat-back.

"Stop congratulating yourself," Gooch said, "and start finding out where them houses are at."

Gooch dialed MeChelle again. There was some sizzling and crackling, but this time they managed to talk without too much trouble. He filled her in on what he'd just learned—that Joe Priest ran the trust that his wife Lane had inherited.

There was a brief pause when he was done.

"He stole the money," MeChelle said.

"What?"

"Think about it. Why would a fifty-something-year-old man marry a twenty-two-year-old blind girl? He stole the money and didn't want her to find out. So he married her."

"Huh," Gooch said.

"It's the only thing that makes sense."

49

"Stay in the car," Gooch said as he parked in front of Leslie Bell's house, a gaudy McMansion in Decatur. The house was nice but the yard was not well tended. There were two cars in the drive, a ten-year-old Explorer, and a newer Mercedes. The Mercedes had a flat tire, and looked like it had been sitting there for a long time.

"Aw, come on, dog!" Raymondo said.

Gooch ignored them, got out of the car, walked to the door, pressed the bell.

It took three rings, but finally the door opened. A woman with streaky dyed blond hair and a great deal of makeup stood there. She was holding a drink in her hand—two ice cubes, four fingers of bourbon.

She gave him an irritated look, then said, "I gave at the office."

She tried to close the door, but Gooch pushed past her into the house. "I get the impression you haven't been at the office today," Gooch said. "Probably not for quite some time, huh?"

"Who are you?"

"Gooch. Cold Case Unit." He flashed his badge.

"Get out of my house."

"You not even gonna ask what I'm investigating?" Gooch looked around the place. Oversized pieces of furniture in bright golds and oranges, giant pillows with gold fringe, Japanese wood-block prints inside overbearing gilt frames—a collection of vaguely Asian stuff that looked like it had all been picked out in an afternoon by a designer with a large budget. There wasn't a sign of imagination or personality in the entire room. Boxes and papers and wadded-up doughnut bags sat on every surface. Gooch got the sense that the woman was in the process of coming down in the world.

Leslie Bell glared at him, her eyes wet with drink and hatred. He wondered if she looked like that at everybody or if it was because she knew why he was there. She had been a beautiful woman once, but had run to fat.

"Kathleen Bolligrew," he said.

Her face turned white.

"Get out," she whispered.

Gooch walked around the room, picked up a Japanese teacup off the mantel, looked at the bottom to see if there was a maker's mark. He'd gotten interested in Japanese ceramics a while back—an offshoot of his interest in Japanese swords. "Fake," he said, putting it back down.

"I'll call the police," she said.

"I just told you, I *am* the police."

"You bastards," she said. She had a fine old Southern accent. It sounded like she'd been in a sorority at someplace like Vanderbilt. "You just want to tear everything down. I see it in your eyes. The contempt. You have no idea what it took to build this place."

A pretty good moral blind spot, I'd figure. But he said nothing.

She turned and walked away from him. She wore very high heels and he had the impression she was concentrating very hard on each step, trying not to stumble. He followed her out the back door of the house into the small, intricately landscaped yard. More Japanese styling cues: a small pond filled with goldfish, bamboo, a rock garden—Zen by way of Home Depot. Again, weeds had grown up everywhere, spoiling the impression.

She walked through the Zen rock garden—which hadn't been raked in a long time—leaving a trail of footsteps in the pebbles, walked all the way to the far end of the property, then stopped, staring into her small stand of bamboo. Gooch could hear the wind in the bamboo. It was just like this dream he'd been having lately, the sound he heard as his daughter called to him. It made him feel all twitchy.

He walked up behind her, stood there, arms crossed.

Just give me an excuse, he thought, not quite sure why he was so mad at this pathetic woman.

"I have nothing to say," she said finally. Under the stress he could hear her accent slipping, the sound of South Georgia redneck coming out. She was *his* people. "If you have questions, you can call my attorney."

"Who would that be?"

"Andre Weiss. From Schumacher, Dillman and Priest."

"I had a hunch," Gooch said. He didn't move.

The wind kept rattling and rustling listlessly at the bamboo.

"Leave me alone!" Leslie Bell said finally

"Not till you tell me why she was killed."

Leslie Bell squeezed into the bamboo, slowly working herself deeper and deeper into the green stalks. Gooch couldn't stand the sound. But he had to get something out of her. He followed her. The bamboo grew dense and he had to push his way through it.

Finally Leslie Bell reached a wooden slat fence and could go no farther. She stopped and stood there with her nose almost touching the mildewy wood.

"Please," she said finally.

The wind kept working at the bamboo. Gooch could feel gooseflesh on his arms. He wasn't sure how long he could stand to stay here.

"What'd Joe Priest offer you?" he said.

She was trembling now, like a dog that had spent its life chained up and kicked regularly.

"Ten percent? Fifteen?"

She said nothing.

"No, I'm wrong, aren't I? I bet he didn't give you anything at all, did he? Some vague promises maybe?"

Her voice, when it came, was quiet and dull. There was no prep school, no sorority, no Vanderbilt left in it. "He was married to his first wife back then," she said. "He promised me that when he left her . . ."

Gooch wanted nothing worse than to get out of this bamboo. But he knew that if he didn't get what she had right now, there wouldn't be another chance.

"Anyway, he didn't steal anything. It was just a . . . loan."

"He took the money."

"No! Joe wanted to develop this property. He was a real-estate lawyer back then. Successful, yeah. But still, he's just an hourly employee, you know? Getting his little hourly wage from all these developers? And he wanted into the game. So he found a property. This was back when things were just starting to heat up again downtown. He wanted to build lofts in an old industrial property. But to do it, he needed five million dollars. He took the proposal around to a bunch of investors and they all turned up their noses. They didn't have the vision that he had. See, he knew where things were heading. But he just couldn't sell it.

"In the meantime, as a favor to a client, he'd set up this trust. It wasn't even his regular line of work. But old man Morris, Kathleen Bolligrew's daddy, knew Joe from way back, so he hired him to set up the trust. Anyway, after Morris died, Joe had this big pot of money that he was in charge of. And it was killing him. So he figured out a way. He used that money to collateralize a loan."

Gooch didn't know that much about real estate. But he knew that you couldn't use somebody else's money as collateral.

"There was an audit of the trust every year," she continued. "All I had to do was overlook some paperwork. No money disappeared from accounts or anything. It was just paperwork. Liens, letters of credit, leaseback agreements. The whole thing was so complex, I never entirely figured it out myself."

"And you didn't try," Gooch said. "Did you?"

She didn't answer.

"Did Kathleen Bolligrew find out?" Gooch said. "Is that why she was killed?"

The wind died down and now everything was silent.

Finally Leslie Bell said, "I don't know anything about that."

"About whether she found out? Or if that's why she was killed?"

Leslie Bell sighed. "Okay, okay, *okay*. So she found out,

yeah. It was actually my fault. We sat down to go over the audit for that year. And she found some things that seemed suspicious to her. She asked some hard questions. I tried to convince her that what was going on was normal. But Kathleen was a smart cookie. She didn't buy it. She said she was going to confront Joe."

"And then?"

"And then she was dead." She was still facing the fence, not looking at him.

Gooch shook his head. "How long you plan to hide out here in the bamboo?" he said.

"I didn't *know*!" Leslie Bell said, her voice rising to a shriek. "I *never* knew. It was just a break-in, just a freak thing! I never thought Joe had anything to do with it!"

"Yeah," Gooch said. "Keep telling yourself that."

He turned and worked his way out of the bamboo.

50

Gooch looked at his watch as he walked out the front door of Leslie Bell's unkempt house. It was a couple minutes past the hour. Presumably he'd be able to make another call. Assuming that the phone was working.

He dialed.

MeChelle answered. "Hank.

"You're right," Gooch said. "It's Joe Priest. He took the money. Kathleen found out. I don't have absolute proof yet, but I know he did it. You figured out any more clues from the stuff that was in the box?"

"Oh my God! I just realized."

"What?"

"The cardboard loop? It's a clerical collar. Get it? A priest wears a clerical collar. Why didn't I see it earlier? I was being too literal!

"It doesn't seem likely that he did the murder himself, does it, though?" MeChelle said. "I bet he hired somebody."

"Yeah."

Suddenly the line was dead.

"MeChelle? MeChelle?"

"I'm here," she said. "The line went kaflooey for a—"

Again the line went dead.

"MeChelle? MeChelle? MeChelle."

"—ere's only one thing left—that we—"

"Say that again."

"—only one thing left that we haven't connected to something."

"Ten to one it's connected to whoever Priest hired to kill her."

"—my guess—it's got something to do with a hitter or hired—"

"That's what I just said."

"What?"

Gooch felt a mounting sense of frustration. "What are the other clues? Tell me more about them."

"—still something wrong with the phone."

"I know. There's the man in the box and the other thing—it's a plate, right?"

"It's a—"

The line went dead. And this time it stayed dead.

Gooch dialed again.

Busy signal. A plate? What did that tell him? Was it a pun? Like Priest and King?

Gooch checked his watch. Just over two hours. Not much time.

51

MeChelle hung up the phone, raised her head toward the cameras that she imagined were positioned around the room.

"Hey! Are you there? We know who it is!"

There was no reply, just the ticking sound.

"It's Joe Priest!" she shouted. "We solved the mystery. It's done. Time to let me go!"

There was a brief delay and then the Voice again: "To gain release, you must have solid proof, admissible in court. You must complete an arrest which has been given approval by the district attorney of Fulton County."

"What?" MeChelle shouted. "What are you waiting for?"

Another delay. "To gain release, you must have solid proof, admissible in court."

"Like what?"

Tick. Tick. Tick.

"Come on, man! Don't be a fool! You can't make an airtight case in thirteen hours. This isn't *CSI*. This is real life.

Unless you got the knife dripping blood in somebody's hand and a signed confession, it's gonna take time. Period."

The room was silent for a minute. She had a sense that whoever was watching her through the cameras was scrolling through a bunch of stock responses on a computer somewhere. They'd pick it off the computer, then play back an audio file. The Voice repeated itself. "To gain release, you must have solid proof, admissible in court."

"We've got a bunch of witnesses, we've got motive, we've got a million reasons. There's plenty for an indictment. All we need is—"

"To gain release, you must have solid proof, admissible in court."

"What—a murder weapon? Testimony of the hitter? How much can you expect in one freaking day?"

"To gain release, you must have solid proof, admissible in court."

MeChelle felt a wave of frustration. The phone wasn't working worth a damn. And now this.

She ran her hand over the clues again, picked up the plate. She held it up to the Silent Man. "What's this say? These lumpy things. Is that a number or something?"

"JSE 4711," he whispered.

"Huh?"

"JSE 4711," he repeated.

It sounded like . . . wait a minute—the plate was a pun. Just like King and Priest. That was it. Not a *plate* plate, but a *license* plate.

The phone rang again. She snatched it up.

"Gooch?"

"—lo?"

"Hank, I've got a license plate number."

"A what?"

"License plate!" She was shouting now. Like that would do any good.

"Wh—"

"J S E four seven one one."

"Say again?"

"J S E four seven one one. Repeat. J S E four seven one one. Repeat. J S E four seven one one."

"I got JSE seven one one."

"No!" She was screaming no. "*Four* seven one one. JSE *four* seven one one!"

"JS—one?"

"JSE *four* seven one one. It's a plate number. Maybe it's the hitter. Run the plate number."

"—whose—"

"The hitter! I think it's the hitter. JSE four seven one. Juliet. Echo. Sierra. Four. Seven. One. One. It's the hitter's license plate number."

The line went dead. *Dammit! Had he gotten the number or not?*

That was their third call for the hour. It would be forty-five minutes before they could talk again. And after that, there'd only be an hour.

This was cutting it too close.

She was going to have to give some thought to escape again. Burning the place down—that hadn't worked so fabulously. Maybe there was something else she could do.

52

Gooch hung up the phone, climbed in the car. "Call 404-555-3899," Gooch said to Raymondo.

"Yes, sir." The young man dialed. "And who am I calling?"

"His name's Detective Cody Floss. Just hand me the phone when he answers."

Raymondo handed him the phone.

"Cody, where you at?" Gooch said.

"Well, they've got me in Internal Affairs. I'm a little concerned here, sir. See—"

"Internal Affairs! Why aren't you making sure that relay box is working?"

"I did what I could. But finally they—uh, they said if I didn't come with them, they'd drag me down here in handcuffs."

The kid should have barricaded himself in the room if that's what it took. But there was nothing Gooch could do about it now. "You close to a computer?"

"Well, I guess, but—"

"Need you to run a tag number J S Something 4711."

"Uh, you mean like JSA, JSB, JSC, JS . . . sir, that's twenty-six plates!"

"Unless they added some letters to the alphabet recently, yeah, twenty-six. Then I want you to cross-reference the owners with the crime computer, see if you come up with—" Suddenly Gooch thought of something. The guy who'd attacked him in the gulch next to Fuzzy's had driven a blue Ford F-150. What if that was the guy?

"Never mind," Gooch said. "Before you cross-reference to the crime computer, look for a blue Ford F-150. Call me the second you get it."

"Sir, I don't have a password for their computers in IA."

"Figure out a way, dammit!"

Gooch handed the phone back to Raymondo.

"Walter," Gooch said, "what you got on those addresses?"

"Nearest one is just a few miles away—936 Grayson Street. Down near Georgia Tech."

The drive to 936 Grayson Street was excruciatingly slow. Even with his light and siren going, Gooch wasn't making as good time as he'd have liked.

But finally they were there—a neighborhood of little cracker-box houses, a mix of gentrification and working poor. Five years ago this had been a really miserable neighborhood. Now it was just mildly miserable.

"936?" Gooch said. They were on the nine hundred block. Gooch scanned the row of houses. Nine thirty, nine thirty-two . . .

"Well," Walter said. "Guess it ain't that one, huh?"

The place where the house should have stood was an

empty lot. A litter of rubble and broken boards had been bulldozed into a heap at the back of the small property. The house had obviously been razed. Not a single piece of an existing structure left—not a shed, not a shack, not a barn. And no sign of a basement where the building stood. These old houses never had basements anyway.

"Next?" Gooch said.

"Next closest one is 808 Wilburn. It's about ten blocks that way." Walter pointed south.

Gooch's cell phone rang. It was Cody Floss.

"Got it. JS*E* 4711, blue Ford F-150. Owner's not a person. Comes back to something a company called Astro Engineering."

"Hold on, Cody." He turned to Raymondo. "See what you can find out about Astro Engineering."

Raymondo started tapping away on his BlackBerry.

"Um, yeah," Cody said, "thing is, they filed a stolen vehicle report yesterday."

"That ain't no coincidence."

"Well, there's more," Cody Floss said. "I called the detective who took the report. They got a suspect. Fellow by the name of Vincent Dale Meredith got fired about three weeks ago. That was his company truck. He still had keys. Day before yesterday, this Meredith guy came around the office complaining that they didn't pay him enough money on his final check."

Gooch couldn't believe it. Sounded like the kid was actually doing police work. Maybe he'd amount to something someday. "Run his history."

"I did, sir. He's clean."

"Got an address on him?"

"103 Majestic Court. It's right off LaVista, just west of Briarcliff. But like I say—"

Gooch hung up on him, started heading toward Vincent Meredith's house.

"So . . ." Raymondo said.

"What?" Gooch said.

"What did you find out?"

Gooch drove, wondering why he should tell these boys anything. "Found a guy who might be involved in this thing," he said finally.

"What's his name?"

Gooch looked over at Raymondo. This kid was thinking he was a real cop.

"Come on, sir! I'll run him through the system!"

"We just ran his criminal record."

Raymondo rolled his eyes. "Dude! Criminal record? Come on, that's just scratching the surface!"

"Did you just call me 'dude?'"

"Sorry, sir," Raymondo said. "What I'm saying is, you got credit reports, employment histories, medical records—all that stuff's floating around out there."

"In case you didn't know, you can't just log onto the Internet and pull that stuff up. It's against the law."

Raymondo and Walter laughed. They seemed to think Gooch was pretty funny. "Where you been, bro? Company out in Norcross got in trouble last year, somebody accessed personal histories on a hundred and twenty-five thousand people. Not just credit. I'm talking judgments, liens, filings, criminal, employment, medical, real-estate holdings—"

"You telling me you can do that?"

Raymondo looked at Walter. "Five bucks I can get there before you."

"Ten!" Walter shot back.

They started pecking away at their tiny computers. Go

figure, Gooch thought. He knew that stuff was out there. But getting to it without a warrant?

Within two minutes, Raymondo said, "I win! I'm in!"

"Bro, please!" Walter said. "I *been* in. I'm running his employment history right this very minute. Here it is! Last five years he's been with Astro Engineering. Two years before that, Elway Security. Four years before that, A&M Security. Before that, King Alarms, before that—"

"Hold up," Gooch said. "What did you just say?"

"King Alarms."

"Can you look up something called the King Corporation?" Gooch said.

"Okay."

More tapping.

"Here it is. King Group. Three divisions. Investigations. Security. Alarms. Your one-stop shop for security needs, blah blah blah. Major clients include Coca-Cola, Delta Airlines and—well, my goodness!—Joe Priest Industries."

"When did this guy Meredith work there?"

"Well, he started—let's see—eighteen years ago."

"Son of a bitch," Gooch said.

Suddenly Gooch was making connections. What if Priest had hired King to arrange the hit? Then paid him off by setting him up in his security business, paying him for phantom investigatory work. King then hired this guy Meredith to be the actual trigger man. That way Priest would have been totally insulated from the crime, and Meredith probably never even knew who ultimately paid for the hit. Meredith was a professional alarm guy. He'd have had no trouble getting around the home alarm. That would explain why Lane never heard the door being smashed in. Probably broke the door after the crime was done, made it look like a burglary gone wrong.

"Hey, hold on," Raymondo said, "I pulled his bureau. This guy owes money to everybody in town. His outstanding Visa balance is—"

Gooch never found out what the Visa bill amounted to.

There was a loud, sickening crash, and suddenly the car began to spin wildly. Gooch wrestled with the wheel, but it was no use. The car spun, smashed into something. Then the air bag went off. Gooch could feel the car rolling. They rolled once, twice, a third time, coming to rest upside down.

What the hell just happened? Gooch wondered. The impact had stunned him.

Everything was silent. There was a smell of gunpowder in the air. Must have been from the stuff that made the air bag explode. Gooch could feel his weight pressing against the seat belt. His left arm was numb.

What just happened?

Then it came to him. He'd seen it for maybe half a second: a flash of bright blue in the rearview mirror. Was it the blue pickup?

"Everybody all right?" Gooch said.

"I think so," Raymondo said.

In the back seat, Walter groaned.

"Walter?" Raymondo said. "Walter!"

Gooch looked over the seat. The young man was bleeding from his nose, his eyes rolled back in his head. He hung limply from the seat belt.

Now Gooch could smell gasoline. If there was a leak somewhere, it was liable to catch fire.

"We need to get out *now*," Gooch said.

Then Gooch reached for his Glock with his right hand, tried to undo the seat belt. But his left arm was in the wrong position to get at the buckle.

"Get me out of the seat belt," Gooch said.

"With what?" Raymondo's voice was high, panicky.

"I got a knife in my pocket."

Raymondo fumbled with the knife.

Gooch could hear footsteps outside the car, boots crunching on glass. The footsteps were coming toward them.

"You might want to hurry it up," Gooch said.

Raymondo finally had the knife out. He started sawing away at the belt.

Outside, through the crushed window, Gooch saw a black boot. The toe wrapped with silver duct tape.

Then bullets started smacking into the car.

53

"You have . . . one . . . hour," the Voice said.

"Is there anything left to read that you haven't read yet?" MeChelle said.

The Silent Man said nothing.

"Come on!" MeChelle said. "Time's running out! What good's it gonna do you to stand there with your mouth closed if this guy's just gonna wander in here after an hour and whack us both?"

As usual, no answer.

She picked up the five items in slow succession. She'd absorbed everything she could think of from them.

"Okay, let's think this through," she said. "Motive, means, opportunity. We pretty much have all that. Motive. Joe Priest is scamming the trust fund and doesn't want to get caught. Means and opportunity. He hired a shooter. Ergo, he doesn't have to worry about either means or opportunity. Somebody else will take care of that. Meantime, he's undoubtedly arranged a rock-solid alibi for the night of the murder. Charity fund-raiser, speech at the Chamber of Commerce, something where a zillion credible people will see him. So what we need at this point is concrete evidence pointing to the shooter. Confession would be nice. But failing that, we need a murder weapon, we need DNA, we need blood—*something*. According to the file, though, the scene was totally clean. No useful hairs or fibers, no semen, no blood other than the victim's. So it comes down to one of two things. Confession or murder weapon."

There was one clue left, the one thing that had puzzled her all this time. It was a rectangular box with a small door. Inside the box, a small plastic figure was lying down with its knees drawn up slightly. There was water inside, sloshing around. Some kind of toy. At first she'd thought maybe it was a toy vampire.

But that didn't make sense. There'd been nothing connected to this case that had anything to do with vampires or the occult or anything else. Plus the guy was lying down in this funny position. And why was there water inside it?

"Here," she said, holding the box out toward the Silent Man. "Read it again."

"On the bottom it says, 'The Holding Company, Ltd., copyright 2000, made in China.'"

"That's it?"

No answer.

"Anything else significant about it? The font, the color, the . . ." MeChelle sighed.

"Well," Silent Man whispered finally, "the spelling."

"The spelling?"

"The Holding Company is spelled H-O-L-D-I-N-apostrophe C-U-M-P-I-N-Y.'"

The Holdin' Cumpiny. It was the sort of jokey faux-redneck thing that you'd find on toys that they sold at faux-redneck places like Cracker Barrel. Which is when it hit her. Not lying down! The little guy in the box was sitting up. She had the thing oriented the wrong way the whole time.

"Oh, my God!" she said. "I know what it is!"

54

Gooch didn't get his Glock free until three or four bullets had thumped into the car.

"Whoa!" Raymondo said. "What was *that*?"

Gooch had been shot at a few times in his life, and there was something about the sound of bullets thumping into wood or metal near your body that was like nothing he'd ever heard. No point answering Raymondo's question; he'd figure it out. It was Vincent Meredith—it had to be. Vincent Meredith, the hitter. Vincent Meredith, Kathleen Bolligrew's murderer. He'd run into them with his truck, knocked them off the road. And now he was trying to execute them.

Gooch aimed for the combat boot with the duct tape wrapped around it, but just as he was about to squeeze the trigger, the boot disappeared from his field of view.

They had flipped over on LaVista Road, a two-lane artery running through a residential neighborhood. They weren't more than half a mile from Vincent Meredith's house. Gooch could see a brick ranch house in front of him. Grass, a multi-colored explosion of petals. They must have landed in a flower bed after they flipped over.

Gooch fired two quick shots, aiming as far from the house as he could. He had no expectation of hitting anything. It was just suppression fire—trying to throw the other guy off his game, drive him into cover, stop his shooting, give himself some room to maneuver.

Vincent Meredith replied with a volley of six or eight shots, the bullets clunking and smacking into the bottom of the upside-down car. One of them passed not more than a few inches from Gooch's head. He wasn't sure if it was a trick of his eye, but he could have sworn he saw it, the misshapen bullet clattering past his face like some angry bug as it tumbled through the air.

If he stayed in the car, they were dead. But climbing out, he would expose himself. There was nothing to do but chance it.

Gooch squeezed out the shattered window, firing another three blind shots with the Glock. In the back of his mind he was keeping track of his shots. Five down, twelve in the clip, two more clips on the belt. He could spare a few rounds. He saw a flash of motion, fired two more times.

Vincent Meredith disappeared behind the blue truck.

It was a strange scene. Around them everything seemed perfectly calm, perfectly ordered. A typical suburban neighborhood—sun shining through the leaves of the old oaks and maples and dogwoods, flowers here and there, pleasant houses, Honda Accords and Volvos in the driveways. Everything normal, that is, except for the two wrecked vehicles in the middle of the neat green yard, scarred now with brown stripes where the tires had torn up the sod.

The blue truck was about thirty, thirty-five yards away. Nothing between them but the trunk of a stately old live oak tree. Gooch could see the license plate: JSE 4711.

There was no cover within forty yards in any direction.

And Meredith? Meredith was gone. The guy knew what he was doing: feet hidden behind the front wheel of his truck, body sheltered behind the engine block. Gooch let fly, more suppression fire, blasting the truck, retreating back behind his own engine block.

Two rounds left: one in the clip, one in the pipe.

Time for a combat reload. Sacrifice the one round in the clip, in favor of the seventeen in the back-up. Gooch had done the exercise a million times. Drop the one in the pistol, eyes staying on the target, pulling the clip off the belt, reloading by feel.

The empty hadn't even hit the ground before his hand hit his belt.

Only . . . his spare clips were gone!

Somehow in the wreck they must have gotten torn off his belt. He stooped slowly to the ground, eyes never leaving the blue Ford, feeling around for the clip he'd just jettisoned. He couldn't find it.

"Might as well give it up," Gooch yelled. "I'm a better shot than you and I'm better armed. Besides, there's about a million cops on their way here right this second."

Vincent Meredith responded by raising up from behind his truck. He had an MP5 in his hand. Probably the best submachine gun in the world.

"So much for being better armed, huh?" Meredith yelled.

Gooch dropped down, listened to the bullets whanging into the hood of the car—full auto now. He scanned the ground, looking for the clip. Nowhere to be seen! Must have fallen under the car.

"What's this all about?" Gooch said. "I think you got me mistook for somebody else."

Meredith responded by firing again.

"Okay, okay," Gooch said. "So it was you, huh? You the one killed that lady back then? Bolligrew?"

Gooch was trying to play for time. If he could hold out for a couple minutes, there would be cops arriving. He hadn't managed to radio a distress call—there hadn't been time for it. But there were cars backed up in both directions now, people frantically trying to turn around so they wouldn't get shot. Probably been thirty calls to 911 by now.

Raymondo's torso emerged from the passenger-side window. "Help me!" he shouted. "Help me get Walter out. He's got something wrong with his arm!"

What could Gooch say? Right now Walter and Raymondo were on their own. "Just get yourself out," Gooch hissed. "We'll get Walter out in a minute."

"But he's gonna get shot!"

"You ain't gonna be helping him by getting shot, too."

Meredith poured another volley into the car. Fortunately he was concentrating on keeping Gooch's head down. Otherwise he would have killed Raymondo for sure by now. Walter, too.

Gooch heard Meredith moving now, running toward the car, firing as he ran. Gooch couldn't see him, but he was pretty sure he knew where Meredith was heading. There was a big water oak next to the road, looked like it was about a hundred years old. Giant trunk, perfect cover.

The footsteps stopped. Gooch peeped over the top of the upended car.

Meredith wasn't visible. He was behind the tree for sure.

In the distance Gooch could hear a siren. High, thin,

barely audible. A mile away, maybe two. On these roads, this time of day? Help was well over a minute away.

Gooch knew that Meredith would hear it, too. If he were in Meredith's shoes, Gooch knew what he'd do: change clips behind the tree, then charge the car, keep Gooch suppressed with his superior firepower, execute him as soon as he stood up to defend himself.

Which meant Gooch had to make the first move.

He came up from behind the cover, started walking across the grass. If he ran, Meredith would hear him, pop out, start blasting. If he walked, maybe Meredith wouldn't hear. The key thing, Gooch needed to get close enough. Thirty-odd yards was too far away for a decent shot.

The MP5 came around the side of the tree, fired blind, a burst of eight or ten shots. Gooch could hear them snapping through the air all around him. In the back of his mind a little voice was telling him to run away.

But he ignored it. *Just keep walking. Silently and calmly as possible.*

He could hear the clicking of Meredith's weapon. He was reloading. Meredith had his magazines jungle-clipped: two magazines taped together back to back so all you had to do was flip them over to reload. Took maybe a second in competent hands.

Gooch imagined Meredith behind the tree, tried to figure out what he was doing. Meredith would finish the reload, take a deep breath, fire one more blind suppression volley, then come out from behind the tree and charge.

At which point—if he wasn't hit by the suppression fire—Gooch would have one shot.

Live or die.

He stopped. Squared himself off. Took careful aim. It was a twenty-yard shot. Had to assume Meredith was wearing a vest. So it had to be a head shot. Twenty yards against a moving target the size of a soup bowl. Gooch was a good shooter. It was a doable shot.

Meredith would come from the right side of the tree. That was the only comfortable way to do it: you rolled around the side on your left shoulder, came out shooting. That way you were firing before you'd exposed your whole body.

Unless Meredith was *really* smart. And unless he'd heard Gooch coming, knew what Gooch would do, knew Gooch was ready to shoot the right side of the tree. Then he might come out the other way to throw him off.

Which was it going to be?

For a moment Gooch just stood there. Pistol raised, front sight fixed on the tree.

Twenty yards. He'd made a million shots like on the range. But he'd missed plenty, too. And when you were shooting at the range, the target didn't shoot back. And your hands weren't trembling, you weren't breathing hard, you weren't scared to death.

Only . . . Gooch didn't feel that way now, either.

His hands were steady. His mind felt clear. The world seemed to radiate out from his own body like some immense crystalline sculpture—everything clear and radiant. The greenness of the trees, the sharp points of the grass thrusting up toward the bright sun, the puffy white clouds moving and changing in the sky, the perfect curve of the road—it all seemed extraordinarily beautiful and serene. So beautiful, so hopeful, so serene, in fact, that he wondered, *Why did I never know this before? How come I never saw it?*

And then the MP5 came out poked out around the right side of the tree and the air was full of bullets. Meredith wasn't exposing himself yet, just trying to suppress Gooch a little. It all slowed down for a minute and Gooch could see the orientation of the barrel, the way it seemed to disappear into the receiver, until nothing was visible but the perfect black O.

And he knew in that moment that he was going to be hit.

The bullet caught him in the ribs. It was the most painful thing that he'd ever felt. Not just the terrible shock, but the needle-sharp pains shooting all over the right side of his chest.

His right hand dropped, no longer in his control, and the pistol slid from view, like a car in a movie going off a cliff.

He reached for the gun with his left hand, caught it, fumbled, brought it back up.

And as he brought it up, he saw Meredith was coming now. *Sneaky bastard! You beautiful sneaky bastard!* He'd fired from his right, but now he was coming from the left side of the tree! Something about it made Gooch feel happy.

Gooch's left hand came up, shifted toward the dark shape emerging from around the tree.

There was Meredith's face. The first time Gooch had seen it, actually. He was a plain-looking guy, neatly groomed hair, soft features, little round glasses like John Lennon used to wear. You saw him on the street, you'd think: college professor, musician, scientist.

Meredith blinked.

The front sight was still swinging toward his face.

One shot.

Gooch squeezed the trigger.

55

A spray of blood bloomed in the air around Vincent Meredith's neck, then disappeared, leaving his shirt soaked with blood. He dropped his MP5 and staggered away from Gooch, clutching his neck.

“Please!” he shouted. “No! Don't shoot me again.”

Then went down to his knees. Gooch approached him warily, gun still pointed at the man. Gooch knew his pistol was empty. But Meredith didn't.

Raymondo ran toward them, his ever-present personal organizer in his hand. “Oh, my God!” he shouted. “Oh, my God! Detective Gooch, are you okay?”

Gooch ignored Raymondo. His attention was entirely focused on Vincent Meredith. The blood was pouring out between Meredith's fingers. Meredith stared fixedly at Gooch.

“Please” he mumbled

“Who hired you?” Gooch shouted.

“Please”

"Do you understand that you're about to die?" Gooch said.

Vincent Meredith blinked uncomprehendingly.

"You got a chance to make this right," Gooch said. "You're about to die. Do you understand that?"

Meredith looked down at his shirt; the entire front of his body was soaked with blood now. Gooch felt a wave of impatience. Impatience and fear. He had to get something out of this guy. Meredith wasn't going to last much longer.

"Did you kill Kathleen Bolligrew?"

Meredith didn't answer.

"Who hired you?"

He mumbled something. Gooch's ears were ringing after all the shooting and he couldn't make out what the man said.

"You want a priest?" Raymondo said.

Meredith shook his head. "Priest," he said again.

"Joe Priest hired you?" Gooch shouted.

Meredith nodded.

"Just now? Or back then?"

Meredith nodded again. "Please," he said. "Call . . . ambulance."

"Where is MeChelle Deakes?" Gooch said.

"Dunno." The words slurring as they came out of Meredith's mouth.

"Does Priest know?"

"If he knew . . . he'd have . . . killed her . . . by now."

Gooch wanted to hit the guy.

"Sent me . . . to kill you. Try to find . . . MeChelle Deakes . . . kill her . . . too."

"Why?"

"Somebody tipped him off. Said . . . that you're investigating the case. Gave him the whole scenario. Deakes trapped in a house somewhere . . . with her eyes . . . glued shut." Meredith's strength was obviously fading.

"Who tipped him off?"

"I don't know. Maybe Elbert King? Mr. Priest was . . . talking about it . . . with . . . King." Meredith was gasping after nearly every third word now. "King said he . . . was pretty sure . . . you'd figure it out."

"So it's true then?" Gooch said. "Priest hired you to kill Kathleen Bolligrew eighteen years ago?"

Vincent Meredith stared at Gooch, blinked. It seemed like he nodded. But it was hard to tell. It could have been that he was wobbly from all the lost blood.

"Where's the murder weapon?"

Vincent kept staring, but you got the impression he wasn't seeing much. Gooch was beside himself with frustration.

"Where's the murder weapon?" Gooch shouted.

No answer.

"Did you kill her? Did you kill Kathleen Bolligrew?"

Vincent Meredith fell over on his face. Gooch frisked him quickly, found a tactical folding knife, tossed it away. Then he felt Meredith's neck for a pulse, his hands going slick with blood. There was no pulse to be found. Gooch cursed.

"Is he gonna be okay?" Raymondo said.

"Does it *look* like he's gonna be okay?"

Raymondo squinted at the dead man. "I guess not."

"How's Walter?"

"He's okay," Raymondo said. "Hurt his wrist. Banged his head a little."

Gooch started walking toward the blue truck. The fender was beat up, but otherwise it looked pretty good.

Raymondo tagged after him. "How come you kept asking him if he understood he was going to die?"

"I wanted a dying declaration," Gooch said. "Hearsay is legally admissible in court if a person has acknowledged that he's about to die. If he'd confessed, then I could go arrest Priest, get this thing over with."

"Excellent. You'll be happy to know, I got it all on here." He held up his organizer.

"What you mean?"

"Built-in camera. I got video of the whole thing."

Gooch cocked one eyebrow, then climbed into the front seat of the dead man's truck. Having video of Vincent Meredith was, in fact, a hell of a good thing. The kid had a head on his shoulders, no question. It wasn't quite a confession. But it was close. All they needed was a murder weapon and they'd have enough for an arrest. There wasn't time to break his arm patting the kid on the back, though.

"Well, for godsake, don't lose the video," Gooch growled. The keys were still in the ignition of the blue Ford. He cranked the engine. "Cops gonna be here in about thirty seconds. I'm gonna leave in this truck. Y'all need to stay here, tell the first responders what happened."

"But—"

"Whatever you do, don't give nobody that video. You just stick that thing in your pocket, hold on to it, okay?"

Raymondo was staring at him.

"What," Gooch demanded.

Raymondo pointed at the side of his chest. "Sir? Wait a minute. You got shot, didn't you?"

"Talk about command of the obvious," Gooch said.

Then he pulled slowly out of the yard.

"Wait! Wait!" the kid yelled. "Don't you think you better have somebody look at your—"

Gooch took off, watched the young man recede in the rearview mirror.

Then he reached for his cell phone, dialed MeChelle's number.

56

MeChelle picked up the phone as soon as it rang. "I've got it! I've got it!" she shouted into the receiver.

"Got what?" Hank's voice came back. No static, no problems, the line was clear as a bell.

"I think I know where the murder weapon is!"

Gooch grunted.

"The last clue. It's an outhouse. You know one of those little gag gifts—you open up the door and the little hillbilly in the shack pees on you? That's what this is. Only, it never peed on me."

"It never peed on you."

"The pee mechanism must be broken. Otherwise I'd have figured it out at the beginning."

Gooch grunted again. To MeChelle's ear, something sounded weird in his voice.

"Hank? You okay?"

Hank didn't answer.

"Hank?"

"I'm fine."

He didn't sound fine. There was something strangely weak about his voice.

"What's going on, Hank?"

"I found the shooter. Or at least, he found me." There was a brief pause. "Guy by the name of Vincent Meredith. Joe Priest hired him."

"You have him in custody?"

"He's—"

The phone cut out for a second.

"What?" she said.

"I said he's dead. This guy Meredith's dead."

"What happened?"

"I shot him."

There was a click and then nothing.

"Hank? Hank?"

But she knew that it was just the phone going out after the allotted time. One minute per call didn't let you discuss much.

After what seemed forever—though it was probably no more than thirty seconds—the phone rang again.

"Okay, okay," she said, talking as soon as she picked up the receiver. "Look, is there an outhouse on this guy's property? Or an old shed? Something like that?"

"I'm just pulling into his house right this minute. According to what I've got right now, he's lived at the same address for twenty years. If he ditched it back when he killed Kathleen—"

Suddenly his voice broke off. Was it the phone going out? No, she could hear something. Engine noise, it sounded like.

"Hank?"

Gooch made an odd sound. Like a groan.

"Hank? Are you okay?"

"I'm at this guy Vincent Meredith's house. But . . . I don't see anything."

"A shed? A bare patch where there might have been some kind of outbuilding?"

A bumping noise came out of the phone.

MeChelle was starting to feel alarmed now. "Hank, what is going *on*?"

"This guy Meredith did a little shooting before he went down," he said.

"Wait a minute. Are you saying you've been *shot*?"

Hank grunted. "Be careful," he said. "Priest knows about us. Knows about *you*. I think he's coming for you. Get ready. Do what you got to do."

Then the signal was gone, replaced by a gentle hissing sound.

Suddenly she felt hot, like the temperature of the room had gone up ten degrees. She pulled on her shirt, making a breeze flow across her chest. Man, it just felt stifling in here now.

Shot. Gooch had been shot.

The crazy bastard. He should have been going to the hospital. But instead he was still trying to save her.

57

Gooch stood in the driveway looking around the property of the man he'd just shot. It was an old house, older than most of the homes around here. Looked like an old farm-housc that had gotten swallowed up by development back in the forties or fifties when the surrounding houses were built. Good-sized lot, a couple acres easy, surrounded by an immaculate lawn, the kind you only got by dumping a hell of a lot of chemicals on the ground. The rear of the property ended abruptly in woods. There was no sign of an outhouse, no bare patch, no nothing.

And even if there had been, it wasn't like he'd be able to dig the thing up in an hour. He looked at his watch. Make that forty-three minutes.

The pain in his side was intense now. He pushed it back. There was no time for being hurt right now. For a second he felt kind of woozy, didn't feel much like making decisions about anything.

He could hear sirens. Pretty soon a witness would mention him to the uniforms—who had probably arrived at the scene of the gunfight by now. "Oh, yeah, the guy who just shot that other guy, he just drove off in a blue pickup truck with a bashed-in fender."

Gooch could hear another sound. It seemed very loud. A wet plopping noise. It took him a second. Finally he looked down, saw the blood coming off his arm, falling in fat, rapid drops onto the ground.

All right, he thought. *Gotta get moving.*

Then he saw it: back in the trees a flash of sunlight on metal. It took him a second to make it out, but the metal was a rusting tin roof. A barn!

He walked slowly across the big yard, feeling the sun beating down on his head, the pain in his side stabbing at his ribs. Everything seemed unusually intense. And the yard seemed endlessly long. There was a catch in his side every time he breathed.

Faster, he thought. *Move faster.*

He started jogging toward the woods. And then he was in the cool shade. There in front of him was an old barn, the rusting roof canted, one wall half collapsed. *Be worth your life to walk in there,* he thought. Then he laughed.

The door had fallen off the hinges. He walked in, scanned the room. A small dogwood tree had sprouted in the middle of the room and vines were crawling through cracks in the boards.

Could Meredith have ditched the murder weapon in here? And if so, why? It would have been smarter to chuck it in a river.

Then again, maybe he wanted to keep it as a trophy or something.

Problem was, there wasn't much here. An old rake was

leaned up against one wall. A wheelbarrow with a flat tire. Otherwise nothing. Just a big empty barn.

Gooch walked the perimeter of the space. It wasn't more than forty feet long, twenty wide.

And there was nothing here. No trapdoors, no old tools hanging from hooks, no hayloft. He felt disappointment and fatigue washing through him. The pain was bad enough. But it wasn't the worst part of getting shot. He knew from experience that when you were hurt bad, your mind started giving you reasons to quit. *I should be at a hospital. I'm just one man—how much can I be expected to do? I'm getting too old for this. Why can't somebody else carry the freight for once? Dammit, I just don't feel like it.* Your mind could come up with a thousand bullshit reasons. And maybe a couple that even made sense.

His mind just wasn't clear.

He tried to put a picture in his mind. *MeChelle Deakes. Think about her. Think about what she's going through.* He imagined her face, the full lips, the little scar on her chin, the arch of her brows. The eyes glued shut.

He walked outside, prepared to make the trek back to the house. Then he noticed something. At first it looked like nothing more than an ancient pile of kindling. But then he saw it was actually a tiny wooden structure, knocked over on its side.

He approached it slowly. Then his mood picked up.

By God, if it wasn't an outhouse! MeChelle had been right!

He grabbed a board with his left hand—his right hand wasn't worth so much right now—yanked on it. The entire outhouse, what was left of it, fell apart with a soft clatter. Probably hadn't been used in fifty years, but it still didn't smell so hot. He kept pulling at the wood, clearing it away until he found the hole.

The latrine hole had silted up a little over the years . . . but it was still there, a depression about three feet deep, surrounded by a small ring of masonry. The ring of bricks was probably the only thing that had kept it from completely filling in over the years, making it so that rainwater flowed around it instead of in it. He looked over the edge. Couldn't see nothing.

He pulled his flashlight off his belt, a small but very powerful light, focused the beam into the hole. There was something down there, a gray lump sticking up out the red clay at the bottom.

He lay on the ground. The pressure of the earth on his chest was almost unbearable as he reached deep into the hole. He scrabbled around, grabbed the gray lump, wiggled it with his fingers until it came free.

A knife!

It was a combat Bowie—the kind every idiot Rambo-wannabe had carried back in the eighties—serrated on the spine, just like the autopsy indicated. The likelihood of there being usable DNA, after the knife spending eighteen years in a hole, was pretty much nil. But the blade type was distinctive, with an unusual type of serration. It was a strong indication this was the murder weapon.

Gooch stood slowly, his vision going dark for a moment. He took a breath, though, and his head cleared.

He began walking toward the house. He needed to preserve chain of custody. But he had nothing to bag the blade in.

It seemed like the yard was endless. Finally he reached the truck. In the bed was a toolbox. He popped it open, looked inside. A paper bag full of nails. He dumped the nails on the ground, put the knife in the bag, closed it, sealed it with duct tape. Then he took a pen from his pocket, signed. and dated the bag.

All right. Chain of custody was preserved.

He climbed in the blue truck, sat in the front seat. His pants felt sticky and uncomfortable from all the blood. He took a deep breath, felt something bubbling in his chest.

That ain't good, he thought. There was a roll of duct tape on the seat. He ran it five or six times around his chest, a searing pain running through him every time he lifted his arm. But when he was done, the bubbling in his chest stopped.

A fleeting thought: *Duct tape. Man, what would we do without it?*

As he was about to crank up the truck, he heard a phone ring. Not a ring, actually, but one of those asinine tunes that everybody's phone seemed to play nowadays in lieu of a normal ring. "Whole Lotta Love," the Led Zeppelin song.

Robert Plant moaning away, about how he was gonna give somebody every inch of his love. It sounded like somebody stepping on a cat in heat.

Meredith's phone lay on the dash, a green light flashing.

Robert Plant moaned again.

Gooch picked up the phone, flipped it open. The read-out said PRIEST, JOSEPH

Robert Plant was still moaning and groaning away.

Gooch thumbed the green button. "Yeah?"

"Vince?"

Gooch was trying not to say much, see if Priest kept thinking he was talking to Vincent Meredith. "Mmm-hmm."

"You sound weird, Vince."

Gooch said nothing. One wrong inflection in his voice would give away the charade.

"Hey, whatever," Joe Priest said. "I don't have time to indulge your petulance. Look, I just got a phone call from one of my property managers. He said there's something odd going on at one of these little apartments we're re-habbing. He rolls up for some kind of routine checkup, finds this weird setup. The windows are nailed shut. New door, lock changed. A surveillance camera has been installed over the door. He thinks maybe it's a crack house or something."

Gooch waited.

"Vince, do I have to spell this out? I don't think anybody has turned one of our apartments into a crack house. I think this cop we're looking for—Deakes—I think she's down in that place."

Still Gooch didn't speak.

"All right, all right, quit sulking. Just get down there and end this thing."

"Where?"

"2626 Fair Oak Terrace in Chamblee. Near the DeKalb-Peachtree Airport."

Gooch flipped the phone shut.

His heart jumped. Could this be it? It had to be!

But then he realized driving this truck was a mistake. He needed another car. By now they'd have a description of the truck out on the radio.

Gooch looked around. Lucky for Gooch, Meredith had a second vehicle, a ten-year-old Beemer, sitting in the drive-way.

Gooch grabbed Meredith's phone, hobbled to the other car, climbed in.

Time to head down and bust MeChelle out.

It was only then that he realized he had a serious problem.

He was out of ammo. He had thirty-seven minutes to make it over to Chamblee, over by the DeKalb airport. No time to stop at a gun shop.

Then he had a thought. A guy like Vincent Meredith didn't roll unarmed. He reached over—pain shooting through his chest—flipped open the glove box. Empty.

What about under the seat? It was excruciating, leaning over to fish around under the seat. But there was nothing there, either.

He started the car. Then, before he put it in reverse, he had another idea. He felt around under the dash. *Yes!* A hard, gun-shaped object was duct taped under the wire harness. He yanked and it came free. A .38 Smith snubby. The old Chief's Special. Not the greatest gun in the world. But not the worst either.

He smiled grimly, put the car in reverse, backed out of the driveway.

He had a choice now: go and arrest Joe Priest, hope that whoever was holding MeChelle would be good to their word and let her free; or go straight to MeChelle and bust her out. It was an easy choice. He headed toward the airport.

As Gooch pulled onto La Vista, a police cruiser flashed by, not stopping, not giving Vincent Meredith's BMW a second look.

The Robert Plant phone started howling again.

Gooch picked up the phone, flipped it open. Joe Priest again.

"Yeah?"

There was a pause. "Vince?"

Gooch waited again. The fewer words he used, the less chance of giving himself away.

"Vince. You there?"

"Mmm-hmm."

"Vince, talk to me."

Gooch thought about it. It sounded to him like Joe Priest

had hung up, then started worrying, thinking that something about his previous call hadn't been right.

"Vince!"

"Hmm?"

"What's your middle name, Vince?"

Damn it! The guy was on to him. Gooch hung up. Let him think whatever he wanted. Problem was, now Priest was liable to head over to where he believed MeChelle to be, try to get rid of MeChelle personally.

Gooch put on the speed, jumping onto the curb and driving on the sidewalk a couple of times. But still the progress wasn't as good as he would have liked.

As he drove, his hand kept reaching for his phone. Wanting to call her, talk to her, reassure her. But he'd already made two calls this hour. Which left only one call. He needed to save it. When he got down there, there was no telling what might go down. He might need to tell her something as he was about to go in.

58

"We've solved it!" MeChelle shouted toward the ceiling. "Come on!"

There was no answer. MeChelle had hoped to get a response from the Voice. But there was no answer. MeChelle felt a tremor in her leg, a muscle jitterbugging away suddenly.

"Hey! Come on! It's Joe Priest. We've got a dying confession from the shooter. My partner's about to find the knife! He may have even found it already."

No answer.

"Come on! What are you waiting for?"

The room was starting feel sticky and stale now. A few minutes earlier she'd noticed that she felt hot. At the time she'd thought it was her imagination, that the news about Gooch being shot had made her feel funny.

But, no, it wasn't her imagination. The place was starting to get hot. It was like somebody had turned off the air-conditioning. Why would they do that?

MeChelle turned toward where Silent Man was standing. At least, where she *thought* he was standing.

"Can you get us out?" she said.

Silent Man, predictably, didn't answer.

"We've done everything this jerk asked," MeChelle said. "We've solved the crime. We've kept it quiet so that other cops didn't get involved. We've played along with this bastard at every stage of the game. But now this guy's not doing what he said. We've got to make a move." She paused. "*You've* got to make a move."

Tick. Tick. Tick. Tick. Tick.

MeChelle counted the ticks. It took one minute and thirty-seven seconds before Silent Man finally spoke. But finally he broke the silence.

His voice, still whispering. "What do you want me to do?"

She, too, dropped her voice. "Find a way through that door. Then lead me out."

A long pause.

"Look," he said plaintively. "What if there's some guy out there waiting to blow us away with a machine gun? Then I'm dead."

"And if you're wrong in trusting this guy? I mean, this is somebody who's kidnapped two people, threatened them with death, assaulted an officer of the law, glued a cop's eyes shut. . . . That's already enough for two life sentences in prison. What kind of moron would trust this guy? There's nothing stopping him from taking the next step?"

"What next step?"

"Killing us! What do you think, you ding-a-ling?"

She could feel Silent Man wavering.

"You weren't supposed to talk on pain of death. Now

you've already talked," she whispered urgently. "Has anybody busted in here and shot you? No."

Still he didn't answer. Finally he whispered, "Look, I'm not some action hero."

"It doesn't take an action hero to open a door."

Tick. Tick. Tick.

"Yeah," he said finally. "I guess you're right."

Then she heard the sound of a key sliding into the door, the door opening.

She felt a flash of scalding anger. "You had the *key*?!" she shouted. "All along, you had the key?"

"Oh, no," the Silent Man whispered. "Please—"

And then she heard a loud bang. Then a pause, then another loud bang. Gunshots. Inside the tiny room the sound pressure on her ears was enormous. Her heart began racing.

Someone grunted, then there was a thump, like a body falling to the floor.

After that someone grunted again. There was some dragging and thumping.

They must have shot him! Was she next?

She shouted, "You son of a—"

She hurled herself toward the noise, pawing at the air with her hands. But she'd forgotten about the table with the clues on it. It was right in her way. She slammed into the table with her thigh, lost her balance, fell to the floor.

There was more thumping and dragging. Like someone dragging a body across the carpeted floor.

MeChelle stood swiftly, then dodged forward toward the noise, trying to throw off the aim of anyone who might be out to shoot her. She was damned if she was going to go down without a fight.

But she was too late.

The heavy steel door thudded shut and the key turned in the lock. She slammed into the cool metal surface, the impact knocking her to the floor for the second time.

She lay on the floor trying to catch her breath. Then she felt something beneath her. Something sticky.

Blood. There was blood all over the floor. She leapt to her feet. Silent Man must have bled all over the carpet when they dragged him out the door.

The Voice came out of the ceiling. "He was warned not to talk. You still have . . . twenty . . . seven . . . minutes. If your team makes the arrest within that time, you'll still walk out of here alive."

"You're lying!" she screamed. "We've done *everything*!"

She lay in silence, waiting to hear a response. But the Voice said nothing else.

"You killed that poor guy for *nothing*!"

Nothing.

She stood silently for a minute, the rage slowly fading. And then the hairs stood up on the back of her neck.

Why?

She couldn't figure out what it was. Something had changed. Something was different. A smell? No. A sound? No.

Which is when she realized: it wasn't a sound, it was a *lack* of sound.

The ticking had stopped.

Why?

The air was getting hotter now. No, definitely not her imagination. Whoever was out there, whoever had just shot the Silent Man—they had turned off the air-conditioning. Suddenly she was aware of just how totally quiet the room was. It wasn't just an absence of car horns and planes and wind. It was an absence even of white noise. There wasn't even the humming of an air conditioner, the shushing of air flowing out a vent.

This must be what it would be like in the burial chamber of the Great Pyramid. An absolute tomb.

A tomb? A tomb was a place for dead people. And she wasn't ready for that yet.

She stood, kicked the steel door. It didn't budge, didn't even move a fraction of an inch.

"Hey!" she yelled. "Hey, why's the air-conditioning off? I'm getting hot in here!"

She felt her way over to the table, picked up the phone. It was dead. Not like it had been before—with a distant electronic hum. Stone dead. Like someone had cut the wires.

They'd cut her off. Absolutely cut her off.

Like they were planning on leaving her here.

She took a deep breath. Maybe that was a good thing. Maybe Gooch was already on his way. Maybe they'd gotten what they wanted and now they were hitting the road, leaving her to be discovered, saved, broken out, whatever.

After all, if they'd intended to kill her, why hadn't they killed her when they shot the Silent Man?

MeChelle sat down on the floor. She had run out of rope, hadn't she? Whatever was going to happen was going to happen. The walls were cinder block; the door, steel. You couldn't kick through them. There were no windows to break out. This might as well be a prison cell. If she had a couple weeks or some steel tools, yeah, maybe she could dig her way out. But not in twenty-odd minutes.

She sat for what seemed a long time, letting her mind drift. For some reason she kept thinking about Gooch. Crazy old Gooch, he'd taken a bullet for her. She never really thought he'd liked her much—and yet there he was out there, putting his life on the line for hers. Why? Out of duty? Because she was a fellow cop? Because he just liked the action?

She could see his face in her mind. Those cold blue eyes always looking through you. But if they weren't looking at you, what were they looking at?

She wondered how his face had looked when they found his little girl all those years ago, when they pulled her body out of the woods. Had he looked through everybody back then, too? Had he cried? Had he raged?

She wished she'd known him better, wished she'd had a chance to know what was going on in his head. A stray thought: *Why? Why do I even care?* It wasn't like he'd treated her all that well.

She wasn't sure why, but suddenly she was feeling all weepy.

She huddled into a ball, ready to cry.

But then she smelled something.

Smoke.

Wait a minute. Maybe now that the air-conditioning had been turned off, she was smelling the remains of the fire she'd set in the kitchen.

No. No, it was getting stronger.

She stood quickly, jarred out of her brief funk, pushed the table against the wall. She had felt air from the air conditioner earlier. Where? There had to be a vent somewhere.

She climbed onto the table, slid her hand along the wall. Nothing. Wait. She tried the ceiling. There it was, a vent cut in the plaster. It was just a bare hole, twice the size of her fist, the edge made of ragged sheet metal.

The smoke was getting stronger now. She could smell it seeping out of the vent—hot air, full of smoke.

Oh, no. Oh, no. They were gonna burn her alive.

Please, Gooch, she thought. *Please, Gooch, come and save me.*

59

Gooch had a sinking feeling as he approached the address for the building that MeChelle was supposed to be in. Grayson Street was a strip of commercial buildings and low-rent apartment complexes on the flight path to DeKalb-Peachtree Airport.

He'd been expecting a street full of little houses. But here—he didn't see any houses at all.

And then, there it was, the address he'd been given. But 936 Grayson wasn't a house. It was an entire apartment complex. A sign outside the property—peeling and canted to the left—read CHICKASAW LANDING. A chain-link fence had been erected around the property and the front entrance was barred by a gate. Behind the fence, several of the units had obviously been bulldozed. But there were still quite a few units standing, large squat brick structures. They'd probably been fairly nice apartments a long time ago. But now they were just eyesores, waiting to be gutted and rehabbed.

Gooch screeched to a halt, checked the gate. It was padlocked shut. He was about to climb over it when he noticed a Cadillac pulled up at a small, low building with a sign that said RENTAL OFFICE over the door.

The door was open and the brake lights were on. The Cadillac had a vanity plate: JP

Joe Priest. It had to be.

Then he spotted the developer. Priest and another man emerged from the rental office. Priest wore a blue suit and a red tie and carried a shotgun in his hand. A Remington 870 with a collapsible stock. It wasn't some little bird gun; Joe Priest was armed for man-killing. The other man, a very fit-looking young guy, wore a loose short-sleeved shirt, untucked—the kind worn by experienced gun owners in the summer to cover a concealed pistol. He carried a large ring of keys.

Beyond the rental office were row after row of scabrous—but entirely intact—apartments.

Priest pointed at the set of apartments on the left as though indicating the second man should check them.

It seemed pretty clear that Priest was there to kill MeChelle. If they could find her. Then Gooch would be next. And the second guy was some kind of hired goon, pulled in to replace Vincent Meredith. Gooch knew he'd have to work fast. Fast and silent. Priest would be expecting Gooch, so he'd be on his guard.

Gooch slowly backed his car up, parked on the street, then sprinted up a short, weedy embankment to the fence. Looking through the fence this second time, Gooch saw that Priest and the second man were gone. They'd be methodically checking the units now. He rapidly climbed the fence, jumped down on the other side, then drew the pistol he'd taken from Meredith's Beemer.

He ran in a low crouch toward the rental office. What once had been landscaped was now a tangle of weeds and bushes. That was good. It gave him a little cover.

He looked at his watch. Seven minutes until the deadline. No time to waste. He counted the apartments. There was a broad expanse of parking lot, with six units lining each side of the lot. And each unit had eight apartments in it—four up, four down; four front, four back. . . . Ninety-six units, total. Eight minutes till the deadline. Dammit. With a dozen men, maybe he'd have a prayer of searching them all in that short space of time. But not by himself, not with two armed men in front of him.

He had to come up with a strategy. Running through the complex kicking down doors, hoping he'd stumble on to MeChelle?—that wasn't gonna hack it.

Think. Think.

What was distinctive about the apartments in front of him? What was different? He tried to put himself in the shoes of MeChelle's captor. If he'd been choosing, where would he have put her? Somewhere in the middle, away from the rental office. Second floor. Backside apartment, the ones facing the trees. Minimize chances of being seen and heard. That narrowed things down to about twenty apartments. But her captor could have made the choice based on something much more prosaic—like which key he'd been able to steal.

What about Priest? Priest probably knew more about the places than he did. Maybe Priest could rule out some of them immediately. Some wouldn't have plumbing, some wouldn't have electricity, some wouldn't . . .

Wait! That was it! Electricity. Priest's company would have cut off the electricity to the units before gutting them. But one of them still must have power. Otherwise they couldn't run the PA system that let them talk to MeChelle.

He spotted it: behind the third unit on the left, rear apartment, he saw a red gash in the ground heading toward a temporary power pole. Somebody had run a trench from the pole—burying a power cable. It *had* to be.

Time to stop thinking. Move.

Gooch felt a burst of confidence as he sprinted to the door of the rental office. Now it got tricky. From here on out, he was exposed.

He surveyed the area again. In front of him were the remains of several demolished units. Beyond that, the intact apartments. In between, one tractor. The unit where he figured she was being held was about a hundred and fifty yards away.

He dodged through the piles of two-by-fours and broken red bricks and twisted I-beams, took momentary cover behind a tractor.

At that moment the man who had been accompanying Priest emerged from one of the units on the left. He had one of those walkie-talkies in his hand, and was speaking furtively into it. Immediately Joe Priest came out of an apartment on the other side of the parking lot. He was holding up a walkie-talkie, too.

As soon as Priest came out of the building, the other man pointed frantically at something. It seemed pretty obvious that he'd spotted the same thing that Gooch had: a temporary power pole that shouldn't have been there.

Joe Priest began running across the parking lot toward the third unit on the left.

Which was when Gooch spotted the smoke. A thin, lazy plume of smoke had begun to emerge from a roof vent at the top of the building. No, Priest and his guy hadn't seen the buried power line.

They'd seen fire.

The bastard who'd kidnapped her was burning the place down around her.

60

MeChelle climbed down from the table, picked up the phone again, listened, hoping for some hint that somebody out there was coming to help her. Stone dead.

The outside world might as well not have existed. All that was left was her tiny prison of a room, the hot air around her, the growing smell of smoke. Before, she had been able to see light through her eyelids. Not much. But just enough to know that she was in a room full of light. There had been times when she'd made out a shape or a shadow. But not now. Now the light was all gone. They'd switched off the lights when they left. She was in a cocoon of utter blackness. Alone.

For a moment she almost felt nauseated with fear. Fear and self-pity. Where was Hank? He'd seemed so sincere all day, so much more human and vulnerable than he'd ever seemed before. He'd seemed like he actually cared about her. But now the crunch had come and he was nowhere to be found.

Gooch had let her down.

And then, just like that, the fear passed. And she got mad.

"No!" she shouted. "I am *not* dying in here!"

She kicked the door. It didn't move. She knew it wouldn't, but at least it made her feel a little better, as though she were actually taking command of her situation—however grim it might be. She tried to think. What about the walls? The walls in the main room were cinder block. What about the kitchen? She felt her way into the kitchen, felt her way along the wall. From the hollow sound and the way it yielded when she knocked on it with her knuckles, it was obvious that the wall dividing the kitchen from the main room was made of soft drywall. But that didn't do her any good. She climbed up on the counter, kicked at the wall over the counter. The plaster gave way easily. But then she hit brick behind the drywall. The brick didn't yield at all.

She kicked it with all her might. Nothing.

Given enough time, she might be able to kick the bricks loose eventually. But she didn't have time for that. And with bare feet? It was possible she'd wreck her feet before she knocked any brick free.

She tried the wall in the other corner, stomping at the wall with the sole of her foot. But it too was solid brick beneath the drywall skin.

The smell of smoke was getting stronger now.

Was it all coming in through that vent? Or was it leaking in through cracks under the door, holes in the walls . . .

Wait a minute!

The vent!

The vent was only the size of her fist. But what about the ceiling itself? Was the ceiling reinforced the way the walls were? Seemed unlikely.

She felt her way into the other room, bumping into walls,

slammed her hip into the table. She was so eager to get up on the table that the pain almost felt pleasurable. She climbed up on the table, aimed her face up toward the ceiling, cocked her fist.

Then she screamed.

And punched the ceiling.

61

Gooch ran.

Not straight toward the smoking apartment building, but around the side of the first unit. If he ran straight up behind Priest and his stooge, they'd hear him. If he looped around the side of the other units, outflanked them, he might be able to catch them by surprise.

Priest's stooge was almost to the stairwell outside the unit. He fiddled with his keys, started opening the closed ground-floor door in the structure.

Gooch reached the first unit, lost sight of him. Now that he was out of hearing of the two men, he could pick up the pace a little. He charged down the row of apartments, his breath ragged. Pain from the wound in his side shot through him with every stride. And he could feel this strange liquid sensation in the right side of his chest. It had to be blood collecting in his lung. But he couldn't think about that. Not now.

He approached the end of the next apartment building,

slowed, peered around the corner. Priest's flunky was walking out of the apartment shaking his head.

As Gooch expected. Not there. She'd be on the second floor. Probably in the unit right above the one Priest's man had just searched.

Priest himself pulled up short. He was well into his fifties. But he was trim and fit, like he could run a marathon without much trouble. Definitely not to be taken for granted. He looked completely in command of himself, not much winded by the trot he'd made to the apartment. Unlike Gooch, he hadn't sprinted.

Joe Priest surveyed the unit. "Up there, Mike," Priest said to the other man. "Look. The windows are bricked up."

Priest was right. Somebody had bricked up the window of the unit on the second floor. There was still glass in the window. But behind it, barely visible through the dirty window, was bare cinderblock.

The man he'd called Mike looked up, squinted. "They changed the door, too," Mike said, then he charged up the steps. "See? Solid steel." He tried the handle but it didn't turn.

"Can you get in?" Priest called.

The man named Mike shook his head. "Nope." Then he stepped back, put his hand above his eyes to block out the sun, and stared up. "Lotta smoke, Mr. Priest," he called. "Maybe we oughta just let her burn."

"Not a chance," Priest said. "They could have moved her. I won't be happy till I see her corpse. Her and that redneck partner of hers. Lemme go grab a crowbar from the trunk of the Caddy."

"Yes, sir," Mike said.

"Anybody comes out that door, you put a bullet in 'em."

"Yes, sir."

Mike waited until he was sure Priest was gone, then holstered his weapon—a Beretta 9mm—and walked slowly down the stairs. He relaxed visibly. As he strolled away from the door, he pulled out a pack of cigarettes, lit one, then paused at the bottom of the stairs. Unable to see the whole apartment well from his vantage, he stepped backward to get a better look at the smoke rising from the building. He was completely unaware that he was not alone, backing closer and closer to Gooch.

Keep on coming, son, Gooch was thinking as the man got closer. *Keep on coming.*

When he was about six feet away from Gooch, Mike stopped. There was still no fire visible, but the plume of smoke coming off the roof had gotten thicker, darker. Gooch could smell the man's aftershave—some kind of bright, fruity stuff. Guy must have bathed in it.

Gooch took two slow steps forward, put his gun near Mike's neck, then pulled back the hammer.

Mike started at the sound, but didn't move.

"Hands on your head, Mike!" Gooch said softly. "Do it now, or I swear to Christ I'll shoot you."

Mike looked around slowly.

"Hands on your head!"

Mike gave Gooch a sleepy smile, his eyes wide open and empty looking. "Hey, no problem, sir."

Gooch knew that smile a mile away. The cold, appraising eyes; the slight tension in the shoulders—it was the I'm-about-to-sucker-punch-you smile.

So when Mike stepped to the side and grabbed for his Beretta, Gooch had no choice. He shot him once in the face, the little .38 letting out a loud, sharp bang.

Mike fell like a puppet with its strings cut.

Gooch ran up the stairs, tried the handle of the steel door.

Mike had been right. That door was not going anywhere—not without a very long, very serious crowbar. Or some C4 explosive.

He looked around for something that he could use. Rebar, something like that.

That was when he noticed the trail of blood coming out the door, running down the stairs. Not drops of blood, but a series of heavy, thick smears. Somebody—either dead or seriously wounded—had been dragged down these stairs. MeChelle?

No!

He had no time to process what he'd seen, though. Joe Priest arrived around the corner, shotgun in one hand, crowbar in the other.

"Mike?" Priest called. "I thought I heard a—"

Priest saw Mike's lifeless body first, then spotted Gooch.

He didn't hesitate even for a second. He just raised his shotgun and fired at Gooch. Gooch fired back once, but the range was too far.

Gooch heard pellets clatter against the brick, then dove to the ground. When he peeped over the lip of the stairway landing, Priest was gone. The crowbar lay on the ground.

Gooch heard a loud noise—WHOOOMPH!—above him. He looked up, saw flames appear in the roof.

No point worrying about Priest. He had to get to MeChelle. It was possible she wasn't in there now, that she'd been shot and dragged down these stairs, taken somewhere else . . . but he couldn't take that chance. He ran down the stairs, looked around the corner of the unit. The crowbar was about four feet past the wall.

Priest was set up on the edge of the lot now, his Caddy pulled up on the weedy lawn. He'd left the crowbar as bait.

Smart guy, Priest.

"It's over, Priest," Gooch yelled. "You're going down for the murder of Kathleen Bolligrew. Might as well give it up."

Priest replied with a volley of buckshot. Gooch looked at the crowbar in frustration. If MeChelle was still in the building, he had to get in there damn quick. But four feet was a long way.

He was just going to have to take a chance.

Gooch reached around the wall, fired once. Priest ducked behind the door of the Caddy just long enough for Gooch to scoop up the crowbar. Gooch reached the wall just in time to hear more buckshot slapping against the brick.

Jesus, that had been close.

Gooch thundered up the steps, jammed the crowbar in the edge of the door frame and yanked. The door frame was steel. It groaned and bent a little—but not far enough for the bolt to come free of the frame. He moved the crowbar higher, yanked again. More groaning from the steel. But still the door held.

How long before Priest came around the corner and blasted him? Gooch leaned on the crowbar again. He could see the end of the bolt now. It was almost free of the door. One more good heave.

This time the door gave way. Gooch ran into the apartment.

It was burning. The heat was unbelievable.

It was also empty.

But on the other side of the room was a second door. It appeared that somebody had built an entire room inside the apartment—a room made from cinder block. Maybe she was in there. The trail of blood led from that door.

He put his arm over his face, ran to the opposite side of the room, tried the handle. There was a steel handle. It wouldn't budge. He stuck the edge of the crowbar in the door frame and heaved.

This door frame, too, was steel. But unlike the outside door frame, this one was anchored in cinder block. It budged—but only just barely. The flames were racing up the walls now. Gooch couldn't imagine how hot it was in there now. A hundred and fifty degrees? Two hundred? He had maybe a minute before he cooked. He tried to take a breath, but the smoke was unbearable. As he ran back out the door, sucked in a deep breath, Joe Priest rose from behind an air-conditioning unit on the ground, gun pointed at Gooch's face.

Gooch ducked back into the fiery room as the buckshot blasted past his face, ricocheted around the room with a fierce clatter.

He ran across the room again. The fire was definitely hotter now. He frantically leaned on the crowbar, moving it an inch at a time, trying to pry the door from the frame. The effort was robbing him of oxygen. He ran to the door, lay down at the edge of the room, took another breath of the cool air that was pouring in now to feed the flames. If Priest had any sense—and it was obvious he did—he'd be on the stairs by now.

Gooch leapt up, ran back to the far door, inserted the crowbar, heaved, moved it, heaved again.

This time the lock gave way, the door popping free.

He grabbed the handle, pulled it all the way open, looked into the next room.

It was a bare cell, the walls lined with foam acoustical insulation. No fire inside, just a haze of thick smoke. In the middle of the room was a table. On the table were a rabbit, a plate, a stack of papers, a plastic peeing hillbilly, a clerical collar, and a little plastic Burger King guy.

Yes! He was in the right place. Problem was, there was no MeChelle.

"MeChelle!"

No answer. He charged into the room. "MeChelle!"

Nothing there.

There was another room, though. He ran through the next door, looked into the adjoining room room. A kitchen. Cheap old cabinets, a scarred sink, some recent fire and water damage. But no sign of a living human being.

He went back into the other room. The ceiling was caving in. He could see up into the attic. Flames were licking at the darkness.

He had to get out *now*. He was running out of oxygen and the roof might go any second.

Gooch felt a stab of anguish. She wasn't here. What about the bloody drag marks? Was that MeChelle? He couldn't think of any reasonable alternative.

His pulse pounded at his temples and he had to breathe. He lay down at the door to the cinder-block-lined cell, took a deep breath. The air was foul, smoky, hot. He choked immediately. Another minute in here and he'd be unconscious.

Time to go.

His vision began to narrow and the world seemed to grow gray. But a distant part of his brain was still working—the combat computer he'd always been able to rely on when things got hairy.

Priest would be coming up the stairs now, shotgun ready, plenty of air in his lungs, plenty of ammo in his Remington. The second Gooch walked out the door, Priest would start blasting.

Which meant there was only one thing to do.

Gooch leapt to his feet, began to run. It seemed like he was running down a long, gray, hot tunnel. He couldn't hear anything but a dull roar, a roar that might have been fire . . . but that might have just been his own blood racing through his veins.

It seemed like it was taking forever to reach the exit to the apartment, his legs gone rubbery, the pain from where he'd been shot running like a sheet of liquid fire up his side. His feet hit the ground in numbingly slow succession.

The blinding white light of the far door seemed to recede as he ran, and for a moment he felt like maybe he'd never make it.

But then he was out into the blazing sunlight, sucking in air. A black iron railing in front of him. He leapt the railing and was airborne.

To his left he heard a loud bang.

Then he hit the ground and heard something pop in his leg. He ignored the pain, rolled once, came up in a crouch.

Something was bad wrong in his leg.

The Remington roared again.

Gooch hobbled to the corner, took cover, pulled in several agonized breaths. The bubbling, liquid thing in his chest was getting worse.

He was pinned down, in agonizing pain, three bullets left in his gun, his ankle major-league messed up and he was slowly bleeding out from a punctured lung.

But otherwise? he thought. *Pretty much glad to be back on the job.*

62

MeChelle was moving through spongy, soft stuff. Insulation. Not the kind that came in rolls, but the old-fashioned kind that they blew into attics through a tube. She was sweating heavily in the extreme heat, and she could feel the insulation sticking to her skin. She kept moving, crawling from joist to joist.

At some point she was going to have to try and drop through. But where? She didn't want to end up back in the burning room she'd come from. She seemed to be getting away from the fire, though. She could feel the heat at her back, so she kept heading in the opposite direction. There was a stream of fresh air on her, coming up through a soffit or a vent somewhere, so at least she wasn't having trouble breathing.

Eventually, though, she was just going to have to make a choice. If she could find a soffit, maybe that would be the place. Kick through it, bail out, hope for the best.

Problem was, she had no idea how tall a building she was

in. It might be a one-story ranch; it might be ten-story apartment building for all she knew. The attic seemed very large. She kept crawling. Then suddenly she bumped into something. A wall.

Behind her she could hear the fire getting louder, a consuming roar.

She pushed her foot through the insulation, found the flat surface below it. A soffit? A ceiling? There was no way to know. She kicked it. It didn't yield much. A little, but not much. Which was good. That meant it was plywood. Which meant it was part of the exterior of the house she was in. Probably a soffit.

She started kicking.

Then she heard something. Loud banging.

Gunfire!

Were they shooting at her? If so, were they shooting from the outside? Or from behind her? With the roar of the fire, she just couldn't tell.

What should she do? If they were outside and she waited, maybe they'd go away. If they were inside, they'd get closer and kill her.

No way to know. She started to kick again, then slipped off the joist she was straddling. Something gave way beneath her and she began to fall.

63

"Hear that sound, Detective Gooch?"

It was Joe Priest calling to him. And, yes, Gooch did recognize the sound. The soft metallic clicking of shotgun cartridges.

"That's me reloading," Priest was calling.

"Give it up," Gooch called back. "Police are on the way already."

Gooch had wedged himself into a corner between an air-conditioning unit and a fold in the wall of the apartment next to the one that was burning. He was safe there for now. But he couldn't move without exposing himself to Priest's fire.

"I don't think so," Priest said. "Cop in a shoot-out? If you'd radioed it in—cop under fire?—hey, come on, brother, if they were coming at all, they'd already be here. No, I think for some reason you and your partner have been flying solo today."

Gooch knew Priest was right. No point trying to convince the guy otherwise.

"You're hit and you're cornered and you're outgunned," Priest yelled. "We could sit here all day. Eventually you'll bleed to death. MeChelle's already burning to death up there."

As if in accompaniment to his argument, a giant gout of flame shot up from the roof of the building.

"Even if the cops don't come, the fire department will," Gooch called back.

"Not for a while," Priest said. "I called my permitting guy, told him we were doing a controlled burn here. He's already called the fire department, told them there's nothing going on here for them to worry about."

"Baloney," Gooch yelled.

"Called the DeKalb cops, too. Said one of my construction crew had left a box of nailgun shells in there. Told them the rounds were cooking off, not to worry if anybody called nine-one-one to report hearing shots fired."

"Good thinking," Gooch said. "But guess what? I'm calling nine-one-one right now myself. I'll straighten 'em out."

Gooch then pulled out his phone and dialed. As he was dialing he saw something strange: a ghostly white figure appeared around the corner of the burning building. It was a woman, her arms outstretched like someone in a zombie movie.

It took Gooch a second to realize what it was. His heart almost stopped. He felt a rush of happiness.

"MeChelle!" he shouted. "Get back! Take two steps back!"

She stood frozen. Totally exposed now. Her entire body was white, covered with some kind of white fuzz. Insulation maybe? She was carrying something in her hand: a piece of brick. Looking like she was ready to clock somebody with it.

Gooch wondered why Priest didn't shoot her. He was probably as surprised by her appearance as Gooch.

"Step back!" Gooch shouted again.

"Gooch?"

"Step back! Two steps back! Before you get shot, take cover behind that wall beside you."

Gooch had no choice now, he stepped out, the .38 extended in front of him. Priest was appearing from behind the concrete stairs leading to the upper floor of the apartment, shotgun swinging toward MeChelle.

Gooch tried to settle the sight on Priest's chest, but he was unfamiliar with the weapon and shooting with his weak arm. He knew instinctively that his aim wasn't quite there. He squeezed the trigger once, twice, three times, saw divots appear in the concrete next to Priest's chest.

Priest ducked back behind the stairwell without getting a shot off.

Gooch's leg buckled and he fell to the ground, pain shooting up his leg and through his chest. It was his ankle. His ankle must have broken—or at least gotten badly sprained—when he hit the ground after leaping the railing.

MeChelle, hearing the shots, jerked backward, her head moving frantically, as though she were looking around. But her eyes were closed.

"You're gonna be okay, MeChelle!" Gooch called. "Just stay where you are."

Gooch crawled back to his shelter, flipped his phone open, dialed 911.

The LOW BATTERY indicator was blinking now. He'd been making calls all day, never recharging. Shit!

"DeKalb nine-one-one," the operator said. Gooch felt a wave of relief run through him.

"This is Detective Henry Gooch, Atlanta Police Department, badge number 3041. I'm involved in a shoot-out at nine three six Grayson. Immediate back-up needed. Repeat, I am an officer taking fire from bad guys. Send backup now."

"DeKalb nine-one-one," the operator said. "Could you please repeat that?"

"Officer taking fire. Nine three six Grayson. Send backup!"

"Sir, I'm sorry. You're breaking up."

"Officer taking fire! Officer taking fire!"

Nobody answered. Gooch looked at the screen. It had gone blank.

"They're on their way," Gooch yelled. "Give it up, Priest."

Priest said nothing.

"You killed Kathleen Bolligrew because she found out you were scamming the trust, right?" Gooch said.

"Who cares?" Priest said. "Happened a long time ago."

"You care," MeChelle yelled. "Otherwise you wouldn't be here."

"How you doing, MeChelle?" Gooch said.

"I don't know," she said. "I feel like my allergies are acting up. Otherwise I'm good. How about you?"

"I'm a little 1053," Gooch said. That was the radio code for officer down. "Slightly 1093, too." That was the code for out of ammo.

"No problem," MeChelle said. "I'll take care of you."

Gooch started laughing. Priest laughed, too.

"What's our status here?" MeChelle called.

"Well, I'm in a corner here and can't move without exposing myself. Priest's about twenty-five yards to your right. He's underneath a set of concrete stairs. He comes out, he's exposed to me. I come out, I'm exposed to him. He's got a twelve gauge, I've got a .38. Mexican stand-off." Partly Gooch was talking for her benefit. But partly he was talking to Priest. "I just called nine-one-one. So he's pretty well screwed. His only chance is to run. All we gotta do is wait it out till the cavalry shows up."

"Cool," MeChelle said.

Gooch sat there, his back against the cool surface of the brick, his feet in the sunlight, his body in the shade. It felt strangely relaxing. It hadn't quite penetrated until just now, but, by God, he felt a little tuckered out.

Man, he thought, *I could just take a snooze.*

"Hank!" A distant voice.

Nice little nap. That would be just the ticket.

"Hank!" It was MeChelle's voice finally penetrating to his brain. "Hank?"

He sat up straighter. *Okay, not good.* The blood loss was finally starting to hit him. He'd gotten through the fire and the shooting on pure adrenaline. But now that the adrenaline was wearing off, he was petering out.

"Yeah?" Gooch called.

"I hear him moving. He's gonna come for us."

Yeah, Gooch thought. *That's probably his best play.*

"You still carry that redneck pigsticker?" she called.

Good point. His tactical folder. He always carried it clipped inside his pocket. He pulled the folding knife out, flicked the button, felt the blade snap out. He pushed himself up the wall, feeling the grit on his back.

His vision went gray and he felt faint. But then it passed.

"The ground between us," MeChelle called. "Is it clear?"

Gooch scanned the ground. It was weedy but flat. He knew what she was thinking. Brave girl. Damnation, she was great. He felt like he should say something. This whole thing was liable to turn out pretty bad. So he ought to tell her what he thought.

"He's coming!" she called.

Gooch heard him, too. It sounded like he was at the end

of a tunnel. But he could hear Priest making a move now. He wasn't running. He was just swinging slowly around, trying to come around the wall at maximum distance so that he could use his superior firepower, take Gooch out. He wasn't worrying about MeChelle. Once he'd popped Gooch, then taking MeChelle out would be nothing. Fish in a barrel. Gooch knew he had to distract Priest. Maybe he could at least save MeChelle.

He stepped out from behind the wall, pointed his pistol at Priest.

Priest swung his shotgun toward Gooch. Gooch slipped back into cover as the gun thundered twice. Another five, six yards and Priest would be around the corner and Gooch would lose his cover. With no pistol and his ankle messed up, he'd be sunk.

Over by the other apartment, MeChelle had her head cocked. She looked like she was listening intently.

Gooch reversed his grip on the knife. He wouldn't be able to make it to Priest before Priest got a couple shots off. But he might be able to throw the knife and hit him. Gooch had pitched in the Single A State Championship his senior year in high school. And he'd fooled around with some knife throwing over the years. How many ruined blades had he stuck in the wall of his shop? A lot.

Worth a shot.

Priest's stealthy steps moved forward once, twice, a third stride.

"Now!" Gooch yelled.

He dove forward, rolled, came to his feet. It was about the most painful thing he'd done in his life. But what choice did he have? Priest was firing, shells flying out the ejection port of his gun

Gooch cocked his armed and threw the knife. As soon as

it left his hand, he felt it. It was like all those years ago, when he knew he'd thrown a perfect slider. Could have closed his eyes and he'd have known exactly where it was going. Low and just knicking the outside of the strike zone.

The knife slammed into Priest's chest with a solid thunk.

"What the—"

For a moment Priest stared. The knife was dead center in his chest. Right in the sternum. It hadn't gone in but maybe an inch or so. Enough to hurt like a bastard probably. But not enough to stop him.

But then, while Priest was momentarily distracted by the knife in his chest, MeChelle surged forward with an ear-piercing scream, brick upraised. Priest's mouth was open, furious.

Good on you, girl, Gooch thought. *You gonna go down, go down swinging.*

Again Gooch wanted to say something to her. But he couldn't even move. Every muscle in him felt useless and limp. That throw had just sponged up the absolute last drop of energy in his body. He felt himself sinking to his knees.

Priest heard the scream and started to turn. He saw the white thing moving toward him, tried to pull the Remington around. But he was a little slow.

MeChelle swung the brick she had clutched in her hand. It connected with the side of Priest's head.

He fell over like a plank, stiff and straight. There was an odd snapping noise. And then he didn't move at all.

Gooch found himself sitting on the ground now, legs folded underneath him.

The white fuzzy figure stood motionless for a minute. Then she extended her arms, probing at the air, swinging wildly with the brick. "Where are you?" she shouted. "Where are you, you son of a bitch?"

"I think it's over," Gooch said. His voice seemed to come from a long way away. Like someone else talking.

"What?"

"Over. I think it's over."

"Hank? Where is he? Where is he?"

"He's down."

"Where are you?"

"Mmm," he said. He wanted to say more than that.

He wanted to say how strange and beautiful she looked. He wanted to say how proud he was of her. He wanted to say something about love—though he wasn't really sure what the words might be.

But nothing would come.

The white ghost leaned over, hands fluttering over Priest's body. She picked up the Remington.

"You called nine-one-one?" she said. "Why aren't they here yet?"

"Nnn," Gooch said. "Nnnnn-nnn."

Her hands fluttered some more, came up with Priest's cell phone. "I can't see the buttons," she said. "You'll have to . . ." She drifted toward Gooch, arms outstretched, probing at the air.

He took the phone, pressed the buttons slowly. It took a lot of concentration, then he handed it back to her.

"Officer down!" she called into the phone. "We've got an officer down." She looked so fierce and beautiful. Even with all that ridiculous white fuzz stuck to her.

He wanted to say something strong, something clear, something pure—something that captured everything that he was feeling all through his body when he looked at her.

"Nnnn . . ." he said. "Nnnn."

Then he felt the weeds against his face and the world turned sideways.

64

"You may be a dumbass redneck," MeChelle said, "but you're tough as boiled owl."

Gooch was finally up and around. He'd rented an apartment off Ponce de Leon, near where he used to live before he retired. MeChelle was sitting at his kitchen table drinking a Coke while he cut up a chicken.

"Seriously, though, this is ridiculous," she said. "You don't have to make dinner for me."

Gooch grunted.

She held her hand out, fingers about an eighth of an inch apart. "*This* far," she said. "The surgeon told me that a bone fragment in your chest missed your pulmonary artery by *this* much."

Gooch just kept cutting up the chicken. This was probably the fifth time she'd seen him since they'd gotten her eyes unglued. He hadn't said more than about ten words that whole time.

"You got out of the hospital like a day ago, Hank. You should be letting *me* fix dinner for *you*."

"Fried chicken," he said. "You ain't gonna take it as some kind of racial slur, get all pissy on me?"

MeChelle shook her head. The guy couldn't be polite if you put a gun to his head. "You just have to make social relations as uncomfortable as humanly possible, is that it, Hank?"

"Shit, I'll make burgers if you're gonna get all ethnic on me."

MeChelle laughed. What the hell could you say to a guy like Hank Gooch? "We got all the documents," she said. "It took this forensic accountant guy from the FBI to sort it all out. But it was all true. Priest had basically ripped off Kathleen Bolligrew's trust fund. That was how he funded his start in real estate. He managed to pay it all back later. But he realized he'd never be safe from an audit, so he put the moves on Lane once she came of age. Marrying her pretty much put him in a position where he could control her finances and wouldn't have to worry anymore about some nosy accountant digging up dirt on him."

Gooch poured milk in a bowl, dumped in some flour, then cracked an egg, dropped it on top of the flour.

"So anything turn up yet to show who kidnapped you?"

"Nothing. All the evidence burned up in the fire."

"Found the body of the guy in the room with you?"

"Decatur Police found a homeless guy by the name of Malcolm Warren out on Memorial Drive, shot in the temple. Dump job. Could be him. Could not."

"Hmm."

"They said I needed to exercise my eyes after they got them unglued," MeChelle said. "So I did some interesting reading."

Gooch turned on the gas stove, started heating the deep fryer, then stirred the batter with a fork.

"I sat down with that trust document, tore it apart. Found a very interesting section. Guess what happens if Lane dies before Nathan?"

"Wild flying guess?" Gooch said. "Nathan gets the dough."

"You got it. Nathan inherits it all. Only exception, if she's got an heir. You take my point?"

Gooch dumped the chicken in the batter, started dredging the chicken with his fingers but didn't say anything.

"Come on, don't be obtuse," MeChelle said. "She's a young woman, prime of life. He knew that if she and Joe had the baby, that was his last chance at ever seeing all that money. I ran Nathan's credit bureau. The guy hasn't got a pot to pee in. His company, NHM? It's been in bankruptcy for a year and a half."

Gooch started pulling out the chicken, dumping it in the vat of hot oil.

"And the kicker? Guess who just left the country three days ago, headed down to Guatemala?"

Gooch looked over his shoulder. "Nathan?"

"Nathan."

"Convenient, Guatemala never enforces its extradition treaty with the U.S.

"Very convenient."

"I'm impressed," Gooch said. "You got it all figured out."

MeChelle laughed. "Hey, I want to *get* this guy."

"Any evidence connecting him to that apartment?"

"Nada," MeChelle said. "Both properties he used were owned by Joe Priest. And anything that might have been in the apartment went up in flames. No fingerprints, no DNA, no nothing."

"So what's your theory?"

"Nathan's been wanting to get back at Priest for years. Probably been investigating him for years. Once he put it all together, he realized he couldn't just go to the police. Priest is totally connected, gave money to the mayor in the last campaign, yadda yadda yadda. The minute the investigation started, Priest would find out. First, he'd probably figure out a way to slow down the investigation. Second, he'd whack Nathan. So Nathan figured that he needed to have all the evidence ready. And then he'd get a good investigator on the case, give them some kind of motive to solve the crime extremely quickly and extremely quietly. Get it all done in a day, so Priest wouldn't have a chance to fight back."

"So he stuck you in a room as leverage to get me on the case," Gooch said. "I'm no longer on the force, so I'd be in a good position to do the investigation quietly and without telling my superiors what was going on."

MeChelle nodded. "You got it."

"I guess we need to warn Lane, huh?" Gooch said. "Be unfortunate if some tragic accident was to befall her. Her grieving brother'd be on the first plane back from Guatemala, file papers to get his hands on that trust."

"As it happens," MeChelle said, "Lane wanted to thank us personally for solving her mom's murder. Invited us both over for lunch tomorrow."

Gooch sighed loudly.

"Hey, it won't be that bad," MeChelle said.

Gooch stared at the chicken for a while. It sputtered and popped in the oil.

"This whole thing was kind of intense, huh?" MeChelle said.

Gooch shrugged.

MeChelle felt her heart speeding up in her chest. "Look, there's something I've gotta say."

Gooch rolled his eyes.

God, he knew how to piss her off! But she had to say it.

She hesitated, trying to find the right words. "Wasn't it weird, us just having that connection by phone? When I was sitting in there, I really felt like you were my lifeline. I felt . . ."

Gooch poked expressionlessly at the chicken with a knife.

"I don't know if I could have made it without you."

Gooch's turned toward the deep-fat fryer, flicked the temperature gauge with his finger like he was all worried that it might be measuring the temperature wrong.

"But, Hank, there were things you said . . . The phone kept cutting out and stuff, and I wasn't sure if you said various things—if I heard them right? Or . . ."

Gooch's back was still turned.

"Can you turn around and look at me, Hank?" MeChelle was feeling all weird. But she felt like she had to talk it out anyway, had to say her piece.

Gooch turned, looked at her. His pale blue eyes, as always, seemed to be looking through her.

Suddenly she felt angry. "You just gonna look at me that way?"

"What way?"

Like I don't even exist. "Oh, forget it!"

He didn't look away, though, or turn his back. Which he could have done. He just seemed to be waiting.

"Did you even think about me after you quit the department?" she said.

"*Think* about you?"

"Or did I just disappear from your mind?"

No answer. Just the pale, empty eyes. And yet . . . there was something there. Something kind of sad. It took her by surprise.

"I don't know." She shrugged, looked away. "It just seemed like when we were on the phone . . . It seemed like something was different. Between us, I mean. Like we'd broken into some kind of new territory . . ." Her voice trailed off.

Gooch looked at her for a second, raised one eyebrow, like—*So?*—then turned back to the chicken, poked at it some more. "You think it's done?"

Man, MeChelle thought. *You just can't talk to some people.* Not even sure if she wanted to. She stood, looked over his shoulder. The chicken parts were bubbling and sputtering in the oil. "Maybe a couple more minutes?" she said.

Bastard, she thought. *Silly unfeeling bastard.*

65

MeChelle had thought Lane Priest would put on the dog for them. Rich woman like that, she could afford a personal chef, really roll out the red carpet. She was imagining lobster and crystal, maybe a glass of nice sparkling wine or something. Make an occasion of it.

But instead it was turkey on store-bought rye with French's yellow mustard and American cheese. The cola was store-brand. Not even Coke or Pepsi. Might as well have brown-bagged it.

Lane Priest sat straight-backed in her chair on her immaculate patio, eating carefully, wiping her mouth after every bite. She wore a simple green dress, beautifully tailored, that showed off her perfect white skin. Gooch seemed uninterested in Lane Priest. He ate loudly, grunting and smacking his lips, reaching across the table for things. But he didn't speak.

To MeChelle, the whole scene seemed surreal. Lane Priest

seemed entirely composed, entirely calm, as though nothing of any great importance had happened in her life at all.

"Must have been a shock," MeChelle said finally, "finding out the man you'd married was responsible for your mother's death."

Lane Priest's face was unemotional. "The day before our wedding, Nathan told me that he thought Joe was responsible," she said finally. "He seemed quite convinced. Of course, I thought it was one of Nathan's usual schemes. Some kind of last-ditch effort at getting his fingers on the trust fund."

"So you never suspected?" MeChelle said.

Lane chewed, wiped her mouth, set her paper napkin in her lap. "No," she said finally.

"You say that like you don't quite mean it," MeChelle said.

There was a long silence. Eventually Lane said, "I'm still trying to make sense of this. I suppose he was quite a terrible, corrupt man. I knew"—she paused again—"I knew something about him was . . . wrong. But he hid it well. It took me a while to see it. Joe was an actor. You knew that the minute you met him. But for a long time it seemed benign. 'Oh, there's Joe doing his shtick again.'" She smiled without warmth for a moment. "But eventually I came to realize that there was someone dark inside of him. It took me a while, but I began to see that. He could be extraordinarily cold, extraordinarily ruthless. Never to me. Not once. But to other people? In business? Yes, I saw it there."

She took a bite of her sandwich, wiped her mouth, set the napkin in her lap. When she finished chewing she continued. "But what's funny is that he didn't want to think of himself that way. He had great aspirations for himself. I always liked that about Joe. There's a little of that Jay Gatsby thing in him. He wanted to think of himself as a pillar of the community, a guy who went to church every Sunday, tithed, gave money to the homeless shelter and the charter school for poor kids, married a poor orphaned blind girl, did the right thing. That's really who he *wanted* to be." She took a long deep breath. "But I guess he just wasn't, was he?"

"You just don't sound shocked that it was him," MeChelle said. "I gotta admit, I find that odd."

For a moment Lane didn't answer. "I suppose," she said finally, "that I'm good at walling off my emotions. You have to be to get through something like I went through when Mom was killed." She paused. "I knew something wasn't right. But I just couldn't go there. When it came out that Joe had done what he'd done . . . well, sure I was shocked. For about ten seconds. And then . . . you remember what Marlon Brando says in *Apocalypse Now*? '. . . Like a diamond bullet right through my forehead.' That's how I felt. It was like a diamond bullet in my brain. It all came clear." She snapped her fingers. "Like that."

They ate their sandwiches in silence.

"So," she said finally, "who do you think put you in that room? Was it Nathan?"

MeChelle nodded. "Do we have any evidence? Not really. But, yeah, I think so. Nobody else really had a motive."

Lane blew out a long breath. "I was afraid you were going to tell me that. Nathan is a very disturbed man. I hope you'll make allowances for the loss that he's suffered. He's had quite a difficult life."

"You're going to need to be very careful," MeChelle said. "We don't think this is about revenge for what Joe did to your mother. We suspect it's about the money."

Lane frowned. "You must have read the trust document."

MeChelle nodded. "If he can find a way to make you die by some freak accident, he'll get the money."

Lane nodded soberly. "Yes, I thought of that." She patted her belly. "I've got a little insurance policy now, though."

"Oh?" MeChelle said.

"I'm pregnant."

"Congratulations!" MeChelle said.

"Thank you," Lane said. "I don't know how carefully you've studied the trust document, but once this child is born, the trust dissolves for good. And I get the money. So I just need to protect myself for another six months. After that, there's not a thing Nathan can do."

MeChelle nodded.

"I'm planning to go overseas. I'll find someplace where I can keep my head low for a while. I've always wanted to go to the Mediterranean somewhere. Greece? Turkey? I don't know. Wherever I go, Nathan will never be able to find me. Then after the child is born, I'll come home."

"Sounds like a good plan," Gooch said. It was the first time he'd spoken since lunch began.

MeChelle nodded. "I agree. In fact I was going to suggest that."

"A good plan," Gooch said, nodding. "Mmm-hmm. A good, good, good, excellent plan. Mind if I make me another sandwich?" He reached over and started assembling another sandwich from the platter in front of them. When he was done, he squashed it with his hand, flattening the sandwich into a thin oozing mass.

Lane looked vaguely irritated, as though she were ready for the lunch to be over. She ran her finger across her little electronic Braille organizer, like she was checking the time.

"Well, then," she said, "I did want to thank you for all your hard work. And for enduring the terrible things that happened to you."

"Hey," MeChelle said, "just doing our job."

"I realize giving you any sort of token of appreciation would probably be illegal and might well be insulting to you. But I've made a donation in the amount of $10,000 apiece in each of your names to the Metro Atlanta Police Disability Fund."

"Well, my goodness!" Gooch said.

Lane gave them a perfunctory smile. "If that's all, then, I have an appointment with my lawyer in just a few minutes. I apologize for being so rude, but I really do need to go. As you can imagine, I have quite a few arrangements to take care of before I leave the country. By all means, do feel free to finish your lunch."

MeChelle stood. "Thank you for the delicious meal."

"Mmm," Gooch said. He took a bite of his horrible-looking flattened sandwich, smacking his lips loudly. He didn't stand.

Lane waited for a moment. "Something else, Detective? Or are you just enjoying your sandwich?"

Gooch squinted. "Yeah, I kept thinking, you know—why the eyes?"

"I'm sorry?"

"The eyes. Why glue MeChelle's eyes shut?"

"Nathan always had a weakness for the theatrical," Lane said.

"Yeah, but . . ." Gooch shook his head. "Nah. Don't think that's it."

Lane cocked her head quizzically.

"I think that Silent Man ain't dead. I think Silent Man was actually the same fellow that was in charge of the whole shebang. Silent Man glued Detective Deake's eyes shut so Detective Deakes couldn't identify him."

"Really?"

"Yeah. I think the whole Silent-Man-gets-shot-and-dragged-out-of-the-building thing was faked. I think Silent Man was sitting there making sure that all the requisite information got fed to MeChelle. He was going to make sure the crime got solved no matter what. And keep an eye on her while he did it."

"And the blood?" MeChelle said. "The gunshots? The drag marks?"

"You heard gunshots," Gooch said to MeChelle. "You heard a scuffle. But what did you *see*?"

MeChelle didn't answer.

"All Silent Man had to do was bang around a little bit, pull out a gun that's been in his pocket the whole time, fire a couple times . . ."

"You have any proof of this?" MeChelle said sharply.

"Not a shred," Gooch said. "Simple logic, that's all. Otherwise, this whole thing's too contrived, too baroque, too . . . well, frankly, too idiotic."

"He tazed me at least four times in a row. Never missed. I don't think so."

"Remember I told you about visiting that school for the blind? The janitor came out, smoked a cigarette, dropped it on the ground, then stepped right on top of it to put out the butt. How'd he do it?"

"By sound," MeChelle said.

"By sound," Gooch said.

There was a brief silence.

"No," MeChelle said. "There's a flaw in your logic. You saw Nathan while Silent Man was standing there right next to me."

"I did, didn't I?"

MeChelle could hear birds calling from the branches of the trees behind the house. There was one bird up there with a very distinctive liquid warble. She had noticed this: after her experience with blindness, her hearing seemed a lot more acute. She found herself listening to things she'd never paid attention to before.

"Detective Gooch," MeChelle said. "We really don't want to overstay our welcome, huh?"

"Hey, she just said we could stay and finish our lunch. I'm just making conversation while I kill off this fine sandwich." He gestured at Lane Priest with the sandwich. It dripped mustard on the white tablecloth.

MeChelle's heart started beating a little faster. What the hell was Gooch doing here? Other than being his usual rude self?

"If I follow your logic," Lane Priest said, "then you're suggesting that it wasn't Nathan who was behind your partner's kidnapping."

Gooch made a whistling noise through his teeth, like he was trying to dislodge a piece of stuck food. "Mmm," he said finally. "I knew was something escaping me. And now you done put your finger on it."

MeChelle felt something twist in the pit of her stomach. "But—"

"Here's what I think. I think whoever was behind this nonsense thought it would all be over in a couple hours. They sent Stormé Venda over there with this cock-and-bull story to get us started. Then they kidnapped MeChelle. What they didn't know was the VO guy they hired was a nutbag who was living this whole secret life. Which sucked us off in the wrong direction right from the start. So Silent Man is in there trying to figure out how to get things back on track."

Lane Priest's finger began tapping impatiently on the back of the chair. Still she didn't leave.

"Silent Man never meant to talk. Silent Man intended to just hang out there for a while, control the computer that played Damon Fergus's voice over the PA system, then scoot once things got on track. But things never quite got on track and so Silent Man had to improvise. Silent Man had to talk. Ultimately Silent Man actually had to read all the clues."

Lane Priest continued to stare expressionlessly.

"So why whisper?" Gooch said.

MeChelle felt a prickle run across her skin. Suddenly she sensed where Gooch was going.

"I've noticed about you, Detective Gooch," Lane said, "that you're quite adept at making yourself sound like a moron. Until, suddenly, you *stop* sounding like a moron."

"Is that a backhanded compliment?" Gooch said. "Or some kind of insult? Sometimes I can't tell the difference."

"A fascinating question," Lane Priest added. "But I really do need to go."

"Hold up, hold up," Gooch said. "Nearly done, I promise."

Lane Priest's fingers ran across the face of her organizer again, checking the time.

"You cut Silent Man with a bottle, MeChelle," Gooch said. "Remember that?"

"Sure," MeChelle said. "Right across the belly."

Gooch looked at Lane Priest. "Say, ma'am, you want to pull up that dress?" he said.

"What are you *talking* about?" Lane Priest snapped.

"I don't think that's a baby in your belly. I think you've got a dressing on your stomach covering up the place where MeChelle shanked you."

"That's ridiculous!" Lane said.

"I'd be happy to step out of the room," Gooch said. "Let you show off your belly to this nice female detective."

Lane Priest's face was hard. She stood motionless for a long time. "I believe it's time for you to leave."

"Quick peep," Gooch said. "If it wasn't you in that room, then you got nothing to worry about. . . ."

"You have an interesting theory," Lane Priest said. "But do you have any evidence? Anything at all?"

"Hey, look," Gooch said. "It ain't like I blame you. I'd of been you, I'd have wanted Joe out of the way, too."

"I'm going now."

Gooch reached out, grabbed her wrist.

"Take your hands off me," Lane Priest said.

But Gooch didn't let go.

"Truth is," Gooch said, "the reason you put MeChelle in that room was to use her as bait. I kept wondering about something. It was obvious that Joe was on to us from the very beginning. I mean, I got the phone call luring me out to Fuzzy's not more than ten minutes after I left your house. So who told Joe about MeChelle? *I* damn sure didn't."

"Let go of my arm."

Gooch ignored her. "I figured, hey, the only person who could have warned your husband was the exact same person who put MeChelle in the room to start with. You set the whole thing up so Joe'd eventually have to go down there with a gun and settle the thing. He probably figured it was Nathan behind it. You were looking for a shoot-out. You never wanted him arrested. You never wanted him charged. You were looking to put him into a gunfight against somebody, oh, maybe like an ex-cop who'd spent time in the Special Forces, trained a little in the martial arts, had a public record of skill with guns. Somebody your husband wouldn't stand a chance against. Somebody like, say . . . *me*?" Gooch smiled. "You wanted to get him plain-out executed. Am I right?"

Lane yanked her arm, trying to get free of Gooch. But Gooch was too strong for her. Her other hand gripped the top of her chair, knuckles white.

"Obviously, being blind, though, you had to have help. Somebody with some manpower. Somebody with some muscle."

"It's all preposterous," Lane said evenly. "Who would have helped me do something this dangerous, this absurd?"

Gooch nodded. "That's the question, ain't it?"

Lane smiled coldly.

"Who'd be the perfect candidate? Elbert King."

MeChelle felt she had to chime in. "Yeah, but Hank, he's implicated in the murder."

"Implicated? Well, there's nothing to prove it. The only people who knew he had any involvement in it conveniently turned up dead today."

"Subpoena his records," Lane Priest said. "Do whatever. You'll find nothing connecting us. Nothing. Because it's not true."

"Or because y'all two aren't fools. I got no doubt that y'all never wrote nothing down, probably communicated using prepaid cell phones, paid for in cash. Any exchanges of money, no doubt they took place way, way offshore."

Lane Priest shook her head.

"Speaking of which," Gooch said, "how much *did* you pay Elbert? A million? Two? Five?"

"You don't have any evidence for any of this." Lane's face was imperious. "Do you?"

"I did a little research on Elbert. Elbert's company got a

little overextended. They're a publicly traded company. Traded on what they call the pink sheets. They've lost money for six out of the last seven quarters. The last time somebody found a buyer dumb enough to buy any stock in the company, they paid three cents a share. Elbert's flat-ass broke. And when Elbert gets broke, he'll do just about anything to get out of the red."

"That's not evidence."

"When you're right, you're right," Gooch said. "You want to prove me wrong? Just lift up that dress, show us your belly."

"You came to my house," Lane Priest said. "You saw me right here in this house. How is it even possible that I could be in two places at once?"

"Yeah," MeChelle said. "But I wasn't aware of Silent Man for at least two hours after I'd been in that room. Maybe more."

"Pfffff," Lane Priest said.

"But after I'd been there for a couple of hours, I had this weird feeling that something had changed. And now that I think about it, see, I went back into the kitchen and had some food. Potato chips, sandwiches wrapped in wax paper, pickles—it was all noisy, crunchy stuff with noisy wrappings. As soon as Gooch left your house, you probably had King drive you down here. I went into the kitchen and started eating, you just breezed right into the main room. The hinges of that door were greased up real nicely, so the door didn't even make a sound."

"Well, it's a terribly entertaining theory. When you get some actual *evidence*, then I suggest you get a court order to look at my belly."

MeChelle felt a slow burn of anger coming on. "You even

wore a man's deodorant, didn't you?" MeChelle said. "Just to throw me off."

Gooch let go of Lane Priest's arm.

"Detective Gooch was right," MeChelle said. "You thought the whole thing would go easier, didn't you? You never thought you'd have to talk. You used that nifty little Braille organizer to control the computer that played Damon Fergus's voice, didn't you? And you figured that would be enough. But you underestimated how hard it would be to make anything out of those clues. You've been blind so long, you forgot how hard it is to 'see' with your fingers. Stuff that's child's play for you was completely opaque to me. I thought the peeing hillbilly was a vampire. Thought the king was a kid with his hair sticking up. And the plate? Forget it. I couldn't *begin* to make anything out of the numbers on that plate. I guess you also figured we'd put all the other stuff together so quick we'd have plenty of time to track down a copy of the trust document, figure out what it meant. So eventually you realized you were gonna have to talk me through it. But how to do that without giving away that you were a woman?"

Lane Priest stared defiantly off into the distance.

"Whisper!" MeChelle said. "You whispered. There's no difference between a woman's whisper and a man's whisper. So that's what you did."

"Supposing that's true," Lane said. "How would I have read the trust document to you? It wasn't in Braille."

"You got some kind of scanner in your organizer, maybe, converts text on a page into Braille? No, I take it back. You've probably the entire text of it stored right there on your little organizer, huh?"

Lane Priest shook her head.

"How long you been planning this?" Gooch said.

Lane's stony face softened and tiny little smile crossed her face.

"You found the rabbit, didn't you? Your husband kept it as a little trophy, didn't he? Couldn't resist. Somewhere in your husband's things you found that rabbit that Vince Meredith took from you the night your mom was killed. And then you knew."

The little smile hung there on Lane's face. But she didn't speak.

"How many years? Five? Ten?"

"I'm going now," Lane Priest said. She walked briskly to the door.

"I never told you about reading the trust document," MeChelle called to her. "The only way you could possibly have known about that . . ."

Gooch interrupted. ". . . is if you were there."

Lane Priest froze. For a moment she looked frightened. But then she composed herself, angled her face toward them. "Lucky for me," she said, "I can afford extremely good lawyers. You'll never prove a thing."

MeChelle stared at her furiously, suspecting that the blind woman was right. They had no evidence. Not a shred.

The hair stood up on MeChelle's neck when Lane Priest spoke. Or, rather, when she *whispered*, "See you when I see you."

66

In the car outside the house, Gooch sat motionless, not starting the car.

"She glued my eyes shut!" MeChelle shouted. "I want her in jail!"

Gooch just sat there, staring out the windshield at the broad vista of Lane Priest's front yard.

"Don't you want her in jail?" MeChelle said. "Come on, Hank. I cut you with a knife, you bleed blue. She kidnapped and assaulted an officer of the law. You *know* you want her in jail. Her little plan got you shot, broke your ankle, punctured your lung . . ."

"I don't know what I want," Gooch said finally.

MeChelle felt her eyes widen. "Boy, that's a first."

"It was raining the day they found my little girl. He'd cut her throat and stuck her in this cane break by a river down at Fort Benning. A couple of guys I knew found her. They trampled all over the crime scene, put her in the back of a deuce-and-a-half truck, drove her to my residence, handed her body to me. It was raining all over me. I didn't cry. I just stood there in the rain with this feeling of cold anger in me. I said to these two guys, 'I'm gonna get him.' I just kept saying it over and over. 'I'm gonna get him. I'm gonna get him.'"

Outside of the case they'd worked that had resulted in the arrest of the man who had killed his daughter, Gooch had never once spoken to MeChelle about his little girl.

Gooch took his badge off his belt, turned it around, set it on the dash of the car. There was a tiny worn photograph of a little girl taped to the back of the badge. The photograph was so frayed and faded you could barely make out what it was. A little girl with two missing front teeth, an explosively happy grin.

"She would have turned twenty-one years old the day after you got snatched. I guess that's why she was on my mind. I guess that's why I was feeling so . . ." His voice trailed off.

"I'm sorry," MeChelle said.

"Years," Gooch said. "I spent *years* looking for the guy that killed her. Didn't go two hours in all those years that I didn't think about getting *him*."

It was MeChelle's turn to be quiet.

"I forgot to shower sometimes, forgot to sleep, forgot to eat, forgot to laugh, forgot to be nice to people . . ." He bared his teeth in something resembling a smile. "Sometimes I even forgot about her." As he stared at the faded little girl on the back of his badge, a tear suddenly ran down his face, dripped off the end of his nose. "But I never forgot about *him*. Not for a second."

"Look," MeChelle said, "Lane didn't have to do it this way. She could have just come to us and told us what she'd found."

"Then what? Put yourself in her place when she found that little rabbit tucked away in Joe's stuff somewhere. Imagine the level of trust you got to put in your spouse if you're blind. And to find out that the guy who's supposedly protecting you from the world is the same guy that killed your mother? Now imagine that your husband is rich, powerful, politically connected, ruthless? Hell, MeChelle, just imagine how desperate she must have felt. How hopeless. How short on options she was. She must have felt like, *Okay, desperate times demand desperate measures.* She sits around stewing and worrying and torturing herself. And then one day, suddenly, it hits her—this whole crazy, desperate, complicated, nutty plan. And she thinks, *My God! Maybe there's a way out!*"

"Look . . ."

"All I'm saying," Gooch said, "I understand where that lady is coming from. She's done. She's tapped out. She ain't gonna do nothing like this ever again in her life."

"That may be but—"

"MeChelle, there's people out there we *can* stop from doing bad things, people that's liable to kill two, three more folks if we don't lock 'em up. Or we can bust our heads against the wall trying to put this one sad lady in jail."

MeChelle was quiet.

"It's up to you," Gooch said. "You want to go after her, we'll go after her. But if it was me . . ."

MeChelle was a little amazed. Gooch, actually consulting *her*? Who'da thunk it? She sat for a while, considering.

Gooch was probably right. a rich blind lady—she'd never do anything like this again. And, God knows, she'd suffered. You could feel for her. But at the same time, what she'd done was inexcusable, wasn't it? Even knowing what the woman had been through, having her mother killed right there in the same house . . . well, it still didn't justify what she'd done. To MeChelle *or* to Gooch. MeChelle still felt mad.

"One thing I still don't get," MeChelle said. "You think she had Stormé Venda killed? Or was that Joe?"

Gooch shrugged. "Stormé Venda owed a lot of money to a lot of people. Some of them pretty nasty people. I talked to that DeKalb County policeman, Constant Reece, just yesterday. He thinks it was a guy who loaned her money, a guy she ripped off for about fifteen grand. But we may never know."

MeChelle thought about it for a while. She couldn't shake the feeling that it just wasn't right for Lane Priest to get off the hook. Just because she was blind and emotionally damaged? Sorry, that didn't give her an excuse.

"I want to go after her," MeChelle said. "I don't care what happened to her, how sad her life was, I want to go after her. She could have done it another way."

Gooch took a deep breath. "You sure?"

She nodded.

He reached down, took his cuffs off his belt, handed them to her.

"What's this?" she said.

"I ain't doing it myself," Gooch said. "But I'll back you up. You go in there and make the arrest."

"What?" MeChelle said. "We got nothing on her."

Gooch reached into his pocket, pulled out a little tape recorder. "It's all right here," he said. "Our whole conversation. There at the end, she more or less admitted she'd done it. It's right there on tape, the thing about reading the trust document to you. It's a fact she knew about it. And it's a fact you never told her. I think that's enough for an arrest."

She stared at him.

"Why you think I was making all that noise, smacking my lips and everything? Blind people hear pretty good. I was afraid she'd hear that little tape motor whirring in my pocket. Had to camouflage it somehow."

MeChelle shook her head and smiled.

Gooch opened the door, sighed loudly. "Come on," he said. "Let's go get her. Before you change your mind."